MW01125452

Cameron Manor

The Meeting and the Magic

Deborah Robillard

Cameron Manor
The Meeting and the Magic
Copyright 2014 Deborah Robillard

All rights reserved.
No part of this book may be reproduced or transmitted in any form or by any means, electronic or mechanical, including photocopying, recording, or by an information storage or retrieval system, without permission in writing from the author

This is a work of fiction. Names, characters, places, and incidents either are the product of the author's imagination or are used fictitiously. Any resemblance to actual persons, living or dead, events, or locales is entirely coincidental.

Published in the United States of America

ISBN-13: 978-1500203757
ISBN-10: 1500203750

DEDICATION

For Nick, Phillip, and Kevin

Not my blood, but my heart.

ACKNOWLEDGMENTS

Thank you, Lord, for your love and mercy in my life. Everything I am belongs to and is a blessing from you.

To my family and friends, my best friend, my mom. God has blessed me with each and every one of you and through you all has given me more love and encouragement than one person can hold in a lifetime. A very special thank you to my husband who has listened to me read for hours, patiently giving me that little push of loving support I needed to pursue my dreams. To my boys who have endured the long hours of work on this project, you have never let me forget all the speeches I have given you about reaching for your dreams and you supported me while I reached for mine. You make me so proud every day I love you.

To my agent, editor, sounding board, and manager of literary crisis, Carol von Raesfeld. You have believed in me for eight years, been my friend and made me a better writer. I couldn't really ask for or find better, I am so thankful for that day you came to see me in Vegas. It wasn't my best day, but you gave me something to shoot for and with that came hope.

To Dorothy Hardy, thank you for seeing the pictures in my head and turning them into art. Your passion and skill gave Cameron Manor's readers a glimpse of what I see in the words. But it is your dedication that makes you so very special to me.

To my Publicist extraordinaire, friend and sister, Melissa Kotz, your tireless efforts and organization amaze me, and your belief in *Cameron Manor* from the very first page pushed me. I love you for that and so much more.

To the musicians I love to listen to whose music inspires, provokes thought, and brings emotion so close to the surface, your art is extraordinary: Casting Crowns, pretty much anybody who sings Country music, Brad Paisley, Keith Urban, and too many others to name. David Cook, your soft side is beautiful genius. I am fortunate to have a father who exposed me to his love of music when I was very young and showed me that it's more than just entertainment, it can be a catalyst for words, pictures, and storytelling. Really listening to music has enhanced my writing and pushed my own desire to make the reader not only see, but also *feel* the words. Thank you, Dad, for passing that gift to me.

To my teachers, who from the earliest years of my education taught me to read and then love it. There are too many of you to name, but know that your influence touches me and bleeds through onto these pages. Even if it was many years ago, I remember you all and how much you cared. Thank you for the authors you shared with me that made the art of writing captivating. I still read them to this day. Your devotion to me, your former student, is a gift that will never be forgotten.

I didn't go to the moon,
I went much further—
for time is the longest distance
between two places.

—Tennessee Williams
The Glass Menagerie (1945)

Chapter 1
"Resolution"

Was I being selfish, hanging on with both hands? I couldn't decide any more than he had been able to for months now. Wanting what I wanted had almost killed her and now it looked like it was killing him. It's true, I guess...I am selfish. I couldn't let go no matter how hard I tried. It wasn't even a choice. I would keep my grip tight until my hands, my heart, and everything in me bled, ached. I had to because I hadn't had any power over anything for so long. I couldn't change the past, but I had to hold out and hold on if I wanted to alter my future. I couldn't let it go; it's the only life I ever wanted...the reason I was born and in every cell of my body I could feel it slipping away. Maybe he wasn't going to be the one to take it from me, but either way there was a storm coming. I could feel it, just like I could feel the lifeblood of this place running through my veins."

"I've been here forever. I can't leave." I lowered my head and my tone before amending that declaration. "I can't leave them behind, Dad. I just can't do it."

He knew me well enough to know that wasn't a dig at him. Maybe he could leave here physically, but his heart would always be at Cameron Manor. I could read his face. I could tell he didn't want to leave any more than I did, but he seemed tired, stretched to the breaking point—a condition that was more than a little out of character for my dad. For some reason, it seemed a little worse today—not that this visit would be any different than the others. His expression was one of hopelessness and despair—or was it anticipation? He was keeping something from me. I could see it in his eyes as clearly as if I was looking into my own because we're the same. Maybe he'd made a decision and didn't want to tell me just yet. I really had to let him know how I felt one more time, but when I opened my mouth to speak, his eyes changed. There was no doubt, he'd decided.

~~~

Our talk was less whiny-teenager sounding than the last time we had this conversation, so he was taking me more seriously—not that he had been overtly patronizing before. This time he was not only hearing me, he was really listening. I took full advantage of his undivided attention, although with every word I felt like I was walking up a steep hill or on a treadmill—getting nowhere fast. After about five minutes, he'd heard enough or maybe he'd decided to stick to his guns. I hoped I'd understand whatever choice he'd made, given the determined set of his jaw. He didn't comment on my speech. He looked away from my face, allowing his gaze to roam around the room that my mother had decorated for me when I was five. It was essentially unchanged as most everything in my life froze when I was five.

Finally, he broke the silence and took a breath. "I'm not saying it wouldn't be hard..."

He paused for a second to think, so I interrupted. "It would be *impossible*." No whining—only the soft fact-of-the-matter tone showing in my inflection. I followed his gaze as it shifted from my light-yellow walls to the window—something that created another memory for both of us. He hated to admit he knew I crawled out my window to sit on the roof, just like he used to do when he was a kid.

He sighed, not in defeat exactly, more like resigned that we wouldn't solve this now. Still that didn't stop me from trying to ferret out whatever feelings he was teetering on the brink of because they were clearly becoming more final. I was looking for any little hint or giveaway in his face, atypical for me...for us as I found nothing concrete, just shadows of assumption that my future hopes were fading away or maybe I was being paranoid. We'd been talking about this for six months and here we were in the same place where we'd started. No progress, just the same old impasse since the funeral. We didn't fight or give each other the silent treatment. We weren't like that, although from what I could tell from watching the kids at school, we were the exception among most sixteen-year-old girls and their fathers. We could disagree, yet remember how much we loved each other. Our loss was too fresh not to. I used to wonder what it might have been like to take anything for granted, but we were too afraid to leave anything unsaid, just in case there were no second chances. Cameron Manor had been unforgiving that way, but I guess every beautiful thing has at least one flaw.

He looked toward the door and took a step towards it, abruptly changing the subject. His expression shifted with the mood of the conversation—not happier, just a shade lighter, like maybe he *wanted* to feel hopeful that things would get better, but in that place deep inside where we never go, we both knew better. Hope can be a dangerous thing, leaving you with boundless joy that's fragile and easily crushed when it's unfulfilled. We didn't do that to ourselves or each other anymore.

Brutal honesty was our policy. We weren't deviating from it now. Still, leaving the subject of leaving behind was a relief that shone deep in his blue eyes, taking with it the paranoid shadows I either saw or imagined there—a stressful topic put away, back into the place where we keep our imagined and unspoken hope.

"Get ready, C.C, let's go see Mom." That had to be where that hope or that hoping against hope was coming from that maybe today would be better. His voice was soft, no irritation in it when he called me by my initials. He was the only one who did it. He'd started using a pet name for me when things really were lighter...hopeful. He changed direction mid-stride and crossed over to where I was sitting cross-legged in the middle of my high four-poster bed. His six-foot-two frame didn't need the stepstool to reach over and muss my hair—another sign of 'no hard feelings.' We'd work it out, or work through it, like we always did.

~~~

He left and I closed my eyes...remembering. I was just a little kid so everything in my daydream looked taller and bigger than it appeared to me now. My mom was spinning her petite body around in circles with her arms outstretched like she was five, just like me. Her sun-kissed light brown hair was swirling around her face, her cut-off blue jean shorts and white t-shirt were spattered with yellow paint, and her deep green eyes were shining. The empty cans and brushes and rollers were on a blue tarp on the floor and all my new furniture was covered in plastic: the big mahogany bed and matching desk, my new overstuffed purple chair, and my fuzzy, multi-colored, tulip-shaped area rug were waiting to breathe again.

She leaned down and scooped me up. "Look, Caimee, isn't it pretty?" She took the plastic off my new yellow bedspread covered with pink tulips.

"Soft too," I said, reaching over to touch it.

"Well, Grammie loves you lots and worked hard to make it. She even tried to find yellow fabric to match the paint color on the walls that you love so much." Each one of the flowers was quilted onto the material and I remember thinking how their puffy shape felt spongy under my tiny fingers.

"We'll have to thank her when she visits." She made me promise to remember as she slid her finger down to the tip of my nose, leaving flecks of paint on my face. Her favorite thing in my room was the huge watercolor painting leaning against the wall that now hangs between the two posts at the head of my bed. She'd found it at *Georgie Mae's Antiques & Collectibles*, one of her favorite stores. We stared at the acres of flowers together. It was the fields of Holland covered in tulips with a windmill in the background. Dad had pulled a lot of strings and traded a lot of flights with other pilots to get to take her there that spring before things changed. The painting's thick, heavy frame matched my dark wood bed and made the picture look massive to me at the time. I often imagined jumping into it.

"It's very nice, Mommy." It had been so long since I'd said the word "Mommy" out loud that it felt weird to think it. I was so little when it happened. I still call her "Mommy" in my memories.

"No more baby room for my baby," she said, running her fingers through my long black hair.

All my life I'd been told how unusual the color of my hair is with its deep auburn highlights submerged in the

5

black-as-midnight strands. My hair is another thing that has never changed. My mother never had the heart to cut it into any style other than long layers, so I never have either. It's thick and has grown down to my waist. Sometimes it's a pain to fix and it takes forever to blow dry it, but I comb through it with my fingers and remember her.

"Almost ready, kiddo?" Dad startled me. I looked across my big square room at my dad standing in the doorway, he was back sooner than I expected. He'd abruptly pulled me from my reverie and he knew it—one of the reasons he wasn't pushing me beyond my limit on the whole extended vacation idea. He knew my face as well as I knew his. He should, given that I look like the female version of him. We were more than just similar, on the inside, we had the same heart, same struggles. He could easily read my expressions and emotions, which is kind of inconvenient when you're ten and had just eaten an entire bag of soft chocolate chip cookies you were told not to touch. We stared into each other's dark blue eyes and he knew immediately. It was easy here. I could remember here...remember her, remember Granddad. He blinked his long dark lashes at the same time I blinked mine. Maybe he'd been somewhere else in that second as well. He needed to get away for a while because of the memories and I needed to stay for the same reason. Same old impasse, only this time it would go unspoken.

"Almost," I lied. I jumped up and ran through my big closet into my even bigger bathroom. I had to go through my closet door and turn right to get to it. My closet was what used to be called a "dressing room." Years ago, when Granddad Nathan remodeled the house, he added the wide threshold on the right-hand side, dividing the room in half and turning the new part into a bathroom. It had a pocket door that I never closed. It was easier to shut the closet door and step out of the shower to get dressed. The one time I had friends over for a birthday party, they thought it was funny that my dad knocked on the closet door to see if I was in there. After that, all the girls at school thought I was rich and lived in a palace with secret rooms leading from one to another. I guess at that age it felt mysterious and magical to them.

Cameron Manor had always felt magical to me. When I was in the second grade, one of the girls, who I had invited to the party, told everyone that I was a snob, so not very many of them were what I would call "friendly" after word got around that the "Camerons had money." It was something people knew, but not to that extent until the kids started telling stories. The worst was April Mantis. Her mother worked at the school and had access to all the kids and their moms, so the gossip spread even faster. Of course, as April got older and changed schools, her mom did the same: elementary, middle school, and now high school—their access to information about my life was endless.

It wasn't long before the parents were giving me dirtier looks than their kids. I used to stand in front of Sycamore Park Elementary School waiting for my nanny, Mrs. Maggie, to pick me up and having to listen to the too loud whispers of what I now know is jealousy. It didn't matter so much about the girls or their mothers because I had my best friend, Ty, who made it bearable. He's a year old than me. He'd stand there holding my hand so we could hold our heads up together. After all, he lived at Cameron Manor too. It didn't matter that he didn't live in the main house, he still got his fair share of the bullying. The boys weren't as bad as the girls, so eventually the stigma was only attached to me. When I skipped the third grade, that put me and Ty in the same class, but it also added "smart" to the "rich" label. I pretty much lost all hope of ever having a real girlfriend in Culpeper. In a small town like it was then, those labels don't ever peel off. I thought as the town grew that things would change, but it turns out there were just more people willing to listen to the gossip. It followed me from year to year, grade to grade. When April moved into the "most popular girl in school" position, even the kids I naturally would have gravitated toward and been friends with wouldn't go against her. The others weren't mean, but nobody wanted to trade places with me and be ostracized too, so they avoided the confrontation and me as much as possible. That ongoing situation was one of the reasons Dad kept giving for us to "take a break." I guess the words "break" or "vacation" sounded better than *leave* or worse yet— *move.*

As I hurried to get ready, I thought about how people perceived my father and me so differently. After all, we had the same blood and came from the same place. I could tell by the way women reacted to him when we were in public that my dad was known as a "catch." Despite the gossip about the Camerons, any woman in town would have loved to be in Dad's inner circle. Today proved no different because it started as soon as we were away from the Manor. On our way to see Mom I caught some blonde looking past her kid sitting in the passenger seat of her car at my dad in the driver's seat of ours. She was so lost in whatever thought...no let's call it what it was—*repulsive fantasy* that she was having that she completely missed the light change. The lustful look on her face was gross, but Dad pretended not to feel the heat from her stare.

Dad's having inherited Cameron Manor wasn't the only reason for their attention. Almost every time we were having dinner in a restaurant or even pumping gas at a gas station, I could hear the whispers. "Caleb Cameron, what a shame about *her*..." and then they'd turn away and say under their breath, "What a waste! He's so good looking, but still faithful to her..." like faithful was a sin or something. Stupid me, I thought it was a virtue. I mean, they'd taken vows in church—for better or worse and all that. I love the way they never used my mom's name, as if *that* would make it disrespectful.

My "favorite" happened at Ted's Barber Shop when some woman was there with her little boy. While Dad was getting his hair cut, she slipped her phone number to him, right in front of me. She'd put her wedding ring in her pocket first...nice. I guess I could see it. Even I didn't think he was old-looking for being forty and he worked out a lot—sometimes at the gym and sometimes jogging with me up and down our dirt driveway. I imagine it was worse when he was traveling and I wasn't with him. I remember one time when we were together at the airport; he brought me to Florida so we could go to Disney for my birthday. He was wearing his pilot's uniform and women were practically stopping to take his picture. That didn't happen here though. Every time we came here to see Mom he looked old and beaten down, like the weight of the world was on his shoulders, pushing him into a slumped, defeated pose. I opened my car door, got out, and followed him inside. Who knows, maybe this place makes me look that way too. Maybe I went from sixteen to sixty aging on the drive over just like he did. He glanced back to make sure I was behind him.

"I'm coming." I sighed. Two short words, but their tone and our expressions spoke volumes.

~~~

Culpeper Baptist Retirement Community. The word "community" makes it sound so optional, like "Hey, come live in our community! The neighbors are great and we barbecue a lot." Yeah, not so much. I hate the institutional feeling of it. Maybe I just hate it because my thirty-seven-year-old mother isn't supposed to be here and neither are we. We kept her at home with a private nurse as long as we could, but about three months later she had a seizure and what little function she had left was eliminated by a stroke afterwards. Any joy in Dad's eyes faded after that day, but not his love for her—nothing could change that. They'd managed to start her heart again, but Dad was too afraid to keep her home after that. He wanted her closer to emergency medical care and this place was only a few minutes from the hospital and also the country club where she used to have friends and Commonwealth Park where she used to compete. Ironically, she wasn't injured during a competition, but while riding her favorite horse at home. People came for a while, some from our church still do, but over the years, people forget, people move on, but we can't because for us life is frozen. "Chronic vegetative state initiated by a closed head injury" was what her doctor called it. We called it "the beginning of our personal misery"—the end of one life we knew and the beginning of another we wish we had never started.

I opened the heavy curtains to let in the sunny day and the view of the Blue Ridge Mountains. It was late May, school had been out for almost a week, so we could stay all day and sometimes we did. I took my usual place on the right side of her bed and picked up her hand. Dad walked around to the left side and gently scooped up her other hand, looking longingly at the wedding ring he'd placed there nineteen years ago. He had loved her even before that—when they were just kids. The square diamond on the thin, elegant platinum band spun easily on her even thinner finger. The old man in him was clearly showing now. The small rays of optimism in his eyes before we left the house, the hope that maybe today would be the day things would be different were darkened by the sadness and fatigue he clearly felt. The "break" he needed was so apparent on his face, I suddenly felt selfish again, but not enough to agree with him. Pretty much all of my memories of her were this way, but every now and then I could see a piece of their past in his eyes, her laughter, the day she had me, the day they got married he ached to have just a little part of that back, nobody would ever be to him what she was, even now when she couldn't speak their hearts communicated. I couldn't imagine how he felt, how he carried those heavy feelings around every day, but worse I couldn't imagine not being here with her. I hated hating myself this way, hated feeling like a selfish stubborn brat. Maybe I wasn't openly acting like a pouting child about to have a screaming tantrum if I didn't get my way, but I felt it inside. I was torn right down the middle between what he wanted and what might be best for him and what I needed, what I wanted more than anything and could never let go of.

~~~

"Caleb, can I see you for a minute?" said Lisa, our favorite nurse.

Ah...now I get it. I'd read him right this morning. He knew something I didn't. They were way past the "Mr. Cameron" phase when it came to talking to my dad here. After all, it was our home away from home. We were here at least three times a week, sometimes more when his flight schedule for Delta allowed. Every now and then I'd see him coming home at dawn, knowing he'd spent the night in the chair beside her bed. He looked up from staring at my mom's face. I tried to feel the tension and temperature of the emotion in the room, but he was avoiding my stare. Lisa had left the room so fast that I couldn't get a read on either one of them. My heart started to race. I was nervous. This was it—whatever he'd decided was going to be carved in stone when he got back. I was trying to catch my breath, but couldn't. I felt like I was drowning. I held my mom's hand tighter in my shaking fingers. I had to stay.

"Sure," Dad replied to Lisa, though she was already out of the door. He gently slipped his hand out from beneath Mom's and left the room.

I wondered what grown up thing they thought my ears were still too young to hear. I think they all still saw me as the five-year-old who used to come here and cry, begging her to wake up. Seeing her increasingly colorless face, the feeding tube, the stack of adult diapers, oxygen hoses, and IVs were second nature to me. Now, the only time we're shocked by the sight of her is when they sit her up to give her a bath. Normally the only position I ever see her in is flat on her back, propped up on all sides with a pillow under both arms and both legs to prevent bedsores. She hadn't spoken or moved on her own in ten years. Sometimes she looks like she's awake, but the doctor calls it "brain stem activity" so she still has sleep cycles and at times appears to be awake, but that's the extent of her function—that and breathing on her own. Dr. Little made it clear to me several years ago that she can't see me, even if her eyes are open, so I shouldn't expect her to know that I'm even here. I read somewhere that she might still be able to hear me, so when we're alone, I talk to her.

I started with the most relevant topic. "Dad brought up the whole long vacation slash break thing again today. He knows I don't want to go. It isn't really practical and he knows it. I don't think his heart is in it either and if he was honest with himself, I think he'd say I'm right, but something seems different about him today. I'm not even going to lie—it has me worried." I smiled to myself at a sudden movie reel of memories playing in my head. "I never could lie to you anyway, could I?" A dozen failed attempts at doing that when I was little and she was teaching me lying was wrong instantly flashed through my mind. "Really Mom, it doesn't make sense. I'd be all alone when he's flying and where would we live? Probably some rinky-dink apartment in D.C., I imagine. He seems to pass through there a lot lately. Mrs. Maggie is against it too, but she'd never say. The only person she ever really bossed was Granddad Nathan and since he's gone, she pretty much tries to give Dad some space. 'I can't make that sad, confused, heartbroken look on his face any worse by

13

telling him what I think he should do,' she says. She's nervous about making him feel bad, or guilty, or whatever. I know she practically raised him, but still she feels a need to butt out, *for the first time ever,* even though I've been begging her to say *something.* She doesn't really think he wants to leave Cameron Manor either, same as me, just the pain from well...missing you and missing Granddad. I guess he *needs* a break, I just don't think leaving is the answer, no matter how long or short a time it would be. It's our home, our family's home. I don't even know how many generations of Camerons have lived there, but according to Mrs. Maggie, it has to be quite a few.

"She's been frustrated lately doing research. She's using the library like we live in the Stone Age or something. I've offered her my laptop, but she's sure the library is just as good as the Internet. I guess you can't change the thinking of an old teacher, but it's going to take her a hundred years to do it her way. She's determined to finish the family tree Granddad Nathan wanted to do before he died. People say it was sudden, but he'd been getting weaker for so long. I guess 'sudden' must mean he didn't have some disease people knew he'd die from someday. I guess I should watch for signs of a stroke when I get old." I smiled knowing she would never be offended that I was alluding to the one she'd had. "It doesn't even seem like it's been six months already. I can still feel him in the house."

I trailed off, watching another movie in my head, remembering Granddad as I'd remembered her this morning—healthy and loving life. If we leave that's all I'll have left—a head full of memories and pictures, only the next ones would be of home.

It only took me a few seconds to realize my alone time with her might be short, so I decided I'd better stop daydreaming and finish telling her what I wanted her to know. "Dad is still chapped about the whole 'Sweet Sixteen' thing and me not wanting to have a party. Who would I invite anyway? He thinks I isolate myself, like all I care about is the farm. He doesn't get it, why would I choose the 'rich, brainy, what's wrong with her mom' title. I might as well wear it like a pageant sash at school. I don't care what they think anymore. There are only a few left who make the effort to be just plain mean. The rest of them seem happy to ignore me. I guess that happens in every school, but I've been the odd man out since I was seven, so why have a party for people who don't really like me? Dad knows what I really want and he also knows you'd give it to me because I tell him so all the time. I've been begging Bo to let me ride and help take care of the horses like he did when I was little, before your accident. I mean now that I'm old enough, Bo could teach me how to train them too, but he says he and Dad have been friends too long for him to go behind Dad's back like that. I think Dad must have figured out that I've been talking to Bo— either that or Bo told him. I've seen them talking a few times and then stop when I walk up—another plus in the 'pack up and go' column. I remind him all the time that Cameron Manor is a horse training and boarding facility and that I'm a Cameron. Dad says it's in our blood, but it skipped him, so that must mean I get it from you. I hate feeling this way, but I'm going to be eighteen in two years and then I'll be able to do what I want anyway. I don't want to go against him, but it's what I want to do: Go to vet school and learn all I can from Bo. I'm so lucky when it comes to that. How many people have the best horseman around to teach them all the tricks of the trade?"

I blushed a little, even though I was basically alone. "Plus, Bo teaching me has the built-in bonus of me getting to be around Ty. I know I've told you like a million times already, but he'll be here soon, so I've been thinking about him more and more lately. Who knew that was even possible? "Anyway, he's been working hard for years and now he's the second-best horse trainer ever. Bo says he's going to be better than him someday. Never mind he is the most beautiful seventeen-year-old male I've ever seen, Abercrombie models included, he has a way with the animals just like Bo, and just like dad says you did." My face felt hot when I thought ahead to when Ty would arrive for his summer visit with his dad. First, we'd have our customary shared birthday party, complete with Mrs. Maggie's half pink, half blue cake. Since our birthdays are May 19th, we always celebrated two weeks late, so we could do it together. It was fun for us when we were small and now it's a tradition. Ty is only a year older than me, but for the longest time he called me a baby. That stopped when I skipped a grade and we were in the same class. I closed my eyes and allowed more memories to come. I flashed on all the recollections of the years we'd had our little family party, the days Ty and I had spent in school together, and how things had changed since we were kids. Normally, I didn't do this much daydreaming. I guess it must be the stress of not knowing what Dad was going to do and the fear that I'd forget even the tiniest thing, and worst of all not see Ty this summer. I sighed and wished that for five minutes

Mom could sit up and tell me what to do. Since there would be no "boy advice" from her today, I went on about something I was already sure about.

"Honestly, it must be in my blood. It isn't only about the horses or the family history, it's more like a pull to it, like Cameron Manor is where I'm supposed to be. I can't really explain it, but I can *feel* it. It just is. Dad never did get Granddad's dream. I guess I do because it's mine too. I want to keep the farm up and running and then give it to my kids someday because it's been that way forever." I lowered my voice to a whisper. I could feel the heat in my face again, knowing I was about to say it out loud. "And who knows, maybe Ty and I can run it together." It felt so good to tell my mom. I'd do it even if she wasn't in a coma, just because all I knew in this town was a sea of acquaintances. I didn't want to confide in any of them because it would be all over town and school by the first day next fall. Mom was so easy to tell, so easy to talk to. Sometimes I could almost hear her words in her faint heartbeats. Now, nothing but silence came from her. I had to imagine what she might say and the older I got the harder it was to hear her voice in my head. According to everybody in the family, Dad and I may have had the same face and heart, but she and I had the same kind of soul and she would have been my best friend. Just then I heard Dad shift his weight from one foot to the other. *Great! What and how much had he heard?*

~~~

Except for the rattling in the old farm truck's dash, we rode home in silence. I stewed over whatever he and Lisa had talked about, mingled with my wondering about how much of what I'd said in private to my mom

17

was now up for discussion. I hoped I hadn't torpedoed myself in the 'going away' argument and given him more ammunition to defend or support any agenda I don't agree with. I didn't really want him to know that as soon as I was of age I intended to get right back up on a horse. I was afraid that if by some miracle he'd decided we were staying, then found out what I intended to do, he'd change his mind. I guess the idea of the Manor and the land was like that. At times it had beaten us, but I didn't intend to let it break me. Mom wouldn't have and he knows it, another part of our conversation I had whispered. It was my birthright and I wanted it. I just didn't want to say it out loud, any more than I wanted him to know how I felt about Ty—not yet anyway. I was kidding myself about whether or not both Dad and Bo already knew, but the denial just bought me more time before we had to have one of our father-daughter chats to discuss it, either that or he thought it was a passing crush and maybe he wouldn't have to deal with it once it went away...yeah right. It was a point not worth worrying about. I'd had no indication that Ty had the same kind of feelings for me, but the thought that he might gave me butterflies. My face flushed and my palms got sweaty just thinking about it, I turned to look out the window, maybe he wouldn't notice...another "yeah right'.

We turned off James Monroe Highway onto Cameron Manor Road. I knew that when I started driving (no doubt another sore subject), that I'd miss the turn into my own home. It was hard to see unless you knew it was coming up. It was about three miles of dusty bumpy dirt that curved into what eventually became our driveway. The house had been here so long that when the highway went in I guess they finally had to give our dirt street a real name. Dad stopped at the bend as it crested the hill, just before the rows of magnolias that ran up each side of the lane for about a quarter of a mile to the iron gate in front of the house.

Great, here it comes," I thought, looking over at him, wanting to prolong the moment before the lecture began. I don't know what I was expecting, but it was definitely something other than the grin he was wearing. He looked ahead and chuckled softly to himself—totally out of context for the conversation I thought we were going to have.

We could see almost all of the regal-looking estate from here—the house, the massive two-story, deep red barn, the horse ring with hurdles of varying heights where Bo trains the competition horses. Behind that was the beginning of the quarter-mile straightaway he uses to work with the racers.

The only thing hidden was the duck pond. It was veiled behind the acres of rolling green hills and grass covered in Virginia bluebells. They were just starting to cover the yard with their beautiful bluish-lilac hues. The thought ran through my mind how they had been here for generations of Cameron's before me to see and would likely be here a hundred years after I was long gone, they were a comforting constant in my world, I couldn't even think of what it would be like to give them up for some concrete apartment parking lot.

It was hard to concentrate on the landscaping. It was almost as if the house was built in such royal fashion as to be a distraction from the natural beauty of the Virginia countryside. It was striking from here. It rose from its foundation steeped in age and history, its tall square-shape softened by the rounded corners of the porch that went all the way around all four sides, measuring exactly six feet from any point in the wall to the railing. For a second my eyes focused on my window where I climb out and sit on the roof that covers the porch. I love that Dad did too when he was even younger than I am so he couldn't be too mad. When he was a boy, he actually took advantage of his room being so far away from Granddad Nathan's. As any teenage male with no fear would, he figured out a way to sneak out that same window and climb down the side of the house to the ground so that he and Bo could slip out at night and meet up with their friends. I never was concerned with sneaking away; I was more interested in the view. There's one perfect spot that gives me just the right line of sight to the barn and the horses.

If Cameron Manor's regal appearance and age gave it that intimidating mansion-like feel, the gray stone exterior gave it balance with the magical fairy tale effect. The square pillars that hold up the roof over the porch are covered with greenish blue ivy, making it look like the front cover of a book of fables. The rounded peak of the tower on the back-right corner was just barely visible from this angle. Mom and I used to play Rapunzel up there amongst the old furniture and antiques that had been owned by generations of Camerons before us. Since the room was round, it was a perfect play place. Now the only person who ever went up there was Bo, since he used it to store all his paperwork about pedigrees and bloodlines. No wonder people think we're rich. If they could see the inside from here, I'm sure the gossip would be far worse. I was used to it and still it seemed like luxury to me. I knew the house appraised for several million, but it's not like we'd bought it or the land—it had just always been in our family. I guess since Granddad turned it into a farm to board and train horses instead of keeping it the apple orchard it used to be, it had become more profitable. We got lucky when Richard Bohannon..."Bo"...Dad's best friend from high school moved onto the land right after graduation and started working with the horses. He left for a while to go to Auburn University in Alabama to get his veterinarian degree, but he came back every summer until he finished. He was a natural and Cameron Manor became well known in the equestrian world for its champions. Now people pay to keep their horses here and have Bo work with them and their jockeys, but it's still hard work and someday hopefully *we* will continue to work hard at it. I closed my eyes and memorized this moment—more pictures to store for later...just in case.

~~~

I waited. He kept looking straight ahead, smiling, it was unsettling not to know why, but finally he started talking.

"I didn't want to come here when I was your age. After never having the chance to know my dad and losing my mom, I knew the only person left to take care of me was my Granddad. Man, oh man, I gave that old guy the dickens for about two years. He worked it out of me though—the attitude, the 'poor me' and the 'why me' are all over this place. Every one of these trees is planted in a hole of my own self-pity. I thought I'd never get them all in—not to mention in a straight line." He laughed a little at the memory and then made a sound in his throat like some of the resentment still lingered, although it wasn't real. He loved Granddad too much to hang onto any feelings other than admiration for him. "Every one that wasn't perfectly spaced, he would make me dig it up and move it. I hated that stupid yellow tape measure of his."

He kept his hand on the steering wheel and pointed with one finger. "I painted that fence around the house with white paint and a whole lot of resentment. You know, that fence is a perfect square around almost two acres. When I was done, I was afraid that he was going to make me do the veranda railing too. It doesn't look like much, but the distance between each one of those stone pillars is fifteen feet and there are thirty slats of vertical wood under each rail. I measured it and counted the support pieces knowing that was going to be my next job. Man, I was mad, but it took all that for me to realize that I wasn't mad at him—I was mad at my life in general. At the time, I thought nothing could be worse." He paused, looking down at his wedding ring—a silent acknowledgement that things could always be worse. "I guess I'm lucky to see that now. I sure do miss that old man, but it was this place that gave me peace from the pain of missing my mom. Until today, I guess I'd forgotten that I'd lost sight of my sanctuary. Most people can't wait for their kids to turn eighteen and go off to college and I can't get mine to leave." He laughed at his dilemma and then got wistful sounding. "I should have never let you skip a grade. Being a senior at sixteen is way too young. It's hard on this old man to see his little girl growing up."

He was still smiling when he turned to look at me. "I think you need to be part of it now as much as I did then and you're right, your mom would give that to you." I looked away, ashamed and a little embarrassed. I had never threatened to defy him before. He'd heard everything. "And even if I have reservations, apparently you already know I could never deny her."

I know my eyes lit up in my self-conscious face as I thought about the other things I'd said that were meant only for my mom—like my feelings about Ty, but I pushed away the complex to enjoy the next moment. They were coming—the words I had waited so long to hear.

"We're staying, Caimee. I'll talk to Bo about letting you go back down to the stables. Keeping you from what you love won't protect you and I'd rather you learn from the best than try to do it on your own later. I think without some mentoring you really would run full speed ahead and fall." I could tell he meant "off of more than just a horse." You're right, you were born to be here, but without Granddad, running this place won't be easy and I'd never send you to do a task like that without preparing you first. If Granddad had tried to keep me here and keep me from flying because he was worried I'd crash, I would have done it anyway. Not knowing my dad because he died over Vietnam put flying in my blood. I was torn between two DNAs and I had to figure out which one was right for me. Now I've found a balance between them. I came back because I belong here too, but I get to follow my dream outside of it." You're really no different." He pointed to our faces so that I'd know he meant it was more than just looking alike.

"Thanks, Dad," was all I could say, even though it seemed like it wasn't enough. I said what felt like a selfish prayer of thanks in my heart. I'd won, but who really wins when someone you love gives up?

He still seemed off when we walked across the wide porch to the front door. The endless mahogany on the other side runs into the large square foyer and continues throughout the rest of the large rooms, door frames, floors, stairs, and banister. The deep rich color was comforting to me, although it did little to calm my nerves now. I had a feeling there was something else we needed to talk about, but at least our impasse had been bridged. I paused in the foyer at the foot of the stairs, hearing the familiar sounds of Hillbilly and Bumpkin. Our coon hounds were barking and howling at something inside that fence that Dad had painted. It sounded like home and seeing Mrs. Maggie's grimace in my mind made it feel that way too. Her room was closest to the back of the house and the sound. The comfort I felt knowing I was going to be able to keep living in the familiarity and asylum of this place faded a bit. My spirit was bruised knowing my dad may or may not feel the same and in my heart I knew he was still keeping something from me. It wasn't that we were leaving, but it was something.

"Lord, I hope it's nothing too terrible. We've had enough terrible for a while."

Chapter 2
"Decisions"

I hung up my purse and my lightweight pink hoodie on the hook above the built-in bench just inside the foyer when it hit me. I pointed my nose in the air to get a better whiff, focusing my eyes on the silver and crystal chandelier hanging from the cathedral ceiling above my head. Mrs. Maggie was baking. I followed the smell down the hall and turned right through the wide square archway leading into the kitchen.

"Please tell me that is peach cobbler."

She laughed her airy, carefree giggle, subtly implying, "Yes, but I'm not sharing."

I couldn't see her face, but when she paused to look out the window, I knew exactly what she was thinking—no implications here. Her thoughts were crystal clear and conveyed with grunting instead of giggling. The noise wasn't necessary, I knew how she hated the sound of all that howling, but she always did it anyway. It was the noise she used in place of words that a proper Southern lady wouldn't say aloud. 'Ugh, those blasted hounds.' That's the strongest language she ever let herself say where anyone else could hear, although many other phrases were usually in her eyes. She turned to face me and went on in her thick, but proper Southern accent.

"It's a good thing I'm not trying to sleep right now. That's ten times louder in my bedroom and yes, it might be my famous..."

"And wait for it, here it comes." I started teasing her like always when it came to this subject, just before she could point out—as she always did, "That's right, little girl, my *award-winning* peach cobbler, but not until you eat your lunch."

"It was rigged," I said, continuing our good-natured kidding. "You won a blue ribbon at a *fixed* church social. You should be ashamed, not bragging."

She didn't dignify me with a response; instead, she glanced past the teak-colored, granite-covered bar where we ate breakfast on Sundays to the matching round pedestal table where we ate proper meals together. Wordlessly, she was giving me my last warning to head towards the table.

The windows at the far end of the kitchen were floor to ceiling. The pure white sunlight streaming through them bounced off the high gloss of the polished table. Mrs. Maggie took good care of the house and before he died, she took care of my great-grandfather too, but she did more than that to her kitchen. She kept it shining, inventoried, and stocked like she was expecting royalty. She'd been involved in its renovation and basically redesigned it with the help of a professional interior designer—Tarah, who came highly recommended by one of her church friends.

Tarah had gone to some fancy art school in Atlanta, but had grown up somewhere around here. The 'frig and cabinets were all built into the walls made from dark mahogany like the rest of the house. She wanted it to all to match. The bar had lights that hung from the high ceiling and the sink, faucets, and stove were shiny charcoal gray, but it didn't seem dark because of all the windows. I hated to give her credit because Tarah, who

26

could easily have been one of the "slipping her phone number to dad women" did a great job. I know she'd never make a move on him because she was trying to build a professional reputation, but she'd tried every subtle thing when she was here. Of course, Dad was oblivious—or pretended to be.

Mrs. Maggie took her eyes off me and turned to get some more glasses so I sneaked around the bar and tasted some of the forbidden cobbler. "I wouldn't," she said laughing, but trying to sound stern.

"I bet your students hated you," I teased her again, thinking how glad I was that she'd retired years ago and was never my teacher. It was a little more than twenty years ago that she'd taken the job here as caretaker of the house and Granddad Nathan right after his first stroke left him with limited mobility, but full mental capacity. She had just lost her own husband to a stroke. He was very young to have had one and I think that's why she understands so well how we feel about Mom. She calls this her "retirement job."

"Sometimes you make me think teachers really do have eyes in the back of their heads. Ouch!" I burned my finger on the gooey peach filling.

"Serves you right." She pointed to the table with her serving spoon with one last playful 'I really mean it' look that said I'd better get on over there. Dad had come in behind me, but my thievery had caused me to miss his entrance. He was already seated. Normally, he'd have jokingly picked on me for getting into trouble, but not today.

~~~

They sat in front of their fried chicken while I sat in front of my salad piled high with vegetables. Mrs.

27

Maggie had given up trying to feed me meat. I stopped eating it when I was about seven and realized what it really was. Dad stared at his food, but didn't pick up his fork. He had that old man look like he gets in the parking lot of the care home.

"Dr. Little called me last night," he said. Mrs. Maggie set down the tea pitcher and by the look on her face, she'd easily picked up on the weight of his words. She silently moved her hefty chair out and sat down. She held my hand under the table. This was it—the secret I'd seen in his eyes today. I'd mistaken it for his decision to leave. I was way off the mark, but he'd unintentionally misled me. He looked at me and in one quick glance he knew I knew.

"Sometimes you're too perceptive for your own good." He smiled a little, but there was no joy on his face and a hint of dread mixed with fear in his eyes. He didn't want to say whatever it was out loud. He didn't want to hear the words himself, because that made them true. He held my gaze for a split second and then cast his eyes down again. "I'm sorry, Caimee. I should have told you this morning, but I wanted to see how things were today before I worried you. They called again early before we left and said she had improved, so I thought maybe things were going to be okay. I guess they just wanted to tell me the worst of it in person. Your mother's heart showed signs of failing again last night. They were able to give her some medicine to help, but..." He sighed deeply. "Today they asked me to sign a form that says whether or not we want them to resuscitate her if it happens again or she stops breathing. I told them I needed to talk it over with you all first."

Mrs. Maggie was family and I knew her opinion would mean just as much as mine. I was guessing he'd already talked to Bo. Over the years, Bo had turned from a being a friend to being a brother to him. He was conspicuously missing from lunch—maybe because he couldn't take hearing it twice. It dawned on me then that when Dad came to my room to talk this morning, he was wearing the boots he only wore to the barn, so of course he'd told Bo first. Now it was our turn to hear the truth. I should have known—usually the "truth" around here is preceded by the words "cold and hard" and we all just accept it and try to keep going. He put his head down like he was plowing through the words and kept talking.

"I remembered thinking after Granddad's last stroke that he wouldn't want to live that way—helpless and hooked up to machines. It's hard to see my sweet Johnna that way because she's so young. I just tried to hold on for what I always believed was her own good, wishing things would change—willing them to be better. I always told myself 'it's for her sake' and it was easier in the beginning, but now I wonder if all this really is for her anymore—that maybe we should do what we did for Granddad and let her go. I just don't know."

He put his hands over his face. I wasn't sure if it was for support or to hide his expression. His posture looked like the heavy-burdened man from this morning times a hundred. I guess this explained the despair I saw in his expression today and a little bit more of the reason he so desperately needed that "break." I felt self-centered and very guilty, yet still relieved we weren't leaving. What if we had and something had happened? I knew he didn't want to face more loss, but I also knew he'd never leave her to go through whatever was coming alone. He'd be by her side as he had always been—faithfully and with faith.

Mrs. Maggie squeezed my hand under the table and reached over with her free one to take Dad's away from his forehead, forcing him to look her in the eye. "Nothing wrong with hoping, Caleb, but it just seems to me like God's been calling her home for a long time now. He's given us plenty of time to say goodbye in the meantime, so if her heart is getting weaker, maybe it's time."

There was nothing unfeeling about anything she said. I knew she had only the best of intentions when I looked at her and saw the tears in her eyes. I berated myself for even thinking for a split second that she meant for us to take the easy way out. She'd been through it all the same as we had. She had been like a mother to Dad since she came to live here and then to me since the day Mom's accident happened. In my heart, I knew that she only wanted what was best, what would eventually be better for him, even if it hurt right now. It dawned on me that's why she'd stayed out of it—the only time since I'd known her that she'd stayed out of family affairs—didn't try to persuade him to stay and didn't try to give him advice. She was trying to preserve his sanity, whatever that meant for the rest of us. A weaker man would have crumbled years ago. I knew better and should have guessed this sooner. Mrs. Maggie could never stay out of family affairs because she was family. She was doing what any loving mother would do for her son—at least that's how she saw him. She wasn't some insignificant face in the chorus of a play, she was central to our story—a main character who just didn't happen to have our blood. In that second I realized that she didn't need Cameron blood to love him. Even more than I had lately, she put him first. Her silence wasn't selfishness or unwillingness to be involved like I'd thought—it was an act of love. I was feeling pretty guilty right about now.

He finally looked over at me for longer than just a glance. I wasn't sure if he hadn't before because he couldn't or wouldn't want to see my reaction.

"I think we should ask Grammie." That's all I could say. No way did I want this decision on my shoulders. I needed a reason why I was copping out; after all, I'd given my opinion on virtually every other aspect of her care and been more than vocal about what Dad should do with his life. I felt like a coward. I was putting my vote off 'til I could hear what my grandmother had to say. "After all, she is her mother. She gave her life, so she ought to have a say now."

There, that seemed well thought out, not on the fly to take the pressure off me like it really was. The truth is just too hard to say. 'No, Dad, don't do it. I need her. I need to believe she can hear me. I love her too much, I'm too selfish. I...I...I.' Yes, I definitely had too many "I's" in my reasoning, only the last ones seemed okay to say out loud. "I just can't be impartial, Dad. I don't know." There, at least that was honest. He nodded in understanding. I was wishing I had some of Mrs. Maggie's selflessness right about now.

"I just want you to know, Caimee. As good as it sounded for a minute, I can't leave either and I'd started leaning that way in my mind before I got the call last night. I had a long talk with Bo and he helped me see things from your perspective a little better." He smiled. That was his way of saying he knew I'd been talking to

Bo behind his back and he wasn't mad about it—and I shouldn't be mad at Bo for telling him. "I just had to talk it out with you one last time this morning before I knew for sure. I guess missing Granddad was clouding my judgment there for a while. The truth is, with my job I'm away too much as it is. I can't take a chance your mom might need me and I wouldn't be here. His tone insinuated he was still feeling guilty that he was away the day she fell, like he could have stopped it. "I don't want to fail her if she needs me now and I think she does more than ever, and your right Grammie should have a say in all this, our decision to go or stay and your mom's care affect her too, after all she would have to take over the decision making alone if I wasn't here. Let's not tell her I was thinking of going she doesn't need that stress on top of everything else."

Wow! There's no right answer here, knowing how I would have resented it if he'd made up his mind to go, I hadn't even thought about how Grammie would have handled that. I just went with the never fails "I love you, Dad" I had been so wrong thinking that he hadn't really thought leaving through, it was obvious now he had done nothing but consider everyone but himself, he loved my mother more than his own life, there was no easy way out here, no clear decision that was right or wrong. Maybe I was being too hard on myself. In my heart, I knew it was true that Grammie did deserve a say, even if I'd brought it up to cover up my own feelings. I don't know anything anymore except that I miss my mom and I wish I could take back that one day. What I wouldn't give to be able to go back.

We sat shuffling our food around our plates for about fifteen minutes. Mrs. Maggie wiped silent tears from her deep brown eyes a few times. Finally, she tucked her short, bobbed, light brown hair behind her ear, got up and cleared the table. The normally perfectly straight bow on the back of her apple-red apron was scrunched from where she'd been leaning against it. She looked so young for sixty-two, flitting around the kitchen, cleaning up the uneaten meal. Must be all those long exercise walks she goes on.

For a second, I wished my thirty-seven year-old mother could look even half as young and vibrant as this woman who was going on twice her age. *It isn't fair,* I thought. Another thought too selfish to say out loud.

She'd had two careers and a lifetime of memories with her daughter, but my mom got none of that. I made myself close my eyes and remember how hard she'd worked taking care of Granddad and realized she deserved every good thing—not that my mom didn't, but still Mrs. Maggie wasn't the enemy here. She wasn't what I was mad about and I shouldn't have taken the brunt of my frustrations out on her, even if it was only in my mind.

I was ashamed for even having the thought. I wasn't upset because she was healthy and had had a great life, I was jealous because her daughter got what I'd always wanted—memories, pictures I'd never add to my limited mental stack.

Maybe I was feeling defeated. Nothing made me feel more helpless than not being able to change my mom's situation. Maybe I was just making myself accept the inevitable. I mean, what did I think—that she'd just lie there forever?

I looked away from them both hoping they couldn't read my thoughts. It didn't help matters much that my eyes landed on a picture of Mrs. Maggie and Phoebe. She'd followed in her mother's footsteps and become a teacher. Her long blonde hair, brown eyes, and beaming smile in their happy moment together at her college graduation was hard on my heart. She was much older now, just a few years younger than Dad and Bo, but the last time I saw her, she hadn't aged a bit, just like her mom. My heart was breaking, wishing, dreaming of what might have been for me. I envied Phoebe. Mrs. Maggie was a good mother and she was lucky to have her. All I wanted was a moment of that with my own mother.

Not one of us touched the cobbler, but we did reach for the silence in our own solitude, each going to a separate corner of our Manor. Maybe people envied our lives from the outside, but they sure didn't want what we lived through in these walls. They avoided it and sometimes us like the plague, it was as if we carried it and it was catching. Nobody wanted or should have to feel that pain, or maybe they just don't know what to say anymore, like I didn't today. Sometimes, in the silence and the seclusion, it's easier and much less likely that we'll say something through the hurt that comes out wrong—a lesson I'd learned watching Dad and Grammie try to have a simple conversation.

Chapter 3
"Grammie"

We walked up the three concrete steps to the small front porch of the little burgundy brick house. The black iron railing on the right with its fancy swirls and flower designs was cold to the touch, almost like it was holding onto winter. The hanging baskets of ferns over the porch were swaying in the light breeze. The woods on both sides made a shadow on the front of the house, making it feel like it was much later than just after lunch. Even in the darkest of shadows or a moonless night, I would recognize it as home. Anywhere I could feel my mom when she was happy, healthy, and loving life was another place I called my refuge. It was the only other place where the memories came easily. I'd stood here a million times, but none like this one. Most of the time I was on the porch and Dad was in the car at the curb waiting for her to let me in. We usually did this kind of thing at the hospital with Dr. Little acting as referee and counselor. Dad rang the doorbell and we heard several musical chimes. It sounded like the organist warming up on Sunday morning. Dad looked a little nervous, knowing what he had to tell her. I can't say I blamed him. He sighed and mumbled, "Help me, Lord."

When Grammie answered the door, she seemed pleasantly surprised to see us, well me anyway. They only really talk when there's a reason and given our situation, something about Mom or me is always the reason. Grammie was dressed in clothes that reminded me of the gypsy costume I'd worn one Halloween. The words I knew would be coming between them started running through my mind and immediately brought thoughts of Mom falling. Although I didn't see it happen, after hearing them talk about it over the years, I know in my heart what it must have been like that New Year's Day. This was going to be tough. I went back to focusing on something else. It wasn't hard my grandmother was...unusual, to say the least. Grammie's outfit didn't really surprise me because it's her style—a long, flowing, rust-colored skirt with a light yellowish-brown loosely crocheted shirt with big holes in it and a matching tank top underneath. Crocheted clothes seemed to be her new thing. I think she'd just learned how to crochet because I'd already gotten my first sweater from her. It looked a lot like the one she had on. I'm guessing there were about thirty or so thin silver hoop bracelets on her left arm and her earrings were matching silver, but they were so long they looked like Christmas tree tinsel. Her long brown-blonde hair was a mess or maybe that was her style today, I couldn't tell because it still looked good around her face. She wasn't wearing any makeup, but she was naturally pretty, like my mom. They had the same eyes—dark green. Grammie's seemed to sparkle with joy at the prospect of seeing me, yet she seemed troubled, no doubt because of the look on my father's face.

She'd been quilting again, even though she'd made enough quilts to cover every bed in town. She said it was her contribution to the church. "Some people can preach, some people can sing in the choir, I can quilt." She donated them to the Ronald McDonald House for sick children. She quilted with the ladies at her church the way Mrs. Maggie played Bingo with her church friends from several different denominations around town. It was more of a social activity than a church sanctioned event, unlike Grammie's quilting. That was definitely an act of love—doing the one thing she felt she did best. Both were devout women who had a hand in raising me, but Mrs. Maggie and Grammie couldn't be more different. Mrs. Maggie gave of her time and Grammie gave of her talents, each willing to sacrifice for anyone in need. I loved them both for so many special reasons. I know my mother would have been grateful to both of them for the roles they'd played in my life.

Grammie was holding her trademark black and silver sewing scissors and had bits of multi-colored thread clinging to her skirt. I stopped focusing on it, I needed to pay attention to the situation at hand, the awkwardness between the three of us flowed like water. I wished they would let themselves know each other the way I knew them both, maybe this situation wouldn't feel so strained if we spent more time together, and they would admit that what bound us together was way more important than the finger pointing that drove them apart. She blamed him for being away when Mom fell. He blamed her for letting Mom ride when she'd had the flu and was still weak and sick and taking medication. Never mind he was working for Delta part time when he was home, but still in the reserves and deployed flying jets in the Navy when it happened, or that no one could stop Mom from riding no matter how sick she was.

Grammie and Dad had been working past the bitterness for years. It had moved from resentment and anger to awkward and strained. I don't think they ever really hated each other, what they hated was the unchangeable, unfixable situation we were in. Both of them needed a reason why such a terrible thing could happen and in the beginning found some solace in pinning fault on each other. It had been going on so long it had become their way of dealing with being around each other. I think it would be fair to say that they had become polite strangers who had one very important thing in common—they both loved my mom.

"Hello Catherine." I guess moms just know when something's wrong or maybe she picked up on our vibes. Maybe she'd heard it in the two words he said. Who knew with them anymore? They'd forged their own style of communication. Her face fell and instinctively she put her hands up, in part to welcome me and gesture for me to give her a hug and in part to block the blow of his words. It wouldn't matter. There was no ducking the emotional punches. We'd all just learned to roll with them.

Dad's timid stance reminded me of being in elementary school, standing on the playground waiting to get picked for a team. She stood there in the doorway staring at us and neither of us responded to her unspoken invitation. Dad was waiting for her to say the words and I wasn't going in without him. No way was I answering any of her questions alone. It was easy to tell that she was nervously wondering why he'd ventured to the door from the curb.

Finally, Dad glanced at me. I think he was waiting for me to say something that might help him. He had that 'could you throw this dog a bone' look. That's when I noticed he had his fingers in his blue jean pockets with his wrists bent forward like the shy kid who knew he was going to be chosen last. He looked as nervous as he must have been when he first came around to ask Mom for a date.

Grammie immediately focused on me, perhaps hoping if she gave in and said the simple words to welcome us inside, his news would stay out. "Come in, Caimee." She waved her hand toward the small living room as if to wave away the tension and to allow Dad to enter too. She always has an accusing look in her eyes for him—not mean, just not welcoming. What she'll never know is that she can't blame him more than he blames himself.

She didn't say anything to me when we got inside; instead she grabbed me and hugged me like I was about to disappear. Yup, Grammie definitely knew there was something up. Nobody spoke. The silence was moving from awkward to super-uncomfortable, but out of the corner of my eye I could see her looking at him over my shoulder, waiting for some explanation. Whatever the news, she resented the fact that he was the "next of kin" and she was the last to know. Like the shy kid on the playground, he looked down as if feeling guilty for having firsthand knowledge. She was the grown up here and my confident father withered beneath her gaze.

I returned her hug. It felt like one of those times when even though you're the most inexperienced one in the room, you're supposed to make them feel better. I'd lived through quite a few of those moments in the hospital. I grasped their hands in mine as if to unite us—at least in what we're feeling now. She smiled, appreciative of my gesture. I love her very much, but she makes this harder than it has to be sometimes, or maybe I am just getting a glimpse at the pain she feels every moment of every day. She walked straight through the house, her holding my hand, me holding Dad's, until we got to the glassed-in sun porch she used for sewing.

We weren't there five minutes before she had me cutting squares of deep ruby-colored fabric. I struggled to use her left-handed scissors, but didn't complain given that she didn't need my commentary on her equipment on top of the news she was about to get. It was a relief to be doing something other than just making idle chitchat. She never asked about Mom, as if that would stop the nightmare from happening.

"Come on, Caimee, you can cut straighter than that." She kept talking and her hands moving, answering her own questions, never allowing whatever news we'd brought to slip into the conversation.

Dad sat down in Grammie's old glider. It used to be in Mom's nursery. It was still covered in the same light pink fabric, quilted with bows and tulips—Mom's favorite flower. They were like the trademark she had left behind on so many things she loved. The chair was in the far corner, away from the window, so he was in shadow. It was much brighter where Grammie and I were sitting by the window, but the bright cheery room did little to lift the mood. The little room had its own air conditioner. She noticed me shiver and scooted my chair into the sunlight that was streaming through the window. It was always freezing in here, but she was so busy in her work she never seemed to notice until company came over and told her she could hang meat in there.

"Here, put this on so you don't freeze," she said, wrapping an old navy blue shawl around me that looked like something she'd acquired from the same band of gypsies that had dressed her today. "Looks good on you...it was your mother's."

"I know, Grammie." My words sounded resentful that she'd felt compelled to point that out, like I didn't know anything about my own mother. She acted like I hadn't said anything. She needed to talk about Mom, like if she made her real enough, none of what happened would be true. She'd tell the same old story for the rest of her life if it would undo it. Talk like there was nothing wrong—that was her weird way of coping.

Dad would give her a while and then tell her the truth about why we were here. We'd done it a million times before. He was giving her a while longer with the peace to which she was desperately clinging because he knew she'd likely never feel it again...and deep down, so did she. It was one of the things he did for her that went unacknowledged. He got the news first, shielded her, softened it, and then found a way to break it to her gently, always gently. No matter how much she resented him knowing first, she needed that cushion and he was willing to take whatever attitude she gave him and be her soft place to fall, always willing to hit the brick bottom first. It was yet another way he showed his love for Mom.

The humming of her sewing machine ceased when Grammie stopped to stare at me before she turned and spoke to Dad. The initial weirdness always wore off after a while and they settled into whatever it was they did just to make it from one day to the next, except for the first time, we weren't at Mom's bedside, we were at Grammie's house, giving every indication that something was coming that she didn't want to face, something bigger and out of what was "normal" in the day to day decisions about my mother.

"Not a speck of Johnna in her, she's the spitting image of you, Caleb. That unique shade of black and auburn." She nodded towards my head. "Dark hair, deep blue eyes, always looks like she has a fading summer tan. None of that on our side of the family."

I didn't look up to see his face for fear of ruining my ruler-straight cut, but I was sure he was smiling at me. We got that from folks all the time. Grammie acted like she resented it, but the truth was she would have been happy to see me no matter what I looked like. I was a part of her daughter and she needed that.

"Make her do it right," he said, nodding toward my simple project, as if cutting wasn't something I'd learned in kindergarten. I reminded them *again* that I had skipped a grade, but Dad kept talking. "She needs to practice on her precision for all Bo is going to be making her do this summer." She paused a second, looking up from the thread she was changing to a different color on the machine and glared at him. She all but slammed the spool into place. She knew that was his subtle way of giving her the first bit of news that he was letting me go down to the stables and near the horses.

She put all of her energy back into her work without acknowledging what she'd heard. She didn't have to say a word—the tension in the air was enough. Hard to say if she was hurt, scared, or just plain mad that he hadn't discussed it with her or maybe she was just worried that whatever else was coming was worse. Her head down low over the sewing machine, so I couldn't read the expression on her face. I certainly couldn't reassure her that I'd be fine over the loud whining of the old machine as she pushed it to its limit. She was the one who insisted that I stay "as far away from those dangerous animals as possible" when we were in the hospital waiting to hear if Mom was going to be okay or not. I remember it like it was yesterday. We didn't even know the extent of Mom's injuries when she made Dad promise he'd never let me near another horse. She was pacing up and down the hospital hallway, carrying me. He was emotionally blind and crippled with worry, exhausted from the emergency two-day trip he'd made to get home and without thinking about anything except for the fact that Mom was hurt, he'd given her his word. Deep down he agreed with her or he never would have made such promise. The idea that I could have been riding with Mom that day was too much for either of them to think about. Most days I would have been sitting on the saddle in front of her, but that day I wasn't because Grammie had taken me for ice cream.

Surely, she had to know the day would come when I'd assert myself and make my own decision. She couldn't blame him entirely. I was getting too old for them to make all my decisions for me. If I had to, I'd find a way to tell her that gently, just like he did.

He sat on the gliding chair, not making a sound as Grammie and I worked. He was peeling the bad news like an onion and knew that if he did it just right maybe nobody would cry. He was a master at keeping his emotions in check, which both helped and infuriated her. The only people permitted behind his wall of pain were me and Bo—and I'd only recently been added to that list. Last year I told him that shielding me was the same as lying and he got it. I was old enough to hear the unvarnished, no sugar coating truth, but like this morning, there were times when he still tried to buffer it, dull the sharp edges, and spare me the deepest part of the cut, as if that was even possible.

I hated quilting, but would have done it all day because having something else to focus on made talking to her easier. I was wondering if that was the plan. Dad stayed quiet for a while to give her some time with me—part of the softening. We all knew this day was coming, but you can't really plan for it and she wasn't ready to know that it had arrived. We had faced her death over and over only this time they were asking us to make the choice. She had simply done it on her own for years, fighting off infections, breathing problems, and now her heart, somehow her little body just kept going.

She moved down the row of squares, pushing more and more fabric through the tired machine. She'd slowed a bit and quieted the whining of the motor so we didn't have to raise our voices to be heard over the noise.

"I'm hoping now that you're sixteen you'll start driving yourself over to visit more often."

Okay, we're going to relieve some of the pressure with the trivial.

"Sure, Grammie, just as soon as Dad buys me a car." I didn't need to look over at him to know his reaction, but we shared a glance for a split second and he responded with *"Humph!"* like 'Dream on, kid.' It was unspoken between us that just having me near the horses was pushing my luck, but driving a car was the same as giving it a big ol' shove right off the nearest cliff. I'd settle for the horses for now.

I focused on my hands as I finished the last ruby-colored square. She handed me a new pile—this one pine green. "Use the pattern to make diamond shapes with those," she said.

Okay, now we're keeping the conversation light.

"I'm guessing Christmas quilt here." I held up the colors to view the contrast.

"No wonder you skipped a grade," she mocked. Since I hadn't brought it up in thirty minutes or so, she threw it in. I gave her that "Love you, Grammie" smirk and kept working.

I sneaked a peek at Dad. He put head back and kept gliding, waiting for her heart to be ready. He always seemed to know when the time was right. I did my job and tried to keep the mood on the upswing. It was working as we made progress on her project. *Okay, more trivial was in order.*

I went back to the car issue even though Dad and I had worked it out in our silent way. "So, Dad, am I getting this right, I'll be the *oldest* walking person ever?" He didn't raise his head, but he gave me a smirk like 'you got it, kid.' "You know that Bo is going to let Ty drive this summer and girls *are* safer drivers."

Even Grammie laughed, still not getting that we had already settled this in the milli-seconds it took us to read one another's eyes. "Maybe there's something I can do about that." She winked at me and nodded toward the front of the house where her car was parked in the garage.

"No conspiring against me you two." I knew Dad was only half-kidding.

Grammie and I were like two little kids in trouble. She motioned like she was buttoning her lip on the subject, but smiled at me though the gesture. Maybe I won't be waiting that long to drive if Grammie had anything to say about it. I'd bet all I had, she wouldn't. I played along. Even if she wasn't serious, at least she was smiling.

I'm sure Dad will have more to say later, but for now focus...focus...focus on the light, the trivial, and ignore the elephant in the room.

With all the car and growing up talk, it started—the same old story we'd heard a thousand times. I sighed to myself. *Here it comes!* Whatever made Mom more present to her I guess was okay with me, there wasn't much choice, it was standard routine now, like so many other things I had just learned to grin and bear it. She needed to hear it aloud as much as I needed to live in my same room. She wasn't even trying to read my face to see how it made me feel anymore, she simply had to re-live it. It only mattered how it made her feel. It was almost like she dismissed the reality for a few minutes and if she pretended hard enough, then everything was normal. From the first sentence to the last, the story never wavered—no new details, no old ones left unshared, except the first sentence—that was a new development, the *only* new development in ten years.

"That watch you're wearing was a Christmas gift she picked out for you and hid over here years ago. I sure am glad I found it last year and you can use it."

I looked at the baby pink band on my wrist. The watch face had a flower background behind a little fairy wearing a purple dress. In one hand, she held a wand that was the big hand and in the other hand she held a flower that was the little hand. For just a minute, I was immersed in my own thoughts, wishing that Mom would've been able to help that fairy teach me how to tell time. It was the last present she'd ever gotten me. I was glad that it was lost all those years because it was such a wonderful surprise to get something from her in my stocking so long after she couldn't surprise me anymore.

Grammie sensed I had drifted away for a moment and cleared her throat to get my attention. I didn't need to listen closely; I could recite the next words with her. "You're named after me. It was just a coincidence that you ended up with your dad's initials."

I took a deep breath and sighed as silently as possible, but I no longer rolled my eyes in typical teenage fashion anymore. I did what Dad asked me to do years ago...let her say it again. She sat up cross-legged in her quilting chair and stopped working.

"Caimee comes from my first and middle names Catherine Aimee. Your mom thought Catherine was too long for a child to learn to spell so she combined the two names. I'd done the same with your mom. She's named after my mom and her father. Johnna was my way of putting John and Joanna together. My mother thought it was silly, but she didn't argue too much. I was honored your mom wanted to carry on the tradition I started. I had your mom when I was only sixteen. Typical immature teenage boy, John left us when she was two. I raised her in this house with my parents 'til she married your dad." She didn't even pause to breathe. She wasn't here. She'd escaped into her story when she was a young mother again. "It was just the two of us for so long, but I suppose you and your dad must know how that feels in some ways."

That realization brought her back for a second and she looked up at me, sensing I was about to say something, but I stopped. She waited expectantly, but I couldn't fill the silence with something I couldn't say. I

47

wanted to say, 'Stop! It hurts too much to hear this story over and over again. It isn't fair you had a lifetime with her and I only had a few years.' Instead I held it inside because she needed the comfort that reminiscing provided. "I'm glad you had Mom young. You don't look old enough to be a grandmother."

She smiled at the compliment and acted like she didn't know I'd had some other thought in mind. She slipped right back into her fantasy of going back in time and being with her daughter again. "When Johnna started dating your dad, she was only fifteen. I thought she was going to follow in my footsteps. I knew your great-grandfather Nathan and he told me a few stories about how your dad was more than two handfuls when he was young." She glanced at Dad to see if he'd heard her.

He pretended that he hadn't and let her enjoy the moment. I could tell from the expression on his face that he was probably thinking the same thing I was, *Stop! It hurts too much. Let's remember later when we can do it without this decision in front of us. These memories of her are making it harder to let go, harder to decide what to do.*

I was praying that I'd masked my feelings a little bit better than he was, but maybe she couldn't see it; after all, she was far away in a time that didn't exist anymore for any of us.

I studied her and I was right. She was oblivious or pretended to be. She was preserving her sanity. Saying the words aloud made them true, real. She went on and on. "It did not take me long to realize that no matter what I did, I wasn't going to keep them apart. It was obvious they loved each other even though they were so young. When your dad went into the Naval Academy at eighteen, right after graduation, I thought maybe they'd just grow apart." For one second she actually sounded like she was proud of Dad given how hard he'd worked to get accepted to such a prestigious school. "He was bound and determined to fly, but my Johnna didn't have a selfish bone in her body. She loved him too much, so she encouraged him to do what made him happy." She was so proud that at age fifteen my mom had supported his dream even though it hurt her so much to see him go—sort of testament to how she'd raised her daughter to be a strong young woman. "I thought she was going to cry a new ocean right here in Culpeper the day he left. As scared as I was he'd come back for her, I was more scared he wouldn't and she'd be left with a broken heart. But he was nothing like her father and he wanted to prove that to me more than anything, so when he came back, even though she was only eighteen, I gave them permission to get married before he had to leave again. I made them promise they'd wait to have a child. They kept their word and waited three years. Your mom was twenty-one when you were born and I never saw her happier than she was that day. You were the light of her life and she loved you more than anything in this world."

She grabbed my hand across the table and squeezed it to make sure I knew she was telling me the truth and that she was back in the present. I'd heard it over and over before, but today it was different. We were about to turn a corner and we were all just trying to hang on during the turbulent ride.

"Thank you for telling it again, Grammie." I hurried to refocus on my task, pretending to struggle more than

I actually was with the left-hand scissors before my face gave me away, and she saw the pain in my eyes. On some level a part of my thanking her was sincere. *Nobody* knew better than I did that someday she wouldn't be here to tell that story again. "Any time, sweetie." She looked out the window, up at the sky like she was talking to me and mom together. That hurt, she was talking like Mom was already gone and maybe that's what she thought. We needed to tell her the truth. I didn't even need to call for Dad because he was standing behind her in the sun. It was streaming in so bright I couldn't focus on his face.

"Catherine, let's go to the den and talk." He put his hand on her shoulder and she slumped beneath it.

She was ready. "Okay," she whispered.

At that point he abandoned his role as "little boy" and became the grown up in their little dance. She led the way slowly, but with a brave face. Realizing what we had done—accidentally misleading her—Dad hurried to tell her the news. Upon hearing it, she breathed a sigh of relief.

"The looks on your faces and you actually coming to my door," she gestured to Dad, "...it scared me to death. I thought the worst. Of course, this is pretty bad in itself." Her voice came out in a hoarse whisper. "But I guess we have a decision to make. Can I think on it, pray on it a while, or do you need to know today?"

He sighed deeply before answering; dragging out the decision was going to be hard on him. "I guess a while would be alright, we can't put it off too long in case...well, in case it happens again, but for now, they'll keep trying to keep her heart going 'til we decide not to resuscitate."

His words brought glistening tears to her eyes, but she didn't allow herself to cry. She was being as strong as that young girl she'd raised. Her face was an odd mixture of resolve and heartache. My father had said the words "not to resuscitate" so gently, he was clearly himself again and not the scared, bullied kid at the door. She had taken it reasonably well and the burden of telling her the news and not having to make the decision alone was off his shoulders. I was grateful for that.

She knew he'd never make a decision without her. I remembered all too clearly the closest they'd come to a fight was just after Mom was transferred to the care home. The doctors wanted to do surgery to remove her uterus after finding she had developed a large tumor. Grammie was afraid Mom would wake up and want another child. That was a tough one until they agreed and approved the surgery to make sure there was no cancer, but of course, there was. It had been there quite a while. They'd found it while running all the tests after her stroke. I guess the fall both took and saved her life. Not an easy paradox to live with. It seemed an unfair trade—find the cancer because you lose your brain function. Live and mostly die all at the same time. It surprised me they could agree on anything after that, but today they would find middle ground.

Dad did all he could to reassure her they were on the same team. "I'm so glad you want to take some time too. I'm thinking it's been so long since she's had any trouble with her heart, it could have been an isolated incident. I just want to make sure, to see if it's going to persist or not before we do anything in haste."

He looked like he was going to reach for her hand, but either thought better of it or chickened out at the last second.

"Yes, let's wait until we both feel right about it...whatever *it* is," she nodded. For the first time in a long time I sat between them in peace.

"I was worried you and the rest of the world would think I was being selfish, no matter what I decided."

She leaned forward in her old rocker and touched his knee, no hesitation on her part this time. "Caleb, I have called you many things since you took my daughter away from me so young," she smiled, "but selfish has never been one of them. Let's give it some time, let's let them treat her for now. Realistically, there may not even be anything new to treat." She looked at me for approval and I gave it with a slight nod. Whew! Not my responsibility. I felt a little better about myself knowing Dad felt selfish wanting to keep her here too. Maybe I wasn't the worst daughter in the world. What a huge weight gone, at least for now.

Chapter 4
"Two Bets"

I jogged up the eight steps that led to the wide square landing. The stairs split from there into two separate stair-cases—one to the right which led to the back of the big square house and one to the left which would take me to the front side and my bedroom. Bo was standing there waiting. He had just come from the back side of the house—the Rapunzel room. I just stood there and waited for it. I knew it was coming. I counted to myself. *One, two, three, four, five.*

"Man, kiddo, I thought as you got older the resemblance would fade, but it's getting down right creepy." He put his hands up like we were about to box. He easily dodged my attempts to block him from messing up my hair. His preoccupation with annoying me didn't stop his chatter. He's like the funny uncle at Thanksgiving, only I get him all year.

"I mean really it's like looking in a mirror—it has to be for you, anyway. If Mrs. Maggie ever finds out anything about the family tree, I hope she at least gets her name. How weird would it be if you two mirrors had the same name?"

He stopped swaying from side to side in his boxer stance and lowered his hands—a sign of a truce or that my hair was sticking up enough to his liking. He kept staring like some big epiphany had dawned on him and he broke into a wide grin. "I think by the looks of it you two are finally about the same age. Guess I can tell Mrs.

Maggie that she had to be about sixteen when the picture was painted. Maybe that will help her pin down the year. She's right, you know—for some things you just gotta use your brain. The Internet isn't everything. It's all about intuition and life skill."

I think I'd just gotten my first horse lesson—either that or he was insinuating that I had neither. It was my turn for a comeback.

"Congratulations! You held out all of five seconds before you brought it up this time. Usually you don't make it that long when you're coming down from up there."

"Well, I can't exactly help it, girlie. She's staring at me, looking out of that great big painting every second. Sometimes I feel like I know her so well I should ask her for tips on which of the stock I should breed."

I resumed my boxing stance while he just leaned back against the railing and relaxed, like "bring it on." Even I had to admit with my thin frame and small fists and the fact that he towered over me, I didn't stand a chance physically, so instead I used my biggest weapon—my mouth. It hit him below the belt.

"Think she's got the inside scoop on your Derby winner?" I didn't even have to swing, I got him good. He hated to say it or hear it out loud to avoid jinxing his luck. I wasn't sure if all horsemen were that way or if we got the most superstitious one in the bunch. He always dreamed of Cameron Manor putting up a Kentucky Derby winner—or better yet, a Triple Crown champ. He didn't even care about the money. For him it was more about leaving a legacy and a name to pass on to Ty and making Cameron Manor a legend, adding his own name to whatever history Mrs. Maggie found. It hadn't mattered to Granddad Nathan though. Bo was just as much a part of this place as any Cameron. Before his death, Granddad and Dad agreed that it was only right that Bo was a permanent part of Cameron Manor, so Granddad left him twenty acres of land where his house sat and then another twenty when he included the pasture behind it. I was so glad when Dad told me. Now, when I inherit Cameron Manor, Ty will most definitely be a part of it.

After my verbal "low blow" Bo slumped against the railing, moved into the corner and held his chest like I had him against the ropes and had knocked the wind out of him. His emerald eyes were only half open like I'd really gone for the knockout. They were as deep a shade of green as mine and Dad's and my mystery twin in the paintings were blue. They reminded me of Grammie's. Bo could have been her other child if she'd had another one. He pulled off his ball cap, leaving a ring in his sandy brown curly hair and used the cap to fan himself as he staggered past me down the last of the flight of steps. He was recovered when he got to the bottom. *Dang! I know I'm gonna pay for that dig.* He spun around like lightning and even though he was thinner than Dad, he was just as muscular and about as tall. I was on the landing, but he could lean back up the railing, keeping his feet on the floor and still be close enough for me to see the payback in his face.

"Hey, by the way, wear something old tomorrow— you know, something comfortable, let's say to *shovel* in."

"*Shovel?*" That came out way too whiny. He knew he got me. "I thought you were supposed to be teaching me."

"Hey kid, everybody's got to start somewhere and you're starting at the bottom—or should I clarify and say the horse's bottom." He laughed a big hearty laugh as he turned to go, putting his cap back on so his hair curled back around the edges of it. Adding insult to injury, he whistled as he walked away.

So it's gonna be like that, is it? No matter, I can take it. I was still gonna get what I wanted and I wasn't going to let him work me into changing my mind. If that's the way he wants to play, I'd play all day long...well shovel all day long anyway. I had to say something before he got out the door. That last word hanging in the air just had to be mine. "I bet I work as hard as or harder than Ty does!"

He didn't turn to answer, but my words stopped his carefree swagger mid-stride. "I bet you can try," he said. His words had a sharp edge. I was expecting sarcasm, but it was off just enough for me to notice it was something else, like doubt maybe. I had to have interpreted the inflection wrong. If there was one thing Bo was always sure of, it was Ty and we both knew he could outwork me any day of the week, unless like Dad, Bo was keeping secrets these days.

The thought of there being something wrong with Ty instantly filled me with worry. *Is he okay? Is he sick...or hurt...or worse?* I wish I hadn't said anything now. *Dang my big mouth and having to have the last word!* The only way anybody could have skills like Bo was to have his DNA and Ty was his only blood. Maybe Bo had taken it as an insult to himself. Nah, that couldn't be it. Bo was too good-natured for that.

I started to get anxious when I wasn't able to figure it out without outright asking Bo. Whatever he meant, it was clear he didn't want to talk about it because he kept walking towards the door. Surely Ty was fine or Dad would have told me. Of course, Ty was coming home on time and in one piece. He had to be. I looked at my manicure and my soft, uncalloused hands. I knew that keeping up with Ty would be impossible. Then the ache of missing him started. It had been too long. I needed to get my mind on something else. Ty was fine. Bo would never not tell me if he was in trouble—at least I hoped so. I would tell myself that until I could see for myself. I hoped I wasn't being like Grammie, lying to my heart because I couldn't face an unpleasant truth. I shuddered and with the motion shook off the thought. "Dad would tell me." I was just being paranoid. I worried about everyone I loved all the time. I knew it was because of Mom. Her accident had wounded us all in one way or another. *"He's okay, so just stop worrying yourself over nothing. You totally misunderstood, so let it go. He's fine...he has to be."*

I turned to continue up the split staircase, but instead of taking the left side to my room, I felt a pull to the right. Just the distraction I needed. I had to see what he was talking about. Could it really be getting more pronounced as I got older? I hadn't been in there for at least a year or longer, so I figured I'd just have to see for myself. The curiosity was killing me. Bo mentioned it often, but had never said it was getting more and more bizarre with my age.

The door creaked open. Everything was just as I remembered it. Bo's filing cabinets and desk were pushed under the window as close as they could be in a round room. He had refurbished the old desk from the Cameron stockpile of antiques. He took it apart one ancient piece at a time, stripped it, sanded it, and stained it to make it look brand new. It was a beautiful work of art when he was done. It was the only piece of old furniture from up there in use. I remember he worked on it for weeks when Ty and I were really little. He would let us come up and watch, while my mom shooed us both away from the nails and varnish. All the other Cameron antiques from generations past—the old tables, chairs, and hutch for the dishes stayed pushed together and unused, half-covered in one of Dad's olive green military-looking tarps.

There it was, the infamous painting, leaning up against the wall. It was done in oil-based paints surrounded by an ornate gold frame that must have cost quite a bit in its day. She was, right in the middle of what I assumed was her family—a woman, a man, and a little boy. My blue eyes, long thick, dark hair with the same unusual blend of black and auburn, just a little less than medium height, slender frame and a slight olive-tan hue to her skin were literally like looking at my reflection in a mirror or a painting of me. She had my face right down to the last detail. People had joked about it since I was little, but it was true—the older I got, the more we seemed to look alike. I slumped cross-legged on the floor thinking how I'd never be caught dead in that velvety-looking green dress or with that ribbon in my hair. I looked down at my jeans, red short-sleeved summer sweater with the big wooden buttons, and tennis shoes, wondering how she would have felt about me.

"Bo is right, it's just downright weird." Mrs. Maggie had sneaked in. I jumped, startled at the sound of her voice breaking the silence. Not quite sure how long I'd been sitting there, fascinated by her, but my jeans had started to cut off the circulation to my feet. "Anytime you're ready to use my laptop and get it all figured out, let me know," I said, holding out my hand so she could help me up.

"I'll keep to my tried and true method, if you don't mind—the library, history books, and the museum have just as many answers as your electronic gadgets. I know those sources work. I've been using them for years. Besides, you can't trust everything you read on the Internet."

I walked around a little, shaking my legs to wake my feet up. I guess maybe your way has worked for generations, but I bet if you offered a cave man a stove instead of a fire, he'd use it." *Man, what's wrong with me today?* My mouth was way ahead of my brain. She gave me a dirty look and turned to go.

"I bet I can find them before you do," I hollered down the stairs after her. *Shut up, Caimee! You're on a roll and not in a good way.*

Never one to turn down a challenge, she called back, "You're on, kiddo! You win and I make you peach cobbler once a week for a year, but I win and you never get to live it down." Since I'd never managed to best Mrs. Maggie at anything, I could see why I opened my big mouth and challenged her again, Obviously, I was a glutton for punishment. I must not have gotten enough sleep last night because clearly my brain was not in full gear. I had just let my mouth run unchecked and gotten myself into trouble—twice. I thought about the humiliation of losing and figured it couldn't be any worse than all the shoveling Bo was gonna have me doing.

"Deal!" I hollered. She too walked away whistling, absolutely sure of herself. "Man, sometimes I need a muzzle," I whispered under my breath. I shouldn't lose with my computer on my side, but Mrs. Maggie was unstoppable when it came to any kind of competition. It wouldn't surprise me at all if she had some trick up her sleeve or more accurately—in her apron pocket. Now, on top of how busy I was going be all summer working for Bo, I had all this research to do and I didn't want to waste a second with Ty or the horses. Unlike Bo, there was no ambivalence—Mrs. Maggie was sure she'd win. That same old feeling of anxiety crept over me as I thought of Bo's remark again. Of course, Bo wouldn't have given it another thought that I could be any sort of a match for Ty. I'd have to figure out what he meant later. After all, Bo hadn't really *said* anything, but it was still bothering me. I felt out of the loop somehow.

I stood there formulating my plan when Mrs. Maggie stopped on the landing. "Oh wait, I guess since we're in a race, to be fair we should be starting at the same place. I did find an old document yesterday at the Culpeper Museum. Did you know that the guy who runs the place is an old school friend of mine?" The corners of her mouth turned up ever so slightly, insinuating that she had an advantage because she "knew people."

"Anyway, in some logs kept by the sheriff dating back to pre-Civil War, there was an entry that said, "the Cameron girl went missing for a while." I don't know if it was the girl in the painting. Funny, he didn't call her by her name, just 'the Cameron girl' like that would be enough for folks in town to know who he meant. Appears there wasn't much of a search party, a few men looked for a few days, but no specific dates listed. The next entry says, 'Cameron girl came back home.' I don't really see how she was missing if she came back home on her own. No explanation of where she'd been, why she'd left, or how long she was gone. Didn't seem like there was any fanfare when she was found—or showed up again, whichever it was. I don't know, maybe she wasn't really missing. Maybe the sheriff didn't make a big deal out of it because it wasn't one. Bit of a mystery, I'd say. Maybe that Sheriff Garrick was just a poor historian. The log book entries stopped for a while, but were picked up later with a new sheriff, but there weren't any dates indicating when the new Sheriff took over. I've had some trouble digging up anything in the town archives because the courthouse was destroyed during the war, but there are some old copies of the *Culpeper Gazette* laying around and that started in 1863, so if there were Camerons here then and this house was even close to what it is now, surely they made the paper every now and then. Given the grandeur of it all, she gestured to our surroundings; I figure they had to be high society folks."

She turned to go again and didn't make it half a step before she laid down a rule for our little contest. "No spending money. All the information I get is free to anyone with a mind who's willing to expend a little energy to find it." She tilted her head as she always does and looked at me with a serious expression, like she would be watching.

Dang, I hate that look. "Okay," I agreed and turned before she could see the chagrin on my face. She had cut off my plan of attack before I even had a chance to get started. "No joining one of those ancestry sites where they do the work for you, I can prove the information I get is right and I expect you to do the same! Just because you find it on your laptop doesn't make it true. *Shoot! Stupid teacher blood still thick as oil in those veins.* She started whistling again. I could hear her all the way up in my room. I closed the door and started thinking about what I should do. After all, I was set up to graduate early and being known as the smart one in the family and with technology on my side, surely I had the advantage. Just the thought was enough to change my mood and banish my moment of defeat. *I'll beat her hands down, no problem!* I told myself, but deep inside I still wasn't quite sure if I believed it or how I would get it done sticking to the rules. Mrs. Maggie's schoolteacher tenacity versus my computer skills—that would be a close horse race by anybody's standards. How did I manage to make two bets in one afternoon with such steep odds against me of winning either one? Me and my runaway mouth.

Chapter 5
"Ty"

Titus Christopher Bohannon. He was my first thought when I opened my eyes. My subconscious mind hadn't let go of the thought that something was wrong. Normally I hated to wake up when I'd just been dreaming about him, but last night I'd dreamed of visiting him in the care home with my mother. I was glad the scene was gone as soon as I opened my eyes and focused on my ceiling. I had all but convinced myself that some tragedy had befallen Ty and that Dad and Bo were keeping it from me because they were scared that I couldn't take losing anyone else.

I leaned over and picked up Mom's picture. "He'll be here in three days. I'll feel better when I see him. I know I misread Bo." It was easier to believe it when I said it to mom.

I went through such a hard time when I was ten and Ty's parents got divorced. He was my only friend and he was leaving me. I'd always had a crush on him, but when I was about fourteen or fifteen it had turned into something more—at least it had for me. Dad always said that he and mom were friends first and then it turned into something else. Why couldn't I have that kind of luck? Ty's mom always hated it here, so he had to go to stupid Alabama with her when she left Bo for a "more exciting life that didn't smell like a barn." It wasn't like his mom moved to a big city as much as she whined about it here because it was boring and she hated animals in her face all day—she went straight back to her tiny home town in Alabama. I think it was more about her wanting to be there than hating it here.

It was the first and only time I'd ever seen my childhood sweetheart—and hopefully future husband cry. Okay, maybe that's a bit overly-dramatic, but we *have* always been best friends. When we were little, I can't remember ever being in school and him not being right next to me. We sat together, even when it was alphabetical seating because his last name started with 'B' and mine with 'C.' My first day of sixth grade was lonely. I cried so much that Dad had to come get me.

"I'm sure he loves me too, he just doesn't know it yet." As if she understood, Mom just kept smiling at me from that silver-framed photo I kept by my bed.

Ty had really wanted to stay with his dad, at our school and with the horses—and I'd like to think with me too, but some stupid judge decided school years with his mom and summers with Bo was best for him. Whatever, it didn't matter now. He was seventeen and old enough to make up his own mind. I was hoping he'd decide to move back here. We always managed to eventually pick up from where we'd left off the summer before, but things were different now. As we got older, picking up where we left off didn't mean playing hide-and-seek in the fields and around the house anymore. The first two weeks were always wasted on that awkward 'How've you been?' or 'What's up with you?' stage like we had to get to know each other all over again. I wanted to get right to the "you're-the-only-one-for-me" and "you're-so-sweet-and funny-and-perfectly beautiful-I-want-to-be-with-you-forever" stage, but we'd never quite been there before. Changing our relationship from how he saw it to how I wanted it to be was going to take some doing. I was willing to swallow all my pride and lose both bets with Mrs. Maggie and Bo to put all my energy into that.

"I love him, Mom. I know people think I'm too young to know that, but you knew it about Dad, so maybe I have your flawless intuition when it comes to men." She just stared back at me, silent as usual. The picture was taken when she and Dad took a cruise to Jamaica when I was three. I spent half of that summer with Grammie. In the photo, she's leaning against the deck rail and the sun is setting behind her. She was so beautiful with her deep tan, the sun highlighting her hair, and her movie star smile.

"I miss you, Mom. I wish you knew everything. I wish you could meet Ty now and see why I love him so much. It's not just because he's so great at everything around here or because he's turned out to be soooooo gorgeous, but because he knows me. He knows why I love this place. He knew you and remembers you just like I do. I don't have to make him part of my life like some random guy I might meet at college. Everything about him *is* my life. I know...after the skinny, awkward braces phase, I'm surprised too, but if you could see him now, I mean WOW!"

I put the picture back on the nightstand and looked at the clock. 8:30. I still had a three-day jump on Ty getting here to prove to Bo that I could do the work. As soon as I flung my covers back and sat up, I smelled it wafting up the stairs—just a hint, but definitely cake. Why was Mrs. Maggie baking cake now when she was going to make our birthday cake in a few days? There was no church social or friend with a birthday or funeral visitation I could think of. *Odd.* I decided to step out of my window and sit on the porch roof to test the spring weather before I got dressed. No excuses. I would spend the whole day in the barn shoveling or hauling feed or whatever other bottom-of-the-barrel job Bo could scrape up I needed to bring my A game. I wanted to be dressed just right and since we still had the occasional chilly morning. First complaint of "It's hot" or "It's drafty in the barn" and I make an innocent request like "I need to run back to the house and get a hoodie," Bo would write me off the first day. I could hear the kidding now. "What's that, little girl? First five minutes of hard labor and you need a break?" and then the teasing would turn to sarcasm. "Well, okay, if you need to file your nails while you're changing your clothes, take all the time you need." I know Bo wanted to teach me. In one of his few serious moments over the past weeks when I'd been begging him to talk to Dad he'd actually admitted he thought I'd be good at his job someday if I put in the hours and the effort, but he never passed up an opportunity to razz me a little.

It was already starting to get warm. I closed my eyes and turned my face up to the sun. No sweatshirts today. Without a doubt, spring was showing itself. Definitely T-shirt and shorts. I could see everything from up here. It was my favorite spot to sit in the evenings, listening to the horses in the field and the birds in the treetops that were so close to the same height as my rooftop view. I scanned the farm and could see Dad and Bo standing just outside the wide swinging gate that closed the fence surrounding the barn. I stood up to get a better view. I'd been watching them for a minute when a repetitive scraping noise started on my right and caught my attention. At the same time, Dad and Bo looked in the direction it was coming from. Curious, I followed their stare.

Ty was on his hands and knees with sandpaper, scraping the old white paint off the bottom rail of the fence that went around the house—the same fence Dad had spent several miserable weeks refinishing when Granddad Nathan was working the attitude and the dickens out of him. Ty was closer to me than he was to them. I could see the grimace on his face and given the used pile of sandpaper beside him, I gathered he'd been there a while. Dad and Bo looked away and continued talking. Ty had arrived early and Mrs. Maggie was baking cake. I was getting a better picture of the loop I'd been left out of. No wonder Bo was acting weird when I brought up Ty yesterday. He knew he was coming early and I wouldn't have the three-day head start I was counting on. Any notion of proving myself was out the window. I didn't have another minute to waste. I hurried to get dressed. He'd probably already had a couple of hour's head start on me. Somebody was *gonna* fill me in. Never in the history of Ty coming here had he ever done anything but work in the barn and train horses. Now suddenly he's a hired hand, sanding and painting the fence? No way.

My dad looked at my clothes with a knowing smirk. He and Bo both knew why I'd chosen to wear this outfit. I think deep down they'd both be happy if Ty and I ended up together—even happier if it could wait ten years. I had on my ragged blue jean cut offs that sat low on my hips and according to Dad were just about worn out, but they showed off the tan I'd been working on since school let out. My wide brown leather belt wasn't necessary, but it matched my well used Timberland ankle high boots that I wore when I was walking to the duck pond or down our dirt lane to the mailbox. My navy-blue V-neck T-shirt made my eyes "pop" according to Mrs. Maggie, but Dad thought the cotton and spandex blend of material was "form fitting." We compromised, given it was the style and covered everything that needed covering. Mrs. Maggie got the deciding vote, pointing out that the sales girl had on the same thing. It was the best I had to suit my purpose today, no way was I not showing off all the running and crunches I'd been doing. It was going to be Ty's first look at me in nine months, so there was no chance I was going to waste my first impression. I was tired of him seeing me as a little girl. I could tell by my dad's face that this outfit hit the mark. I pulled my hair back into a ponytail and put on my usual "just enough make up to not look made up" face. I remembered watching my mom. She always said subtlety was the key—to your face and your clothes. Too much on the face and too little on the body were never a good combo. They were the only girly tips I ever got from her. Mrs. Maggie never let me forget that she was right and truth be told, neither did my dad.

The thick-soled boots and the hair up and out of the face like I was ready to work didn't fool anyone. I knew it wouldn't so I let Mrs. Maggie bake and I sneaked out before she could see me. One less "I can see right through you" look to deal with, except Mrs. Maggie never just looks. She most definitely would have a comment or two. At least Dad and Bo wouldn't whistle or ask me to turn in a circle so they could get the full view. Mrs. Maggie was another story entirely. Bo was the first to speak, but not to me. He was talking to Dad when he paused mid-sentence to take in the sight of me walking up the path to the barn. Bo was leaning on the gate, barring my way to the horses. I looked behind him and understood why. Dad was right beside him, arms folded. *Great, they're already being over-protective.* He and Bo moved together in front of the gate the second they heard my footsteps. I decided not to say anything yet. I was more curious about why Ty was here early and doing grunt work than I was interested in the massive reddish brown thoroughbred, "Thor's Thunder" that was running amuck around the hurdles inside the arena. He was a runner, not a jumper and normally Bo or Ty would have been working on his speed on the straightaway track. From what I'd heard, he was young and unpredictable, and still needed some breaking in, but he was as fast as a cobra strike and a handful even for Bo.

"Like I was saying," Bo continued, not quite turning his face back to Dad, but still assessing me and the innocent look on my face, like I didn't know they were both thinking I was trying to look older.

"He's been miserable with his mom. He tells me she doesn't care about him or what he thinks. He wants to come back here to live. I talked to her on the phone last night. I guess he finally admitted to her he called me yesterday morning and that he wanted to come here early. She says she's tired of trying to handle him and is leaving it to me, like I'm some deadbeat dad who's never been there for him or something.

"I hate to say it, but she started flouncing around that tiny town with one of his teachers, for Pete's sake. What did she think was going to happen? I'm just saying with her position as a detective, she's supposed to live by some higher law enforcement official standard, right? Well, in one fell swoop she's managed to ruin her reputation and his. He's embarrassed and ashamed. He's been getting into fights at school. Kids are calling his mom names. I guess this last one was the worst— the other kid ended up in the hospital with a broken arm.

"As long as he stays here, the parents won't press charges against him, but they don't want the two boys in the same school together. I guess his mother used what was left of her pull in the police department just to keep him from getting arrested. She's lucky she didn't lose her job over this mess.

"Right now, he is mad at the world, well Rainsville and Alabama mostly. I've been there and the people are good church-going folks. This doesn't have anything to do with the town, or the high school, they've always been good to him there.

"It's really his mom and a few gossips that blew this whole thing up, but, unfortunately, he feels like he's taking the fall alone. His mom doesn't take any responsibility—at least she didn't when we talked last night. She says she has a life to live too and she deserves to be happy. Never mind the way she went about it brings him nothing but misery. I really had to bite my tongue to keep my thoughts about her to myself in front of him. I know someday he may want a relationship with her and I won't stand in the way of that ever.

I'd never heard Bo so passionate about anything that didn't have to do with pedigrees and bloodlines. He wasn't emotional very often.

"I know it's a lot to ask, Caleb, but I need to spend the extra time with him. I know he won't be causing any trouble here."

I put it all together before my dad could answer. All I could think of was the group of snooty girls at school who already hated the "rich, brainy nerd" and now Ty would be staying here for his senior year. They'd either hate me more because I know him or suddenly want to be my BFF because they want to get to know him—but either way, I'd have to share. *Umm... NO WAY!*

I'd be the one getting into fights at school if one of those phony teen magazine model wannabes who hang in their own 'we're-better-than-the-rest-of-the-world' herd tried to sink her fake nails into *my* Ty.

I was ashamed, putting my feelings into the words shouting inside my head. I instantly realized how selfish that would have sounded out loud. I should have been thinking something more along the lines of 'Wow, what a terrible thing for Ty to go through' or 'Sorry for all your stress, Bo.' I guess love really can make you do crazy things you think you'd never do. Never in a million years would I dream of fighting in school, but I could definitely see myself defending my territory. I sneaked a glance back at Ty. *Oh yeah, I could do it easy, finally a wish come true... he was staying, I would defend that to the death.*

"I'm glad he's moving back, Bo. I feel terrible you'd even think I'd be hesitant about wanting him here. You know I love Ty like he was my own son, same as you love my girl here." He pulled me tight against his side for a forced hug and in typical teenage fashion, I acted like I hated it, but knowing what I now knew about Ty's mother, I also knew how lucky I was.

"I just wanted to discuss it with you given the trouble he's been in. I wanted you to hear it from me so you would get the truth. And you're right, even though she's kind of prissy and girlie, I have to say I'm rather fond of this one." Bo reached over and hugged the other side of me, acting like he was struggling with Dad to hug me more.

"I don't think you say 'I love you' by giving someone a shovel and putting them at the back end of a horse," I said, looking at Bo.

I knew it was coming. Dad started the sentence and Bo finished it. "You need to learn there are other things to do on a place like this other than ride." Bo let me out of his vise grip hug and mockingly wagged his finger at me. "It isn't all fun all the time." They laughed at my expense and their shared thought, and then Bo went on. His mood was much lighter.

"Well, as of late last night, we got us a little change of plans. I think you're really going to like this." *Heavy sarcasm.* He reached in the back pocket of his old jeans and handed me a stack of sandpaper from one side and a paint brush from the other. "I think my boy there could use some help."

"What did I do? I'm not in trouble." I was protesting as my dad turned me loose and took the tools from Bo, put them in my hands and spun me towards where Ty was working.

"Yes, but you're gonna be if you don't mind Bo and do whatever he tells you to do." He had a huge grin on his face and I knew exactly why. I could read it like a book. A few weeks of me sanding and painting would get him out of hot water with Grammie. He'd let her know right away that he and Bo had decided to wait a little longer before they let me back into the barn and near the horses. I would be "learning how a real horse farm runs first." *Great.*

"See you at the party tonight," Dad said, insinuating that stopping before dinner was out of the question. I was walking away when I heard Bo say under his breath, "If he'll talk to anybody, it'll be her."

I smiled to myself as I walked away. I had all day to spend listening. Sure, I'd protest and "insist" Bo let me ride. I was an open book and they both knew what I wanted, especially since Dad heard me say it to Mom the other day. I still felt embarrassed just thinking about it. I had to shake it off and get my blushing under control. I had to make myself not revisit that moment of humiliation. Okay, I'll put on my 'let them think what they want' attitude. Whatever, I'll play their game. Whatever kept me near Ty was going to work out just fine and they couldn't keep me away from training forever, although I'd never tell them I didn't want to start with Thor.

~~~

Ty was sitting in the damp grass still sanding the same part of the bottom log of the fence. If he'd actually been really trying, he'd have been done with that rail by now, but he was only half-heartedly moving his hand back and forth. I got it right away. Bo had talked to him yesterday morning. I knew the lackluster performance my dad had started with when Granddad was working him. I was right when I made my first guess. For one split second, Bo had doubted Ty, not because he couldn't do the work but because he didn't want to, all of his energy was going into being mad at his mom and whatever else happened to him, I got the quick rundown listening to Bo, but I was sure I'd get the details from Ty. Hillbilly and Bumpkin were wagging their tails like whips, sticking their heads through the wide gap between the bottom log and the middle one, licking his hands and further slowing his progress. Ty loved all animals, but ignored them both. I could never figure out why they didn't just walk through the space between the logs and wander the fields, but they never did. I looked down the long fence line. There were three horizontal logs about ten inches around with about two feet between each one and thick round posts about every fifteen feet. No wonder it had taken my dad so long to do this last time. We were going to be here a while. Two acres was an awful lot of fence.

"Hey!" I folded my arms in front of me so he could see the sandpaper and the paint brush and at least know I was there to help. I swung my right leg over and tapped his knee with the toe of my boot so he'd look up.

The bill of his blue ball cap was rounded with age and the top was a little tattered. Years ago, when I told Ty he needed a new cap, Bo explained, 'That's when a cap starts to get comfortable. Ty's was in worse shape, so I imagine it has a few good years left in it, according to his dad's theory.

Ty stopped his repetitive back and forth motion with the sandpaper and looked up, squinting at the sun behind me. Even though his eyes were half closed, my heart still skipped a beat. They were so beautiful—light, warm, liquid caramel with dark brownish-gold flecks, like his mother's. I'd surmised from the conversation I'd just heard, were the only good thing she'd ever given him. His hair was all Bo though, sandy brownish blond and curling around the edges of his hat. His jeans were every bit as worn as his ball cap and his T-shirt wasn't in much better shape. He was too dirty for having just been sitting here sanding all morning.

"Your dad have you shoveling out the barn this morning, too?" Normally my intuition would have made him smile, but not today. He was resentful.

"Oh, just since about 5 a.m. I got here at midnight and the guy has me up before the sun...nice."

I crossed my ankles and sat cross-legged in front of him as gracefully as possible. Now that we were face to face, I could see there had been some changes in his. His beard was heavier and he needed a shave, his jaw was much more defined and the boyish baby fat was definitely all gone. His chest was much broader, his waist thinner, and although he was sitting, I could tell he was at least six feet tall. The sleeves of his T-shirt strained around his muscles, flexing with each swipe of the sandpaper. I had three words floating around my brain to describe him—*smoking white hot.* He was gorgeous last summer, but now he was just straight perfection.

Maybe he'd see that I'd changed too. I just hoped it was in all the right places like he had. I sighed and picked a piece of the rail he was working on that he hadn't reached yet. "Well, now you've got some help."

I started sanding and didn't say anything until the silence was screaming between us. "You want to hear something funny?"

He was still in no mood for chitchat. "Do I have a choice?"

Okay, so he was a little more than crusty from lack of sleep and being mad at the whole world. He was treating me like a stranger or worse yet—like one of the

75

kids at his old school who would judge him. It was unnerving, not any part of the relationship that had ever been "us." I felt like I was starting from farther down in the hole than I'd expected. I gave him a 'hey, it's me, not some stranger look and he knew instantly his pushing me away was hurtful. The harsh, impatient look in his eyes softened a little. He stopped again so I wouldn't have to talk over the scraping. "Okay, Caimee...what?"

He came across a little less irritated, I could tell it took some effort for him to push those feelings down, and he still wasn't smiling, but at least there were no sharp edges on his words. "People, especially the girls here, hate me because of this place, but mostly they whisper because my mom doesn't get around at all and well..." I hesitated, not knowing how he'd take the next part. I mean we were doing that 'let's start again' thing we do at the beginning of every summer, but I wanted to skip it. I figured if he knew that I knew what was going on, we might be able to leap frog ahead.

"I hear you have to move here now because your mom gets around too much. I guess you just can't win no matter what sometimes." I could see by the shocked look on his face we'd gone fast forward past about two weeks of "awkward" and jumped right into our "relationship"—whatever that was. I'd been trying to define it and shape it my way for at least two years. You'd think he would've caught on already. This time I was going to just jump right in, if I waited for him to come around to talk about it I would be here way longer than this fence had been. It was a risk bringing up all the hurt he was feeling in the first five minutes, but I figured I would take it.

I couldn't tell by the smirk if he was mad or about to laugh, but if anybody understood Mom troubles, it was me. Surely he knew I didn't mean to upset him. I held my breath a little hoping my little plan would pay off. He went off, but not on me. He started talking like we had just talked yesterday. I was so relieved. Step One: "speed things up" was a success.

"I can't believe how selfish she is. I'm just sayin'... really, dating a teacher? A teacher who was flunking me, no less? All those parent-teacher conferences were just some excuse for her to run up to the school and see him. Oh, and hey, while you're there, Mom, why not get caught sitting on his desk, leaning over and kissing him while he's sitting in his chair? That's a *great* idea. I'm sure none of the other kids—not to mention teachers who I *have* to look in the face every day will care when guess who? Another teacher's son walks in and sees it all. Big mouth punk ran his fat pie hole to everybody who'd listen and his dad—an "educator and student advocate" at the illustrious Plainview High School couldn't tell the entire faculty fast enough. All of a sudden Coach wants me off the football team because I'm a 'distraction to the other players' and 'maybe if I keep a low profile' the gossip will stop." So even though the season was over, I was off the team for next year. The only person on my side with enough guts to say anything was my friend Seth, but he's a senior and won't be there for summer tryouts, which would have left me alone on the field. I probably would've started getting tackled by my own team. All the talk might have died down if she hadn't been making out with him in his car in the school parking lot with her shirt half off. The teacher got fired, which somehow turned out to be *only* her fault and I got to be the town tramp's son. I hope I never see the borders of Rainsville, Alabama again as long as I live and if I never see my mom again, it'll be too soon. I hate that place, you sneeze once and the whole town blesses you. Everybody knows everything." Bo had been right about that, he definitely blamed the whole town and state for something one person did...that wasn't really like Ty, he was more level headed than that, but then again this was personal and it sounded like his feelings about taking the fall for what his mom did were right on the money. I held my tongue like Bo did, I couldn't believe he had gotten kicked of the football team, I was mad at his mother myself for getting him caught up in her selfish choices, but I figured there was a difference between getting him talking and giving my opinion....at least for now.

I laughed. "Well, I'm hoping you don't think that since you've been gone, Culpeper has turned into some big city where you can avoid that. I know it's bigger than that postage stamp-size town you just came from, but we aren't exactly in New York City or something. They may not know about Alabama, but this place isn't much on secret keeping or keeping your opinion about everybody else to yourself. We may have a bigger population, but that just means more people know your business—at least if you're in high school. Wow! And I thought I had problems."

I was staring and thinking about how incredibly perfect he was. That certainly wasn't going to help right now and I didn't want him to catch me.

"Well, the scoop around here is your dad and mine have finally decided I can be near the barn again. I'm guessing only with supervision." That seemed to change the whole tone of the conversation and really made him smile. I could tell he was thinking he was going to be my babysitter and boss...no words necessary the look on his face was plenty.

"And my dad and Grammie finally agreed on something where my mom is concerned, but she's getting worse, so I don't know how long the truce will last. If anything has to be done sooner than later, they may not agree on what or when to actually do something." He dropped his tools for a second and took my hand, like some buried instinct had taken over, he missed her too. My heart skipped a beat.

"Sorry, Caimee, I think that's way worse." He looked down and realized that not only was he holding my hand, he was stroking it, so he quickly let go—not like he was dropping a hot potato, but more like he'd shown too much of his feelings and felt awkward about it. At least that's what I wanted to believe, but maybe he was just being a friend. The lines were so blurred with Ty.

We started working again, only this time the silence wasn't screaming. It was just me and just Ty, same old friends, same old 'where-is-this-relationship-going' tension that was simple compared to everything else. I knew we'd work it out because we'd been doing it for years. Now that I knew he was staying, I was determined to stake my claim before school started. I shuddered as I thought about some other girl turning his beautiful head. I hated to admit it, even to myself, not all of them were the mean, nasty type. Some of them simply didn't know how to be my friend in a town where being a Cameron meant being different. *Who knows, maybe one of them might get to him?* The thought of that happening was painful.

He stopped again. "Oh, by the way, I was up in the Rapunzel room earlier and I saw the painting. Dad's right, the older you get, the creepier that is."

I smiled. "You and me and Mom are the only ones that ever call it that." He smiled too. Finally, he was lightening up a little. There was something about our shared history that brought us both unspoken comfort, so I brought up another memory. "I hope you're hungry for cake 'cause Mrs. Maggie is baking."

"Great!" He rolled his eyes and his tone was full of heavy sarcasm. 'I am *so* in the mood for a party." The resentment wasn't real, but we pretended anyway.

"Put on your festive face," I said, playing along. Given the moods we were in, it was easier to act like we didn't like it right now than it was to show any joy in the familiarity. I sat there sanding, looking over at the barn knowing my being Ty's wingman on working out his problems would take forever. I had a bad feeling we were about to do a repeat of my dad's youth. I couldn't regret the part where we'd get to spend time together no matter how crummy the task, but I didn't want to waste my whole summer being a field hand when I could be riding. My mind wandered to thoughts of riding off into the sunset with Ty. I'm not sure how long I'd been hanging onto that notion when I noticed him staring at me.

"That goofy grin and the pace you're keeping is going to keep us here forever. What are you so happy about all of a sudden?"

I felt the heat of the blush rising to my face. "Nothing."

He looked at me like my dad and Bo had when they saw my outfit this morning. I don't think he knew my thoughts were of him, just that he'd caught me thinking of something private that I didn't want to share.

He grinned again, showing off his perfect teeth. "Sure it is," he said, catching me in my fib. "Just get to sanding, girlie." There was a playful challenge in his command and the race was on.

Chapter 6
"Going Back"

I laid in bed sore, exhausted, and thinking about Ty. We'd worked all day in the heat and the sunshine. Mrs. Maggie insisted we take showers before we were allowed to come into her kitchen. We were covered in old white paint shavings, dirt, and dog slobber. When Ty came back from the log cabin-style house Bo had built on his property in the fields to the right of the barn, he looked handsome and he smelled better than great.

Everyone saw me blushing and fumbling in his presence. I tried hard to control it, but the olive-green T-shirt brought out his eyes and did little to hide his muscular build. I was right again. When he was standing next to my dad, I could tell he was easily six feet tall or maybe even an inch taller. His faded blue jeans fit him just right, or maybe he was just the only guy I knew that could throw on worn Levi's and pull them off like they were a tux. I had to force myself to concentrate on my pink half of the cake in order to blow out my candles.

It was official. This was way more than a crush—it was the fulfillment of a lifelong destiny. We were meant to be together—at least that's what I kept telling myself, but then the negative voice would kick in. "Just wait 'til he gets a load of the short skirt, plunging neckline shirts and high heels that walk the halls of Culpeper County High School that push the dress code to the edge of its limits, ok so maybe it wasn't all the girls but I could picture at least three or four right off the top off my head. When we leaned towards each other and blew out our candles, I caught a whiff of his cologne again and that didn't help matters at all.

Now that his memory was keeping me from sleep, even though I was exhausted, I rolled over and talked to Mom about it for a few minutes. Same old smile, same old unchanging expression, same old silence. The sound of Hillbilly and Bumpkin howling and barking up a storm pulled me from my one-sided conversation and my daydreams, which I was hoping would soon put me to sleep and last all night. I rolled over, trying to ignore it and move on to my next memory.

~~~

After we'd eaten cake, Dad and Bo spent the evening poking fun at Ty and me for all the hard work we'd done today and how much more we had ahead of us. I couldn't help but ache a little. This was another birthday party Mom had missed. I wanted to make her a part of it.

"Dad, will you take me to see Mom?" I interrupted the laughter over a snide comment Bo had made.

I saw the understanding and pain in his eyes when he said, "I can't, Caimee. I'm flying tomorrow. I have to get a few hours of sleep before I leave for Dulles. I have to be there at 4 a.m. There are a few hundred people counting on me, sweetie. I'll be back in four days and we'll go then, I promise."

The silence that followed dampened the festive mood. All thoughts turned to Mom. No one knew quite what to say. The awkwardness wove through the silence. As always, Mrs. Maggie ended it by getting up and clearing the dishes. I knew he wanted to go. It was tough when he had to leave knowing I wouldn't get to see her. It was only six o'clock, but Dad stood up and announced he really did have to get some sleep. He was standing in the doorway when Ty spoke up, almost hurriedly, like he was trying to get permission before Dad left the room.

"I can take her." He realized he'd spoken too soon, as he hadn't asked Bo first. He gave his dad a sheepish grin, obviously embarrassed about his assumption that he could use the farm truck. "That is, if nobody minds and I can borrow the truck," he clarified, looking away.

Bo leaned back in his chair like he'd eaten too much, but didn't seem to give it a second thought. "I don't have a problem with it, Caleb. He's been driving for a year and hasn't had so much as a speeding ticket." I was bursting with joy. Was Ty really volunteering to take me out? Granted, seeing Mom was no date, but it wasn't staying home either.

Dad sighed and thought for half a second with his eyes on Ty. "Bring my baby back in one piece, young man," he said and then turned to go. I jumped up and ran after him.

"Thanks, Dad! See you in a few days. Promise to be safe."

"I always am, C.C." It was our custom. I made him promise every time he flew.

~~~

Watching Ty drive made him seem so mature and well...manly. It felt like he was taking responsibility for me, but not in a babysitter sort of way. He let me go to the room alone for a few minutes to talk to Mom. I quickly told her all about my day, Ty's unexpected early arrival, and the fact that he was living at Cameron

Manor again. The last thing I wanted was for him to walk in and hear me gushing. When I'd finished telling her all I had to say, I went out into the hallway and motioned for him to come in. We stood side by side at the end of her bed watching her, watching her shallow breath come and go. It had been almost a year since he'd seen her and I could tell he was shocked. I realized for the first time how much I had to tilt my head to look up at him now.

"Does she look worse to you? It's getting harder for me to tell because I'm here so much."

He didn't answer me. He reached over and took my hand for the second time today and silently shook his head "yes." I could tell the gesture was purely one of sympathy and comfort. We'd been talking about Mom both times he held my hand today. It wasn't the time or place for me to think it meant anything else, but still, it felt nice.

~~~

I pulled my covers up and closed my eyes, hoping this would be the moment my dreams would take over and turn into something more. It was quiet again—time to let fantasy and sleep take over. Just when my brain started to relax and I started to drift, the dogs started barking again. I looked at the red glowing numbers on my clock. Eleven-thirty. I knew Mrs. Maggie would wake up and be on the verge of making coon hound stew if I didn't get up and do something about it; plus Dad had to get his rest and I didn't want them waking him up either. I threw on my work clothes from today, grabbed a flashlight out of my desk drawer and headed downstairs.

They heard me as soon as I opened the front door—the sound of my boots against the wooden porch called them and they came flying around the corner, heads back, tails wagging, and howling. "*SSSHHH*, stupid dogs! You want Mrs. Maggie to come out here? You'll be sorry if she does. She'll get her broom out and shoo you clear to the pound!"

I reached down and started petting them. They led me around the corner of the house to the back yard. The moon was full, shining clear bright white light all the way around the house. Its silver rays made the black sky look deep blue, while the stars lit up the clouds. It was the kind of sky I could crawl out my window and stare at for hours, especially in the summer, but not tonight. The dogs stopped just where I feared they would—a much darker place where I knew the beautiful moonlight would not reach. For a minute, I thought about turning and running for the duck pond, my other favorite place to sit and look at our big piece of the sky. I loved to see the pale blue glow reflecting from the heavens and spilling across the dark water; I was betting at this hour, without the sun's sinking rays, it would be shining silver. I wondered as I had about the bluebells if the generations before me thought it was as breathtakingly beautiful as I did, another comforting constant of the Manor shared between Cameron's over who knows how many years? I wanted more than anything to go sit on the little dock and enjoy it, but I knew as the dogs licked my hands that if I left now they would start howling again. Neither of them would be happy until I flushed out whatever was keeping them awake.

Around the bottom of the house, all the way across the back side and running the length of the porch, there was a white wooden lattice fence used to cover the crawl space that had been dug years ago. It ran the length of the house to provide access to the underside of the foundation when the plumbing, heating, and air-conditioning had been installed. I'd seen service workers slide it aside to crawl under there to work on the pipes from time to time. There was only one small corner that wasn't thoroughly nailed down to allow easy access. It never failed, every spring some critter or another got under there and had babies. Last summer it was a cat; the year before it was a family of squirrels. I crossed the fingers on both of my hands, yet still managed to hold onto the flashlight as I slid the fence aside. "Please don't be a snake. Please don't be a snake."

Coward that I was, I shined the flashlight under the house, first checking for the eye shine of an animal to be reflected back at me, hoping for a puppy this time. No luck, I didn't see anything. Hillbilly and Bumpkin were too tall to belly crawl under there, so I knew I'd have to go alone. They stood behind me, ready and waiting to chase whatever poor creature I was about to flush out for them. They'd pursue it clear across the yard and under the fence; but, of course, anything that made it to the fence line was safe. Dang dogs wouldn't go outside it if their lives depended on it.

I knew if I could see beyond the flashlight's beam, I would never be under there. One spider would be enough to have me on my way back out as fast as I could crawl backwards. I used my most soothing voice 'Come here, little baby animal. Whatever you are, I won't hurt you." I thought about how dumb that sounded and tried a new approach. I decided to whistle first and once it was in view, then talk sweet to it. Of course, there was no response to the whistle. *Okay, back to the sweet talk.* "Okay, here little baby animal and mother, please don't bite me." It sounded just as stupid the second time, but maybe soothing to whatever it was that was watching me in the darkness by my flashlight beam, which was starting to grow dim because I'd forgotten to change the batteries. "It's alright, little buddy, I won't hurt you. Come out."

I swept my light left and right, trying to see through the pitch black. *Great. Here I am crawling under the house in the middle of the night when I should be upstairs dreaming of Ty.* I would definitely have to take another shower, but at least the dogs were quiet.

It felt like I'd been crawling too long. I had to be reaching the end of the space. I'd gone around pipes and the concrete posts that held the house up, now it was just dirt and small rocks. I figured whatever was there was either backing away from me or had run out around me. As far as I could tell I was still going in a straight line. I could hear the dogs starting again with low whines on the other side of the small fence. They seemed too far away and were getting impatient.

When I put my hand out in front of me to crawl forward, I almost fell flat on my face. There was nothing in front of me. I shook the flashlight in an attempt to get the light to shine a bit brighter when I saw it. There was one quick really bright flash, but that seemed to be the batteries' last bit of power. It went right back to dim, but that was all I needed to see.

Chapter 7
"Falling"

There was a hole about three feet in height and diameter right in front of me. It was like the ground came to an end and the wall that was supposed to mark my having made it the length of the underside of the house had been compromised by a wearing away of the foundation. I'd been under here many times, but never all the way to the other side, so maybe it had always been there. My light went very faint again and just as I reached through, expecting the hole to be shallow and find more dirt or concrete on the other side, I lost my balance and fell forward through the hole and down about four feet. I landed on my palms in a dirt room about the size of my closet. Thankfully, I didn't break my stupid neck. All I could see clearly was the shape of a ladder a couple of feet in front of me. I shined what was left of my light upwards and discovered a wooden door. I walked toward the bottom rung, tripped over a large burlap sack and a bunch of potatoes rolled out. There were several more just like it stacked all around me, each labeled with some type of vegetable or meat. I immediately figured Mrs. Maggie must know something about this—after all, she was the cook. *"Stupid dogs, barking at nothing, keeping me awake and making me fall."* If Mrs. Maggie was going to palm them off on someone else I was just in the mood to help her.

I climbed the ladder, which was oddly held together with some type of wooden pegs instead of nails. The door above my head was flat, like a storm door in the ground. I pushed as hard as I could and managed to swing it halfway open before it fell back down and nearly hit me in the face. It was heavy and solid. I squinted at the flash of broad daylight and the sun directly over me shining into my eyes. I pushed the door again, harder this time and it flipped all the way over and hit the grass surrounding the opening with a dull thud. It had to be about high noon. Surely it hadn't taken me all night and half the day to crawl the length of the house. I was sure it was eleven-thirty when I left my room. It hadn't felt longer than thirty minutes. It should be about midnight. I was confused, trying to shove twelve hours into thirty minutes and make it fit somehow.

It was dead quiet except for the gentle sound of the wind. I smelled something. It wasn't unfamiliar, but it was out of place—not something typical for the Manor, but I couldn't quite place it. I didn't hear the horses or Bo whistling or the roar of the truck engine. I heard nothing. The breeze blew by and I smelled the odor again. Apples, like a lot of apples. I was facing an empty field, but when I turned around there were rows and rows of apple trees all in a perfect line. They were covered in beautiful white blossoms. I figured by harvest time this fall somebody was going to have more than a few pieces of fruit to pick. It didn't dawn on me 'til just that second I had no idea where I was. My brain was trying to make it make sense. If anyone lived near Cameron Manor, I think I would have found some way to the neighbor's yard, but we didn't have any neighbors. Our house sat in the middle of at least a hundred and fifty acres.

I walked away from the edge of the trees, not wanting to get any more lost than I was when I rounded the corner of the last row. There was a wide clearing and I nearly fainted. The sight brought me to my knees. My head spun and I started gasping for breath. I braced myself with my hands in front of me, clinging to handfuls of grass so I could register something real. The dirt, the grass beneath my hands, it was real. I could feel it, but the sight before me had to be an illusion. It was Cameron Manor—at least it was an older, more rustic replica of it. I squeezed my eyes tight before I looked up again to make sure I wasn't losing my mind. It was still there—my home, only different. My window, my porch, but no fence, no dogs, I looked to my left where it should have been and I was right—no barn, only more apple trees. What was happening? *I have to be dreaming! This can't be real.* I was digging so hard into the grass now I was breaking my nails. The pain was real. The smell of the dirt was real.

"I have to be dreaming" I barely whispered feeling strange about breaking the silence, but saying it again, willing it to be true, didn't really help. There was no other explanation. I'd never left my bed. But this was not the fantasy about Ty I was hoping to have. This was odd. Maybe I'd eaten too much cake too. I got up and started walking. Funny, I didn't have that heavy leg sensation I usually get when I'm walking in dreams. I only made it about twenty-five feet when I saw her. She'd been hidden from my view by the last few trees on the corner. Her long black hair was partially pulled back and tied with a peach-colored ribbon. Her matching dress came down to just above the tops of her odd-looking black shoes. I could just barely see something that looked like fancy long johns and the hem of what I thought might be the bottom of a nightgown that matched her dress coming out from underneath cream-colored lace around the bottom. The back of her collar was also lace. The sleeves puffed a little in the middle, but otherwise looked tight on her thin arms. It looked like a really uncomfortable Halloween costume or a little like the dress Mom had worn to a masquerade ball at the country club one New Year's Eve before I was born, before she fell, before New Year's Day wasn't worth celebrating anymore. I had to stop and catch my breath before I could try to make sense of what I was seeing in front of me. Even in this strange dream, absently thinking of that day—my worst day—was painful. Taking in deep breaths of hot humid air to ease the squeezing sensation in my chest brought on by the memory of Mom's accident made me realize that the girl's outfit was way too heavy for the sweltering temperature. I noticed the sun beating down from directly overhead. My mind hadn't registered the stinging heat on my unprotected skin 'til the moment it was relieved by the breeze that carried with it the light scent of the apples. Vaguely, without conscious effort, I was thinking how lucky I was that I didn't burn easily. My brain was on overload. My thoughts seemed to pass through me without any willful use of my mind. My arms and legs kept moving without any conscious intent on my part. I slowly drew closer to her with no idea who she was or why she was standing in my yard—at least it looked like my yard. Well, kind of anyway.

She was doing something I couldn't see, furiously working with her left hand. I was quiet as I sneaked up behind her, curious to see what she was working on.

Maybe it would give me a clue as to what was going on—at least until I woke up. When I was about five feet away I could see a picture of the house over her shoulder. She was sketching with a charcoal pencil. I recognized the likeness immediately. It was the canvas picture we had in the Rapunzel room with the rest of the family heirlooms. It was a rather good likeness of Cameron Manor. I gasped louder than I intended. She stopped moving and stood rigid. I couldn't be sleeping or sleepwalking. This was real. That picture was real. I'd seen it before, dozens of times. Maybe I was sleepwalking. I'd just seen the picture today, so maybe my subconscious was seeing it again. *"Great Caimee argue in your own head that will help."*

She turned around slowly, like she was afraid of what she might see. She turned about the same speed I had crawled when I first went through the fence, frightened of an insect or reptile jumping out at me. I had unwittingly startled her and she made an unintended stray mark on the picture when she jumped. Every time I looked at that picture, I always wondered why there was a random wandering line coming off of the porch railing on the right side of the image. Now I knew—or in my dream state, I just made up a reason. She continued to turn very slowly and I realized I had more than startled her—she was genuinely terrified. I guess she had every reason to be. The more her face came into view, the more my mind shut down. I was stuck in wordless, motionless shock. I was numb all over. It was her—my twin—the girl in the painting. We were the same height, had the same face, even the same hands. As best I could tell under her strange clothes, we were also about the same size.

93

She saw me and turned ashen gray and then pale white. I didn't know what to do. It was like she was falling in slow motion. I thought of my mom and the jagged rock where she struck her head and immediately went from numb to moving in a flash. I put my arms around her waist and caught her about two feet before she hit the ground. We both ended up rolling onto the thick green grass. In that instant I realized my falling was far more significant than hers or my mother's. I had tumbled through more than just a hole in the wall under the house. I'd fallen into another time. *If I'm sleeping, shouldn't I be able to fly or something?* It was just enough on the edge of magical to be a hallucination. I could see the strings behind the illusion, but the whole experience—the sunshine, the breeze and the heat, the smell of the apples, the sight of Cameron Manor, it was just crazy enough to make me feel insane for thinking my senses were capable of deceiving me to this degree. Admitting this was possible to whatever part of my brain that was still functioning almost made it seem true. I felt like I was stuck in a fog that I couldn't quite see beyond. Was I in the middle of a dream or on the outermost limits of concrete reality? My head was swimming trying to accept it. The logical part of my brain that told me what was right and real was slipping away, I forced myself to try and hang on to some type of reason, while the part of me that dreamed, wished on stars and wanted to believe in fairytales pushed itself forward. I pushed it back; realizing if I didn't my sanity might leave me altogether. There had to be another explanation. As the conversation with my delusion ensued, I realized I was wide awake...and very confused.

Chapter 8
"Joyelle"

"Hi, I'm Caimee." I had to say something. I didn't mean for them to, but the words came out shaky and nervous.

I went for the obvious, hoping that even in this strange and familiar place it would be a benign enough greeting. I decided to leave off the Cameron part. I had no idea what would send her back over the edge and I was just barely hanging on myself. I spoke gently when she opened her eyes. She squinted into the bright light trying to see me again. I was sitting cross-legged in the thick warm grass. The sun was high over our heads.

It hadn't been long, but sixty seconds was about all I needed to take in the sight of it. Cameron Manor was just as stately looking in its early days as it is now. True, Granddad Nathan had made it regal and modern-looking, but this original condition was beautiful. Everything was authentic and the picture of perfection, like it had risen from the natural surroundings instead of the history it belonged to in my time. There were no fences, no barn with horses, no lane lined with magnolia trees or an iron gate, but I'd know that gray stone anywhere. It was definitely different now, whenever *now* was. The structure was the same—the turreted rooftop visible in the back, the wide front porch. The glass was different, but the placement of the windows was the same. She could crawl out and sit on the porch roof as easily as I could.

Instead of the house being comparable with a million-dollar horse farm as I knew it to be, it seemed to blend just as easily as the center of this beautiful, humble apple orchard. Looking at it, I got that same sense I'd had in the car the other day on the hill. Cameron Manor still appeared as though it was the center of attention here too, as if bragging about its own beauty. In the shadow of its glory, the Virginia backdrop seemed to disappear. I was curious about the inside, but figured I'd better wait for an invitation. I thought of running inside to take a peek, but I didn't know who might be in there and she'd awakened so quickly I was glad I didn't chance it.

Her eyes, my eyes in her face, my face, were wide with fear. She stuttered a bit with her voice shaking. "Who are you? What do you want with me? Why are you here? Where did you come from?" She looked over her shoulder at the house as if she might scream for help, but when she turned back around to face me, something in her expression told me she was alone. Nobody was home. I could see the longing for its sanctuary in her eyes when in the next flash of a second I saw her move her legs as if she were considering trying to jump up and run away from me. At least she was sitting up and not still out cold. Her color had started to improve, so at least I hadn't scared to death. I reached across what I thought was the safe, non-frightening distance I had put between us while I was sitting there waiting for her to come around and touched her ankle just above her peculiar slipper-like black shoe.

"Please wait. I don't know how or why I'm here either. I fell into a cellar over there."

I turned and pointed toward the corner of the orchard by the trees where I'd come up the ladder and out of the ground. I figured that was enough information for now. I guessed if I went on with what I was thinking—*This is my house too—only about a hundred years or so from now,* she might faint again.

"That's our root cellar. Ma stores food in there. Did you hurt yourself when you fell? The door should have been shut, but sometimes it's hard to see in the tall grass."

How odd. She had gone from total terror to concern for my wellbeing in a matter of seconds. I made a mental note—she was kind and compassionate. I wanted to ask her a million questions, but maybe this way was best at first—learning about her through her own words and actions rather than quizzing her into a state of panic, raising more questions in her mind than I could expect her to answer. After all, I was still fighting off my own terror. Pushing my feelings aside, I realized that she had misunderstood. She thought I'd been walking along and fell into the root cellar from the top. All the while we'd been sitting there, she was taking in the sight of my clothes, just as I had hers while she was unconscious. Her eyes roamed over them and her face flushed with embarrassment at the display of my bare arms and legs. I must have looked half naked to her. *Okay, stick to the usual plan and keep it light. Minimize the stressful and awkward,* just like with Dad and Grammie.

"No, I didn't hurt myself." I looked down at the scratches on my palms from where I'd put my hands out to catch myself. They weren't too bad. *Oh, by the way, I didn't fall through the open door. I fell through a hole in the wall from another time.* I kept that to myself too.

We sat staring at each other, both searching for what to say next when it occurred to me that since I had no idea how I'd gotten here, I suddenly had to see that my way home was certain. I had to look at it again to touch it and know for sure it was still there—that I hadn't imagined it. After all, this whole thing was pretty unbelievable. I was suddenly terrified that it was the strange part of a dream that unexpectedly disappears. The thought of being stuck here made bile rise to my throat. I felt like someone was pouring hot water over my head and my heart started to race. *This must be what a panic attack feels like.* I'd seen Grammie have a few over the years since Mom's accident. This was not a good time for my first one.

Focus, Caimee, get back home! That was all I could think about. I forced myself to push the fear aside and figure this out. I'd become good at that over the years. Maybe it was a skill I could use in life, *like when I figured out the answer to time travel that even the most brilliant minds couldn't grasp.* My sarcasm was working, so at least my brain was turning back on and I was realizing that I might have more than a slight problem here, all the while praying that I wasn't. I stood up, but my legs felt like rubber. I did my best to hide it, but as she kept her position—half reclined, propped up on her elbows. I could tell by the look in her eyes staring back at me that she knew something was wrong with me.

"Come on," I said as casually as I could muster. "I'll show you."

She got up slowly and cautiously followed me. She was kind of like a kid invited to get into a stranger's car—wary and not totally willing, but cooperative out of curiosity. When we reached the tree at the corner of the first row, about twenty feet away from the door in the ground, I realized I should asked her a few questions before I go...talk to her for a few minutes; otherwise, I'd make her wonder forever if this was real or some crazy fantasy, and since I was about to leave this dream, vision, half reality that had confused and terrified both of us I figured I might as well get something out of it.

She seemed pretty steady now—either that or she was faking it like I was. Maybe just a few answers to take back with me wouldn't hurt. I mean, talk about your firsthand information. I'd have to make up some website to give to Mrs. Maggie to prove how I'd gotten it, but at least I'd win the bet. That thought...allowing myself to believe this all might be true, was in some strange way beneficial to me. It took my mind off the scary unknown and what I hoped would not soon be precarious circumstances. I told myself I was leaving but still deep down that little voice inside wondered if it was really true, after all it had pretty much been screaming since I got here vacillating between a crazy sugar induced dream and belief that magic suddenly existed without the curtain and camera tricks, it had settled on magic, she was, this place was too real for me to still be tucked in waiting for sunrise and another day with Ty. I made myself keep moving forward, solving both problems in my head—getting home and what to tell Mrs. Maggie when I did. I'd nearly convinced myself this might be an incredibly, albeit *unbelievable* stroke of luck. As we made our way across the tall grass in the fragrant field, I was realizing that this may have just saved me an entire summer's worth of research. *Excellent! More trivia to focus on, less concentration on the anxiety.* I decided to try and keep it up.

"What's your name?"

She looked down, embarrassed, as if I had asked her something far more personal.

"Well, the doctor who was with Ma when she gave birth to me had a French wife and Ma really liked her name so..."

Ah! I understood immediately—something different and unique that she wasn't used to telling strangers and likely made her a target for her peers. I tried to make my face look empathetic and her shy smile told me she knew it. Maybe it was just genetics, but we seemed so connected already. I decided that whatever her name was, I'd just act like I'd heard it a thousand times. Really, how bad could it be? Certainly no worse than celebrities come up with for their poor kids. She finished explaining before she told me.

"Ma told me when I was born, Pa looked at me and assumed that I would be very plain and unattractive, she believed in her heart that he was wrong, but instead of saying so she gave me a name she said was as pretty as I was and would be respected. She gave me the French lady's name—Joyelle Adrianna Cameron is my full name. Pa says it's too fancy for me, but Ma insisted that I would grow into it, she is the only one who really uses it everyone else just calls me Joy. The girls at school tease me. Ma says they're jealous because it's different and pretty, but really it just makes them pull my hair or completely ignore me." I didn't comment on the other kids right away my thoughts were stuck on her dad, she didn't even seem surprised he had said those mean things about her, I could just hear it now.... *"Guess what dear you have just given birth to an ugly baby, whose name is stupid."* I couldn't help but be a little offended myself after all we were clones, and I had been called a lot of things but ugly was never one of them.

"It *is* a pretty name and *believe* me, I understand those other girls more than you know, so I will let you choose. What would you like me to call you?" She didn't hesitate. I like Joy better, not because I agree with Pa but because I am used to it from everyone except Ma, now Joyelle is kind of our special name. I nodded. "I understand special things with your Ma too."

Establishing a sense of camaraderie seemed to relieve her uneasiness. Her posture became more relaxed and she seemed to follow along of her own free will—at least she didn't look like she was about to bolt in the other direction at any second. I didn't know which question she'd raised in her answer to ask first, but since we were at the door in the ground, I decided to wait and solve my biggest problem first.

With the door open, I could see the ladder and the contents of the room far more clearly than I could with my dim flashlight. It was a bit bigger than I thought with dirt walls and a dirt floor. There were small bits of rock and roots mixed in, which would explain how I scraped my hands. I hadn't thought of my flashlight since I'd dropped it to push the heavy door open. It was still on the ground at the foot of the ladder. I kicked it and it rolled into a dark corner. I didn't want to have to explain how I could flip a switch and magically make light appear from a small black tube.

Joyelle came down behind me. I stayed focused on her feet as she carefully navigated the steps. I was afraid to turn around and see the hole gone. Who knew how this worked? It was weird enough to think I'd fallen into this world. I was still praying that I'd be able to just turn around and climb my way out. I pivoted slowly— like ripping off a Band-Aid. Scared it would hurt, scared to see what I would...or worse yet, what I wouldn't find. I don't know why, but in my heart I just knew. When my eyes found the spot, I rushed the few short steps to the wall—feeling it, pounding on it, pressing on all the loose stones...but no hole. This was no hallucination I wasn't going to wake up safe and sound. Everything around me was definitely concrete solid and hard to the touch, the wall most of all.

I didn't care about having to explain anything now. I practically leapt over to where I'd kicked the flashlight, dropped to my knees and frantically felt around for it in the dark. As soon as I felt its cold metal in my hand, I turned it on, shaking it, jostling the weak batteries to make the beam brighter. I shined it on the wall, searching for any crack or crevice that would give away where I had fallen through, but there was nothing. I turned around, dropped my arm, and aimed the light at the floor.

A look of shock appeared on Joy's face. She was staring down at the round beam of light. I wasn't really focused on the "you must be magic" look in her eyes, I was too busy trying to get air into my lungs. My breath came out in ragged gasps as I fought back the tears. If I lost it, I knew she would too. I put my hands out to support myself against the solid wall. I closed my eyes and took the slowest, deepest breaths I could. My mind was racing, but I had to force my breathing to slow down, passing out would not exactly be helpful at this point. After about a minute, it worked. I had pushed as hard as I could against the truth so that I could figure out this moment. She was staring at me, not far off the panic mark I had just hit dead center. The only thing I knew for sure is that nobody here could see me, it was instinctive. Changing the past wasn't an option and neither was answering a bunch of questions from strangers who would be curious to know how Joy suddenly had a twin.

"I need to tell you something. Can you keep a secret?"

My voice was shaking through the terror. What if I was stuck here? I felt pieced together at that point, trying hard to hold my form like one of Grammie's quilts that's only pinned and hasn't been stitched yet. Even that inner voice that helped me stay calm at the hospital was silent. I was forcing the calm, willing it to come against my own will. What I really wanted to do was dash away screaming. I wanted to run—that always cleared my head at home, but I was afraid if I took off sprinting, she'd think I was crazy. The small room felt like a coffin and I had to get out. I couldn't breathe. I needed daylight and something familiar. I rushed passed her and raced to the top of the ladder. She followed my swinging light and came up right behind me. I could tell she wanted to ask about it, but something about the way she stared, but then remained silent told me that in this day and age it would have been rude not to wait for an explanation—either that or she was just too shy or afraid of me again.

Chapter 9
"The History and the Mystery"

"Is there a duck pond here?"

In daylight, I turned off the beam, but gripped the round barrel of the flashlight, clinging to anything that felt real. I had to get my emotions fully under control. I was making myself hold onto the hope that there had to be a way home. I needed something recognizable, something I *knew* was home—a place I would be familiar with, but for the first time in my life, Cameron Manor brought little comfort. Yes, it was the same, but way too different. All I could think of that might still be unchanged was the duck pond. I figured a walk and a quiet place where we might not be seen would be best. The only plan I had was to stay out of sight. I had no idea where I was going and with my sense of direction, I'd likely not find my way back. There were no landmarks, no familiar paths, and no house where Bo and Ty lived, nothing that was really home.

Her expression was somewhere between shocked and confused. She was trying to put the pieces together, except unlike me, she'd never seen the whole puzzle. There was no picture, no painting for her to go by.

"How did you know about the duck pond? Ma and Pa don't even know about it. I go down there all the time when the bluebells come up. I was just there this morning after they left for town."

I didn't answer her question. I had so many questions of my own from our earlier conversation and now about a million more. I had to get my head together, but what she'd just said didn't make any sense to me.

"How is it that your family has never seen it?" I asked.

She turned and started walking an invisible path she had obviously been down a million times before. There was no clear-cut trail, just grass and one apple tree after another. It all looked the same to me. I might as well have been in a scary movie trapped in a cornfield or something, but she navigated it with ease. We were both squinting into the bright cloudless daylight. I wished I'd brought some sunglasses, but I'd started out at night. Then again, sunglasses might scare her as much as the feeling of being lost on my own land scared me. Maybe blackening my eyes so she couldn't even see my face wasn't the best idea right now.

"Well, Pa never comes into the orchard. Ma always has my brother with her and she's afraid of water. She almost drowned when she was a child. After we came here, I never told her about it so she wouldn't be afraid and keep me away from it. The grass is tall around it so I can sit for hours and never be seen." Her cheeks flushed with the same embarrassment as when she told me her name.

"Ma thinks I'm taking a walk, but I really go down to the pond. I don't mean to lie to her; I just never actually say where I went so she won't ask. I never come back with wet or muddy shoes. I am very careful."

She justified herself immediately, like she cared what I thought a little too much. Now I knew she was kind and considerate, and despite her omission, she was an honest person—or tried to be. Her list of

105

virtuous characteristics was growing. In the face of my dilemma, I smiled a little for just one second, I genuinely liked her.

"Well, Joy, believe it or not, teenagers haven't changed much."

Her head cocked to one side. She looked like she wanted to ask me a question, but like me, wasn't quite sure where to start. She was puzzled, but I knew after our conversation she wouldn't be for long. It crossed my mind for a split second that if I was staying here, we'd be good friends, but I immediately shook the thought away. Anything that didn't point toward home wasn't something I could deal with.

"Oh man, I can't believe it! It's prettier in real life than any of the pictures and so much bigger than I had imagined it. The cottonwood Granddad Nathan told me was old and starting to fall apart when he was a kid was young and strong and beautiful. It stood right by the big pond, just as he'd described it to me a million times. The branch that hung out over the water had a rope swing on it when he was a small boy learning to swim."

I stopped and closed my eyes, imagining him swinging and splashing down into the water. The faded black and white photos I'd seen of it didn't do it justice. Joy didn't respond. I wasn't even sure she'd know what a picture was, at least not the way I was describing it. I had to ask her what year it was, only I was a little afraid to know myself. I decided something she could see and quantify and knew was real would be the best place to start, so I continued with the story of the cottonwood tree.

"Granddad Nathan had to cut the tree down when he was about fifteen because it had started to die. His father decided they didn't want anyone to be swinging from the limb up there and have it break." I pointed to the one I had been staring at that went out the furthest over the pond that I knew the old knotted rope had hung from—or from this perspective, *would* someday hang from. "He made a gazebo out of it and put it right over the spot where the tree is now. Then he took the leftover scraps and made a small dock and put it right here so we could sit and watch the ducks. My favorite is when the sun goes down and the moon makes shadows on the water." My voice sounded wistful, remembering the thought I had about running down here and seeing the moon last night, now I wished I had, barking dogs or not.

She interrupted me like a little kid might when they caught another kid in a playground lie. Her tone was one of annoyance—she didn't believe me. "What do you mean he cut it down? It's standing right here. Are you blind? Why are you trying to confuse me by making up stories? Who is Granddad Nathan? I don't know anyone around here with that name. If he came here and tried to cut my favorite tree down, I would tell Pa." The conviction wasn't there. She would never tell her father about this place. I could see the bluff in her eyes, but it didn't take away from the fury she was feeling.

She was adamant, to the point of anger, about not changing anything and keeping the tree. This place apparently meant as much to her now as it would to me someday. *Man, that's a strange thought to have— thinking of myself as not even born yet.* I reined in my thoughts and slowed down; after all, I still had to figure all this out and I wasn't entirely sure if any of her information would help me. What good would it do if it couldn't get me home? What was the point of trying to win the bet with Mrs. Maggie? I'd never see her again. The thought made me physically sick. *Focus! Stop freaking yourself out!* I was trying to stay positive in my head. I pushed the thoughts aside again and managed to keep up my calm façade. I slowly walked to the cottonwood through the tall weeds and willows and sat beneath it in a place where the grass was flattened. She'd worn her spot in well.

"I'm sorry, I got ahead of myself. It's just that I've been missing Granddad so much lately and he used to talk about this tree all the time." There, that sounded reasonable enough.

She came and sat beside me. She was a little excited. The anger was gone, but turned to confusion and questions. "Oh, did your grandfather grow up here? I thought since we moved in that we were the first to live in the house."

I sighed. I had to answer, but I didn't want her to faint again. "Yes, Granddad Nathan was raised here, but not how you think. Just let me tell you and then I promise you can ask me anything you want."

I stopped talking, trying to decide where to start. She opened her mouth to rush me, but I held up my hand and she stopped. Glad to know that still meant the same thing. "I just need a second."

I decided to start with the barking dogs and my crawling under the house because it was something she could see and touch, like the tree. I stuck with my original plan to keep the concepts as concrete as possible. I left out as much of the time difference as I could. I saw her turn pale and a few shades of green a couple of times, so I stopped that line of thought and tried another, hopefully putting it to her as gently as possible. When I was done, all she understood was that I had somehow gotten lost in a tunnel and that I knew a few things about her family and her house in ways she couldn't quite grasp. That seemed to be enough for now.

"This isn't as strange for me as it is for you, I know," I tried to reassure her. "After all, I've seen you before. I mean I saw a painting of you. It's an oil painting of you and other people who we have always thought to be your parents and your brother."

That did it, that one sentence. She leaned back against the trunk of the cottonwood and started to hyperventilate. Telling her I had seen her before now without her actually having met me was way too much. I took her hand the way I had Grammie's when I'd seen her breathe the same way at Mom's bedside. "It's okay, Joy. You're okay."

She got her gasping under control long enough to ask, "What does "OK" mean?"

I rolled my eyes and laughed. "After all I've just told you, that's what you want to know? I guess that isn't a word yet."

"I don't understand the painting hasn't been done yet. It doesn't make any sense." She was rubbing her temples like I was giving her a headache. I tried to be reassuring.

"I know it's hard to make sense of it. I'm still trying to make sense of it too. Please, just trust me when I say I *have* seen it and that's all you need to know." She nodded. Trusting to the point of being almost childlike— another character trait on the mental list I was making.

She stopped rubbing her thumbs in circles on her head and got serious again. She was almost resigned to it, accepting my impossible words as possible, like I did with the Easter Bunny or Santa Claus when I was little. She was looking down at my hand on hers, seeing they were the same. Somewhere in the back of my mind, I was glad I'd taken off my nail polish.

"I know what you're saying must be true. Pa didn't want to do it. They fought over it for quite a while." She lowered her eyes, ashamed she had let that slip. "But finally Ma convinced him that having such a fine rare thing like a real portrait would help what people in town whispered..." She cut herself off there and I didn't press it. She was uncomfortable enough. Ma hired an artist in town to paint the picture. She didn't take me shopping when she bought the fabric to make the dress, she wants me to wear, she wants me to wear a dress I don't like, I doubt Pa knows she spent money on it, she is good at things like that." I knew what was coming next.

"Green velvet" I said the words for her. The look of astonishment on her face was almost funny. I tried to imagine some kid from the future showing up in the barn one day and doing the same to me. She seemed to be recovering from her initial shock, but she still had the look of someone who had just been in a car accident or something—dazed, confused, and upset. She'd almost be to the part where you walk around your vehicle and assess the damage, wondering how this happened to you.

I changed the subject again. I discovered that belaboring any one of my points in the story proved to be too much, so I skimmed over a lot of it, only lightly touching on the parts that seemed to confuse and frighten her the most. I knew because her light tan skin became pale, when it did I moved on to another topic. I decided enough about me for now and got back to asking questions about her.

"What did you mean when you said your dad never goes into the orchard? Why does your mom think you needed a rich-sounding name? You live in the finest house in the county—at least as far as I know." She looked embarrassed again.

"Sorry, I know that's a lot of questions at once. I didn't mean to pry."

She shook her head. "That's alright, I don't mind since you already seem to know so much about me." Her embarrassment changed from blushing to hanging her head in what...shame?

"We haven't always lived here. We came here from Georgia, just after the last harvest season. Ma didn't want me to tell—she told me never to tell."

Whatever it was, I was right—she was ashamed. I hoped she could see the sympathy on my face. I leaned forward, eager for her words. "Tell what? What could be so bad about moving from Georgia that you have to hide it?"

She took a deep breath, like she was about to jump off a cliff and her words came gushing out. "Pa got a job working for the railroad last year. He was hired on to help finish the Richmond, Fredericksburg & Potomac line. They started laying it a few years ago, but Pa only started to work for them recently. He met a man in Georgia who had done railroad work and told him he could get hired. He was glad because employment is so hard to find."

I interrupted. I had to know. "What year was that exactly?" I held my breath, wondering just how far that four-foot fall had taken me.

"He started working in the end of September, 1839. It's May 1840 now, just one week and it will be June."

I quickly did the simple math in my head. "One hundred and seventy-three years," I said slowly, whispering the words to myself. I leaned back against the wide tree trunk. She definitely wasn't ready to hear that, but I had to—I had to make myself believe.

"That hole pushed me back one hundred and seventy-three years." It was too much. I couldn't get my head around it. *Concentrate for now, there's a way here. There has to be a way back. Just focus on her for now and figure out the rest later.* This time my thoughts were calmer. They had to be. I was begging my subconscious mind to obey, trying to hold myself together—to force the pins to stay in place, still pieced together, but unrelenting in pleading with my mind to hold onto my reason. I had to see my family, my mom, and my Ty again.

She heard my whispered statement, but still she didn't quite understand. How could she unless I took her back with me and showed her with her own eyes? It was like the whole time thing wasn't registering with her, like she had no concept of the far off future or the long ago past. I suppose it was a more common topic in my day with movies and television and books. I couldn't think of a way to explain, so I didn't even try. I just asked her to keep telling me her story.

"Please go on." I looked sideways at her, not quite turning my head and gave her the best reassuring look I could. "I'm okay...I mean, I'm fine," I tried to comfort her, not sure if she bought it or not, but she kept talking anyway. I closed my eyes to listen.

She took another deep breath as if she was getting closer to the edge of the cliff. She was feeling guilty because her mother had forbidden her to tell. She was getting to the big secret. Her voice started to shake. I couldn't tell if she was afraid of what her mother would say if she knew she was betraying the family trust or what I would think of her once I knew it.

"Well, Pa was never much of a farmer, so when the opportunity came for him to work on the railroad, he thought it would be easy. Ma was upset by the prospect of it. It was the onset of winter and he was leaving us alone in our small cabin with next to no staples to see us though the cold weather." She paused and lowered her eyes, then started to whisper. I sneaked a quick sideways glance but didn't turn my head in response. I sat as still as the stagnant pond water and listened. I didn't want to make this any harder on her than it already seemed to be, and I didn't want to act shocked or disbelieving, I knew if I did she might stop talking altogether.

"Ma made the best of it for Nicholas and me, but it was a hard time. She worried about how Pa fancies strong drink and card playing and every day she expected him to come home penniless. He was gone for two weeks. Ma has always been ashamed of it—the way he lived his life. She says he hid things about himself before she married him, that had she known she might have married another boy who was trying to court her, but Pa was charming *then*. I didn't miss the emphasis on the word "then" but didn't interrupt. I had my own thoughts on that, but I figured they were better left unsaid.

"When he came home, he hadn't sent any money back as he'd promised. One evening at bedtime he burst through the door, whooping and hollering about how he'd finally 'hit it big.' He showed Ma the deed to the house and told her to pack up my brother and me—that we were moving to Virginia.

He'd spent all his money gambling with the other men who were working on the rails. He was down to his last few dollars when a wealthy friend of the man who owned the railroad came to visit and see the house for the first time since he'd commissioned its construction.

He stopped by where the working men were camped for the night, looking for a card game. I believe Pa said the man's name was Clarence Winthrop. They spent hours drinking and gambling. The game was almost over when his luck turned. By sun up, he'd won the house and all the land.

"Mr. Winthrop never did ride over and see it completed before the card game. The story was he had it built for his wife and children. It took almost five years to build because having to haul the stone added a great deal of time to its construction. He'd used all of the savings he'd inherited and all the money he had earned in the banking business. He was so sure Pa would lose, he bet all he had on one hand of cards. Pa won.

"I hate to think where the Winthrop family is now. Ma says his wife must be as ashamed as she is, living with a man like that. When Pa got home to Georgia, he told us that he'd never seen such a fine estate before, not even in all his travels before he met Ma. Ma didn't want anyone to know the story of how Pa had gotten the house, so she burned all the evidence that it had ever belonged to anyone else. All the bank notes showing who had originally purchased the land were destroyed. The new deed with Pa's name on it is the only thing she kept.

"Mr. Winthrop signed it in front of Sheriff Garrick here in Culpeper to make it legal. I'm not quite sure what they told him because all the townsfolk think the house and the land were a gift to my family from a distant relative, who none of them know. I think that must be the story Mr. Winthrop told Sheriff Garrick because he doesn't seem to be any the wiser. Maybe he was too ashamed to tell the sheriff he'd gambled it away and pretended to be related to Pa.

"Ma just keeps saying one thing so we don't get confused in telling our own tale. 'It was a gift to my husband from his favorite uncle,' she says over and over, so people have come to accept it. She loves this house. She says it's the best thing Pa ever gave her besides me and Nicholas. Now she says the only thing that could ever make her leave is if one of the two of us didn't live here anymore. She says she will always be where we are, wherever we go."

She seemed comforted by the idea of never being without her mother. I supposed if I told her my whole story she'd know exactly how I felt about mine. She sighed, relieved that they finally had a stable place to live seemed to come from deep inside her.

"Nobody knows the truth and I don't think we'll ever get caught after all of Ma's careful planning. I guess it's a lucky thing Clarence Winthrop never came here to meet the people. No one seems any the wiser about Ma's fable and Pa says Mr. Winthrop will never tell because he took his family and moved out west somewhere. The only others who were there were the rail road workers and pa said they had all quit playing hours before, it was just Pa and Mr. Winthrop when he won."

I never opened my eyes and looked at her during my history lesson. I didn't want her to think I was judging her father. There were times when she used the word "Pa" with a harsh tone in her voice. I got the feeling she resented him and was maybe even a little scared of him. She hated the lie. I could hear that in her voice as much as I could hear the love and compassion she had for her mother for having to tell it.

"Ma makes him promise when he leaves he won't ever gamble it away. She says Nicholas—that's my little brother, should have it someday. He's only three, so it will be a long time before he's grown enough to take this place over and make it a real farm. Ma is just hoping that Pa won't lose it all in the meantime. We've had to start over so many times." It was a shame we got here so close to the harvest last year. Some of the apples had fallen to the ground and we didn't have anyone but me and Ma to gather them. We saved what we could and lived on them over the winter."

That brought me to another question I had for her. "How old are you?" I shifted my position, pulling my head away from the tree and managing to snag my hair on the rough bark. She leaned over to free it.

"Fourteen. Why, aren't you? We look the same age, don't you think?" She was waiting on my answer when I noticed her looking at my hair in her hands. "It's the same odd mix as mine—dark black with Pa's color showing through, like the dark reddish color that makes the fall leaves look burnt."

I smiled a little at her assumption about our ages and for her help untangling my hair. At least she didn't seem terrified of me anymore. I did the genetic math in my head for a second before I answered. We were the same size, came from the same gene pool, and were identical in every other way. Grammie was wrong. I did get something from my mom. She was always petite, which proved I was some part of her. Joy was big for her age and I was small for mine. Something of my mother was in me and it made me smile wider than necessary to answer such a simple question. "I just turned sixteen." She was confused by my expression, but didn't ask. I think her subconscious was protecting her brain from too much information.

She did as all kids do when comparing ages and pointed out that she wasn't all that far behind me. "I'll be fifteen on January first. It's easy to mark time that way when your birthday is the very first day of the year."

"So, I guess that makes us just about a year and a half apart." I flinched at the unlikely coincidence of the date—New Year's Day. That was three times now—once at Grammie's and twice since I'd been here. It had sort of come out of the blue. I tried not to think of it, but it being a holiday, it comes up more often than any ordinary day. Mrs. Maggie tried to keep it normal for me and for Ty in years that followed. She knew Mom would have wanted it that way, but still it always loomed over the festivities. Every year, after the sparklers and fireworks had fizzled out and the sun came up on January first, the memories and the sadness came flooding back. I shook it off and refocused on Joy.

Her eyes shone light and optimistic, like she had finally let go of a heavy weight. Maybe telling the truth and finally saying the forbidden words aloud didn't make her feel guilty; instead, it made her feel free—like she had a friend.

"You promise you won't tell?"

"I promise your secret is safe with me. Nobody in Culpeper has to know." That was basically true. I didn't plan to tell anybody in town when I got home—except Mrs. Maggie.

"I really do believe you won't tell. Somehow I feel like I've known you for a long time. Maybe it's because you seem to know so much about me. I've always wanted to have a friend like that—a good one where there was no need to hide anything. Will you come and see me again soon? I want to hear more about things on your side of the hole in the wall."

It was weird to hear her say that. She was so trusting. She hadn't seen any hole in the wall, yet she accepted it as fact, blindly believing in me. Her face lit up like she'd suddenly figured something out. I prayed in that split second it would get me home.

"I guess now I know where that tunnel would have come out if the man who built the house had finished it. Pa says he was a strange man. I guess he would have to be to gamble this place away. There's another small room just off the back corner of the house. There was supposed to be a tunnel that led from there to the root cellar that was never finished. It only goes about twenty feet or so. Pa knew about it right away. It was the first thing he went to see when he brought us here. Ma made me promise never to show it to Nicholas. He likes to hide. He's too little to climb down there now, but he might when he gets older. Nobody knows exactly why he was digging it, but Pa says it's unstable and could cave in. He forbids us to ever tell anyone about it, so nobody will ever go inside. You must have opened it somehow. That's the only thing that makes sense to me if you started under the house and made your way all the way out to the orchard underground."

"But if the tunnel isn't finished, how did I get through it?"

We both stared off in the direction of the water trying to come up with our own theories. Of course, only silence followed as none of this made any sense. A few of my brain cells were still not entirely sure I wasn't still asleep, safe in my bed, in my time. I had accepted the truth, but just like with Mom some tiny part of my inner self still waits for things to suddenly be normal again. I wished January first hadn't come up. I didn't need to dwell on that right now too.

"I have to go," she said, suddenly jumping up. I heard it then too—the whinny of a tired horse in the distance coming from across the field towards the house.

"Go back to the root cellar. I'll come when I can. You'll be safe in there." I nodded in agreement.

"Don't tell anyone. I don't know how we would explain it and I really don't want to change anything here. That might change how it turns out for me in the..." I decided to use a word other than "future" to keep from freaking her out again. "It might change things on my end of the tunnel."

"I promise," she said before she took off running. Watching her run in that heavy dress and those weird shoes, I had no idea how she was going so fast and not passing out from heat stroke.

Chapter 10
"The Tunnel"

The root cellar was cold. The temperature in the subterranean vault had dropped substantially after the sun went down. It was easy to see it was night, although the room was as dark as a tomb anyway. The full moon I remembered lighting my way around the house to the backyard was shining through a small crack in one of the boards in the door. I wished I could just sleep and wake up back in my bed. I was remembering how I'd taken my watch off and put in on my nightstand just before I went out to quiet Hillbilly and Bumpkin. I wished I knew what time it was.

"Great, no iPod, no nothing." I had to think about anything but the fact that I was still here with no way home. Then it hit me like a ton of bricks—nobody there knew I was gone! They'd be finding out soon and it would kill my dad. I imagined Mrs. Maggie trying to track him down if he'd already left for the airport. This would push him past his breaking point. Losing Granddad, Mom getting worse, and me just up and disappearing would be too much for anyone. Tears started to run down my face just as the door creaked open.

"Hello?" She whispered so loudly it wasn't really a whisper at all. The big round silvery moon shone behind her and I almost started sobbing out loud. It was so full I thought I could touch it, just as I'd thought last night.

"I brought you something to eat." She leaned down the ladder and handed me a slab of ham wrapped in a cloth. Thanks, but I don't eat meat."

She was so confused my tears almost turned to laughter. Her eyes went wide as saucers with shock and bewilderment. "Is that common over there?" She nodded toward the wall to the non-existent hole where I had fallen through.

"Sometimes." That was all I could say without her hearing the tears in my voice and knowing I'd been crying. She'd kept her left hand on the door and closed it gently. We were in the pitch dark again except for the ribbon-thin rays of the soft moonlight coming in above her head. I'd memorized their pattern on the floor. The space in the boards was shaped like a spear head and the other a diamond. I turned on my flashlight. I had been sitting in the dark trying to save the batteries, every second wondering how much longer they would last and what I would do when they failed if I was still hiding here.

"Do you use your left hand to write in school?" I'd noticed it seemed to be her dominant one, I guess since Grammie was a leftie it stood out to me. I'd stuck that fact somewhere in the back of my head for later and it was later so I was asking.... but only to fill the silence.

I just kept chattering, trying to keep either of us from stating the obvious—I was stranded. I'd managed to steady my voice, although I'm sure she could see the tears shining in my eyes as I blinked to hold them back. She did for me what I do for Grammie—kept it light and trivial. We were more alike than I thought.

"Yes, Pa doesn't like that very much. He tried to make me use the other one when I was little. He said left-handed people aren't smart, but I never could make the change." There was more resentment in her voice, the same as this afternoon. She seemed to teeter on how she felt about him versus how she wanted people to think she felt about him, like she was constantly trying to save his reputation or something. Talking him up and still down at the same time, I didn't even have the brain power in my current state to analyze how complicated that must be.

She walked toward the light and sat down beside me. "I'm sure there has to be a way."

I just nodded before she could finish the thought. I knew I couldn't talk about it. I was scared, my insides were starting to shake, I missed my family and I missed Ty.

I opened my mouth to tell her all about him when the room started to spin and the walls started to twist, changing the shape of the small space. At first I thought it was just my anxiety and that my mind and my will to stay calm had finally broken, but then the walls righted themselves again and the one I'd fallen through started to shimmer with its own light. The edges of the hole came faintly into view, getting brighter and more distinct over the next few seconds. I realized somewhere in the back of my head the flash I had seen before I fell hadn't come from my flashlight, it had come from the wall. She grabbed my hand and we both gasped. She'd taken my word on blind faith, but seeing it for herself was another thing entirely. She looked at me with eyes wide, believing and doubting at the same time. I could tell she was feeling that "I must be dreaming" feeling I'd been having all day. A sense of urgency flooded me. I knew she had a million things to say, but I was too afraid to take the time to discuss it.

"Help me quick, before it closes again!" I yelled, not caring if anyone heard me.

She got down on all fours. "Hurry, go now!"

I took a few steps back and made a few big strides, making sure I had my flashlight. I didn't want to leave anything of the future here and I *really* didn't want to go back in the dark. I bounded up, hoping I hadn't hurt her. I managed to get myself inside the hole up to my waist. She jumped up and gave me a boost the rest of the way.

"Please promise you'll come back," she said in a sad, pleading voice. In that second I realized she likely had about the same number of friends I did. She was the odd kid in Culpeper too.

I turned to tell her I would try, but by the time I managed to maneuver myself around to see her, I was staring at a dirt wall. It was open for about two minutes and then it was gone. I crawled as fast as I could toward what I hoped was home. Everything had been so crazy, it crossed my mind I might come out somewhere entirely different this time. For a second I was afraid there was another time or place waiting for me on the other side. I started to hyperventilate as I forced my arms and legs to crawl faster.

~~~

The dogs' noses were pressed against the white lattice fence and their tongues were licking my face through it as I pushed it out of the way, but not before what I saw what all their fuss was about last night, a mouse scurried towards a few tiny babies in the corner as I neared it. I couldn't believe I had just been through all that because those two hounds wanted to chase a mouse and babies so small they couldn't even walk yet. I hated vermin of any kind so I pushed the fence harder to get out of there. The sun was once again blinding, like it was high noon. I was confused and suddenly very tired. It dawned on me all at once that I had missed a full night's sleep. With the stress of being stranded suddenly gone, there was room for the exhaustion to set in.

I sneaked in the front door with zero success. My head was spinning and I was still reeling from shock. The stress and anxiety leaving me all at once left me feeling strangely numb, the way I had when I first met Joy, like my limbs were hollow. I almost had to convince myself it was real. It was over and I was home. Mrs. Maggie, Bo, and Ty were all in the kitchen eating lunch and, of course, Mrs. Maggie, a better bird dog than either of our two, immediately came into the hallway and saw me trying to slip off my shoes. I did my best to hide my shaking hands. Coming to terms with hearing their familiar voices, the relief came in crashing waves. I thought if I was in my stocking feet she wouldn't hear, but of course, no such luck.

"Where've you been? You missed breakfast and half a day's work." She nodded toward where Bo and Ty were sitting at the table. "We were about to send Ty out to find you." She sounded genuinely worried. I realized I'd made it back just in time. She had a phone in her hand, probably about to call Dad. I dropped my other shoe, but the only answer that came was one I couldn't say. *Um...1840. Where've you been?*

Okay, a quick lie that Mrs. Maggie couldn't sniff out—nearly an impossibility, but I gave it my best shot. "I got up and went running super early this morning. I sat down under one of the shade trees up the drive and the next thing I knew I woke up to birds singing and the sun in my face."

She looked doubtful, but since I had no car yet and was wearing the same clothes I had on yesterday, she kind of had to believe me. She knew me well enough to know I wasn't likely to sneak off in public somewhere as dirty and disheveled as I was where anyone would see.

"Well, for somebody who napped half the day away, you sure look tired."

I ran up the stairs past her so she couldn't see the lie in my eyes. "I told you, I got up super early." That didn't make any sense. Why should it matter if I'd had a good long nap? Of course, Bo heard everything. I could imagine only too clearly the smirks between him and Ty about my skipping work half of the day—the first day that my dad is gone. No doubt they thought the only reason I showed up on time yesterday was because he was here. They probably think I planned to sleep today because I was too tired from yesterday to be of any use.

"Got sandpaper waiting for you. The stack from yesterday was barely used, so you all need to make some progress on the fence today."

I was at my door by the time he finished hollering after me. I could hear the stifled laughter in his words. I leaned over the banister and called back down. "No problem." My sarcasm was almost a challenge—like I was threatening to finish the whole thing in the next few hours. *Fat chance.*

Bo's silence as I waited for his response told me he was thinking the same thing. *Nice.*

I'd managed to mess up my "I can work as hard as Ty" even faster than Bo thought I would.

Chapter 11
"Confrontations"

I didn't tell a soul about Joyelle Adrianna Cameron or the wall or the history of the house. I did what I was good at, what I had mastered—I put it out of my mind, partly because I had nightmares about still being trapped there and partly because I had almost convinced myself it wasn't real, like a mirage in the desert, but I knew I was lying to myself.

I found Clarence Winthrop online and he was real. He built this house and had his own ulterior motives for doing it. I guess it was a good thing the tunnel was never finished in his day. He died shortly after he lost the house. Its real purpose would've never come to light anyway. All the web page said about his death was, "...deceased circa winter 1839, no cause or place of burial mentioned."

Every morning I would shake the dream away, but that didn't stop it from coming back every night. I was devising a plan to make up a fake website to at least win the bet with Mrs. Maggie, but I wasn't ready yet. The dream or the nightmare, whichever it was, depended on whether or not I actually made it home, never let up and anything that brought it to mind during the day made it more real in the dark. Every night I closed my eyes and there I was in the root cellar, waiting to get back. Sometimes my worst fears came true in my dreams and I couldn't get out, it always ended the same with me pounding the wall screaming for Ty, waking up in a sweat gasping for air. I went from day to day biting my tongue. I wanted to tell Ty, but it sounded too crazy, even to me. The only person I spoke to about it was my mom and even then I whispered.

It took two weeks for Ty and me to sand and paint every splinter of that fence. Even though I wore gloves, my hands were blistered and my nails were a mess, but on the upside, my tan was coming along nicely. Dad had come and gone for one short visit, and then later had a week-long break in his schedule the day before we finished. He whistled low as he casually strolled up to us where we were working on the last section of beams. His hands were tucked in his overall pockets, a big switch from his uniform.

"Wow, only took the two of you fourteen days together." The impressed look he was trying to pull off was totally and obviously false. "I believe I did it all by myself in less than ten." Ty and I both stopped at the same time and squinted up at the sun to give him a dirty look. It didn't stop him. "Seems like there's been a lot more lips moving and tongues wagging than working going on here."

It was Ty who answered just as Bo was walking up.

"Well, Caleb, maybe if you had let us use tools that were not from the Stone Age and let us use the electric sander like I offered to rig up across the yard, we wouldn't still be here on our hands and knees working like slaves. He threw down his worn sandpaper and held up a pathetically worn tool before adding, "And maybe if you had sprung for more than this one brush that we had to share when the sanding was done, that might have sped the painting up. Sorry your inferior utensils aren't letting me work up to your standard."

His tone was acidic. He never called my dad "Caleb." He'd always called him "Cal." Ty was like a son to him, so he was the only one who used it. When Ty was two he couldn't quite get the "b" in Dad's name out, so the name "Cal" stuck. Bo didn't say anything, but he was in earshot long enough to catch the sarcasm. Dad just smiled and took it. The dirty look I gave him was slightly meaner, than Ty's tone. I could read him like a dime novel. He was going to use this as an excuse to "work some more attitude out of Ty" which would keep me away from riding. He'd antagonized him on purpose. The old Ty would have laughed it off. Man, I missed the old Ty because right now this new Ty's mouth was getting me in trouble too—like I can't do that just fine all by myself. No doubt about it, Ty was definitely still chapped about his mom and everything he had been through. That had to be the reason. Nothing else would change his personality so negatively.

Dad kept that stupid grin on his face and shook his head, but Bo jumped in. He'd come closer in order to throw in his two cents after hearing Ty's disrespectful rant to my dad.

"Well," he said with a deep sigh. I knew it would be bad. I just closed my eyes and waited for the bullet to hit. "That old barn roof is looking pretty shabby. Shingles need to be replaced. Caleb, I believe we should go down to the roofing place there on Stonehouse Mountain Road. I s'pose they got all the shingles a fella and his assistant could need." He gestured to me when he said "assistant." Great, I'd been demoted from future owner of this place to assistant.

Bo and Dad were laughing. "I bet we can work it out so they'll be delivering those shingles in the morning, so you all best finish up this last little bit here so you can get started on the barn tomorrow."

They turned and walked off together. Bo slapped Dad on the shoulder as they headed off towards the truck and the roofing supply place. I kept my eyes closed, shaking my head. Just the thought of spending the next however many days on the hot roof of the barn ripping off the old shingles and putting on new ones made my heart sink. I could see my summer plans getting so far away I wouldn't be riding again 'til winter. I looked up just in time to see Ty jump up and start to walk away in what I mistakenly assumed was a huff.

"Hey, get back here! I know you don't think I gonna do this last twenty feet alone."

He kept walking like he was on a mission. "I'll be right back." He took off faster, trotting to catch Dad and Bo. They talked for a few minutes beside the open truck door when I saw him reach out and offer my dad his hand. He had gone to apologize. I was sure it had nothing to do with getting them to change their minds. He'd never talk to Dad or anyone like that. It just wasn't in him to be mean or rude.

I realized he wasn't in a huff, he was in a hurry. He wanted to say he was sorry before another minute had gone by with him at the top of Dad's brat list. My dad didn't shake his hand. He took it like he was going to shake and then pulled him in and gave him a hug with the other arm. I sighed again, but this time for an entirely different reason—my sweet boy was still in there. I didn't have to be in the truck to hear our fathers talking about how their little plan was working;

129

however, their victory would be short-lived.

At dinner, Bo did something he never does, he answered his phone at the table. Her name must have lit up the screen. Ty knew who it was the second Bo started talking. I could hear him gritting his teeth. He wouldn't look up from his plate. I was sure Bo had a few choice things he would have wanted to say, but was always about setting a better example for Ty.

"It's your mother. She says she's been calling your phone, but you don't answer and she was worried."

Ty shook his head "no" and left Bo with his phone in his hand stretched across the table with Dad, Mrs. Maggie, and me watching. Bo's tone was gentle, but still had the authority of a father. "Go on son, take it."

I think we all expected Ty to leave and put his dinner on hold before he started talking to her, but we were beyond hiding the situation now. He shrugged like 'Okay, whatever Dad, you asked for it' and started talking right there in front of all of us. We didn't need to hear her side of the conversation. It was all too clear.

"No, I don't have the phone you gave me anymore. That's why I didn't answer it. No, I didn't lose it. I threw it in the pond." He paused for a second, listening. We all realized we weren't eating, we were staring. As soon as Ty looked up, all four of our heads bent back down to our plates. "Well, you being sorry doesn't get me back on the football team now does it? No, I don't want to come back. I'm going to do my senior year here."

My heart was pounding. She was trying to get him to go back to Alabama. *No way!* I was screaming in my head. *Don't go!* I knew that deep in his heart she was still his mom and no matter how mad he was now, he would always love her, but *please* don't leave! I chanted it in my head over and over, concentrating so hard on my own thoughts and worries that I almost missed the rest of the conversation.

"Well, I am seventeen now and I think I'm old enough to make up my own mind. ... Yes, I can. ... I'll just come back. ... I live here. ... No, Dad isn't forcing me to stay."

Bo didn't look up, but I caught him rolling his eyes when I looked sideways at him. Dad saw it too.

"Well, your breaking up with him doesn't really have anything to do with my decision. The damage is already done at school and all over town. No, I don't think going to a private school there will help. Besides, I think everybody made it clear since the fight I kind of have to stay away from the school. ... Yes, I know that's not the only school. No, I don't think it would be fine if I came back and apologized because I've made up my mind this is better for me right now. I have to graduate and start making my own choices anyway."

Ah, so that was it. She'd lost her new boyfriend and wanted Ty to come home. He sounded like Bo, like a grown man. He wasn't sarcastic or raising his voice. His tone was smooth and even. He sounded sure of himself. It was like she was the child begging him for something and he was the adult saying no. His words were not a lie, but a cover-up of his disappointment in her. His true feelings were raw and honest with the hurt showing when he talked to me or Bo. He'd learned this coping skill with her years ago. This exchange had the feeling of an old pattern. It seemed easier for him and less of hassle to disguise how she made him feel so he could end the interaction sooner. He made his decision clear and didn't prolong the agony of the discussion.

"I'm staying, Mom. This is where I want to be.

"Yes, I'm sure I can work out something with Dad to get a new phone. When I have a new number, I'll text it to you. ... Okay. ... Okay...bye."

Man, I wished I could hear her so I knew what else he had agreed to do. He hit the end button, which somehow seemed symbolic and handed the phone back to Bo. Nobody said a word about it. The silence was heavy, but not uncomfortable. We were a family and used to being in each other's business. This would just be another adversity we shared, this time to make the load easier on Ty. Although he'd handled it well and wasn't at all childish or disrespectful, he still hadn't agreed to work anything out with her. As far as Bo was concerned, Ty not making things worse wasn't the same as him making them better, so that didn't change the attitude adjustment he needed. Dad and Bo looked at each other, wordlessly hatching new plans. *Man, this is going to be a long summer.*

Mrs. Maggie finally couldn't stand it anymore. "Okay, well I made peanut butter fudge for dessert, so save room." Like her peach cobbler, her fudge was legendary. Everybody started joking, claiming how many pieces we each got based on the size of the pan we could see on the counter.

Chapter 12
"Midnight Visit"

June faded into a hot, humid July. Bo decided to put off the barn roof for a while, but only because they had to order the specific kind and quantity of shingles he and dad had selected. Ty and I were kept busy with more "pressing" projects, none of which seemed to be making me look glamorous enough to make him fall in love with me. I was beginning to feel like his employee. We had been mowing the tall grass on the side of the long driveway with a push mower instead of a tractor, no less. "I'm surprised they didn't give us each a pair of scissors," Ty commented.

When that was done, we started trimming trees and hauling away dead branches, replacing the splintered and broken boards on the duck pond dock, and any other chore Bo could come up with. It was like he was going down a list or something. I only had about six weeks of summer left and looking around the farm, I could see Bo easily filling all of them. In my mind, I was sitting on my freshly painted fence somewhere between frustration and anger, but working for Bo never gave me the chance to actually sit anywhere. I was way too busy for any sitting these days.

It was midnight when I heard it—the sound of a horse's hooves hitting the ground. They woke me from a familiar, yet impossible dream. I was sweating and clutching the blanket. As soon as I opened my eyes, I realized that tonight's dream had been one of the nights

I was stranded in the root cellar. When I saw the red numbers glowing on my alarm clock in the darkness of my room, I knew it wasn't Bo riding. It was the middle of the night. I couldn't get to the window fast enough. I was half in and half out trying to get to my spot outside so I could see. I felt a light breeze and inhaled deeply to savor it. Unlike the apples that first day, this was a scent I recognized right away. It was pitch black so I couldn't see the low clouds, but I knew they must be covering the stars and the moon if there had been one that night...I loved the smell of the coming rain. For a split second, the impending storm made me realize that we'd get a reprieve from putting up shingles for a day or two. Bo had decided we needed a change of pace—that we had sanded, painted, and landscaped enough. He laughed a little when he told us the barn roof would be a nice change. The guy who owned the roofing place had called, our order was in. Ty and I just looked at each other when we got the news. No words expressing our displeasure were necessary. It was going to be a hotter, dirtier, worse place to work. It was too late to protest. We'd known for weeks that this was coming. The rest of my summer was bought and paid for in the form of several bundles of heavy black shingles.

I didn't want to think about that or anything else unpleasant right this moment. I was perfectly at peace, content with the sight in front of me. I took my well-worn spot on the porch roof and breathed in the smell of the bluebells and the approaching storm. The floodlights were on over the massive round training pen. Ty was so strong and in charge, commanding that horse that my breath caught in my throat. He looked perfectly gorgeous in his old ripped jeans and what I assumed was his old football jersey. No ball cap tonight. His hair was cut shorter now, but still long enough to curl in the humidity of the warm thick air. He was riding a horse Bo said was going to be a champion. She came to us for him to train about three months ago.

"She jumps like she can fly," Bo said the day he unloaded her from the trailer. "A bit unpredictable though. Most appaloosas are like that, but we can get that out of her." He patted her side and let her go to explore her new home.

Of course, Dad wouldn't let me near enough to touch her, but I wanted to. She was amazingly beautiful. "She's a true white appaloosa," he said. We were awestruck, watching her as she ran and bucked all over the pen. "She was born this color and will never change. You can tell by her pink skin and her hazel-brown eyes," said Bo.

"What's her name?" I asked, inching closer with Dad barring my way. Bo rolled his eyes. He hated it when people who had a potential champion gave it some pretentious name like that would enhance its ability to perform. "Misty Magical Moonlight," he said. Dad shook his head, knowing how Bo felt about calling her that. "Let's just shorten that and go with 'Moonlight,'" he suggested and Bo agreed.

Since there was no moon tonight, she was shining the brightest white I had ever seen under the lamps above and against the darkness behind her. Seeing Ty on her now I was torn between which one of them was more stunning. She was like putty in his hands, following his every command. They jumped like a fluid pair, flowing like water over every hurdle in the ring. I sat watching, wishing I could be down there with him.

Moonlight's graceful beauty only contrasted and enhanced Ty's strength and control.

Seeing him in that jersey from his old school made me picture him walking down the halls of mine. I could see the entire female student population following him around like lost puppies—especially the ones who made my life miserable. I'd been thinking about what approach they'd take and decided I was probably right to begin with—they'd all try to be my friend just to get closer to him. Suddenly, the rich, snobby brain would be the most popular girl in school. No thanks! He was meant to be mine, even if he didn't know it. If I have to write a handwritten letter to every girl in that school, they're going to get the message: "Claws off! He's taken!"

I pushed away the thought of having to fight for him and go up against the popular crowd to stake my claim because surely he would see right through them. I didn't have time to decide. In the split second it took to shake my head back and forth to clear away those thoughts, a silhouette standing to my left caught my eye. It startled me and I gasped so loud it sounded like a yell. Like the lightning that was approaching, the shape came from out of the darkness, flashing on stored away pictures from my dreams and nightmares. The fluffy dress and strange shoes, it had to be her. All I could see was her shape, an outline standing in the dim light coming through my window. I knew in my heart, but like the thoughts of the other girls I'd dreaded seeing again soon, I tried to shake it away by closing my eyes, willing the image to be gone...wishing it away, hoping it wasn't real.

"Hi," she said meekly. She must have seen the color drain from my face. "I'm sorry, I didn't mean to scare you." She smiled after she said it. "Hey, that's the same thing you said to me, remember?"

Of course, I remembered. How could I forget? My attention quickly shifted to Ty and then back to her and then back to Ty again. I jumped up and practically pushed her back inside. I was afraid he might look and see two of me up on the roof. This was not a dream or a nightmare—she was here ... in my time ... in my room. My fears about getting back and forth or being stuck in one time or the other were quickly swallowed up with thoughts of how I was going to hide her. I didn't have a root cellar.

Chapter 13
"Hide and Sneak"

She stood in the dim glow of my bedside table lamp looking around in what I could only interpret as awe on her face.

"This is my room too. I can't believe how different everything is. Your dogs are nice. They greeted me at the gate on the other side of the tunnel. The gray stone looks the same, but the inside is all different. I almost got lost 'til I saw the bottom of the staircase. I think I figured out how the wall in the root cellar works."

Her thoughts flowed together in no particular order, much as mine had in the orchard when I saw her standing there drawing. I totally got the surreal feeling she was having as she walked around my room. She put out her hand a few times to touch some of the unfamiliar things around her, but hesitated and stopped short each time. My head was spinning almost as fast as she was around my room. The only thing I'd heard her say was that she'd figured out how the tunnel worked so maybe I wouldn't have to hide her. Maybe there was some secret to using it as we pleased. That would be good news, but apparently I wasn't due any.

She finally picked a spot and sat down on my fuzzy area rug, not sure if she chose it because the texture looked so unique to her or she was unsure how to roll out my desk chair. She had been eyeing my bed, but the look on her face made me think she was trying to avoid my personal space until I invited her to share it.

"It was sunny on your side of the tunnel, but dark when I left. I waited 'til now to come out." She brushed off the dust on her dress to show me she had been under the house all day. I saw you around noon when I first got here. You were with that boy you were watching ride the horse just now. You were hauling tree limbs.

I was worried the dogs might give me away, but I slid out of their view in a little corner. They lost interest after a while, I guess because I wouldn't let them under there with me, but they don't fit anyway. I have a boy at home I like. I wish I could be as comfortable around him as you seem to be with the boy you were with today. He must think quite a lot of you the way he kept helping you and picking up the heavy branches, and lifting even the small ones you dropped.

I made a mental note of that, truth be told I acted like I needed his help a little more than necessary, just to be near him. I guess I was giving off vibes, which meant Ty was nice enough not to call me on it because he wasn't interested. I couldn't think about that without wanting to cry. I tuned it out and tuned back in to her rambling. The boy I like, his name is Kade. His pa is the sheriff. Sheriff Garrick. He's Scottish, like my pa."

I had to sit down in front of her to make her stop talking, but I did pick up on the Sheriff's name in her chatter. It was the same name on the log that Mrs. Maggie found, the same man who she told me had witnessed the signing of the deed to the house; she hadn't mentioned he had a son the day we spent together. Maybe I could get some info on the good Sheriff and his family too just to prove to Mrs. Maggie I had found out something about him she couldn't.

She was shy in her time. Now that I was on her eye level, she stopped talking and took a breath. I realized she was going on and on because she was nervous. She inhaled with jagged uncertainty, held it in for a few seconds, and then let out a sigh that sounded like it had tears behind it.

"I don't think I can get home until the next full moon, but I had to come."

There it was—the bad news I was expecting. Yeah, this wasn't going to be good. That fleeting feeling that we had control of the tunnel was gone in seconds. I didn't really have time to mull it over because she was talking again. "I hate leaving Ma alone, but the last couple of times Pa left to go to work on the railroad, he came home with no money and smelling of whiskey. Ma's been crying a lot because he's been yelling at me about nothing really. I figured if I left for a while then maybe things might get better. As soon as the wall closed behind me, I wanted to go back because Ma will worry."

I took it all in, trying not to look panicked. I had no idea when the next full moon would be. I'd have to Google it to be sure. "Don't worry, at least we know a little more than we did when we thought I was stuck on your side."

I wasn't quite sure I was believable with the reassuring act I was trying to pull off. I got up and climbed the two small steps next to my bed. "Come on up here and let's talk." I tried to sound encouraging, recalling too clearly how freaked out I was and the nightmares I'd been having about being away from my family and stuck in her cellar. When she was in front of me, I grabbed the pad of paper and the pen on my bedside table and started writing down what we knew. It always helped me to see things in black and white.

"Okay, so we know that if we leave at night, it's daytime on the other end, so I think there's about a twelve-hour difference. I left around midnight and when I came out of the root cellar, I'm guessing it was around noon. Is that about how you did it?" I waited to write down her answer so we could compare our experiences.

She was staring at my pen like it was a magic wand. She thought for a minute and then spoke slowly and carefully, wanting to be accurate.

"I looked at the mantle clock when I sneaked out. It was close to eleven. I'm sure I sat in the cellar for about an hour when it happened—you know, that spinning feeling in the room, the walls twisting and then the light around the hole gets brighter and brighter." She blushed a little before she continued. "To be honest, I was so curious about you that I went back every night and waited." Her words just kept coming in a nervous jumble. She actually looked ashamed, like I would think she'd been stalking me or something.

"I sat there night after night, thinking about how things were when you came. I had almost given up hope and stopped going. I felt silly sitting in the dark, staring at a wall. I thought it would never happen again after about the first week, but then I started to figure things out. I tried to remember what might have been different about that night when you left. All I could picture clearly was how big and bright the moon was. I remembered because after you were gone, the path to the house was lit and easy to see.

"I was surprised when it happened again and there was no moon. It was pitch black outside. I decided not to go that next night, even though I figured the tunnel would be open. The moon was dark for two nights in a row, so I just assumed...." She hesitated a moment. "Things were...uncomfortable in the house. I didn't take the chance that time. I was afraid if Pa caught me sneaking out he'd be mad.

"That didn't stop me the next time, I didn't want to lie, but I decided that if I got caught I would just say I was sick and needed the outhouse. I studied and waited, week after week, whenever I could get out to the cellar without being noticed, trying to figure out the pattern. You left the last day of May. I watched the wall shimmer and the tunnel open twice in June, the last time the moon was full. I knew then the next time would be when the moon was dark. I counted the days. It's about fourteen between the full moon and no moon at all. The tunnel appears for two nights when the moon is darkest and when the moon is brightest." She was watching intently as I wrote, it was getting easier to keep up, the longer she talked and I didn't react as if her coming inconvenienced or angered me she both calmed and slowed down.

"This time I finally decided to go. Pa left this morning for another railroad job, so I hoped Ma would be safe for a couple of weeks or until he decides to come back again, but he's been so out of sorts lately, we never know how long he'll be gone. I figured if he came back early it might be better if I wasn't there for a while. I took Pa's lantern. I had to leave it under the house when I got to the end of the tunnel. The first night the wall opened I was too afraid to come, but the second time I did it. I don't know how, I just closed my eyes and jumped in. I was ready. I had Ma's milking stool to help me up."

She stopped talking waiting for me to say something. The look on her face made me think she had slipped back into being scared of what I was going to say. I kept it positive. She already looked and sounded like she felt guilty enough for leaving her mother.

"It's really helpful to know that it stays open two nights in a row. At least now we know if we miss the first one, it will open again. Can you imagine if I had fallen through on the second night of the full moon? We wouldn't have known it would open again." I shuddered at the thought. Being stranded was scary enough but how would I have explained it when I got home.... twelve hours I managed to cover but missing two weeks that would have been impossible.

Before she could answer, I grabbed my laptop and put the paper away. I could see a million questions in her eyes, but I didn't take time to answer. I wanted to understand it myself first. I was forming a theory given what I'd found out about Clarence Winthrop and the reason for digging the tunnel in the first place, tying its use to the moon was making more and more sense. I looked up information about the earth's orbit and the moon and started reading. The facts I found were exactly what she had already figured out, only this time with scientific proof from Google to back her up. "Well, you're right. There are about fourteen days between the full moon and the dark of the moon and each phase lasts about two days. I don't understand why we leave at night and come through to the other side in the daytime, but so much of this is a mystery. Crazy how some things are the same no matter what, like the seasons and the cycles of the moon." I decided not to bring up the "over a hundred years apart" point I was about to make because her stress level seemed maxed out. She nodded in partial understanding, mesmerized by the light from my laptop screen and my instant access to all things lunar.

"You came through on the second day." I was mumbling more to myself now. She knew before she left how long she would have to stay, but I was the one who was going to have to work out the details. I was talking it out, trying to put together a plan to hide her. "So, you have to wait until the moon is full before you can leave again. That's two weeks." I was amazed she had come knowing all of this beforehand. No way would I want to be stuck back in her time for that long. For all she knew, this side could be worse than hers. She might have jumped out of the frying pan and into the fire without even knowing it. If she was that desperate to leave, I reasoned to myself that things must have been pretty bad for her there. In my reverie and planning what to do next, I realized she was still explaining herself and I had missed part of what she was telling me.

"All through June when the light came through the rock and the roots on the wall, I got scared and ran back to my bed. I just knew if I didn't come last night, I wouldn't have another chance for a long time, so I came." She looked down, shame-faced again. I could almost feel the guilt coming off of her in waves. "I know Ma will wake up and wonder where I am. I should have left her a note."

I wanted to be comforting. Even though she had chosen to come, she looked like she was on the verge of losing it, like if she could choose again right now she would still be at home, she had come on an impulse.

"Don't worry, I promise we'll get you home, but I think I know why the tunnel opens and closes when it does." For a moment, she was able to put her anxiety aside because I had piqued her interest, using another old trick I use on Grammie—redirecting her attention.

"How could you possibly know that?"

She was even more confused when I replied, "Well, you kind of gave me the biggest clue."

"Me? How? I didn't know anything about any of this when we met."

"You knew more than you thought you did. See, look at this." I pulled up the page I had found on Clarence Winthrop and started explaining. I pointed to his picture and that was all it took, I lost her in seconds. Unsure if she was captivated by his image, disbelieving how I could see him so magically at will, I had to shut the lid. "You told me that Clarence Winthrop built the house for his wife and children and that he was penniless after he lost it to your father. None of that is exactly true. He didn't have a wife or children and he died a very rich man. He left all of the money to his brother, who was much younger than he was, but I couldn't find his picture. In your day, the Winthrop brothers were criminals, breaking the law, any family they would have had would have been in danger if they'd been caught, but they protected each other. I am guessing that is why he lied to your father about having built this house for a fictitious family; he didn't want anyone in Culpeper, especially a sheriff to know the truth. I have searched and I can't find anywhere that either of them had any kin but each other" I sat up cross-legged and she did the same, mimicking my posture and facing me.

"His work? What work and what danger?" She sounded distressed, not quite speaking in whispered tones soft enough for the middle of the night. I had scared her a little, like there might still be some type of threat still lurking around the Manor on her side of the wall.

I reached across the two feet that separated us and patted her hand, partly so she would stop talking so loud. "Let me explain." I thought for a minute about the best way to put it. "Have you ever heard the expression 'hidden in plain sight'?" She didn't answer. I could tell by the look on her face that her response was "no" before she started shaking her head. "It means that if you have something really important you want to hide or keep secret, sometimes the best place to put it is not in an obvious hiding place where people might think to look, but right out in the open where it blends in and people won't notice. I always wondered why this house was so grand that it seemed to swallow up the contours of the natural landscape around it. Now I know why.

Clarence and his brother built four houses like this one, all huge mansion-style homes all throughout the South. All of them were destroyed except this one and all of them had a tunnel that led to a cellar. He used the tunnels to help runaway slaves escape to freedom. Now that we know that the tunnel is only open when the moon is full or not visible at all, it makes sense. My best guess is those two times during any month would be the only time it would need to be used. If the moon was full, the slaves would be easily seen and need to hide. If it was dark, they would have to stop traveling and wait for some sliver of it to come back so they could continue on their way. I think the tunnel only opens now when they would have used it in your time had it been finished. Clarence didn't get to finish it because your father won the house in the card game before he could. Our tunnel was shut down, which is likely why this house wasn't discovered and destroyed. They found the tunnels in use in all three of the other houses. I don't know maybe we leave at dark and come out in daylight on the other side for the same reason, the slaves would have hidden during the day and left it at night just like we did, we both left our sides at midnight and I hid in the cellar all day and you hid under the house and came out at night."

Joy's eyes were wide with understanding and shock. "But we don't have slaves. Pa says we can't afford any, but he'd have them if he could because he hates working the fields." She hung her head, finally whispering, but out of humiliation, not because I needed her to be quiet. "I have never seen Pa do any farm work."

No doubt she was telling me that he was lazy on top of everything else. I didn't know what to say, so I moved on. "Well, Clarence hated slavery and did all he could to help slaves escape. I think he told your pa he didn't have any money because he didn't want anyone to know he was the one who built all the other mansions. He tried to hide what he stood for and if people knew he was wealthy, he would have been caught much sooner. He had the means to help..."

"...so he hid it in plain sight." She finished my sentence. She understood.

"Yeah, sad he died before he could use this house." I should have guessed how she would have seen it.

"Even sadder he gambled his chance away to even

try." Again, I didn't know what to say, so I just nodded. Clearly, her problems with her dad pretty much colored how she saw all men. I changed the subject again.

"I think we have to do a little better than that. We can't hide you in plain sight. You're going to have to stay in there." I pointed towards my closet. It was the only place big enough where she would be comfortable and private enough that even Mrs. Maggie didn't go rummaging through it. When I was ten, Mrs. Maggie told me that she would wash my clothes, but I was plenty big enough to put them away. For once I was grateful for housework she didn't do. At least she wouldn't be poking around up here.

Thinking of her, it suddenly dawned on me. "You know, I really can promise you that you'll get home again, no problem. See, I have this bet going with Mrs. Maggie." Joy looked at me confused and a little accusatory. I hadn't explained our family yet and I'm sure the word "bet" made me sound like a gambler, just like her father or Clarence. *Great.* I waved my hand like it wasn't important and told her I'd explain later. I continued to give her the quick version now, omitting the gambling reference.

"Mrs. Maggie lives here. She's part of our family. We were trying to see who would be the first to figure out who built this house and what members of the Cameron family actually lived here. I think the only reason we never solved the mystery before I met you is because we thought a Cameron built it. She would never find Clarence Winthrop in her research because your mother fixed it so he didn't exist—at least in any written records related to the house. Anyway, Mrs. Maggie found an old Sheriffs log about how "the Cameron girl" disappeared and then suddenly returned home with no real explanation of where she had been."

Joy was quick as a perceptive look flashed in her eyes. "Because I'm here, but I think we need to come up with some reason why I left. Ma will ask.

"Well, we have two weeks to think about it, so I'm sure we can come up with something. Come on, let's fix you a place to sleep."

I hopped down off the bed and she followed. I showed her to the closet, found some extra blankets, padded the wood with a couple of my old sleeping bags and made her a bed in the middle of the floor. "I have to get some rest too. If the rain holds off, I'll have a busy day tomorrow."

Joy looked embarrassed again before she crawled into the covers. "I don't have a night dress and I need to go to the outhouse." She said it so quietly I almost didn't hear. Great, the absolute last thing I thought I'd be doing in the middle of the night was "potty training" a fourteen-year-old. Awkward.

Chapter 14

"Orientation"

The dull gray light of the stormy day shone through the plantation shutters covering my windows. The thunder rumbling along with the rain pounding on the roof startled me awake. The clock said nine-thirty, but I wasn't worried about it. Storms like this pretty much brought everything to a halt on the farm.

It had become obvious with their "working my way up plan" Bo and Dad had no intention of letting me anywhere near a horse, so I knew Ty would be working alone in the barn today. I imagined he rode last night because he knew the weather wouldn't permit him to do it today. Just the thought of our first day apart since he got here made me miss him. I sighed, wondering how long the storm and our separation would last.

"What's wrong?" Joy asked. I sat up surprised, wondering why there was a strange voice in my room. Suddenly, all that had happened last night started coming back to me in a blurry flood. She was standing at the foot of my bed, wearing my pink sweat pants and my Culpeper County High School Spirit Week T-shirt from last year. It had a picture of a blue devil on it. She totally did not get the concept of a mascot. It was way in the back of the closet with the rest of the stuff I never wore. I remembered the uncomfortable moments from the early morning hours trying to teach her how to dress in modern clothes.

"Nothing," I said, sitting up and trying to act like she hadn't startled me again. "You must be hungry," I said, trying to change the subject, while somewhere in the back of my mind realizing that in her time it was well past dinnertime. I had embarrassed her yet again. She looked at the floor, not wanting to meet my gaze. I sat up straighter and moved my covers out of the way so she'd know I was serious.

"Look Joy, if you're going to be here for two weeks, you're going to have to speak up and tell me these things. We're family, so there's no need to be embarrassed about asking for something from another family member.

She smiled and nodded. "That's right, we are family." She said it like it had just dawned on her. "I think we should try and figure out exactly how we're related while I'm here... and yes, I'm hungry." She hesitated a moment, before adding, "And you should know that I am more than hungry I am starving." She tried to sound confident and a little bossy the way I had to show me she got the point—either that or she was copying me like she did last night. Great...a stubborn little sister. I was waiting for the next part when she started following me around. That wouldn't be awkward or impossible at all. I could hear what I'd say to Mrs. Maggie. *Oh her? Yeah, she's a clone I picked up while time traveling.* Yeah, that would go over well.

"Wait here, I'll go figure out what we can eat."

She nodded and I left thinking how strange it was to suddenly feel like I had a sibling.

~~~

Mrs. Maggie wasn't happy I had missed breakfast, but since Dad had gone to the gym and Bo and Ty went to Peppers Grill for the breakfast buffet, there really wasn't anyone to cook for, so I wasn't on her "missed a meal" list alone. I felt sorry for Ty, given the weather putting off work and the fact that Bo wanted to be alone with him to eat had "lecture about his mom" written all over it. Mrs. Maggie scowled. She hated all of us eating in scattered places. Thankfully, she went into the study off of her bedroom to work on the family tree before she could see what I was doing. As I was leaving the kitchen, she called to me. I almost dropped everything in my hands. For a second I thought she'd come back out and would see that I had two of everything.

"Don't make a mess or leave my dishes up there to get all crusty or you'll be washing more than just those," she threatened as I hurried up the stairs. I rushed out answering over my shoulder before she could come out to make sure I'd heard her.

"I won't," I said, hoping that would be enough to make her stay put.

Watching Joy eat cereal while sitting on my closet floor was something I would have loved to post on YouTube if the entire world would not have thought I was crazy or been stacked up on top of each other on our porch trying to get a look at our magic tunnel.

Apparently Frosted Flakes are not appreciated by every generation. 'It is very sweet and crunchy." She was trying to sound intrigued and thankful for the food, but it came out tentative and perplexed, like she didn't like it and couldn't figure out why anyone else would. I imagined it was something like the average American might sound if they were eating some exotic jungle food—she was doing her best to politely choke it down. I didn't call her on it so as not to make her feel shy again.

"I'm glad you like it." I kept eating mine so she'd know that after she finished her cereal it was okay to drink the milk from the bowl.

We sat in relative silence, except for our crunching and her false *Mmm...* sounds. I took the break in the conversation to think about last night's tutorial on the use of toilet paper and flushing when something caught my eye. I realized there was more awkward to come. I could see the skin on her leg between the bottom of my sweat pants and the top of my sock and realized a shower and a little leg shaving action was definitely in order. I had no idea how to break this to her gently, but given the skin I could see, I knew it was most definitely necessary.

She finished about the same time I did, copying my every move with little sister precision and set her bowl on the floor next to mine. *Okay, new and delicate subject, how to do this with tact?* I wondered.

"Joy, there's something else I want to show you. I think you're really going to like it."

Her face lit up with anticipation and then just as quickly she glanced at the empty bowl, swallowed the last bit of the taste of the cereal, and became wary.

I pulled up the loose leg of my polka dot sleeping pants and showed her my leg. "Feel right here." I ran my hand up my smooth leg.

"Why, that seems like an odd thing to do." She pulled her hands back into her lap and laced her fingers.

"No, really, it's okay. I want to show you something." I was going for the "look and see for yourself that my way is better" approach. I figured it sounded less like criticism if I could make her come to the conclusion on her own. Still no less awkward or weird, than last night's dressing and potty lesson, but I was pretending for her sake it was perfectly normal. *Man, raising a teenager is tough."* She was very hesitant, but did it anyway.

"So?" she said, after she touched me for a micro-second.

"Now feel yours," I said, slowly reaching over and exposing more of her leg beneath the pants.

"So?" she said again. This time there was a "what's your point" tone to her answer. She saw the difference, but wasn't catching my drift. I was going to have to spell it out.

"Well, do you see how smooth my legs are and yours are well...not?" *Dang!* She was instantly embarrassed and self-conscious. I was going to have to figure out a way to stop doing that to her.

"I guess we're not so identical after all, but my ma is the same way as me, so maybe I'm more like her."

I smiled at her assumption. There was no solution. Maybe I had a chance to save her pride after all.

"No, that's not exactly true. Can I show you?"

She thought for a minute, looking back and forth between her leg and mine. "Well...I guess so, if you're sure it's alright." She was scared. I was feeling the pressure not to cut her and then it hit me. I could teach her. Less stress for me, more opportunity for her to keep up the "monkey see, monkey do" act.

I jumped up, excited now. It was like giving a cave man fire. I dug through my drawers and found two bikinis. You need to put this on." I gave her the one that did not require tying, hoping she could figure it out and went to turn on the shower. I was glad I had a big tub so we could both sit on the edge. I was back in a flash and she had tears in her eyes. "I can't wear this. People will see me and laugh. Ma would be so ashamed of me."

"Wait here, just one minute." I did something I never do and closed the door between the bathroom and the closet. I felt terrible leaving her there with those big tears about to flow, so I hurried and put on my bikini. True, it was a bit skimpy, tied on each hip and around my neck with thin strings, but hers was way better—just a standard buckle in the back across the strap and French-cut sides. I opened the door and let her see me. Her eyes got bigger than saucers and then she covered them.

"What are you doing? You're nearly naked!" She was almost yelling.

"*SSSSSHHHHH!* I covered her mouth as fast as I could. "Do you want someone to hear you?"

Thankfully, between the rain and the shower running, it drowned out her voice. "I promise, no one will see you except me. We look so much alike, I've practically seen you already just by looking at myself."

It took her a couple seconds to think about that, but eventually she shrugged, admitting that was true. I cautiously took my hand off her mouth.

"I don't know how this goes," she said, holding up the two pieces. I held them up to her over the clothes she was already wearing and turned around. She did a good job, except with the clasp part. "I can't buckle this." She was frustrated and about to give up on the whole idea just when I had her committed to it. I couldn't let her back out now.

"That's alright, you turn away from me. I promise I'm not looking." I was trying so hard to be positive and reassuring. "Every girl has trouble putting on a top like that the first time."

She obeyed and turned around, and then let me turn around once she had her back to me so that I could help her with the plastic ends.

She seemed to like the warm water from the shower and was in awe, just like she'd been when she saw the inside of my room. She liked that the water appeared at the top and disappeared at the bottom. She looked at me like I was a liar when I told her we could use as much water as we wanted. I explained it was like a bath before she would actually get in.

"Ma fixes my bath in the tin tub in the kitchen and heats the water in a pot over the fireplace." Her tone was questioning whether or not this was actually a legitimate way to get clean.

I rolled my eyes. "Trust me, this is way better than a tin tub and the water stays warm as long as you want it to." She was disbelieving, but followed my lead.

After about a two-minute lecture on how not to cut yourself, she once again followed my lead. She used twice the amount of my pink foamy shaving cream as necessary, but when she was done, her smile was beaming from ear to ear. I realized that teeth-brushing would be next on my list.

I took the shampoo and stood up, and then washed and conditioned my hair, feeling stupid doing it in my bathing suit while giving step-by-step instructions. I got out, closed the curtain, and after a lot of coaxing, she threw her wet suit over the curtain and agreed to wash everything else without it.

"This hair soap smells sweet, like fruit or something." She was talking loud over the sound of the water. I was so afraid she'd be heard downstairs, I ran into my room dripping wet, wrapped in a towel, and turned on the radio, carefully dialing a volume that wouldn't send Mrs. Maggie up to tell me to turn it down, yet loud enough to cover our conversation.

When I got back to the bathroom, I answered her with a short "yes" or "no" so she'd stop talking and start washing. I also told her if there was anything else she wanted to shave it was okay as long as it wasn't her head or her eyebrows. I didn't ask, but she was in there for another thirty minutes. I'm guessing she was noticing I was pretty much smooth everywhere while we were shaving our legs.

She pulled back the curtain just enough so I could see her face and told me she was done. I put my hand over my eyes so she could see I wasn't looking and then reached in and turned off the water. "Put this around yourself." I handed her a big fluffy yellow towel. When she got out and was standing on the rug, I put another one around her hair and handed her the lotion.

"Dry yourself off with this one, leave the other one on your head and put this all over your skin." I showed her how to use the pump handle on the top of the bottle of my Shea Butter moisturizing Jergens. She nodded, appearing to trust me a little more.

I closed the door and went into the closet to find us both something to wear. I was dressed in a second. She was a different story. It was exhausting—almost like taking care of a baby. I looked at the underwear situation and shook my head. I felt defeated. All I had was pretty scanty in the amount of fabric department and everything was silk, satin, or lace. Surely, she'd hate it. I opened the door a crack and handed her a matching top and bottom. I went with the pink lace. It was the closest color I could find to the dress she was wearing when she arrived. I told her to put it on like the bikini and to my surprise she didn't question me. She came out and put on the jeans and short-sleeved sweater without complaint.

She tried to swallow the toothpaste, but after I explained to her that even though it tasted good it was not food, she brushed her teeth and gargled with the mouthwash just like I did. I didn't even ask how she kept them clean in her time, I didn't want to know. I wasn't even sure she got that she was in a different time and I continued to avoid the subject. She just kept saying that this side of the tunnel is so different. I remembered our conversation by the tree and how confused she was when I tried to mention the number of years between us. I was going to have to figure out a way to break that to her gently.

"Okay, so we do this every day only we don't start in clothes and then take them off, we take them off then put on clean ones. Now you know that you can do it by yourself, but you have to wait until I'm here so if anybody hears the water, they'll think it's me, okay?"

Excited at the prospect of taking another shower, she nodded "yes." I didn't have the energy to blow dry her hair. I was definitely thinking twice about those four kids I imagined having with Ty. I brushed it wet and fishtail braided it instead. She didn't mind that it took so long because she was fascinated by the music coming from the radio, wondering where the instruments. She picked up the radio, twisting and turning it around like she was looking for an orchestra to come out the back.

After we were done, it seemed to have brought us closer. I thought maybe now might be a good time to ask. There was one word she'd said last night that I was curious and a little worried about. I hadn't been able to shake it.

"You said that since your Pa was gone, your Ma would be 'safe.' I don't mean to pry, but what does that mean exactly?" She looked away from my eyes and shook her head. She didn't want to talk about it. "Sometimes he's not a nice man." That's all she was going to say.

"Oh," I said casually and let it drop. The silence that followed was awkward and weighted, at least for me. I felt a little like she didn't know me enough to fill me in just yet and I had crossed a very personal line. When she was ready, when she more than believed but really felt we were family and I cared about it, she would tell me. I remembered my mental list. She's trusting.

Chapter 15
"The Test and the Contest"

I decided to fix my hair the same as Joy's, even though it was more play dress up than my actual style. It was a fun way to kill the rest of the morning. Now that we were both in regular clothes and had our hair styled the same, it looked pretty strange even to us how much we looked alike.

We laid with our legs dangling over the edge of the bed, watching the ceiling fan go around. She was hanging off one side and I was hanging off the other so our heads met in the middle of the bed. She didn't ask any questions when she was finally bored with the fan, but when she turned to me in her deep blue eyes I could clearly see that she had some. She was trying to read the answers in mine. I figured I'd better say something.

"Remember how I told you when I tumbled through the wall that I fell a hundred and seventy-three years?"

She nodded slightly, her eyes wide with anticipation. She was intelligent, and quick to catch on to pretty much everything I had said or done. I got that when she told me how she had figured out the tunnel. I don't know if I would have connected it with the moon as fast as she did. I could sense from her that she was trying to think ahead of me and figure out what was coming.

"Well, when you jumped through it from the other side, you came forward the same number of years. It's June in the year, 2013. She shook her head slowly from side to side like she didn't believe me, but inside she knew it was true.

"How did we do this? How could this happen?"

She was genuinely sure that given all the gadgets in my room, the hot water that appeared out of the wall and disappeared down into the floor, the razor and the soap in a bottle, that I must have had the answer. Her face fell in disappointment when all I could say was, "I don't know."

She was starting to look panicked like I had. It was all over her face; just because I told her I was sure we could get her home didn't make the number of years an easier pill to swallow. I guess this whole house must seem like a bunch of magic tricks to her. I knew the blow dryer would be another amazing wonder I would have to explain. She was scared, but enthusiastic about everything. I figured the noise would frighten her nearly to death, but once she felt the heat, like the water I was sure she would be okay with it.

I had an idea, but I'd have to check something first. I noticed last night it would be a problem, but I wasn't sure how she'd feel about fixing it. Another touchy subject. I sat up, hopped down off the bed, and headed back to the bathroom. "Come on." I waved her to follow behind me, like that was going to be difficult? She was practically in motion before I told her to come. "If we're going to do what I want to try next, I need to...well, I need to cut your hair." She grabbed the end of her braid and pulled it in front of her.

"No! Why? Why would you want to cut it?"

"Well, it's about four inches longer than mine. Look." I turned around to show her. That still didn't explain why I would want to. We were already perfect reflections of each other; she didn't even ask why I would want to make us more exact copies. I felt bad, like I was manipulating her. I suppose all older siblings have done it a time or too, but if she didn't want to be so much like me she might not have cooperated so blindly.

"Oh," was all she could say. She looked down at the floor. She was sad to cut it. I could only imagine how she felt. I'm not sure if I were I her I'd have let her come anywhere near mine with scissors, especially given how my mom felt about it. She unclenched it and swung it back over her shoulder, giving me unspoken permission. I think if she had taken the time to think it over she would have chickened out.

"Sit here." I patted the bright flower pattern on the cushioned top of my tall makeup stool that sat in front of the vanity. I took mine down and combed it, showing her how my long layers flowed together down my back and around my face. She nodded, knowing I was going to do the same to hers. I took my brush and stroked it all very carefully and then did exactly what my hairdresser did at Marlene's Hair Salon when she fixes mine. I turned her head face down, gathered her hair into a ponytail on top of her head, and cut about four inches up.

"Wow!" she said, her face red from having held her head upside down for so long while I shook and tried to cut straight. I was glad she couldn't see my hands. I looked like a nervous surgeon.

"I like it and we look even more alike now." I stood beside her while she remained on the stool, looking at our long hair flowing. We were still a bit damp, so I sighed and got out the hair dryer. When I was done with both of us, it really was creepy, just like Ty said. She was more than my twin—it was like having an identical double. There were literally no differences now. Most sets of twins had some distinguishing feature or mark that their parents could use to tell them apart, but between Joy and me there were none. Well, maybe one, hair up or down, we had the same face, and now that she had worn my clothes I knew we were the same size, but there was one difference. She reached with her left hand to use the brush she had just seen me use on my own hair.

"We have to be careful of that," I said. "That could get us caught."

"What could? What are we doing that we might be caught?"

I picked up another brush with my right hand and she watched us both in the mirror—mirror images of each other. Her eyes lit up when she noticed on the second stroke. "Oh, I see. Let me try it your way." She switched hands and it was awkward for her, but she did it. "This feels strange, but if I practice, maybe I can get better." Remembering what she had told me about her father trying to force her to be right handed I figured I better show her she wasn't the only one trying I didn't want to come off like I didn't accept her just the way she was.

I switched hands to show her I was willing to learn her way too. After all, I'd made her conform to a lot today. She smiled and we brushed until all of our thick black hair was ruler straight.

She started talking with more confidence than I had ever heard in her voice. She was about to teach me something and she knew it—knowledge she would easily have that I never knew and wouldn't be able to find without effort. Family history.

"We both have thick hair like Ma. Her family came to America when her mother was a little girl. She's Italian. She has three younger sisters and a brother, but they live up north and we never really see them.

"Pa is an only child. His father's parents and his parents came to America as servants. They worked very hard to earn their freedom and own some land of their own. Their dreams came true, but only for a short time. All four of them died of pneumonia one winter and left everything they had to Pa.

"Both Ma and Pa have very strong accents, even though Pa was born in Virginia, his pa told him he should speak like a true Scotsman so he learned young. Ma didn't learn English until she was about ten. Sometimes I hear people in town say they have a hard time understanding either of them.

"Ma has been teaching me Italian since I was little. Pa doesn't know because he doesn't want us saying things he can't understand. Ma says she is lighter-skinned than her sisters, but her skin is still a little darker than us and her eyes are brown like theirs.

"She says Nicholas and I have even lighter skin because Pa's is light, like his Scottish parents. He has very dark blue eyes like ours, but like I told you when we were out by the pond, his hair is reddish, like the leaves in fall with brown mixed in—not orange like one of the girls who gets teased in school."

I smiled at her reference and the fact that she had managed to tell me all that without taking a breath. It was funny, she just assumed I'd know an orange-haired kid in school who got picked on. Sadly enough, I did. Truth be told, she was a very pretty girl, but like me, her label stuck.

"Yeah, people tell me all the time how unusual my hair color is. Deep auburn mixed in with raven black. My hairdresser told me she hopes I never go gray because she can't even mix anything like it." I saw that I'd confused her again. "Never mind," I said, "It's too hard to explain."

She had cleared up so many of our questions about the painting. We were right that it portrayed her parents standing there, her brother held in her mother's arms. Even thought it was fairly easy to figure, it was nice to know we were right. Nicholas was the same mixture as Joy and me—black hair, slightly olive-tan skin, and blue eyes.

"I want to show you something." She got excited and started looking around for what it might be. I caught her hand to get her attention. "First I have to go downstairs. It's almost lunch time and I haven't even been out of my room. They must be wondering what I've been doing all day. I can't exactly tell them I've been 'playing beauty shop' with you." That puzzled her, so I broke the next part down. I really needed her to get this right. You'll have to stay very quiet in the closet." I enunciated each word slowly and distinctly. "You cannot be found, which means no noise. Got it?"

She nodded solemnly, giving me her silent promise. I walked over to my bookshelf and grabbed the first thing I saw. "Here, read this. I'll be back soon." I handed it to her, noticing the front cover was a picture of Niagara Falls. It was my *America, the Beautiful* picture book that my dad gave me years ago. She took it, but was clearly impatient for whatever was coming next. "Alright, but then you promise I can see."

I smiled and nodded "yes." It was like talking to a little kid. She didn't even know what it was, but she really wanted to see it. I waited until she got in the closet before I headed downstairs to the sounds of Dad, Bo, Ty, and Mrs. Maggie in the kitchen.

I stopped on the landing and gathered my thoughts, quickly reviewing my story in my head. This was about to be a whopper of a tale and I had to get my game face on to tell it. Weaving half-truths together was harder than just straight up making something up from scratch and I'm a terrible liar: one, it's wrong, and two, I always get caught, I was still amazed I had managed to cover that twelve hours I was gone. Everyone was already seated, waiting on my dad to start and he was waiting on me. He had his hands folded, along with everyone else. Great, I'm holding up grace. I trotted across the kitchen as fast as I could and pulled out my weighty chair. Ty smiled at me like "you're in trouble." I smirked back at him just before I closed my eyes. Why couldn't we progress beyond this childish friendship so he could just fall in love with me? Dad must have been hungry because he didn't give me a dirty look. He just said the blessing and dug right in.

Mrs. Maggie started. I'm sure they were already talking about it before I got here, so she was pretty much repeating what was on everyone's mind. "Haven't seen hide nor hair of you this morning."

Ty picked up on her remark. "Yeah, I had some shoveling I could have used your help with." He looked down at his dirty white T-shirt. I was surprised Mrs. Maggie let him wear it to the table. I imagined his jeans didn't look much better. His hair was a mess too. Normally, he would have covered it with his hat, but even if she let him wear work clothes to eat in once in a while, "no hats at the table" was a hard and fast Southern rule she wasn't willing to break.

"That's two days you been slackin' now, girl," said Bo, winking at Dad. He'd already spread the news, so I had to come back with something. "Well, I would've helped Ty this morning, but I know nobody here has any intention of letting me within a mile of a horse, at least not until I've worked myself to the point where I'm too weak to ride one."

All three of them smirked at each other. I'd nailed it. Ty was in on it too. Whatever their plan was for me, he knew it step by step. Instead of giving another excuse about work that I had no hope of thinking of right off the top of my head, I went with the story I had already rehearsed. If I couldn't beat Ty at working, I could let Mrs. Maggie know she was about to make me some peach cobbler.

"Sorry, I figured because of the previously unspoken "no horses for Caimee rule" I might have a few extra minutes this morning to work on a project I've been trying to finish. I got distracted and caught up in it."

Ty didn't understand. "Project? During summer? No wonder you skipped a grade, ya nerd." He gently kicked me under the table. Any touch from him made my brain a little fuzzy with warm thoughts of him touching me again. Yeah, my next plan was definitely to begin "Operation Win Ty's Heart."

"It's not for school, genius. What teacher gives projects over the summer?" I took a bite of my veggie burger so I wouldn't say something else that put us on a childish friendly teasing level. I was going to start taking every opportunity to get past that.

Thankfully Dad was curious and broke up our mocking each other to have a real conversation. "Okay, C.C., what's the big project?"

I looked at Mrs. Maggie and smiled. "Clarence Winthrop." I pointed at her with my fork. My smile turned to a gloat as I reached for my tea. "Who?" Both she and Bo said it at the same time.

"Oh, just the man who built this house and four others like it to hide runaway slaves. See, the problem here is you've been looking for a Cameron, but a Cameron didn't build this house. Clarence Winthrop did. A Cameron who worked for the railroad won it in a poker game in the winter of 1839. It was going to be a cover for sneaking slaves to the north."

Mrs. Maggie looked shocked and then beaten. The story was just elaborate and simple enough to be true and she knew it. She hated to lose at anything—cooking, bingo night with the ladies from church, whatever it was she always had to be blue ribbon best. Everyone else had dozens of questions in their eyes, but they were too busy looking between me and Mrs. Maggie, like watching a tennis match. Dad had a grin a mile wide. I knew he was about to brag and he did. "That's my girl!" He leaned over and put his arm around me, giving me a high five.

I glanced at Ty. He was eating like the horses he'd just fed, but through the chewing I think even he looked impressed. Mrs. Maggie didn't quite know what to say. I'd blown her research back to the Stone Age, but little did she know I had to go back there to get it. She picked up her mason jar and took a sip of her tea before she answered. Indignation was all over her face. She was definitely not a good loser.

"I suppose you have proof of this, some type of documentation, I can read for myself." Her tone, which she tried to hide without success, was annoyed and a bit uppity, like she was playing off how bad she hated to be beaten, like maybe there was a chance I was wrong. Shoot, I didn't expect her to ask for proof right this second. I'd put my cart in front of my horse again—or better yet, my big lie, about all the "research" I had done, before my way to not get caught in it. I should have known better than to try to pull one over on Mrs. Maggie. No good ever came of it and I always got trapped. *Poker face, look calm,* I told myself. I had to roll with it now. I put my chin up like I was offended that she would question my integrity; after all, the only part that wasn't true was that I didn't exactly have proof, other than the eyewitness in my closet.

"Of course, you will have my full report once I'm done with all of my investigation."

Bo piped up first, "Well there, Mama Maggie, looks like you have some peaches to peel and bake."

Dad laughed. They hadn't called her Mama Maggie since they were kids and were trying to suck up to her for something they wanted.

This next pill was gonna be a little tougher to swallow than the taste of the victory I had just pulled off. I looked at Bo, about to admit defeat. I hated doing it in front of Ty, but if he heard it firsthand, it would be better than if he later heard Bo's embellished version of how I groveled, which I most certainly would NOT. All I had to say was a few simple words and Bo would know immediately that I was conceding the other bet.

"Well, I guess you win some and lose some." That was all it took. The word "loser" might as well have been in red neon flashing over my head. Bo put down his beef burger and gestured grandly towards Ty like he was on display on a showroom floor. "And that's my boy."

"He looked at Dad after copying his sentence. "I guess you got the brain, but I got the brawn."

Dad nodded in agreement. "Good combination, I think." He said it, not realizing how it sounded 'til it was already out there. I liked it and I knew it...subconsciously he already thought of us a couple. Okay, maybe that part was wishful thinking. It was probably more like "good combination they can get a lot done around here, if they work together."

Ty was offended. "Hey, I got more than brawn over here just because I am not a grade-skipping, house-researching geek. I had a B average in Alabama, well except for that one class." We all knew he was referring to the teacher his mother had gotten to know on a very um...personal level.

He quickly changed the subject and looked at me. "And I knew all about your little bet, you...outwork me! He snorted a little. "Yeah right, that'll be the day."

He playfully flexed at me in a "no hard feelings" kind of way. In my mind, all I could think was *Man, I sure am lucky my future husband has a good heart, is sweet and smart, and has a pretty face and great body, what more could a girl want?"* I was beginning to turn deep scarlet and was grateful Mrs. Maggie immediately started quizzing me to stop the playful banter between the four of us. Normally she would have joined in, but not today—not after she had done what to her was unthinkable—she'd lost at something.

"How did you get all this information anyway?"

Her tone was still suspicious, wanting to make one

hundred percent sure I hadn't cheated. "What made you look for this Clarence Williams?"

"Winthrop," I corrected her. *Well, the girl in the painting is hiding upstairs in my closet and she told me all about him.* That put a smirk on my face, raising her suspicions even further that I wasn't being quite honest.

"Well, I just figured that if *you* weren't able to find a Cameron that built this place, then maybe there wasn't one. Instead of looking for a relative, I found the house, *boy if she only knew I really found the house right smack in the middle of the apple field it stood in.*" I felt better about putting it to her that way; it gave her a little credit. Her expression told me she had accepted the sideways compliment. "Hang on a second. Let me see if I printed that page I was looking at." I hadn't thought that this would be the time, but since I had to have some type of proof for Mrs. Maggie now I would go ahead and try out my little scheme and send her down, it was as good a chance as any, although the prospect of actually going through with it made me nervous.

I ran up the stairs. My heart was pounding. I couldn't wait for the second part of my plan. We hadn't thought of doing it in her time, but I wasn't going to pass up the chance to do it now. I flung open the closet door when I got to my room. She was so intrigued by the book, it didn't even surprise her when I barged in.

"Did you know that there were such tall mountains outside of Virginia? Look at this." She was holding up a picture of the Rockies covered in snow. I only had a few minutes to get this done and print the picture of Clarence Winthrop.

"Fascinating." Which it likely was to her I wasn't sure that part of America was even on her map.

She was bewildered, or maybe even a little hurt by my tone. I don't think she used a lot of sarcasm in her day. I would have to remember that when I wasn't in a hurry. I ripped the book from her hands. She looked at me like I was the rudest person ever. I had to explain fast. I hadn't told her about the "test" I had planned, I thought it would be later this afternoon and just on Mrs. Maggie. "Quick, switch clothes with me. We're going to try something. It is kind of the reason I cut your hair."

She didn't even budge. "I'm getting awful tired of having to change my clothes in here."

"Just shut...I mean stop talking and do it." I wasn't sure if she'd ever been told to shut up before and I didn't want to be the first one to do it. "Do you want to see what I promised to show you or not? She looked wary, unsure if the reward was going to be worth the effort. "I'm going to give you a piece of paper and I want you to go down stairs and hand it to Mrs. Maggie. She's the only lady at the table and she's wearing a red apron so she should be easy to spot. Don't say too much, something like 'Here you go' and then leave."

I was stripped down to my underwear talking a mile a minute. She was just standing there, still dressed, but now thoroughly confused. I slowed down and sighed. "We're going to see if they can tell the difference."

She looked worried. "What if they can? You haven't told me a thing about any of them. What if they start talking to me?"

"Don't worry about it. There is no reason for them to question you, why would they even think you weren't me? I don't imagine they'll suspect that the girl from the painting is living in my closet." She was confused again.

"I said I'd show it to you later and I will."

Thankfully she put the pieces together rather quickly. "Oh, *our* painting. I forgot you said it was still here."

Suddenly my excitement was catching on. I threw my clothes at her and ran to my computer to find the page I'd found earlier, wishing now I'd saved it. It took me a minute, but by the time I was done she appeared wearing the clothes I'd just taken off—the Delta Airlines T-shirt that Dad had given me and jeans with the holes in the knees.

"This really isn't very practical, you know, having clothes with holes in them."

She was studying my tattered pants, looking down at her legs. I couldn't help it. I rolled my eyes at her.

"This is not the time. Now go to the kitchen. If you can't find it, then follow the voices and hand this to the lady. Remember her name is Mrs. Maggie. Just say, "Here you go," and then say, 'I'll be right back down.'"

The kitchen looks way different, so try not to be looking around and acting surprised to see everything like you did in here. Can you do this?"

She smiled a devilish little grin, odd for her being so shy. Another character trait—she was brave. I was surprised I hadn't thought of it earlier. She would have to be to jump through that wall into the unknown.

I paced around in my underwear, waiting for her, wishing she would hurry. I knew I'd have to get my clothes back on and get back down there the second she made it up the stairs. I was beginning to regret this whole thing and getting nervous, how odd is that for her to just hand her the paper and leave? I was hoping she wasn't making me look like I'd totally lost my mind or something. It seemed like forever. I'd made about ten laps around my room when the door opened. She was smiling and started quietly jumping up and down, clapping her hands.

I quickly shut the door and grabbed her shoulders to calm her down. "Well, what happened?"

She was beaming, her face all aglow. "I did it."

"And..." I coaxed, trying to get her to hurry up and spill the rest. "They believed me. Nobody knew. I did exactly what you said. They didn't look at me too much because they started passing around the paper." She started to blush deeply. "Well, at least no one except that handsome boy. He's the only one who really noticed me. He smiled when I walked into the room. He saw me before anyone else did."

Instant jealousy. What if on some subconscious level, to his stupid man brain, she was prettier than me? I'd forgotten this would be her first good look at him.

"Okay, first of all, his name is Ty. He was the one riding the horse that first night you surprised me, remember?"

She nodded. "Second of all, he's all mine. And third, I ushered her to the bed, totally forgetting for the moment that I still needed to get my clothes back and get down there. "What do you mean he smiled? What kind of smile?"

She shrugged. "I don't know, like he was glad to see me, I mean you. That kind of smile."

I ran to the door and then turned around, realizing I was about to dart out into the hallway in my underwear. I didn't need her to say it—the look on her face was plenty. I turned and looked at her—this time a little embarrassed myself. She was giggling, covering her mouth with her hand at the thought of what I had almost done. She was kind enough not to full on laugh at me. We were getting good at this non-verbal communication thing. I just shot her a "hurry up" look.

"I know," she said, a martyred inflection coming through. "Change my clothes again and go back in the closet."

I thought about it all the way down the stairs. Ty was probably smiling because I had proof and beaten Mrs. Maggie. Well not proof exactly, not much of what I said was actually written anywhere and I was hoping this lie about rock solid research wasn't going to come up again for a while after today. I didn't really want to spend my time making up fake web pages, now it was time to work on Ty. *Yep, I'll bet that was it,* I told myself, feeling defeated about ever winning him over. He was smiling because I won and he got to see Mrs. Maggie get bested for the first time ever. I would have to be looking at him when I went in, just in case he did it again. All these years we've been trying to get one up on Mrs. Maggie and one of us finally did it. I'll bet he's going to mess my hair like Bo does and say something like "Proud of you, kid."

She didn't look up right away when I sat back down at the table. She studied my handout for another couple of seconds. "This only gives a brief history of Clarence. So, he built houses and helped slaves, died young and left his brother." She paused to check the name again. "Michael Winthrop, a very wealthy man," she said, waving the paper back and forth.

"It says nothing about any poker game or this house specifically."

Here I was, staring down Mrs. Maggie, stuck in a story I'd told way too soon just to win a stupid bet and now I had to *prove* the truth. Another quick lie. "I found the rest, but I didn't realize I forgot to save it. I'll have to find it again and print it for you later. I hoped that would be enough to put her off for now." She looked skeptical, but turned her attention back to the information in her hand. Ty had a mouth full of food again, of course, a typical teenage boy bottomless pit. He smiled at me, keeping his lips closed. He swallowed hard, reached over, and messed my hair. "Proud of you, kid."

I rolled my eyes. We couldn't be any more right for each other if we'd been born married. Clearly, I knew him like I knew myself, like I knew my dad. Ty was my family already. I sighed. *Why, oh why, can't he see it?* At least he was sincere, not meaning to treat me like a baby by calling me "kid." I knew he was genuinely proud of me. It was a victory for both of us. A lifetime of getting one-upped by Mrs. Maggie finally brought to an end. When we were little, I don't believe we'd ever won one bet or board game, or gotten away with any ill-advised plan she hadn't caught us in. This was a corner we were turning. We were growing up and playing more on her level. I wanted so badly to tell Ty the truth. Once again, I wished my mom could give me some advice.

Chapter 16
"The Favor"

As soon as I thought about her, Dad pushed away from the table. He took a deep breath like he was excited to go on a first date or something. It breaks my heart to know that the only place he can be with her that way is in his memory. "I'm going to see my sweetheart. Caimee, you coming? This is my last chance before I start a two-week run. One guy's wife just had a baby, so he's out for a while. We're all rotating, taking his flights."

I finished my last bite and nodded, worrying about leaving Joy in the closet for another couple of hours. Mrs. Maggie conveniently provided me with a way out of that one. Bo spoke first. "Do you mind if Ty and I come?" My eyes immediately shot over to Mrs. Maggie's face. She looked guilty, even though I couldn't see all of her expression. She was staring down, pretending to read about Clarence Winthrop and his brother Michael some more, like she'd suddenly found the insignificant brother, who was not a very big part of the story, fascinating, there was almost no information on him on this page or anywhere else. She and Bo had definitely been talking. This was a "we want to see her one last time in case something happens visit."

Mrs. Maggie composed her expression into a forced smile. "Let's all go." She looked sideways at Dad. "That is, if you don't mind, Caleb."

He stood up and took his keys out of the front pocket of his blue jeans. "I don't mind a bit, but I'm going to leave now and I'm not sure if everybody is ready. He looked at Ty. "I'm sure Ty wants to take a shower. Caimee, you want to come with me or do you need to get ready too?"

I was more than ready, I'd fixed my hair twice today, but I had to talk to Joy. "Um...I might need a few minutes."

Bo stood up and took his plate to the sink. "Well, I'm ready now and since we'd be crowded all in one car, why don't we take your Jeep and let Ty here take the girls in the farm truck? I'd like to take a ride in that old Wrangler before you make a decision and trade it in."

Dad nodded in agreement. "Sounds good. Yeah, we got a lot of miles in that rusty dusty jeep, don't we?"

Bo agreed, sharing some teenage memory from years ago. Dad looked at me and nodded. "See you all up there then."

Maggie interrupted them as they were about to walk out. "Caleb, I'm going to clean up here, so if it's okay with you, I'm going to take my car and let the kids go on ahead of me. I was going to meet some friends later for bingo anyway, so I want to drive myself."

Dad agreed. "Sure," he said. "I think Ty can handle it. He seems to be proving to be a pretty good driver."

Ty took playful offense at the words "pretty good" and said, "Don't you mean excellent?"

Both of our dads just rolled their eyes and didn't dignify his little joke with a response.

Ty pushed back from the table, looking at me after our fathers had gone. "I'll meet you at the truck. Is twenty minutes okay?"

"Sure, that should be plenty of time."

Mrs. Maggie started clearing the table so she could do the dishes. "How long do you think before you come up?" I tried to sound casual, but I don't think I pulled it off.

"I won't be far behind you, maybe half an hour at the most."

She probably thought I was asking so I could plan my time with Ty, but for once she was wrong. Ty wasn't my focus, but she knew me too well not to know how much I cared for him. I was glad she'd never call me on it. She always waited for me to come to her about the big stuff. As soon as she turned away, I grabbed as big a handful of fries as I could and put them in a napkin.

I ran up the stairs to my room about to burst. Mrs. Maggie had just unknowingly done me two favors by convincing Bo and Ty they needed to go, I got to drive there alone with Ty and by deciding to come along, she left the house empty for Joy to explore so she could get to know the place as it is now.

Joy was dutifully and quietly following instructions. She hadn't left the closet. I handed her the fries. They were a little squished in my haste to steal them. She looked at them a little skeptically.

"They're good, I promise."

She tasted a tiny bite very slowly and then smiled. "It's a potato," she said like she'd just discovered cave man fire again. I nodded. *It really is like having a baby,* "I thought. I didn't have time to stand there like a new parent and be fascinated by her every move. I picked out my low cut, fit-in-all-the-right-places jeans and since I'd just done my toenails, a cute pair of brown leather sandals that showed them off. A fitted white short-sleeved shirt with a wide scoop neck with the snug bottom hem made of lace that came down just an inch above the top of my jeans it showed just a hint of my midsection, along with a belt to match my sandals completed my ensemble. I didn't want to be flashy or fake, or revealing, but I also wanted to give him something to think about.

Joy watched, shaking her head, "I can't get used to the clothes here. They seem so... I don't know, strange, I guess. They don't cover everything like my dresses do and you change them so often." I went into the bathroom and combed my hair back into a ponytail, then pulled it through the back of my ball cap, making the outfit just casual enough to look like I wasn't trying too hard. I put on some lipstick and blush and then did my eyes. They were dramatically wider and deeper blue when I was done. Joy just stood there with her mouth open.

"You gotta lighten up Joy. This is all normal, I promise." I waved my hand over my face and my outfit so she'd understand.

She said something that totally shocked me. "Can you teach me? You look so pretty."

"Thanks." I hugged her for the compliment. I needed it. It shouldn't, but being alone with Ty made me nervous. Like taking a test, I was sure I was going to fail no matter how much I had studied. If he was never going to feel the same about me, none of this mattered. I was beginning to think we'd never be more than what we were and it was bumming me out, after all we had spent every waking moment together and he hadn't even given a hint he felt the same as I did, hadn't even touched me really except the two times he held my hand to comfort me about my mom. I had to put my mind on something else before I started worrying myself sick.

"Come here, I want to show you something."

Her eyes lit up. "Is it time for the painting? I didn't get to see it finished. The artist said he wanted to frame it first, before we were allowed view it." I walked to the window, shaking my head "no." The tip of my long ponytail brushed against the thin strip of exposed skin between the top of my jeans and the bottom of my shirt.

"No, I promised I'll show you the painting and I will, but for now I need you to do something for me." She rolled her eyes, as I had before. This copying me thing was kind of cute, but a shade on the weird side.

"Do I have to change clothes again, too?"

"No, just come over here." I sounded impatient, so she hurried. I didn't want to make Ty wait. I opened the plantation shutters over the window, angling them just enough so we could see the ground. "See that...um thing there—that white thing?" I pointed at Mrs. Maggie's car. She had no concept of what it was or what it was used for and I didn't have time to explain. In a little while, I want you to look out this window again. When that white thing is gone, it'll be safe for you to go and look around the house. Don't go in the round room yet. I want to see your face when you see the painting. But I want you to learn your way around and see the rooms as they are now. Don't touch *anything*. I just want you to get familiar with how things look. I don't want you to try and figure out how things work until I show you. You will have about an hour to look around, okay?"

She looked at me like I thought she was stupid or something. "Of course," she said, repeating her instructions. "I look out the window, wait until that big square white thing is gone and then I can go."

"Right, but if you hear anyone coming in the door or coming back up to the yard, hide in here right away."

She nodded. "I promise, I can do it."

"Even if you don't hear anything, to be safe you only have one hour." She nodded again. There was a firm understanding set in her eyes and the hard line of her lips. "I promise."

I had a little more confidence in her since she had done so well with the switch earlier. I put the worry away and went to go meet Ty.

~~~

It had stopped raining, but the dirt drive where we parked the truck near the barn had turned to mud. Ty was sitting in the driver's seat, waiting for me to take the last ten steps to get in on my side, but I was standing on the last island of wet grass before the minefield of dirty puddles and sinkholes started. I didn't want to get my feet all muddy and ruin my sandals. I motioned for him to back up, but he just laughed and shook his head no. *Great, more games like when we were kids.* I sighed and gave up on ever changing our relationship, or saving my shoes. If I thought about the first part too much, I would have started to cry, so I just concentrated on not falling and giving him more ammunition to laugh at me later. I started to take a step when I heard his door close. He sloshed around in his already dirty work boots and stood about five feet from me.

"You mean you can't jump that?" He looked at me from across the great divide assessing the distance to the truck. He couldn't even get the words out, he was laughing so hard. He stared at my flimsy, but too cute shoes and shook his head.

"Sure I can, you're standing in my way and I don't want to knock you over with my Superman leap." The sarcasm and frustration was so thick in my voice I think he actually thought I was mad at him. Maybe deep inside I was, since he wasn't doing what I *know* he should be and that was falling for me.

He looked so cute in his button-down shirt. It was blue and black and gray checks, left open over a matching gray T-shirt he had tucked into his Levi's and, of course, the standard worn leather belt and ball cap. He took two big steps and was mere inches in front of me, sharing my little safe patch of grass. I looked up into his beautiful caramel eyes with the sprinkles of deep brownish gold around the edges, shining in the overcast light.

"Can't you just back the stupid truck up a few feet and help me out here?" He didn't say anything. He just grinned and shook his head "no" again. I sighed and moved to go around him. I'd just have to scrape my shoes off later and rinse my feet in Mom's sink. He moved to his left and blocked me as I moved to my right to go beside him. "But I will help you for a price." I sighed and tilted my head back. I couldn't be as mad as I wanted to be and look at his beautiful face. "A price? Okay, Ty, what do you want? Lemme guess, I get to take off all the shingles on the barn by myself and you get to help break in Thor."

He smiled. "Now that's an intriguing bargain, let me think on it." He paused, taking in my aggravated expression, but he had no idea why I was so frustrated. I didn't want a bargain, I wanted him. Finally, he came up with his terms. It was simpler than I thought it was going to be, but left me wide open to something horrible later.

"Just as long as you know you owe me." He didn't give me a chance to answer, but my frustration changed drastically into something I hadn't expected—pure happiness, the extreme pleasure of being so close to him I could feel his heat and smell his cologne. He scooped me up so fast I lost my balance and had to grab his shirt to keep from falling out of his arms. He threw me up a little like he was threatening to drop me once we were squarely over the middle of the mud.

"No, please!" I was begging and squirming, not really trying to get away; as if I could have he was infinitely stronger than me. As much as I hated to admit it, it was easy to get lost in our childish games when I was in his arms. He squatted down 'til I was about two feet above the mud, the tip of my ponytail almost dragging in a puddle.

"Say you owe me." I tipped my head back laughing and he moved his arms from my shoulders to the back of my neck so my hair didn't reach the dirty ground. "You're gonna go in, girlie, so say it." He was laughing through his words and I was afraid he was going to lose his focus and drop me. "Okay, okay, you win! I owe you." He stood up easily carrying my weight and walked through the muck to the passenger side of the truck. He lifted me over the side and I stood up in the bed while he took the key and unlocked the door.

"I have begged Dad a million times to get a newer truck for this place. I'm glad at least he's thinking of trading in his old Wrangler for that fancy new Range Rover he likes so much."

Ty disagreed. "Nah, this old thing has character.

Besides, where else are you gonna find a baby blue and rust mix as perfect as this?" He stood back appraising it like it was a work of art. The heavy door creaked on the rusty overused hinges as he swung it open. "Can you climb in from there?" I looked at the side of the truck for whatever invisible foot holds he wanted me to use to scale from the bed into the door and then up onto the seat.

"Sure, just let me shoot my web and swing over." I turned my wrist like Spiderman and made him laugh again. He sighed and rubbed his shoulder like my weight had strained it. There are no words to describe the dirty look I gave him.

"Aw, don't be mad, my little sack of potatoes. Come here." I wasn't sure how to climb over the side and into his arms. He saw I was stuck trying to squat down and figure it out, but the side of the truck was still between us and in my way. I didn't want to sit on the edge because it was no cleaner than walking through the mud. He raised his arms up and bent his fingers forward encouraging me to lean from the waist. I put my hands on his shoulders. He grabbed the back of my legs and flung me over his shoulder. I had to grab my hat so I didn't lose it.

"There," he said, setting me right side up in the seat. Can we go now?"

"You could have just moved the truck and let me get in and we'd be there by now."

"I know, but that wouldn't have been any fun and now you owe me."

As we were backing out, I saw Mrs. Maggie standing on the front porch. She'd gotten ready faster than I thought and had been watching the whole thing. She gave me a little knowing smile when we went by. Had she heard the conversation, she wouldn't be thinking what I knew she was thinking at all. Ty's little display was not to show me special affection, it was all about the work we had to do on the barn—not about the work I was trying to do on his heart. All the way to Mom's, I sat there wondering when he was going to call in his favor. Either way, favor or no favor, I got to be close to him and it was like many a dream I'd had, only better.

Grammie was visiting today too. The only person in the world she'd overlook me to greet first was Ty. She'd always claimed him as the boy she wished she could have had.

"Ty, I have missed you so much! You've grown half a foot! Now get down here and give your Grammie a hug."

Her bracelets jingled as she reached her arms up to him. She was wearing the same ones from the other day, but the outfit was a work of art, depending on your definition of art. Cream-colored crochet leggings under a multicolored flowing skirt that came down to her knees in the front and her ankles in the back, topped off with a solid burgundy colored blouse that matched one of the many hues in the skirt. Her hair was in the same style of wispy disarray. Dad and Bo had to turn away from the strangled look on Ty's face when she threw her arms around his neck.

It was a rare occasion, but Mom was sitting up in a high-backed padded chair with straps around her waist and chest to hold her upright. Samantha from Marlene's Hair Salon had come by to cut her hair. She always styled it just like she did when Mom used to go to her shop.

"Hey Caimee! Hey Ty! Glad to see you're finally back in town." Her thick Southern accent and charm made going to get my hair cut like therapy. There was something so happy about her it was contagious. She didn't say much today. I could tell she got right back to work because it was rare we were all there and she didn't want to intrude on family. With her Southern manners, she would have considered that rude. She usually tried to come when Mom was alone, so as not to impose on Dad's time with her. Mrs. Maggie walked in next. Surprised to see Mom sitting up, she stopped in the doorway with her mouth open.

"Doesn't my baby look great? No signs of any new problems and a fresh new 'do." That was Grammie's way of letting all of us newcomers know that there hadn't been any more trouble with Mom's heart since the incident in May. We already knew, but I would never tell her that. Dr. Little must have stopped by while she was here alone. He had reassured us several times that he hadn't seen any problems, but it was good to know he was doing the same for Grammie, it put her and dad more on an even playing field when she got to talk to him for herself. I breathed a sigh of relief. Grammie flitted over, almost giddy and put her arm around my waist. Finally, it was my turn. It didn't matter who came or went, I will always be the one she clings to longest. "I don't think there will be any need to sign any papers, all that worry for nothing. She looks like she's about to get up and go out for a night on the town." Okay and now we all knew she'd changed her mind about considering the Do Not Resuscitate order.

Dad looked at Bo. Their unspoken conversation told me they thought she was deluding herself and if there was a need to decide whether or not to restart her heart again, my poor dad was on his own. I was sure there'd be another fight. After all these years, she still couldn't accept it. Her broken heart had started to fool her mind now. Samantha kept her hands busy and her eyes on Mom. She cut Grammie's hair too. Like any therapist would, she knew Grammie couldn't hear the truth and no way was she going to comment on that and neither was anyone else, it hurt too much. In some ways, Grammie's thought process was as sick and weak as Mom's body. She wasn't seeing the same pale, frail, strapped into a chair, comatose person that the rest of us saw.

Everybody sort of found a chair or a corner and watched Samantha work. The silence was comforting; nobody felt the need to fill it. We were all just so glad to see Mom sitting up and doing something that looked normal. We all knew it was just a dim shadow of the reflection of what her life used to be—everyone except Grammie, who looked at it like medical progress, like maybe tomorrow she'd sit up and comb her own hair. It killed me, but inside, the only place I could say it, the deep place where Dad and I keep our hope, or lack thereof, I knew better. After a cut and blow dry, Samantha packed her things and said a quick goodbye. She was so generous. Years ago, she had insisted that she was volunteering her time and refused to take a cent for her work. "Johnna was my friend and she would do the same for me." I remembered her saying the first time she ever came.

I couldn't help it. I didn't know it would upset Dad and Mrs. Maggie. I didn't even think about it when I opened my purse, took out my lipstick, and put some on her. I spent a few minutes on her hair. Samantha did great work, but Mom didn't like too much poof. I tucked her hair behind her ear on the left side like she always wore it. When I turned around Dad, Bo, and Ty were all watching. Grammie and Mrs. Maggie were wiping tears from their eyes.

"Sorry, I just thought she might like it." I looked down, feelings ashamed, but not quite sure what I'd done wrong. "I didn't mean to make her look bad. She wore this color all the time. Maybe it's too much though."

I grabbed a tissue off her nightstand to wipe off the lipstick. Before I could make it back across the room, Dad took it out of my hand to stop me. "She would love it, baby. My sweetheart looks beautiful." He was standing back and admiring her. I don't think he even saw the hospital gown or how it draped on her thin shoulders or the feeding tube hanging on the pole next to her, waiting to be reattached. He still saw the girl he'd fallen in love with when she was just a teenager. The thing was, we all knew the difference. We'd all come to a place of some type of acceptance. I wished Grammie could get there too.

We stayed for another hour, talking and laughing like Mom could hear, like she was part of the conversation. I noticed several times I caught myself looking at Ty, sitting between my dad and his. He looked so grown up. The boy I knew was gone. He looked every bit the man they did. I ached to go sit on his lap and have him put his arms around me like he did when he carried me over the puddle. I wanted some alone time with Mom to cry over him, but I knew I wouldn't get it today. The sun was going down outside her window when Dad leaned over and said something to Bo. He nodded and punched Ty in the arm, like "let's go," and then passed on the gentle nudge my dad had given him. He obviously wanted to be alone with Mom.

"Maggie, what time does bingo start?" Mrs. Maggie took the hint. "In about half an hour. I'd best be heading that way. Catherine, can I interest you in joining me? You might just win big."

Grammie shrugged and said, "Sure, I'm always up for an adventure. It might be out of the way for you to drop me home afterwards. Bo, would you mind taking my car out to the house? I'll ride with Maggie and pick it up later." Maggie agreed that would be easier and save on gas for both of them.

"I think I'm going to spend the night with my girl here, so it might be a while 'til I can get back." Dad took his place in the big fold-out chair. Just then the nurse came in to put Mom back to bed. It wasn't Lisa this time. Jenny was working. We knew them all so well. She looked at Dad for an explanation as she walked over to Mom. It wasn't like him to not see her for extended periods of time.

"I have a new schedule at work for a while," he explained. She nodded and went to the call button to get the orderly to lift Mom. She was so petite that they didn't use a hoist on her like they had to do with some of the other patients. It was just easier to carry her. Dad put his hand up to stop her and picked her up himself. I wished Ty could have been looking at me that way when he did the same to me earlier. The love on Dad's face was immeasurable.

Chapter 17
"Cashing In"

"Ty, you get my girl home okay," said Dad, hugging me goodbye.

"You know I will," Ty answered in a tone more formal than necessary, like he was babysitting me or something.

"I'm sixteen now, you know. I could learn to drive myself." I hadn't mentioned it since Dad and I went to Grammie's the other day. Couldn't hurt, so I gave it another futile shot. Ty and Dad looked at each other and rolled their eyes. "When you're willing to sit down and let me teach you to read a map so you're not driving around lost in your own hometown, maybe we'll talk about it, okay? Just let your old dad get used to one thing at a time."

I nodded in defeat. He was right. I had absolutely no sense of direction. It was pathetic. The only thing they could tease me about that was true, although I would never admit it to any of them.

"Wanna get some ice cream?" Ty asked as I slammed my heavy door shut. I was so embarrassed I didn't know what to say. I was beet red, which confused him. It wasn't exactly a normal response to that question, so of course I made a joke.

"Unlike you who gets *paid* for the slaving we do at Cameron Manor, the only thing I have in my purse is makeup and a cell phone."

He laughed as he swung the truck around to face the road. I didn't realize how the sound of his laughter made me feel before now—happy and excited.

"Don't worry, I got you," he said, amused by my poverty. I sighed, wishing I could say the same about him.

"Brewster's okay?" he asked, knowing it was my favorite. I nodded, trying not to think of all the kids that would be hanging out there since it was summer. It was just a few minutes to Rogers Road and when we pulled up I could see the parking lot was nearly full.

"We can go somewhere else if you want," I suggested.

"Nah, I don't mind waiting. I want to get a hotdog too and they're the best here."

I flipped down the mirror and fixed my bangs under my hat before we got out. I was expecting him to be halfway to the door by the time I was done, but he waited and didn't say a word. I realized that I hadn't given him enough credit, of course he would sit and wait just because we weren't a couple didn't mean he wasn't still a gentleman. Of course, I knew he'd wait for me and it made me wish he were mine all the more, I was starting to get bummed again and right now there wasn't one single thing that would distract me from the pain of loving him. I sighed deeply "You ok?" he asked picking up on my mood as he always did, "Fine" I lied "I'm ready, we should go before it gets any more crowded in there. There were only a couple of tables to choose from so I just followed him to the one by the window. We weren't there two minutes before I could feel their eyes on me. Girls from my school were crowded around a nearby table, staring at us. It wasn't that they were mean to me like when we were in middle school. Teasing and name calling was a bit juvenile. We had moved on to teenage hostility, now that we were all in high school, so now they just ignored me, but not anymore apparently—Ty looked good to them too. There was one table of girls who smiled and waved a little, the ones who were nice, but avoided the attention being my friend would have gotten them.

April Mantis, my arch-nemesis, the one who started all the rumors when we were little, didn't even let the waitress come to our table before she made a bee line towards us. She looked like Barbie—only prettier, of course.

"Hey Caimee! Haven't seen you since school got out." *"Um...that's because you make my life miserable and you're mean."* "You should come around more often and say hello."

Wow! How very fake of you, I thought. Thinking the bogus smile and short nod I gave her in return betrayed my thoughts, she quickly turned to Ty before I had a chance to say what I was thinking out loud.

Who am I kidding? I wouldn't put a spotlight on myself by picking a fight with April, at least not until I saw what she was about to do. Had I known, not only would I have picked that fight, I would have announced it and gathered an audience to watch. Even if I'd lost, it would have put in a good effort.

"Who's your friend?"

Of course, Ty knew her. We were all in the same fifth grade class together and he'd been here every summer since, but I guess he'd really changed.

"It's me, April—Ty." She acted all shocked, I saw right through it from the first fake shriek. She's such a phony! She knew who he was, she just wanted an opening line. In my mind, I was picturing a new toy—"Broke Nose Barbie." Comes with her own bloody shirt.

"Oh my gosh, Ty! It's so great to see you!" The squealing almost hurt my ears. "How long are you here for? You'll have to come hang out with us sometime."

Convenient, I thought. No invitation extended to me at all. I picked up a packet of sugar from the table and occupied myself with it so I wouldn't jump up and kill her. I knew right then that this was something I'd just have to get used to. Ty was gorgeous and the girls in Culpeper who were anywhere near April's circle would know it by morning. *Great.* Yes, he was handsome, but I loved him for so much more than that all April wanted was a trophy and a pretty prom picture. I wanted him forever.

"I'm staying with my dad now. I'll be a senior here next year."

Her face went from lit up to glowing like a lighthouse beacon. I could not believe her next move.

"That's so great! Can't wait to see if we have any classes together."

She started by putting her hand on his shoulder and then ever so casually she slid right down on his lap in the small space between his chest and the table.

He pulled his face away from her and put his hands up like he was being held at gun point.

"Yeah, that would be great. Maybe we can suffer through a few classes together."

He was casual and calm, but she laughed like he was an animated standup comedian who had just told the funniest joke ever. He relaxed his posture either because he liked her there or realized she wasn't going to get up. I blinked back the tears I had been fighting for too long and went to the restroom, passing by the table where April's friends were sitting, all of whom had a little smile for me as I went by. The table of nicer, shy girls just shot me looks of sympathy.

I knew once I got in the stall that if I started crying my make-up would be everywhere and someone would tell April she'd gotten to me. I'd give anything to go back to just being ignored. I couldn't help it. Silent tears ran down my face, I grabbed some toilet paper and dabbed as fast as I could before I had mascara lines down my cheeks. I knew I had to get back out there. Ty wouldn't order without me. If I was gone, hiding like a coward for too long, he might think I was sick or something. Even if it wasn't a date, I hated to make him sit there starving while I was stuck in the bathroom feeling sorry for myself. At home, he never started to eat until Mrs. Maggie had started. Bo and Dad had always been big on men having manners and Ty took it to heart.

I checked my face in the mirror, pulled my cap down a little, held my head up and walked back to the table. April was writing her phone number on the palm of his hand with the waitress's pen, a permanent marker no less. I mean really, what waitress writes with a Sharpie?

"Well, don't let me keep you from eating. Call me, okay?"

I pulled my chair out and sat down. "Yeah, I am kind of hungry." My tone said, *ummm...*you can leave now. She shot me a dirty look and sashayed back to her table. I was hoping that Ty wouldn't watch her leave. The view from the back was just as Barbie-like as the one from the front.

I kept my head down when my ice cream came, swirling the warm caramel and thinking of his eyes, which led me to think about his gorgeous face, which led to his body. I had to stop myself there. I was thankful for the ball cap to hide my blushing, but he seemed more interested in the hot dog he was eating anyway. I'd lost my appetite, what difference did it make how much I loved him with April's number written on him like he was her personal property already.

"I thought you were hungry?" As soon as he said the word I happened to look at my watch, my mind went from his perfection to Joy in the closet. She was probably starving by now. A handful of fries wasn't exactly a meal.

"Not really, I'm kind of ready to go."

He finished his last bite. "Me too." He picked up the bill and went to pay.

I walked out to the truck with my audience still watching. I could see from the parking place we were in through the big window in the front of the shop that as soon as he walked out the door, my audience quickly became his. I had a minute to really look at April without her knowing. It wasn't like she buried me in the looks department, she was just bolder and more brazen than I could ever be, especially around guys. There was literally no limit to how far she would throw herself out there to get my Ty. The ride home was awkward. Not only had I not had a chance to win his heart with that kind of in your face competition, I felt like I'd just lost my best friend. Normally we would have talked about it, maybe even laughed about it, but his silence was telling me he was thinking about her, mulling over asking her out. Since he probably would be dialing the number on his hand soon, I didn't want to insult her and make him defend her. I couldn't stand to hear that, so I said nothing and neither did he.

I almost pictured him diving into the duck pond, hoping by some miracle that his cell phone would come back on and he could call her tonight without having to tell Bo and ask him for his phone. I knew that was ridiculous. He knew the phone was long gone and wouldn't be fishing it out, but I just figured whatever he had to do to hear her voice again tonight, he'd do it no matter how stupid I thought it was. More likely he'd be driving back to Brewster's later hoping she was still there, maybe waiting on him. The thought turned my stomach.

I hated the weighted wordless quiet between us. It was almost worse than bickering. We usually didn't let either last long, but the short ride was agonizing and seemed to go on forever. He didn't slosh through the mud to park the truck because he would have had to carry me again. Instead, he pulled up next to the dry dirt near the porch steps. I couldn't get away from the heartache fast enough.

"Thanks." That was the only word spoken between us as I climbed out and closed the heavy door behind me without meeting his eyes.

I slumped down the wall in my closet and told Joy everything. I didn't even ask how her exploring the house went. There was an apple core and a banana peel and a couple pieces of bread next to her, so I knew she had eaten. "Are you still hungry? I can get you some real food."

She seemed confused...surprised by the term "real." Seems like everything I said to her was like if she'd suddenly started speaking Italian to me—she didn't understand any more than I would have. I felt selfish. I only asked if she wanted anything when I was done with my story, but I was still wiping the tears I had held back in the restaurant restroom. Now I couldn't help it, I just let them flow.

"No," she said, shaking her head. She expressed her opinion and comforted me. "I can't imagine a girl being so forward like that. She seems like someone no boy would want to even be seen with."

"Well, things are a lot different now than they are in your time," I decided that since I was already crying that I'd just tell her everything. I started at the point when I was five and Mom had had her accident and continued to the part when Ty left and how I'd always loved him. We talked for hours. For the first time in my life I felt like I had a girlfriend who was a true friend. For a minute, I selfishly never wanted her to leave.

"Caimee, I think you are so brave! I'm glad I came here now. You're my family and I want to help if I can." *Brave*, I thought. *Nobody had ever used that word to describe me before. I didn't feel like it was true now. She was the one who literally jumped into the unknown and came here. I would never have done that. For all my big talk, I certainly didn't fight for Ty. When it came down to it I didn't want to have to I wanted him to choose me because that is what his heart wanted as much as mine does.*

I shook my head. "I don't think anybody can fix all this. I'm sorry, I've been totally telling you all my problems and I know you're missing your mom and worrying about her. I promise tomorrow night is your turn and I'll be a better listener and a better host. I won't forget to bring you meals tomorrow.

She laughed a little. "I did want to tell you about how I looked around today, but it can wait. You look tired."

"I am." I got up and went to the bathroom. My eyes were red and I'd pretty much cried all my makeup off. I washed up, brushed my teeth and put on my favorite pajamas, satin, Chinese red, spaghetti-strap top with fitted, low-waisted matching shorts. I loved the sweetheart neck line outlined in lace and the way the top fell about two inches over the top of the shorts. Mrs. Maggie bought it for me on my last birthday and gave it to me in secret. I always felt pretty in it and the color looked good in contrast to my skin. I figured, 'why not try to make myself feel better and wear something pretty and girlie?' it was usually a good start down my broken heart road of recovery. I made sure Joy was comfortable and I crawled into my bed.

I wasn't really sleeping. I was still pretty upset and feeling so defeated every time I started to drift off, I imagined myself actually having the intestinal fortitude to say what I was really feeling to April, but then I imagined Ty coming to her defense. At this rate, I'd be exhausted in the morning. Maybe they'd believe it if I went back to bed sick after breakfast; after all, I was heartsick over all of this. It wouldn't be a lie, not that Mrs. Maggie wouldn't investigate and catch me in it anyway, but she'd raised me better than to tell the half-truths I seemed to be living in these days. I sighed, missing the days when I didn't have to hide anything.

I tried not to think about April anymore, opening yet another door in my mind: memories of when Ty called me the day we buried Granddad. I very nearly told him then. The words "I love you" were on the tip of my tongue when we hung up. Joy was wrong about me. I wasn't brave. I'd chickened out a million times when it came to Ty. I could still hear his voice from that day in my thoughts. He was so soft-spoken and sweet on the phone, despite his anger over his mom not letting him attend the funeral.

The closest I thought we'd ever come to him saying anything to me was last summer when we sat out on the dock at the pond, fishing and talking. My dad found us at midnight and woke us up. I'd tried to leave him that night and walk home to bed, but there was something unspoken between us holding me there—at least I'd hoped there was, but clearly I was wrong. I did appreciate him taking the blame the next day with Dad, promising it would never happen again. I guess he was right, it wouldn't.

I rolled over and started crying again, not hard like before, just left over tears that eventually wore me out and forced my eyes closed. Of course, even in my half-sleep state, I dreamed of him. I was lost in the moment when we won at Foxfield races in the fall of last year with Bo's champion, Beretta. I missed that horse—so strong, but sweet-tempered. I guessed somewhere in the back of my mind he was like Ty. It was almost the same story—his owners had to move and took him to California. Ty had trained him. It was the only time his mom ever let him come back after his school had started. He'd had to beg her. He wanted to see the fruits of his labor and it was well worth it when Beretta thundered across the finish line first. We were in the stands. Ty picked me up and hugged me, but my victory didn't even last as long as Beretta's name was in the paper as the winner. Ty went home and it seemed that the hug was just a moment of shared pride, just a second of lapse on his part, nothing more. He was celebrating and I was the closest one to him at the time so I got the hug first. I couldn't imagine I had any more tears when I realized that my pillowcase was wet.

I sat up, alarmed when I heard the faint tapping at the door. All my walking down memory lane was abruptly brought to an end. I looked at the clock—a few minutes after 1 a.m. My first thought was my mother; my second was waking up Joy. I peeked through the crack of the closet door, but she was sound asleep. I crept to the door, expecting to see my dad and hear more bad news. Today at Mom's had been too good. Surely my good fortune in that area couldn't hold out. I hadn't heard his car drive up, but I was sure he'd left her to come and get me. If I was right, this was going to be bad. I didn't want to open the door. I didn't want to know. I stood there, hesitating. The soft knock came again. I turned the knob and swung it open slowly so as not to make any noise and startle Joy. The last thing I needed was for her to come bolting out of the closet half asleep, scared and confused.

It was Ty, wearing the same clothes he'd been wearing earlier. I started to speak, but he put his finger up to his lips and took my hand. He reached down with his other and picked up the first pair of shoes he saw— my white canvas Keds. I noticed he was wearing his tennis shoes. They were much cleaner and quieter than his old work boots and they wouldn't leave a trail of footprints for Mrs. Maggie to find in the morning.

He turned and started down the hall, never letting go of my hand, gently leading me the whole way in the quiet darkness, using the banister for a guide. Had my dad called Bo and told him and Ty to come? If so, why were we trying so hard not to wake Mrs. Maggie? When we got to the landing, he pulled a small key chain light out of his pocket and put my shoes down in front of me.

"I need socks," I whispered." He smiled like "Of course, I knew that." He knew I hated to wear lace up shoes without socks. He reached in his other pocket and handed me a pair of his. He put his finger back over his lips and held the light on my shoes so I would put them on. I sat down on the top step trying to keep quiet. I was fumbling with the laces; I hadn't untied the knots in them the last time I'd taken them off. He knelt down in front of me and untied each one with the small light in his mouth and then I put on the socks. I could tell he wanted to hurry so I put on one shoe and he put on the other. We sneaked the rest of the way down the stairs and out the front door. I was thinking I'd be going to the hospital in these pajamas and I wanted to tell him I had to change, but he never gave me the chance to say anything.

When we were safely away from the house, I had to ask. "Did my dad call? Is my mom okay? Did he say not to wake Mrs. Maggie and tell her?"

He held the flashlight up so that I could see his face clearly. What I thought was excitement in his eyes faded. He was horrified. He'd given me the wrong impression.

"No, no, Caimee. I'm sorry! I have a surprise for you. He took my hand again, trying to avoid the leftover puddles, nearly dried up now, but still scattered around in the dark. Finally, we were close enough to the barn I could see he had turned on the flood lights on the side opposite the one that faced the house. It wasn't like the other night when he'd turned them all on and lit up my room. It was funny how our last encounter ended on a strained note, but we were able to move past it with no mention of the tension at all, because it had simply disappeared into our friendship...like always.

He let go of my hand and said, "Go see." I walked across the wide hurdle ring and around the corner of the barn. There she was—Lindie, my mother's horse, saddled and ready to go. She was a beautiful quarter horse with black and light gray markings that made her look like a cow. Her unique appearance and her gentle nature are the reasons why my mother loved her so much. She wasn't a jumper or a champion, just Mom's pet and constant companion around here—at least until I came along. Lindie was nearly seventeen years old now. Mom had gotten her while she was still pregnant with me and couldn't even ride her 'til after I was born. The first picture I have a conscious memory of us taking a ride together was when I was about three and we were sitting on Lindie. Ty walked up beside me. The tears were starting to flow again. Maybe he'd think they were red and swollen from these fresh tears and not the many I'd shed over him earlier.

'I'm sorry, Caimee! I thought you might want to see her. What I'm trying to say is I know you've seen her, but not up close since...that day."

We were standing half in the shadow, out of the circle of the bright light that shone down from the top corner of the barn, but I could still see the pain on his face, pain thinking that he'd caused me pain. Good thing he wasn't in my room a few hours ago or he'd have been really upset with himself. I knew now I could never tell him. The last thing I wanted was for him to be with me out of pity.

"No! No! I'm so glad you brought me here. I've missed her so much. She's part of my mom. I turned to look at her again like she might disappear; I had that same dream-like feeling I had when I came up out of that root cellar. I couldn't take my eyes off of her. The tears were coming, but my voice was even and steady. It wasn't like uncontrollable grief—more like unexpected joy, mixed with memories of happy times. Ty didn't say anything. He stood quietly beside me and let me soak in the moment. I dried my eyes so I could talk to him without blurred vision and a runny nose. Maybe he didn't love me, but I at least didn't have to ruin the moment being a blubbering mess.

"Did you know that the last words my mom said were to your dad?"

Ty didn't speak, he just shook his head. My eyes were fixed on Lindie, but I could see him in my periphery, looking, glancing down at me and then looking back at the horse that shared the memory I was about to let him in on. "She made him promise not to let anyone shoot her. 'It wasn't her fault! Protect my Lindie, promise me!' Your dad promised. It was the closest he and my dad ever came to blows—like brothers, I guess. Dad wanted to blame the horse. Just like Grammie, he needed someone...*anyone* to be responsible, but Bo had seen the whole thing and knew it was an accident. He didn't tell me that until last year. I guess he figured it was time I knew her last thoughts. She whispered my name just before she lost consciousness." I smiled, but there was no joy behind it, just wistful longing that I could have heard her say my name one more time. Bo was lucky to have been the one to hear her say what turned out to be her goodbye."

Ty took my hand so tenderly I had to look to make sure he was actually touching me. "Come on."

We walked up beside her and gentle Lindie never even so much as flinched. I didn't realize what his intentions were until I felt his hands grip my exposed midriff between my nightie top and my shorts. He helped me get my foot in the stirrup and I automatically reached for the saddle horn, like I'd done it yesterday. I remembered. He took the reins, steadied her, and then climbed on behind me. It was magic. We rode around the unlit part of the ring by the light of a sliver crescent moon and a million stars.

After about thirty minutes he stopped her back under the lights. I couldn't help it. I leaned back against his chest and closed my eyes. "Thank you."

He didn't respond like I thought he might with a "you're welcome." Instead he said, "Take your right foot out of the stirrup." I sighed, expecting this was to be my dismounting without killing myself lesson, but as soon as I did, he put his hand under my leg, helped me turn, and then put it over the horse so I was facing sideways in the saddle. "Take your left foot out of the stirrup," he instructed calmly, sensing this would throw me off balance and I might be afraid.

"But I won't have a way to help me down." I was already confused, knowing if my satin shorts slipped on the leather saddle I was going to fall flat on my face from the height of the horse. I didn't want that. It scared me to think of it, Lindie was much bigger than your average horse which contributed to my mom's injuries.

"I promise I won't let you fall." He put his right arm

around my waist and bent his wrist over my hip and held me tight, all the while keeping the reins in his hand. Slowly I complied and took my left foot out of the stirrup. He put his left arm under my leg while holding me tight with his right and the next thing I knew I was facing backwards on the horse—face to face with him.

Lindie never moved. He held her reins firmly, but I could feel him pass them to his left hand behind my back. I didn't notice that one of my thin little straps had fallen off my shoulder, but he did. His eyes never left mine as he reached to put it back where it belonged.

"You know what I love about you the most, besides this?" he said, pointing to my heart. I was so shocked at the word "love "and by the question so out of context, I just dumbly shook my head "no."

"You can put on makeup and nice clothes and fix this pretty hair 'til it shines and you're gorgeous." He stroked the length of my hair and then ran his fingertips around my shoulder bringing some of it forward. He slowly slid his hand down to my waist with the pieces entwined in his fingers, as if he was memorizing it, as if he were waiting all this time for permission to touch something fragile for the first time. I barely felt it; I was nearly numb all over, like the fog or dream state I was in when I fell through time. I had to shake it away to hear him continue. "Or you can wear those muddy boots, ripped up shorts, not a drop of makeup, pull your hair up on top of your head and somehow you're still gorgeous." He took a deep breath not like he was nervous, but more like he was about to reveal a secret. "But I see you for so much more than that."

He looked directly into my eyes, so I could see the truth in his. "I've known lots of girls like April, even dated a few of them." That stung. He could see it on my face and deep in my eyes, but as soon as he noticed, he looked down and hid his face underneath his hat. He was embarrassed, the same way I'd been at Brewster's. I thought I'd hidden my feelings, but he'd seen them all.

He waited a second and then continued. "But every one of them eventually broke up with me. Know why?"

I still couldn't speak. I dumbly shook my head again.

"Because all I ever did was talk about you and Virginia and how much I missed you and wanted to be here." He was blushing! I could see the faint pink glow under his tan.

"I lost more girlfriends that way. I tried so hard to find a piece of you in all of them, but not one even came close. When you didn't speak to me all the way home, I figured you were mad at me...I mean *really* mad and I didn't know what to say. It tore me up to think I'd hurt you, or just sat there while someone else did, I'm sorry, I didn't want that...any of it to happen that way. I don't ever want to be the reason you cry again."

He knew, of course he did, he was my Ty and he knew me. I wanted to look away, but his eyes held me there. He stroked my face wiping away the last of the tears.

He paused like he was in deep thought and finally nodded his head "yes" like he'd decided something really important. "I think I'm going to have to call in that favor now."

This time I looked away from him, not sure if his words had fully sunken in. I'd envisioned it a million times and it didn't feel real.

"I can't imagine anything I could do for you that's better than what you've given me tonight, just being here and so close to Lindie, so close to memories of my Mom."

I felt his calloused hand lightly touch my chin and turn my face back to his.

"I can," said Ty. "I've been thinking about it for a long time now." He kept Lindie firmly under control with his left hand and slid his right up my back under my hair, the feeling of his fingers through the thin satin made me shiver under the heat of his touch. He froze and cautiously appraised my reaction in case that shiver meant "no."

I couldn't take my eyes off him and there was no hiding the "yes" through their deep blue and into my soul. Once he had my unspoken permission, he kept going, slowly sliding his hand up my back until the fabric ran out just below my shoulder blades, never taking his eyes off mine. He didn't stop until he reached the back of my neck. I couldn't move, I couldn't even breathe.

He leaned forward and turned his cap around backwards, letting the reins slack for a second so he could reach it, with nothing but the air of the hot Virginia night and the smell of the bluebells between us, he leaned forward as much as the saddle would allow and he kissed me. It was soft and sweet. I put my arms around his neck and enjoyed every second of it. It didn't seem long enough. I thought he was done when he moved away, but instead he progressed from my lips to my face and I couldn't help it, I leaned into his chest, wanting to be closer to him. I had loved him for so long. He pulled my hair aside and buried his face in my neck, relaxing his whole body. We sat there leaning on each other.

Lindie got a bit restless and started to lift her feet like she wanted to take off. I felt him tense all over and get her back under control, but he had to lean away from me to pull on her hard enough to get her to be still again. Both of his hands were around me, behind my waist, holding her steady now and as promised, protecting me from the fall I would have taken if it had not been for his arms to secure me.

"You know, you're a really good kisser for a first timer." He was back to the teasing. Tears welled up in my eyes; I was surprised I had any left. I couldn't remember wanting to cry or being this emotional since the day my dad sat me down to explain to me that my mommy wasn't coming home. Another memory of Ty—he'd been sitting next to me at the time. I stopped the flow and blinked them back, but it was too late. He saw them glistening under the lights. He looked deeply surprised and horrified that he'd hurt my feelings.

"How did you know and why are you teasing me about it?"

His face became soft, his eyes gentle. "Because I know my Caimee—and I know she's been waiting for me to make up my stupid mind for a while now. I'm sorry it's taken me so long and I'm sorry you thought I was teasing you. I promise—no more baby games. Sometimes it's just easier for me than saying what I really feel."

I had to know. I had to hear him say it. "And how do you really feel?"

"Don't you know by now, my sweet girl? I love you! I've always loved you. It just took me some time to figure it out, but when I saw your dad with your mom tonight, I knew right then and there that if that was us, I'd do the same for you. I'd stay with you and take care of you. I'd still want to be with you forever. You are my other half. We were meant to be together—and lucky me, you're beautiful too!" He touched my face again, tracing its outline with the fingertips of his left hand.

I slid my hand down his forearm, towards his right hand behind me. He squinted his eyes, looking a little puzzled. It was an awkward way to turn my arm, but I managed to find his hand. Sensing what I wanted, he stopped memorizing my face with his touch and put the reins in his left hand and brought his right around in front of him between us. The dark black phone number was lighter than it had been, but still clearly readable. "And that?" I asked. "That isn't going to go away when we get to school? It might even get worse. You'll likely be covered head to toe in ink."

He laughed and shook his head. "That washes off eventually. You're not a phone number on my hand, you're in my heart and there's no washing that away—ever." He took my hand in his ink-covered palm and placed it flat on his chest over his heart, I could feel it beating. I didn't know what to say. It was like standing at the pot of gold at the end of a rainbow. What do you say when you finally get there and find out it's real? There are no words for that. My heart felt like liquid that had burst into a thousand teardrops—happy, grateful tears. I took off his cap with my free hand, leaned in and kissed him again, running my fingers though the soft curls at the back of his neck.

Chapter 18
"The Barn"

He jumped off Lindie like an acrobat, like he'd done it a thousand times. It made me a little sad for two reasons: He *had* done it a thousand times and it was going to take me so long to even come close to learning everything he knew about horses—and two, our ride was over. He saw right through to the heart of me. He could read me so easily and I had misread him so thoroughly all these weeks. He reached up to help me down. I swung my left leg over the saddle and he slid me easily to the ground. He put one finger under each of the straps of my nightie and began to run them back and forth over my shoulders, my skin underneath the pads of his fingers and the smooth satin on top. Absently, I wondered how he could be so strong and so gentle at the same time.

"We'll go again, sweet girl. I promise."

"You're going to get us in trouble, you know." He tilted his head back, laughing quietly. "Haven't you heard? Apparently, I stay there."

I scoffed. "Yeah right, like your dad could ever stay mad at you for defending yourself. He needs you too much around here for more important things than what we been doing."

"Yeah, but I did get in a fight and I did break that kid's arm." He wasn't at all proud. His face fell just saying it out loud to me.

211

"On top of that, Dad thinks I *need* to talk to my mom and give her another chance, so until we come to some agreement, you're looking at Cameron Manor's new caretaker. He made that clear when he took me to breakfast. I think he thinks if we don't do this, he's like letting me get away with something. I already know the big *lesson* here, but he has this thing about 'raising a man right' and all that."

"Bo may be pretending like he doesn't know it already for the sake of this whole 'lesson thing,' but I believe he already suspects he raised a pretty great man."

"I hope your father thinks so," he said. He bent his head to kiss me again in the circle of bright light. Now that we were on solid ground, he put his hands on my face and in my hair, not stopping 'til he'd made his way down my arms to my hands, holding them in his.

It took me a second to catch my breath before I could ask him, "Are you actually nervous? You really think my dad wouldn't give his blessing or whatever?"

He didn't answer, but I was right—his face said it all. Calm, collected Ty had found something he was worried about and at that moment it felt like he wanted my father's approval more than he wanted Bo's.

I stayed behind while he walked my mother's horse past me and into the barn.

"Come on, I won't tell." He smiled. His words came across like he was ten, but no sign of childish teasing this time, just our shared history of never telling on each other remembered. The barn was cooler inside than the warm Virginia night had been. Bo kept it temperature controlled for the comfort of the horses. I remember Granddad Nathan thought that was silly and going to be expensive. "You can't coddle them like that, they'll never be champions."

Bo said, "Just trust me Nathan, just this once. I got it figured where it won't bankrupt us, but the horses can't stand the extreme heat and cold. We won't use it year round, just now and then...and you're wrong on this—they will perform better."

Granddad lost and Bo was right—the horses did win that year more than ever before. Each stall was equipped with large box fans in the ceiling for the hottest parts of the day and flameless torches for the winter months. Bo had the fans running tonight to help them tolerate the heat and humidity left by the rain storm.

There were twelve eight-foot by eight-foot stalls on each side of the wide aisle. Lindie went in the last one on the left. "A lot of new faces in here," I said, putting my arms across my chest, trying not to tremble. The air circulating was great if you had horse hide, but not so much if you were wearing thin satin and lace. He had opted to turn on the dim lights attached to the post on the outside of every other stall instead of the large overhead lights. Moonlight was asleep. I stopped and looked at her glowing in the soft white light. He realized I wasn't right behind him and stopped and turned around with Lindie. "She's my favorite," I said and then looked at Lindie. "Present company excluded, of course." I walked over and stroked the side of her face. He saw me unfold my arms to pet her and realized I was chilled.

"Sorry, I forgot Dad left the fans on tonight. I think he turned them on early to dry the place out a little." He was taking off his top shirt while he spoke. He didn't wait for me to reach for it. He dropped Lindie's lead rope and walked around her to put it on me.

It was like he couldn't touch me enough, now that he'd finally admitted how he felt out loud. He swept my hair out of the way with his fingertips and put the shirt around my shoulders. I put my arms through the sleeves, which were about a mile too long. The length of it hit my legs about three inches above my knees. It smelled like his cologne. I turned around and he was smiling. The ring of deep brown in his eyes glimmered in this light.

"Not exactly a great fit, but it definitely looks better on you. He took my left hand and then my right and rolled up the sleeves.

I tried to stay out of his way as he put Lindie's tack away. There was a spot on the back wall for it and he made sure it was exactly as Bo had left it. Thor heard the noise and started getting restless, pacing back and forth in his stall, next to Lindie's. Even though the five-foot doors were closed and locked old-fashion style with a board slid across them, he could still look over them with ease.

"He's a fussy one tonight, isn't he?" Ty could tell he scared me a little. "Dad says I'll have him tame by the end of the summer, but I don't know. He seems like it may take a while to work some of that wildness out of him, especially since I won't have that much time with him.

"Sounds like he's treating him like you."

He grinned. "Yeah, kind of does, doesn't it? Dad thinks this may be the one."

I turned my face away from Thor and looked up at Ty. He was standing a few inches behind me. He slid his hands under his shirt and held my waist from behind.

"This might be your dad's champion."

"Who owns him?"

"Well, that's just it. We all do—my dad, your dad. I even took the money I had saved up from working the past two summers and helped buy him. He isn't a well-known bloodline, but Dad thinks his DNA is perfect. It's his temperament that needs work. He is only seven months though so that gives us time to get him calmed down and winning before he turns three and dad tries to get him in the derby, he is big for his age, he will be a monster when he is full grown."

Thor stood up on his hind legs and hit the doors with his front feet, shaking the thick wood. I leaned deeper into Ty's chest.

"Oh, stop showing off, you old bully," he chastised the horse, who seemed to understand. He calmed down long enough for us to turn and walk away, but I wasn't ready to go.

"Can I say goodbye to Lindie?"

Ty glanced at his watch. "You know, we have to be back here in four hours." I gave him a look that just said "please."

He'd already given in before I had to promise I'd be on time. He let go of my waist and aimed me in her direction. I walked over to her stall.

"I'll be fast, I promise."

She came right over, putting her head over the half doors in front of her stall. I stroked her face. "Your mama misses you, baby." Without knowing what I said, she nodded her head in agreement. Maybe somewhere inside she understood.

On the way out of the barn, we walked past the horse that Mom used during the jumping competitions at Commonwealth Park. He was old now, nearly twenty-two. Bo had taken a special liking to him over the years and kept him around because he was a calm influence for the other horses. He was beautiful, albeit faded with age—a buckskin colored Appaloosa. Mom called him Peter Pan because she said he floated over the hurdles without effort. It was the only time Bo agreed on a horse's name. Mom had a gift, like an extra sense when it came to choosing winners—just like Bo and Ty. I hoped I'd be like that someday and also maybe ride as well as she did.

Ty walked me to the porch. He laid the little flashlight on the railing next to the steps. It gave off just enough light for us to see each other, but was swallowed by the darkness after just a few short feet. I tucked his shirt under me like a dress and we sat down on the top step. I knew what I wanted to say, but didn't know how to start.

"What is it?" he asked, seeing something unspoken in my eyes.

"I think that maybe we should let them see us together slowly—you know, the family. I mean what if you go to school and meet someone else?" He started to stop me right there, but I put my finger on his lips. He kissed it and then moved to my palm while he let me keep going.

"I know you don't think it will happen, but just in case, I don't want you to feel trapped or obligated to me because you live here—and I *really* don't want it to be weird between us and have everyone else giving their opinion. You know Mrs. Maggie and Grammie will have one and neither one will be too shy about saying it. I'd hate to do anything that would upset our fathers' relationship. I wouldn't want them to take sides."

He looked down like what he was going to say was hard for him. "I think I waited so long to tell you that now you don't entirely trust me. Sweet girl, don't you know I'm not going anywhere? I would have never told you if I wasn't sure. I promise I'm not looking for anyone else and even if I were, I wouldn't find her because there's only one you."

I just about laughed out loud thinking of Joy asleep in my room. *If he only knew...* I almost told him. "Ty," I whispered his name and made him look up. "I love you too—so much you don't even know."

He patted his lap and I moved over and sat on it. It wasn't like with April, who just took advantage of the fact that he was a gentleman and wouldn't throw her off, I was invited. It was my place to be. As soon as I was comfortable, with my head leaning on his chest, feeling his soft breath come and go, he explained.

"I know. I've always known."

I opened my mouth to speak. I was going to say 'Then what took you so long?' but then he returned the favor and put his finger over my lips, anticipating my question.

"Because I wanted to be sure, because I would never ever take a chance and hurt you if I didn't know we were forever. I needed to know the feelings I had were about us, not this place or our parents or any of it, just me and you. I know they are. When I saw you that first morning I got here, I knew. The second I saw your pretty face and heard that sweet voice and felt your warm spirit all around me, it hit me. It took me a few days...okay a few weeks to get it together. I was sort of scared you might say no. I would pick you out of any crowd, even if we had never met." I leaned my face down and kissed him again, but then I hit the bill of his hat.

"Like I'd say no, you big moron." He righted it again so he could look into my eyes. He caught the sarcasm and the sentiment that I would be his forever—no question about it. We sat like that for a long time. Eventually, he turned and leaned up against the gray stone pillar and let me slide over in front of him, me leaning back against him, our legs stretched out in front of us. He combed his fingers through my hair until eventually I drifted off to sleep. I heard him reach behind his head and turn off the small light.

We startled when his watch started to beep. "It's five in the morning. I have to get back before Dad realizes I'm gone." He took advantage of my position and my hair swept to the side. He kissed the back of my neck. "I guess I should go," he said, with no conviction in his voice that he was actually going to get up. Neither of us moved.

"Okay," I breathed, knowing that if I was standing, my legs would have given out on me.

"Tell me something, anything," he said between kisses.

"How much grunt work do I really have to do before Bo will start teaching me again?" He let out a deep sigh. His breath tickled me. I turned my head and laughed a little in response.

"Well, let me put it to you this way. After your dad said whatever he said to your grandmother about it, she called my dad and gave him a good talking to. It turns out that neither one of them is as afraid of you getting hurt with all this supervision," he said, pointing to himself. "...as they are of Grammie. So, the three of them came up with a compromise." You learn from the ground up, I get to work out my "anger," he made air quotes around the word, my sentence is up as soon as I work things out with my mom, which means that I'll be doing this forever. On the upside for all of them, they have cheap labor and Cameron Manor gets a facelift.

Starting with the fence we did, then all the landscaping we've been doing, the barn roof starts tomorrow..." He looked at the sky. "I guess I should say today and then I believe next on the list is the fence around the jumping ring. It needs new weather-proof stain and so do the hurdles. I think I heard something about building some type of shed down around back similar to the barn for Hillbilly and Bumpkin that's cooler and warmer than their dog house. Dad says maybe then they won't bark so much and keep Mrs. Maggie from making hound stew.

I laughed, remembering telling the dogs the same thing the night I first met Joy. "Yeah, Granddad loved having hounds around. I kind of figured once he was gone she would find them a new home, but I think deep down she keeps them for him."

"I think you're right," Ty agreed. "She tries to come off all teacher-like, as if she's in charge of all of us like her classroom, but I think inside she is just a big softie."

I turned fully around to look at him. "That list is going to take all summer. By the time I get to learn anything from your dad, I'll be going off to college."

He nodded. "I think that's Grammie's plan. She kind of has them over a barrel. I overheard my dad on the phone the other day, promising her that the same thing that happened to your mom won't happen to you. They both feel so bad for her. You're all she has, all any of them have of your mom." I nodded in defeat.

"Don't worry, though, your dad really does have your back on this one. My dad told me that your dad told Grammie that he made you a promise about helping run this place someday and he intends to keep it. I think he's just easing her into the idea with all this delay.

"And what about you? I don't want you fighting with your mom, but if you make up with her, can you keep that your little secret so I don't have to be the Manor's field hand all alone?"

He leaned toward me, boring his eyes into mine, never diverting until he leaned a little to my right. He put his lips up to my ear. Alternately kissing and talking, he whispered, "I will *never* ever leave you."

I nodded against his lips, reached down and took his hands in mine.

He held my fingers, but turned his wrist and looked at his watch again. We were tangled together the way we were sitting, so he slid his legs out from around me and eased to a standing position so I wouldn't have to move and so he wouldn't knock me off the step.

"I'll see you at breakfast, sweet girl. Wear light-colored clothes and those boots you've been working in. It's going to be hot up on that roof and you'll need the traction of those thick soles."

I stood up and walked into his chest putting the top of my head against him.

"I can't believe they're worried about me falling off a horse, but have no problem with me being on top of that barn. I pointed at the height of it without even looking up. I felt his laugh vibrate inside his chest.

"I know, don't worry. Not only will I not leave you, I

won't let you fall either."

I put my arms around his waist, sensing he was about to leave. He gently removed them. "If you want to ease them into "us" then I have to go before my dad wakes up. I'm going to have to sneak in and he might already be up. The early rays of the sun were starting to light the far eastern sky.

"Will you do one more thing for me before you go?" I looked up and he melted when he saw my pleading eyes and smile.

"What?" He playfully rolled eyes his like I was imposing on him.

"Kiss me one more time so when I go upstairs I'll know all this was real."

He turned his hat around backwards again, put one hand gently on each side of my face, and kissed me like it was the last time he was ever going to kiss anybody. "Real enough for you?" he asked when he was done untangling his hands from my hair, trying not to pull it.

I couldn't answer, I numbly nodded yes.

He turned to go, not waiting for me to regain my composure. "Oh, and pull your hair up today. I want you to be able to see where you're stepping, okay?"

I waved in understanding and watched him jog back across the field to Bo's house.

Chapter 19
"Joy's Friendship"

I sneaked inside, still glowing, still numb, still so happy I couldn't believe it. I made the quietest thing I could think of for Joy to eat without waking up Mrs. Maggie—oatmeal and toast. I took off my Keds and crept up to my room after making sure to clean up my mess in the kitchen so she wouldn't know I'd even touched "her area." Joy was still sound asleep. I couldn't help it. I had to tell her I was bursting inside. I wrapped Ty's shirt tighter around me. I wanted to be able to smell his cologne and feel his arms still at my waist when I told her the story.

"Wake up! I need to talk to you." I shook her to hurry the process. I had to get in the shower and get ready for my day and I didn't want to leave out even the smallest detail. Her expression was that of alarm when she opened her eyes and focused on me. "What is it?"

My face must have been showing the frenzy I felt inside. She instantly looked worried. "Is something wrong?"

I handed her the breakfast I'd fixed for her and shook my head "no" with a huge smile on my face. I could feel my eyes shining. It was all so new to me—having a real friend to tell all my secrets to, at least one that could talk back. Mom knew everything up 'til now and I couldn't wait to tell her this, but for a split-second I felt guilty telling Joy first—but I had to. No way would she have not seen it all over my face.

"So much has changed, you won't believe it." She took the spoon and started to eat. Finally, some food she seemed to recognize.

I started with the knock at the door and ended with the kiss on the porch. By the time I was finished, so was she. She set down the bowl and hugged me.

"Oh, Caimee, I'm so happy for you! I wish I could have a night like that with Kade." Her shyness came out as soon as the words did, "...at least I think I would like it."

"He is the Sheriff's son, right?" I remembered, but I wanted her to know I'd been paying attention."

She nodded a hopeless 'yes.' "I don't think he even knows I'm alive. Doesn't matter because I don't think his pa would approve of me anyway. He's seen my pa in town, gambling and drinking with some of the other railroad men. Ma was buying supplies and said she overheard him say he was tired of them raising a ruckus and wishes they'd finish laying the tracks near town and move along."

All of a sudden I remembered something Mrs. Maggie had said about the Sheriff. It dawned on me all at once, clear as a bell why he hadn't made a big deal documenting Joy's disappearance. Given how he felt about her father, I imagine he didn't put much effort into finding her. Sure, she lived in a big fine house, but that would not have changed how they were seen, as "less than civilized" for that day and time. That had to be it. Why would anyone except her mother and maybe a few compassionate people care if she was missing? The daughter of a trouble maker, living just on the edge of the law, I imagined not too many would be all broken up about it. *Man, I thought we had it bad with the gossip; but it's nothing compared to the reputation her father must have been carving out for her family.* She looked at me curiously, catching the intuition in my eyes. I didn't want to tell her what I was thinking because it would only make her ashamed and I'd promised myself I'd stop doing that. I turned the look to encouragement as if that's what I had always intended it to be.

I hugged her back. "If it can happen to me, it can happen to you. We'll just have to come up with a plan before you leave to help you get started."

Suddenly she looked hopeful, "Well, he did walk me to school almost every day. My house is on his way, but he didn't have to offer to carry my books, right?"

"Definitely a good sign," I assured her and I didn't even have to exaggerate. Maybe Kade did like her and was as shy as she is. We were chatting and giggling like little kids when I heard Dad talking to Bo and two sets of footsteps coming up the stairs. My first thought was that Ty had gotten caught and they knew everything.

There was a hard pounding on my door. I started to answer it, but then realized that I had Ty's shirt on. I took it off in the closet as fast as I could. My hands kept getting stuck in the sleeves because he'd rolled them tightly so they wouldn't slip.

"Get up, girl! You been late one day already and today's a'wastin'. "Breakfast is almost on the table. Got you some good ol' bacon," Bo said, teasing me about my eating and work habits. I could hear Dad laughing in the background. I put on my best sleepy, just dragged out of bed face and cracked the door open.

"I am up. I'm getting in the shower right now." I shifted my gaze to my dad behind him and opened the door a couple of inches wider. "How's Mom?"

"She seemed okay this morning when I left. I'm beat, though. I'm going to bed for a few hours. I have to be at the airport by midnight." He saw the bummed look on my face. "Don't worry, I'll see you at dinner. You'll be so busy over the next couple of weeks you won't even have time to miss me." I rolled my eyes at both of them and gave a sarcastic nod of my head before I closed the door.

"Come talk to me while I'm in the shower. I want to hear what you thought about the house."

Joy looked wary. "But you won't have any clothes on."

"*You're* not getting in. *I'm* taking a shower you're going to do the talking." I pointed to the makeup stool, climbed behind the curtain, threw my clothes over, and waited to hear about her adventure. It must have been like a walk on the moon for her. Besides, with everything that has been going on, I felt like it had all been about me. I hadn't kept my end of the bargain and taken her to see the painting. I opened the curtain and stuck my head out. "I promise, first chance we get we'll go see the picture and all the stuff up there."

She nodded anxious to get on with her own story. "All the rooms are here, but they're so different. There is so much I don't understand. I can't wait for us to be alone in here so you can show me. I was lucky when I found the food. I was starving, but I didn't want to say. I know, you told me to tell you, but you weren't here, but I remembered what you said about family and started looking through things. I wish you could come home with me and see how Ma keeps the house. This all looks so strange. The pictures on the wall are so pretty. There seem to be so many pretty things everywhere. I don't how you look at them all. I was overwhelmed. I wanted to touch some of them, but I remembered my promise. I really want to learn about everything before I go back. We have to make some time when everyone is gone. There were a few things in the kitchen I think I figured out, but so much more I want to know."

The excitement in her voice was palpable. I was going to have to make some time soon.

"The worst part was when I almost got caught. I had to move my head out from under the water to make sure I heard her right.

"What do you mean you almost got caught?"

"Well, you told me I could leave when the lady moved that white square thing out front, so I did. I made sure she was gone, but as soon as I got into the kitchen, she came back again. I ducked behind the big sitting chair in the bedroom Ma and Pa use it was the closest place to hide. It's next to what Ma uses for Nicholas's play room, but now it's full of books."

"That Mrs. Maggie's room!" I gasped.

"I know. She came in there, picked up a bag she'd forgotten, and hurried back out again. I was sure she was going to see me.

I turned off the water and she handed me a towel the way I had done for her.

"The new rule is no going out without me. I don't know how in the world we'd explain it. If anybody comes in here, you hide behind this curtain." She nodded gravely, realizing the trouble it would cause if she were seen.

I got dressed in light blue-jeans shorts and a light pink T-shirt just like Ty had told me to do. I dried my bangs, put my hair in a ponytail, put my cap back on, pulled my hair through the back, and braided the ponytail just to make sure it wouldn't be in my face. "How do I look?"

Joy stood back and appraised me. "Why are there patches all over your pants?"

I realized that these were the ones that had holes in the back pockets, and one on the hip. I didn't care, but Mrs. Maggie stole them one day and put pink heart-shaped patches on them before they ripped straight through. The good news for me was I'd been needing something to match the T-shirt I was wearing and the color of the patches seemed to tie the outfit together.

"Mrs. Maggie thinks it's more proper this way." She nodded, understanding "proper" like she'd heard it herself a time or two.

"Well, everything here looks so small and short, but I'm starting to like it, so I think you look fine and Ty should think so too."

She was happy for me, but I could see a deep sadness in her eyes. "You're missing your mom, aren't you?"

She nodded. "I wonder what she would think of me approving of strange clothes and eating strange food, but mostly I wonder if Pa has come back and how she must be feeling, missing me and worrying about what has happened to me." I noticed she didn't mention her father missing her.

I tried to imagine my dad in the same situation. He'd be going crazy and I knew it. I had to come up with something. "Don't worry, we'll get you back. It isn't much longer now." I sat with her my arm around her shoulders as long as I could.

"I know you have to go. I'd feel worse if I kept you, but I would like to see the picture of my mother soon, if we can manage it."

"I won't forget," I promised again. I was torn. "I want to stay and keep you company, but I have to go. I'm hoping to be back early, but you never know with Bo and Ty. They can work 'til sundown. My dad is sleeping across the square in the other bedroom, so you'll have to be extra quiet.

"I know, but I get so lonely and bored."

I wanted to offer her my iPad or something, but I would hate to think of her staring at a blank screen all day trying to figure it out and I didn't have time to show her. "I have a ton of books, read anything you want. I'll sneak back up at lunch and bring you something to eat." I really did hate to leave her. She was good company and so easy to talk to and confide in. Mrs. Maggie had tried to be that friend for me, but this was different. I heard Bo calling from the bottom of the stairs.

"Now I really have to go." I looked back at where Bo's voice was coming from and then back to her. She could tell I was caught in the middle. She seemed to understand that I was feeling guilty and made it easier on me.

"Hey, what are friends for? Now go see Ty and tell me *all* about it when you get back."

"Promise," I said over my shoulder as I was halfway out the door. I'd just seen what a true friend is from someone other than Ty—sacrificing and unselfish.

Chapter 20

"Partners"

Ty was at the breakfast table, waiting for Mrs. Maggie to sit down, same as always. I saw that he'd done what he told me to do. He was wearing light-colored clothes—camouflage shorts with huge cargo pockets on the side and a light tan T-shirt. Today he was hiding something—his hand holding mine under the table.

Bo walked in and took one look at my pink shirt and matching shorts. "You really didn't need to get all gussied up to do roofing work, but whatever makes you move faster is okay by me."

Ty let go of my hand and put both of his in plain view, I guess so Bo wouldn't suspect anything.

"I'm sure she'll do fine, she has an excellent teacher." He pointed to himself and started to say something else, but Bo scoffed at his son's playful arrogance and gave him a warning to be serious.

"Just don't let her fall off the roof. The tarps to cover the ground around the barn are already out. The shingles and the felt should be delivered sometime today and the dumpster guy should be here in an hour or so, so you need to get the tarps laid."

It was all in perfectly good English, but I didn't understand a word of it. Ty nodded like "no problem."

"Well, nobody is going anywhere 'til they eat something, I don't do all this for my health, you know," said Mrs. Maggie, setting down a huge stack of pancakes, bacon, juice, and coffee. As soon as Bo said grace, he and Ty made quick work of almost all the bacon. She loved to see them eat. She always sat back with a satisfied look on her face and watched. I had a couple of pancakes and some juice.

"I'm guessing this job will require no less manual labor than the last?" I sighed. "My nails are never going to be the same. They look like they've been put through a shredder."

Bo got up and slapped my back. "Well, look at it this way, kiddo, they can't look any worse."

"Thanks, that makes me feel so much better. Maybe if my fingers fall off altogether, you'll have a permanent reason not to let me ride."

Bo looked thoughtful like he was considering how he could work that into his plans. I gave him as dirty a look as I could muster and took my last bite. Of course, I finished first and left Ty sitting there like I normally do to scarf down his meal. As much as I hated to do it, I went and put on my work boots.

I was sitting on the bottom step tying the second one on when he rounded the corner. "Ready?" He reached his hand down to help me up. When I was upright, he grabbed me around the waist, taking me off guard and setting me up on the second step so we were almost face to face. "Morning," he said and kissed me. It was too fast to really enjoy, but Mrs. Maggie was just out of sight and could walk around the corner at any second.

"I guess I'm ready now." I said it loud, sounding morose for Mrs. Maggie's sake, but then I whispered in his ear, "I still love you, even in the light of a new day."

He smiled and hit my cap like I had his last night, almost repeating my words. "Duh, like you wouldn't."

Then he went one step farther and gestured teasingly, like he was a prize no girl could resist. I shook my head and walked out the door in front of him, not realizing that in a few hours I would see how right he was.

Bo heard us walking down the porch steps, our heavy boots striking each step in unison. He was on his way back down to his house when he turned to us. He tapped his watch. "You all best get that plastic rolled out before the dumpster gets here." Ty waved at him like "got it."

~~~

There was a huge roll of thick black plastic by the back corner of the barn. "What are we doing with that?" Ty didn't answer. He put his arm around my shoulders, leading me in the direction of a job that I knew was going to be terrible.

"Can't we hire someone to do this? You know, like a crew of men with some experience?"

He laughed. I was measuring my size compared to the roll of tarp. It was almost to my waist, like a giant truck tire. "I am the man crew and I do have experience. Now, be a good little assistant and help me unroll this." He patted my head and I stuck out my tongue at him. Okay, maybe the little kid stuff would always be a part of our relationship to some degree. Now that I knew he was mine, maybe it was a part I didn't really want to lose because it was our way, but I wasn't going to tell him that—not yet anyway.

I decided right then that maybe I kind of liked the kid stuff. It was part of us.

I learned that the tarp was used to protect the ground from all the falling shingle debris, sharp edges, and nails. "This will make clean up easier and protect the horses and you if you come out here wearing those shoes that show off your cute little pink toes." He tone was sarcastic and a little teasing, but the look on his face was telling. He liked my pink toes. I smiled back at him so he'd know I knew it.

"Oh, well as long as it serves a purpose and I'm not out here sweating at nine in the morning for no reason." No hiding the sarcasm there. "It makes perfect sense, protecting a twenty-dollar pair of shoes is totally worth the thousands my dad will have to spend to repair the hernia I'm going to get pushing this ton of tarp."

We stood side by side in front of it and started to unroll it. For me, it felt like inch by inch, but he was pushing so hard it was more like a few feet at a time.

"Come on, ya big strapping field hand, show me some muscle," he said, putting all of his weight into each rotation. He was easily taking on about eighty percent of the load. No way was my one hundred and twelve pounds of pressure pushing more than twenty. We both pushed and unrolled the thick heavy plastic the length of each wall of the barn and then I stood on the corners while Ty used a box cutter to slice off each piece and then tacked down the loose corners with sharp metal rods that looked like tent stakes. We finished the last side just as I heard a huge truck coming down the drive.

A wiry man with red hair and a red beard was leaning out the driver's side window of a huge truck with the name "Big Red Box Dumpster Rentals" painted on the door.

Ty pointed with his gloved hand. "Alongside the barn!" he yelled over the loud thundering of the truck's engine, showing him exactly where he wanted the driver to position the huge metal box. The man nodded and maneuvered the massive dumpster into place. It had to be at least sixty feet long and about fifteen feet high.

Bo ambled over and shook the red-haired man's hand after he'd finished dropping the giant container into place. The name on the man's shirt said "Mickey." Bo seemed to know him. "Morning," he said, walking toward him with his hand extended. "We spoke on the phone yesterday."

"Yes sir," replied Mickey. "I was a little worried about you all doing this with all the rain yesterday. Thought maybe you wouldn't be able to get started 'til tomorrow, but it dried up pretty quick."

"Hallelujah," "I said just loud enough for them to hear my cynicism.

Bo ignored me and Ty laughed. Bo shook Mickey's hand with his right hand and took the clipboard he was being handed with his left. "Yeah, I sure am glad of it. I got two workers here who would've been disappointed to have to wait another day." Bo looked over at us and smiled as he signed for the dumpster. Ty and I just stood there, arms folded, hands gloved in heavy duty leather and suede, waiting on the truly sweaty, dirty, horrible part to begin.

As soon as Mickey drove off, Bo said, "I have some work to do in the round room, but not to worry, I'll keep myself company talking to your painting."

Well, if you want you can stroll over to my closet and meet her for yourself, I thought, but knew the disdain and the urge to tell was only coming from my wanting to put off the work of scraping all the shingles off the barn.

"Got some rolls of felt coming in a few hours," he added. Be sure you leave yourselves enough time this evening to cover the areas where you get the old shingles off." More instructions as he walked away, leaving us to the task. "Ty, harness her up tight and *don't let her fall;* otherwise, I'll have to turn the other way while Caleb has a "talk" with you about that." Ty knew Bo would let my dad push him off the roof after me if he let me plummet to my death—that is, if heat stroke didn't kill me first.

"I got it, Dad! She won't fall unless she stops working," Bo playfully threatened him one more time.

"Well, if she does, you'll be praying for another place to live come Sunday—either that or a real good place to hide." They laughed together at my expense.

I punched Ty a little more than playfully in the arm. "I thought you said no more teasing." He flinched somewhat over-dramatically like I'd hurt him. *More kid's stuff...yeah, I'd take that any day, gave me an excuse to touch him,* I thought, smiling to myself. He caught me, but we didn't need to say anything. It was clear between us.

"You know, I'd get you back there, girlie, if I wasn't sure you'd bruise like a peach." He pulled my hat up so he could see my face. "I have to tease just a little." He tried to look all innocent, but his beautiful eyes were full of mischief. "I mean, you know...to keep up appearances."

He knew I saw right through his convenient excuse and tried to pretend like he didn't notice. "It won't be a secret forever, but it was your idea to "ease" them into it. If you'd let me, I'd shout it from the top of the barn." He waved his arms, emphasizing the height he was willing to go to spread the news.

Sarcasm on a grandiose scale, that's new!

He grabbed my slumped, unwilling shoulders and turned me around. Come on, let's get going. It'll be hot up there in a few hours and you're right, telling them slowly and letting them figure it out is best."

There were two ropes and two piles of what I thought was rope on the wall with the horse tack at the back of the barn. Ty went to get them while I spent a stolen minute with Lindie.

"Okay, come here, sweetie. I think this is as small as it goes." He was holding the thick straps out and I wasn't quite sure what he wanted me to do. He saw the confusion on my face. "Step your feet in here." I followed his instruction, trying to balance and fit my thick dirty boots into the circles he had laid out on the ground. He pulled the loops up over my shoes to the top of my legs, making sure the hem of my shorts hadn't wadded up between me and the strap and then took the straps that were left hanging and put them on me like a back pack.

"Sweetie, this may not fit you. We're going to have to do some adjusting here. Don't take it the wrong way, okay? I promise I'm not taking advantage here. It has to fit right. If you fall and it doesn't fit right, you could get hurt." He was serious for the first time all day.

At first I thought he must be kidding because I felt so stupid standing there wearing that ridiculous rig, but he was genuinely worried I'd think he was touching me like that on purpose. Things got very personal. Once I saw where all the buckles were and how he had to tighten them, I understood. I don't think he was even looking at me when he started to adjust the straps. He wasn't seeing my body the same way he had on the horse the other night, he was totally focused on the task at hand. Still, my heart was pounding a little with every touch.

"Sorry, this will only take a second." I stood still and let him walk around me. My arms were extended and my legs shoulder width apart, just like he asked.

"Okay, I don't think you're going anywhere." He tugged on all my straps and buckles one more time to make sure. He couldn't really look at me after he was done. No longer concentrating on my safety, his relaxed face gave away his feelings. I'd never seen him self-conscious about anything before.

I hugged him to let him know I wasn't offended. "You're right, I'm *never* going anywhere."

He'd shaken off his embarrassment when he put his hands around the straps just below my shoulders and pulled me closer to him, "I could get used to having you at my mercy like this," he said, knowing that I was tied in so tight I couldn't pull away, even if I wanted to—and there was no question about it—I didn't want to.

The next thing we knew Bo was clearing his throat, he was standing halfway up the barn aisle holding a squared off shovel in each hand. Ty stopped kissing me, let go of the straps, and stepped about two feet away immediately.

"I forgot you needed these, so I made a trip to the tool shed before I went upstairs to start working."

"Dang! So much for letting them find out slowly," he whispered to me under his breath. He put his hands in his back pockets, a subliminal signal to his dad that he wouldn't touch me again in his presence.

Bo had a look on his face I couldn't read as he approached. I knew this was going to turn into far more than him handing over some special shingle removing shovels. I was looking down at my dirty boots, but Ty impressed me more than he already does. He looked his father square in the eye and was ready to take whatever was coming for both of us.

Bo looked at him as serious as I'd ever seen, that is, best as I could tell from my cowardly glances upward. He paused, appraising each of us before he spoke, but he didn't address me—at least not until he made sure his son was in check. "Don't do something you don't mean, son." He wasn't mad, or stern, but very serious.

Ty took his hands out of his pockets and took one of the shovels. "No sir," he reached for my hand with his free one. "I mean it more than you know." It was easy to hear the thick layers of sincerity, like he was making his dad a guarantee.

Bo stared at him, not saying another word, but he didn't need to—Ty got it. They'd always had an honest relationship like that, but there were clear lines drawn. As Ty got older it had turned from one of discipline and instruction from a father to his son, to one of mutual respect. Bo nodded once, giving his permission. It was the first time I had the courage to really look up and look him in the eye.

"Well, then let me say to both of you, I don't mind it. I can't speak for the others, but you tell them in your own way. I will say, boy, and to you too, Caimee, you all need to mind yourselves and keep a proper distance. I know how this works." He nodded in Ty's direction. That was code for "you have my support, but don't be making no babies."

I figured it was my turn to take some of this responsibility; otherwise, how would he know we were both going to be responsible?

"Bo, we weren't trying to hide exactly, we just didn't

want to do anything that might divide us as a family, but I do love Ty very much." I stepped closer to him holding his hand tighter. "We're sorry you found out this way. We weren't trying to lie or sneak around. We just weren't sure how everyone would react."

He handed me the other shovel. "I suppose that's your own decision to make, but just remember—no matter what happens, we all have to live here and we'll still be family no matter if you two end up hating each other.

"Dad, I promise I have thought long and hard about this. I never would have told Caimee how I felt if I didn't think we were going to be together, it was me that admitted my feelings to her first." He seemed to be struggling for the words. "I mean, I know we'll stay together long term."

Bo seemed satisfied that we had considered all the consequences. "Well, nothing would make me happier, but just be careful. No matter what, nothing is worth hurting one another, because when you cross some lines you can't go back."

He turned to go, but turned back to add one more thing. "Just remember, son, if you love her, you love her and only her. You know firsthand how destructive doing things wrong can be." Ty nodded. I kept silent, not wanting to get involved in their cryptic words about his mother. I figured that had to be who they were talking about.

"I know, Dad. *Believe* me, I would never hurt her that way. I don't want anybody else." He looked at me and said, "Only her for the rest of my life." He didn't say it sappy like some lame movie. It came out like a grown man who was taking on a new responsibility.

Bo had a look of doubt on his face, some part of him still saw us as little kids. "Only time will tell, so just be careful—both of you."

Abruptly the conversation turned. It kind of had to because Bo can only take so much serious. "Now stop all that time wastin' and get to shoveling."

Ty dropped his shovel and put on his own harness. "Yes sir," he said, but I could hear the double meaning. He was going to get to work, but he was also going to take what his dad had said to heart. I knew he loved me, but insecurity crept in and Ty could see it all over my face. He was only half looking at me, focusing on his own harness, but still he could tell. "What's got my beautiful blue eyes looking like that?"

I shuffled my feet again, not wanting to look at him. "It just bothers me a little that your dad thinks that only time will tell how this will last." I gestured with my finger back and forth between us.

He pulled his last buckle tight and walked over to me. "Look at me." It took me a couple of seconds, but he waited patiently. He took my hands and wrapped them around the straps under his shoulders, the same place he had been holding mine before. "I'm not going anywhere either." Deep in his sweet soft caramel brown eyes, I could see it was true.

Chapter 21
"April's Place"

Ty tethered a twenty-foot rope to the clip on the back of my harness, wound it up, and put it around his arm with about five feet of slack between us. He pointed to the ladder that went up the back of the barn wall all the way to the ceiling. I didn't realize how high it was 'til I was about half way up.

"It's okay, I'm right behind you if you fall." As soon as he said it, some wet mud on the bottom of my boot hit the metal rung and I slipped. I hung on with both hands and Ty instantly pinned me to the ladder with his full weight. He was so calm—never a moment of stress in his voice. "I've got you. Hang on, you're okay. I won't let you fall. Get a good grip and then move your left foot up about six inches and feel for the ladder."

The metal bar hurt my hands and I kicked frantically trying to get my feet back in line. He kept his leg bent underneath me and instead of the ladder, I accidentally stepped on him. He was holding onto the sides of the ladder instead of the cross rungs like me, pushing me into the wall with his chest.

"I'm sorry!" I said when I realized I was stepping on him.

"It's okay, I've got you. Just keep going up. Don't worry about me. You're not hurting me at all. Use me to brace if you need to...I've got you." The encouragement just kept coming until I got calm, stopped flailing, and started climbing. I managed to get my right foot back on track and then used him as a stepping stone to get my left one on the same step. I realized I had slid about three rungs down when I managed to catch my breath and assess the situation. I also realized we balanced on more than just the thin metal bars of this ladder. I panicked and he stayed calm. I stressed, but he never did. I over-analyzed everything, while he just jumped in and did it. Between his strength and calm and my mouth and evaluating everything, we fit. It took less than a second for all of that to go through my head, but it made me hang on, smile, and keep climbing.

When we finally got to the top there was a flat, rectangular-shaped knob above my head. "Pull down that silver handle then twist it like a door knob." I pulled on it as hard as I could, but it wouldn't budge. He saw me struggling. He held his position, protecting me from another fall which at this height would have been much scarier. His patience was endless. "Come on, babe, you can do it. Pull hard." I tugged for another minute or so. My hand was turning red from the effort.

"Okay, trust me for just a minute and *don't* move. Get as close to the ladder as you can." I put my hands on the side railing as I had seen him do and pulled myself towards the wall. "Put your feet together." When I did that, I felt him climb up behind me, putting his boots on either side of mine. "Don't lean back, baby. You're doing fine, stay just like that." He reached up over my head, pulled the knob, and twisted it easily. I felt defeated, like when I had to take a pickle jar to my dad to open. "Okay, sweet girl, push it open."

I had flashbacks of coming out of the root cellar. That memory that had turned from a terrible dream to an impossible reality was shining in my face, like the sun over my head all over again. So many things brought it back now that Joy was actually here. Truthfully, I was glad I had gone through the fear of it to have her as my friend now. This time, there was no fear or confusion when I stepped though, Ty was with me. The barn roof could have suddenly become moon rock and it wouldn't have scared me.

I climbed up onto the roof all the while Ty held onto my rope. I stood up and walked a few steps and he came up right behind me. It came out a little whinier than I had hoped; I didn't want to seem like a baby, but *dang*, I just couldn't hold it in. "This is going to take forever," I said, looking around at the massive size of the roof."

He laughed. "I figure at least two weeks with just the two of us." I looked back when I felt tugging on my harness. He had tied the rope to a steel loop that was screwed into the top of the barn at the rounded peak where it sloped down on either side. There was another one where I assumed he'd tie off himself. I walked over to examine the knot, it was complicated looking and I was trying to figure out how he had done it so fast.

"Okay, sit down. I'll be right back. I need to go get the shovels and my rope."

I sighed. "Okay, I guess it's a good thing I'm not afraid of heights. You gotta be fearless to be a farm hand around here." I couldn't help it. The cynicism started flowing when I realized the magnitude of the task ahead. "Hey, I have an idea. Why don't we just build a new barn, save them the trouble of replacing the roof on this one? Ouch! As soon as I sat down, I felt the stab. He turned quickly, standing on the top of the ladder we'd just come up. He was leaning out of the hatch, balancing on the ladder for a second. I was worried he would fall, precariously teetering up so high. It seemed like he forgot his own safety the way he was turned so he could see me. "What's wrong?"

I stood up and saw the trickle of blood coming out from under the jagged hem of my shorts. "I've been up here exactly fifteen seconds and managed to cut my butt on the corner of a loose shingle. *Nice.* He jumped back up onto the roof.

"Turn around." The look on my face must have been filled with the horror I felt. The thought of him looking at it was going to fall in my "no way" column. I turned around as fast as I could, pressing my shorts against the wound to stop the bleeding. "I got it, just keep on moving, proper distance—remember?" I shooed him away with my free hand.

I could hear him laughing as he went back down the ladder. "Just don't move, babe. I'll be right back." How could he be so optimistic? No way were we going to get all this done in two weeks and now, in addition to everything else, I'd cut myself in a place that I'd feel every time I sat down. *Great, a scar to remind me of this day forever.*

It was still early, but obviously he was right about getting started as fast as we could. It was already hot out and standing on these black shingles was not going to help that situation come noon. He was gone about fifteen minutes. "I hate this. I'm tied here like an animal. What if I had to go to the bathroom right now?" He was squatting in front of me, unbuttoning the large cargo pockets he seemed to have stuffed to capacity while he was gone.

"Do you?" I was lost in thought watching him, not even realizing I was still complaining.

"Do I what?"

"Have to go right now, 'cause if you do, now is the time."

"No, let's just get going." He started pulling stuff out of his pockets. I understood now why he had chosen those pants. It reminded me of Mary Poppins' suitcase—things just kept coming out.

"Okay, here's your water." He unclipped a sports bottle full of water from his belt loop and attached it to the one on my shorts. He had another one on his other side. "Drink a lot so you don't get dizzy and dehydrated." He clipped his rope onto the other anchor so he could walk around.

"Now, come on over here." I took a few small steps towards him. My face was glum, my mood worsening by the second. The word "dehydration" was ringing in my ears. This was going to be tough.

"Come all the way over here, little sour face and close your eyes." I didn't even bother to ask what he was about to do, because I didn't care anymore. I felt his fingers on my face. I could feel the coolness of the lotion. It smelled like the beach. He was taking such great care to touch me so gently I wondered how he was actually rubbing it into my skin.

"I don't usually burn."

"I know, but you'd be surprised how fast you can up here."

Next, he pulled out two gauze pads—one was dry, the other pre-soaked in peroxide. I stepped away from him. "No way! You want me to die of shame? You won't have to explain how I fell to my death, you'll have to explain how I keeled over and died of embarrassment."

He just stood there, unrelenting. Mrs. Maggie went to the grocery store, so it is either me or my dad. You're still bleeding a little bit, some of these nails are rusty, and all of these shingles are dirty. They're a little rougher than the ones you sit on outside your window." He had a smug look on his face. He was letting me in on the fact that he was perfectly aware I watched him ride. He knew exactly what to do to make me comply. He knew I would want to cut off the conversation about the porch roof more than I wouldn't want him to clean my cut. *Dang, he's good!* It was either turn around or keep talking and comparing rooftops which would be the same as admitting what I had been doing, so I turned.

"Come on, babe, I've seen you in a bathing suit. It's no higher than that, I promise—and it has to be cleaned." I tried to stare him down over my shoulder, but I couldn't see how bad it was and I knew he was right. I didn't say anything; I just stood still and let him work. He lifted up the left side of the bottom of my shorts about three inches to assess the damage.

"Well, it doesn't need stitches, but you did a pretty good job back here. It's not a cut, it's more like road rash."

When I felt the sting of the medicine, I realized the wound wasn't quite as high up as I'd thought. He was right again—it was no place he wouldn't see if I was wearing a bathing suit. He washed and dried it and must have reached back in his pocket because I felt him put one of those extra-large Band-Aids on it. He was trying so hard to be gentle, and make this whole thing as physically and emotionally painless as possible. I realized right then that my attitude might be hurting his feelings. He was going to so much trouble to make this bearable and I was complaining. At least I got to spend my terrible day with him and I needed him to know a terrible day with him was better than a fantastic day alone.

I turned to face him as he was standing back up. "I'm sorry, I've already grumbled a million times, stepped on you on the way up here, cut myself, and given up hope of us finishing before we even start. I'm not trying to be a pain, I promise. I'm really just mad about the whole conspiracy thing between our dads and Grammie. I feel like they're treating me like some stupid, reckless kid when I've never given them reason to. I'm just saying, if you can teach me how to do this..." I gestured to the roof "...way up here, I might add, why can't we work with the horses a little?" He grunted a laugh and sighed. "You seem to forget, I'm in trouble here too. Why do you think I've been riding at night? Dad has forbidden me to do anything that might be even remotely enjoyable until I answer one of the million calls he keeps getting from my mom. One thing he didn't figure, though, I can do all the grunt work they want as long as I get to do it with you. It can't last forever. I think he realized that this morning. I mean, yeah, I get the lesson they want me to learn and all that, but they didn't count on me enjoying it."

I thought about that for a second. We'd been in trouble so many times together when we were little, it was always better to sit in the corner with him than by myself. As we got older, Mrs. Maggie realized that and started separating us, but now she couldn't. "I love your logic." I hugged him close and he squeezed me back. Okay, let's get all dirty and sweaty together, if you can I can. Besides, this would be much worse for me right now if you hadn't come clean. I'd be up here hating this job and stewing over whether or not you'd called April yet."

He rolled his eyes. "Whatever. You're the only girl I'd want to call...that is, if I hadn't thrown my cell phone into the pond." He gave me a sheepish look. "Okay, one more thing to make this somewhat less of a prison." He pulled a small radio out of his pocket and tuned it to my favorite country station. He was just about to show me how to start using the shovel when I grabbed his hand to stop him.

"One more thing, okay?"

"Make it a quick."

It's going to be noon before we know it." I took the shovel out of his hand, reached up, and turned his hat around. "I thought I'd let you decide if it was quick or not." The emotion behind his smile was unmistakable. Pure shock, pure joy, pure love. "You know, I don't always turn my hat around to kiss a girl."

"Well, since I am the last one you'll ever kiss—and the best kiss I ever had was just like this, I'm thinking we can make an exception just this once and then maybe next time, I'll let you decide."

"It was the only kiss you ever had," he pointed out and then I think wished he hadn't. Given all the complaining I had already done I gave him a pass and let that one slide. I wanted to start on a positive note.

"Well, I'd rather be your last than your first."

He didn't need any more prompting than that and it definitely wasn't quick. We only stopped because we heard a car crunching on the dirt, Mrs. Maggie was back. We pulled apart and looked at each other, not quite sure if we should care if she might have seen or not. "I'm thinking we might not have much luck at that "let's tell them slowly plan, it just doesn't seem to be working out."

He picked up the shovels and handed me one. "I'm thinking you're right."

Once I got the hang of it, the shovel made removing the shingles faster. We still had to go around the vents in the roof that let the fans work, twelve on each side. That was hard. After about three hours I was filthy, sweaty, and out of water. I looked at our progress, knowing he had done most of it.

"What's the next step?"

"You know that felt Dad said was coming? We have to put that down before the new shingles, but any area we scraped today has to be covered for tonight. I stepped to the edge and looked down at the dumpster, we had gotten most of the old roof shoveled into it, but there was still a lot of debris we'd have to clean up later. I felt him holding my rope.

"Please come back here. You might not be afraid of heights, but you're making me nervous."

"I've never seen you rattled over anything before."

"Well, I never told a girl I loved her before either. It is a week of firsts for me."

He reeled me in like a fish 'til I was back up to the peak of the roof. "We have to get down from here—it's getting too hot. We can come back up later in the day. I don't want to get too far ahead of ourselves before they deliver the covering anyway."

Just then we both noticed a song we liked on the radio. He didn't say anything, he just took my hand put one on his waist and the other around his neck. We slow danced to the open hatch, he unhooked our ropes, and we climbed down the ladder.

Mrs. Maggie stopped me at the door. "Oh no, missy, you're not coming in here all covered in that black dust and filth. You all are having lunch on the porch." I had to get past her to see Joy and bring her some food.

"Please, I've been drinking water all day. If you want, I'm sure we can build an outhouse in our spare time, but right now I gotta go."

Ty burst out laughing. "Sure, I think we have time to dig a fifty-foot hole and make ourselves an outhouse, just put it on the list." He sat down on our big wide porch swing, it tilted back a bit so it was more like our outdoor hanging recliner, and waved his hand like the extra work would be nothing. He'd gotten her attention so I pulled off my boots as fast as I could and ran around her.

"Any mess on my floors and you won't have time to build any outhouse, you'll be in here scrubbing."

I knew I only had a minute. There were sandwiches already made on the counter. I grabbed two, not even looking to see what was on it and a glass of tea, and ran to my room.

She wasn't in the closet reading, she was in the bathroom. What a mess. She'd found my makeup. She'd been working on her face for a while. She was somewhere between a mime and a circus clown. It took all I had not to laugh, but I didn't want her to retreat back into her shy shell. I loved that she was interested in it at all. She was slowly getting over her aversion to all things 2013.

"I brought you some lunch. I think you look great. Maybe later we can do it together," I lied and came up with a plan for more girl time all in one breath. "We've been so busy talking about so many other things, I still haven't shown you around the outside either. Her mouth was full of sandwich so she just nodded enthusiastically. I could see the cabin fever starting to set in, I should have noticed it sooner, but of course she didn't complain, maybe I should take a lesson from her on that. Sometimes I had to remind myself that she was almost two years younger than me. It didn't seem like a lot in years, but she was also one hundred and seventy-three years behind me in life. She really was like a little sister—great for friendship, but also needing entertainment and attention. She was trying to be like me, which was flattering, but messy. *Another job for me for later.* I suddenly felt guilty. I'd been leaving her alone too much, but in my defense, it had been a life-changing couple of days. I had to remind myself that she was part of all of it.

We ate our lunch outside on the porch swing while Mrs. Maggie was rescrubbing the floors she said I'd "completely ruined." She was right. We were pretty much covered in filth from our heads to the dirty toes of our boots. When I looked at my big scrape in the mirror, I realized it was the only part of my body that was clean. The outline of the Band-Aid was clear. Ty was just trying to make me feel better when he said it didn't look so bad. It was a pretty impressive graze, but he was right about it not needing stitches. It looked like I'd been skinned and there was nothing left to sew. The shingles were rougher than sand paper and had just ripped a bunch of my hide off.

"So much for riding for a while anyway. Talk about your saddle sore." Joy nodded in agreement when I had shown her.

Bo finally came down stairs from the Rapunzel room. He'd been up there all morning studying the horses. He'd been evaluating their chances for the upcoming competition season at Commonwealth Park, going over the results of the blood work he had done on each one making sure their diets were perfect and that they were healthy. He loved to win, but he loved the animals more. We were swaying slowly back and forth in the breeze enjoying the shade—Ty on one end of the swing with his arm and head resting on the back. I was lying with my head on his leg, almost asleep. Our staying up all night last night was catching up to us both.

"I think Moonlight is going to be our champ this year." Neither of us moved, but Ty was still awake enough to respond. "What about River?" They're from the same blood line—cousins, right?" Bo sat on the railing across from the swing. "Man, Carlton Meriwether has all the money in the world to buy these pedigree jumpers and lets that *hoity toity* wife of his give them the dumbest names. I hate to even enter a horse named "Blue River Baby" next to the Cameron Manor logo on the ticket. It makes it sound like the animal was born in the Potomac or something."

We were both tired, but leave it to Bo to wake us up enough to laugh. "Well, he is that bluish gray color, so maybe she had a good reason," I said, trying to make him feel better about it.

"There's no reason good enough to stick some kid or some poor animal with a stupid name they have to wear the rest of their lives."

He continued his conversation with Ty as we'd had this discussion before and he just ended up frustrated. "River may have a chance, but there's something special about Moonlight. She has a better gene pool on her mother's side that River doesn't have. Both jockeys have been working hard though, so it may come down to the better rider. Either way, Cameron Manor will do well this year. Some of the others will place. We've got some good jumpers this season. Have to wait 'til racing season to see about Thor though."

I opened one eye and looked over at him. "I guess me and my co-worker here won't have time to go to any of the competitions, will we?" I could see it on his face so I don't know why I even bothered to ask. Here comes the sarcasm.

"Are you kidding me? We have to keep this place fit for those champions," he inclined his head toward the back pasture where he'd moved the horses this morning so they wouldn't be spooked by all our noise. Just think how it will look if we let our cash winning, top bred, expertly trained horses live on skid row." He'd just managed to give himself a compliment as a trainer and tell me we weren't going all in one smooth sentence. I was too tired to argue. "That's about what I was thinking." Ty just shook his head and tilted it back onto the rounded edge of the back of the swing.

The three of us sat there in silence that nobody felt the need to fill, taking in the cool breeze when we heard the crunching of a vehicle coming up the dirt lane. Ty and I sighed, knowing it was the delivery guy from the roofing place bringing the covering for the barn. Break time was over. Neither of us moved. I think we were hoping it wasn't true.

"This ought to be interesting," Bo said, standing up to greet our guest.

"Ty, I'm thinking this has your name written all over it." I would have preferred to sit up, open my eyes, and see a thousand trucks carrying shingles and felt instead of that stupid, red Volkswagen bug with the top down and Barbie behind the wheel with her posse, Jenna Wheeler (or as I liked to call her, "Mrs. Barbie runner up" and her twin sister, "Mrs. Homecoming queen,") Ericka Wheeler. They hadn't been here since the disaster of my birthday party when I was little and Bo obviously knew they weren't here now on a social call to see me. The dust was settling around the car and all three of them were fixing their hair just before April cut the engine. Bo looked at Ty and laughed. "Good luck with that." He was about to leave, but then gave Ty a meaningful look, reminding him of their conversation this morning about me. Ty didn't even let him say the words.

"Oh please, gimme a little credit," he said, insulted that his dad would even insinuate that he'd go after some other girl while he was still committed to me, much less the same day Bo had warned him about it.

"Sorry, you're right, you handle it, son." Bo strolled off the porch and back down toward the pasture whistling—his subtle, unspoken way of telling Ty about the carefree life of a single man.

Luckily, Bo firing up the four-wheeler drowned out my next sentiment to everyone but Ty. "You have got to be kidding me." I sat up feeling humiliated. I was filthy, there was still a blood stain on the back of my shorts, and I was still wearing that stupid harness. Ty was every bit the mess I was, but somehow it looked manly on him. "What does she want?" I regretted it as soon as I said it. The look on Ty's face was answer enough, but he said it out loud anyway. "Me." Obvious resentment. He didn't want to deal with this any more than I did. He was too much of a gentleman to go against his nature and be flat out mean or rude, but he was also no pushover and wasn't about to let me get trampled on.

He grabbed my hand. "Come on, babe."

I pulled my fingers out of his. "No way! Look at me! I look like a dirt farmer."

"Yes, but you're my dirt farmer and I don't care who knows I love you, no matter what you look like. These people don't get to find out gently, they get it right in the face no questions about it. Besides, it will save me having to scrub more ink off myself later."

We smiled at each other, but it was different. It wasn't just on our faces, it was in our eyes—at least it was in his. I looked up and all three of them were sitting there staring at us, satisfied that they had fixed themselves up adequately and they were waiting on him to come to the car.

"Okay, but you stand in front of me so they don't get the full view—I mean, look at me."

"Babe, I've been looking at you all day—sometimes in ways that might embarrass us both." He walked forward, leaving me with that knowledge to follow behind him.

I stood about two feet back with my arms folded, almost too embarrassed to look at them. I glanced up trying to focus somewhere else when I caught a quick glimpse of Joy looking down from my bathroom window. At first I was terrified she would be seen, but then I realized I had a girlfriend in my corner too and in that second I was comforted and found some courage. I took another small step forward.

"Hey April," said Ty. Only I caught the "let's hurry up and get this over with" that he didn't say. She was too mesmerized by his looks to notice; otherwise, that smile would have melted right off her plastic face.

"Hey Ty," she practically sang his name and then, of course, her backup singers joined in the chorus—all three of them greeting him like they were auditioning for the part of "the girlfriend" in the play of his life. I wanted to puke. The posse sat back in their seats while April took the lead. Clearly, she'd called dibs.

"You look like you've been working hard." She shifted her gaze to me and it instantly became judgmental.

"Caimee, you look um...nice." *That's it! I was going to have to kill her. Broke Nose Barbie, coming soon to a store near you,* sounded better and better every time I thought it. The others snickered at her "compliment."

All three sets of their eyes roamed over Ty with about the same speed that Bo had gunned it out of here on the four-wheeler. He was kind of the hard-working, masculine, *fell-off-the-pages-of-a-calendar-type* now, but still their oh so obvious lust was gross.

"Well, me and my sweet girl here have been taking shingles off the barn all morning. He half-turned to face the barn to draw their attention to the dumpster and the work we had done. Instead, all three of them used the opportunity to check out his backside. The fact that he'd called me his "sweet girl" went totally unnoticed by all three of them, like that was my stupid horse name or something and he was using it to be nice. When he turned fully back around to face them, he knew they were completely undaunted by his term of endearment towards me. He was just about to make the whole "sweet girl" thing clear, but he didn't get a chance. Someone else had already heard it for what it really meant and was about to step in, or I should say, step in it.

I should have known there was one person who was not going to let this go on. One person that despite the fact we hadn't said it aloud to anyone but Bo would know exactly what the deal was. Both Ty and I looked down and waited for whatever was coming when we heard Mrs. Maggie's footsteps on the porch. We kept silent because we knew it would be so much more entertaining this way. We knew her well enough to know it would be very polite, very southern and ladylike—and the message would be unmistakably clear. She didn't come down the steps; instead she just stood there holding her broom, leaning on the railing where Bo had just been sitting.

"Afternoon, ladies." I snorted a little at the term "ladies." She greeted them graciously. They all knew her. She was friends with their grandmothers who I'm sure played as much bingo as she did. She didn't give them a chance to respond, she simply looked over at the car and then at me and Ty as if they had suddenly disappeared. She knew how long I had waited to be with Ty and wasn't about to sit quietly while someone tried to take that happiness away, as if they could. In Mrs. Maggie's estimation, I'd lost enough in life.

"You know, you two would finish a lot faster, if you spent less time up there making out, holding hands and dancing around and more time shoveling. The delivery guy just called. Said he was on his way with the felt to cover the bare parts. You might need more of it if you had made any progress."

None of them had caught Ty calling me his "sweet girl" but they sure didn't miss the words "making out." Ty wasn't one to let someone else fight his battles, but in order to spare me anymore glaring from any of them, he stood back and let Mrs. Maggie go. No way would they treat me bad in front of her, but they'd try to humiliate me in front of him.

Mrs. Maggie kept up her charade like she might really be angry. We'd wasted time up on the roof and she'd stood there watching, but the barn roof wasn't exactly going anywhere and she'd rather see us content than productive when it came to a chore that wasn't on her list. She'd been looking after both of us most of our lives and wasn't about to let her "kids" be picked on in her own schoolyard.

She was subtly using her authority to tell April and her crew to move along, but Volkswagen Barbie was arrogant and wasn't going out like that in front of her girls. With clear understanding written all over her shocked face, she looked at Ty and then appraised me like she was looking at an ugly outfit or had just smelled a can full of garbage. Her eyes went right back to Ty with all confidence.

"You'll change your mind. After all, she's convenient right now, but soon enough we'll all be together," she said, reaching to turn the engine back over. He walked the few feet to the car and leaned over her door. She looked hopeful, like he'd already "changed his mind." She picked up the hand she'd written her number on with the permanent marker and stuck her lip out like she was sad when she saw it was gone. He took his hand back and smiled, shaking his head at her silly, pathetically fake hurt look.

"It comes right off if you have the right stuff," he said. "No, I won't ever change my mind."

Always the gentleman, he added, "Sorry." I looked down at the dirt so she wouldn't see my self-satisfied grin. April Mantis had just been put firmly in her place—and it sure wasn't in Ty's lap.

Chapter 22
"Telling Ty"

We both stood there in the cloud of dust left behind after April's hasty departure. When it cleared, Mrs. Maggie was standing there looking all superior. "I knew this was coming someday. I love you both and I don't want to see either of you get hurt. Her tone became very serious. She looked at Ty the same way Bo had and then said the exact same thing he did. "Just make sure you keep your proper distance." She shifted her gaze to me so I would know the warning applied to us both equally. We answered in unison, "Yes, ma'am." She gave us "the look" and then walked away.

"I guess we were kind of stupid to think we could even come close to hiding this."

Ty looked at me sideways, disbelieving we'd even tried. "Well, I guess if you could keep your hands off me for five minutes we might have had a chance, but I guess I can understand that I'm irresistible to you."

He didn't have to look up to see me coming. He outran me easily. We stayed right there in a fifteen-foot circle in front of the porch, chasing each other. I didn't even come close to tagging him once. Mrs. Maggie had gone back inside, but I had no doubt she was watching us play.

Finally, he caught me around the waist and swung me around in a circle until we were both dizzy. "Come on, let's get out of the heat before we have to go back up there and finish." He gave me a piggyback ride up the steps and we settled into the porch swing.

About fifteen minutes later Bo came thundering back up on the quad. He ambled past us to go into the house. "Thanks, Dad," Ty said just as Bo was reaching for the door handle.

"You're welcome, boy. So, what wonderful thing did your old man do for you this time?"

"Telling Mrs. Maggie. Somehow she knew and spied on us all day while we were up on the barn. We were kind of hoping we might not have to be on her radar so soon."

Bo put his hand on Ty's cap and shook his head around. "Son, you ought to know by now nobody has to tell Maggie anything. She can sniff out what's going on in this house way better than either one of those hounds she loves to hate."

I knew it was true as soon as he said it. I realized right then I was fooling myself. If Ty and I couldn't keep a secret for a couple of days, how was I going to hide Joy for nine more? I was going to need help. I had to tell Ty. I didn't have time to think about it before the rumble of the big moving truck from the roofing place came up the drive.

"Man, we ain't had this many visitors in a year." Ty and I nodded in agreement, but didn't get up.

Bo turned around to go deal with the delivery man. Ty didn't even flinch at the noise. He was so tired he'd closed his eyes, trying to get some sleep right after his conversation with his dad. His slow, steady breathing was soothing. I focused on it to stop thinking about the situation with Joy.

It took two men an hour to unload all the shingles and the felt padding that went between them and the roof. Ty slept through the whole thing. I drifted in and out, every now and then startled by their loud voices. I remembered hearing Bo thank them and the truck drive away. He must have taken pity on us and let us be.

The next thing I knew it was five o'clock and Dad was shaking us both awake. He had a knowing grin on his face, seeing us cuddled up together on the swing the way we were. "I've got to go C.C. I'll see you soon okay?" He glanced at Ty. "You'd better wake him up and get started. You can't leave that roof uncovered."

"I'm awake," said Ty. "We'll get it done. It was so hot earlier, we just didn't finish."

"Well it's always hot after a rain like the one we had." Dad looked at him with a warning behind his smile. He jumped right into it, same as Mrs. Maggie. "I expect you're going to be good to my girl here. She's just like her mama. Johnna knew what she wanted younger than Grammie would have liked, but once she made up her mind I was it, she never turned back. I couldn't have asked for a more faithful girl or a better wife. She waited for me to chase my dreams and was always there when I came back, true and steady as the sunrise. I know my Caimee and I don't mean to embarrass her, but she's had her heart set on you for a long time now, same as her mom did on me."

Dad looked at me. "Come on now, baby girl, you didn't think your old dad wouldn't notice, did you?"

I hung my head and nodded. He had me there. I never was any good at keeping things from him. I shouldn't have been surprised that he knew, probably long before he had heard me say it to mom before Ty even got here.

He turned his attention back to Ty. "You treat her good and this will be the last father-son talk we ever have to have. I have always accepted you as family. This won't change that even if things here don't work out," he said, nodding back and forth between the two of us. "But you should know that Cameron girls fall hard and for keeps."

Ty stood up to face him man to man. "I know, Cal, and believe me, this is for keeps. You have my word on that. I promise you, I will never hurt her." Dad seemed to respect his honesty and put his hand on Ty's shoulder. "Okay, then you all have my permission—just keep your proper distance."

Ty and I looked at each other. "They had to have had a meeting."

"No," I said. "I think they all just think exactly alike. Either that or there are three people here who definitely don't want to be grandparents any time soon."

He reached down and helped me up. "Come on, sweet girl. Let's go finish that roof before we're working by moonlight. I know Dad probably wants to get the horses back up anyway.

He opened the door and yelled down the hall so as not to track up Mrs. Maggie's floor. "We'll be eating dinner late, so we may go get pizza or something when we're done."

I heard her yell "okay," which meant she got the night off. I was sure that meant she was already on the phone, getting her seat saved for bingo.

~~~

We worked until nine. Hauling the new rolls of felt up the ladder and making sure the old felt was completely scraped off was hard work, but not nearly as much for me as for Ty. I couldn't lift the rolls. They were too heavy, so he rigged a pulley system up the ladder and through the door in the roof. That took an extra hour, but by the time he was done, I had all the wood stripped and ready. When we were done laying the covering, Ty used neon orange duct tape to mark the places where there were openings in the ceiling where the fans vented so we wouldn't accidentally step there and fall through. Not only were we dirtier and more tired than we were earlier, we were also starving.

"So, since everybody here is about the proper, Ms. Cameron, may I take you out to dinner?"

I acted like I had to think about it. He acted like he didn't notice and kept unbuckling my harness.

"Um...can we go to Osaka Japanese House? They have veggie plates there." He put away the last of the equipment and then wound and hung up our ropes.

"We can go wherever you want as long as you can hold out long enough for me to take a shower. I think Japanese is good. They're open 'til eleven, so if *we*, meaning *you* hurries, we can make it. He reached in his pocket like he was going to look it up on his phone, but then quickly realized he'd done it out of habit. He breathed a frustrated sigh. "And tomorrow I'm going to the cell phone place."

I kissed him quick and ran toward the house. "I can hurry." I was already taking off my hat and loosening my hair as I ran up the porch steps. Just as I thought, Mrs. Maggie had gone to play bingo, so I ran in the kitchen and got Joy something to eat. It dawned on me again that I had to tell Ty sooner rather than later. Mrs. Maggie was going to notice someone had been rummaging around in her kitchen. She kept it inventoried like Fort Knox.

"I am so hungry," she said as I handed her leftover fried chicken and biscuits. "Sorry, they're hot. I left them in the microwave a little too long." Of course, she had no idea what I'd just said. "Just be careful not to burn your mouth." I handed her a glass of milk, hoping that would solve the problem. I went into the bathroom and closed the door halfway so I could talk to her. She started asking questions before I could tell her I was going to let Ty in on our secret.

"Who were those girls that came to visit today? Are they friends of yours?" She sounded a little jealous because I'd told her she was my best friend. "Hardly, they came to see Ty." I wrapped up in a towel and opened the door wider. "I need to tell Ty about you."

Instantly, she looked worried. Her expression was somewhere between hesitation and fear. I was going to have to do some fast talking to convince her it was a good idea.

"Trust me. There are at least two very good reasons. One, I'm afraid Mrs. Maggie might find you...and two, I really want you to meet him. You always tell your best friend about the guy you're dating." She looked slightly comforted by that. Anything I told her was "normal" here seemed to be okay.

"We thought we could keep our dating a secret—at least for a little while 'til we got used to it ourselves, but then typical of everyone in this house, everybody seemed to find out in one day. There really aren't any secrets in this family. If Mrs. Maggie keeps finding missing food and dishes she knows she didn't use, she will eventually ask, so I'm thinking Ty will be able to help me cover up any evidence of you being here to keep her from finding out." She nodded in agreement. "It does seem to outweigh the risk of changing things here or on my side." She was intuitive and thinking ahead. For a second, even though she was so much younger, I wished I had some of her strength and fearlessness—not that I was a wimp, I comforted myself, but she seemed to have spiritedness about her that I just didn't have. I made a mental note something else about her I wanted to pick up on while she was here. I realized I had been arrogant thinking that just because she was from the past I couldn't learn from her. Technology was great, but something about where she came from had built quite a strong character in her.

"I'm going to tell him tonight at dinner. I don't even know how to begin to explain really. We're eating out together in about half an hour, so I need to hurry." I looked over at the mess she had made of my makeup and knew that was going to slow me down. I tried to put a positive spin on it. "I can't wait 'til we can do this together," I said, holding up a blush brush in one hand and my eyeliner pencil in the other. She still had streaks of the disaster left under her eyes.

I went with a tiffany blue spaghetti strap sundress and matching flip flops. Ty seemed to like the straps on my nightie, so I wanted to stick with what I knew caught his eye. I made sure that since my nails were a mess, at least my toenails were still painted and not chipped. I spent a little longer on my hair, making it perfectly straight. Putting on makeup with Joy trying to "help" substantially hindered my progress. I finally made it to the truck at ten. Ty was sitting there, waiting patiently. The aroma of his cologne filled the cab—not so much that I was choking on it, but I wanted to sit in the middle of the seat and be closer to him.

"Sorry," I said, glancing at the little fairy on my watch as I climbed in and slid across the bench seat towards him.

His eyes were bright and excited. "You're actually earlier than I thought you'd be."

I was playfully indignant. "I can move faster than you think," pointing to myself with all five of my fingers spread across my chest. "I just don't happen to be the fastest *shingle shoveler* ever born." He nodded in agreement.

"That you are not, my sweet girl, but..." He looked me up and down so I knew we were not talking about shingles anymore. "...I don't mind waiting."

The Japanese place was just off Madison Road, so we were there in minutes. "Of course," he said when we walked in and saw April and her parents eating a late dinner.

I sighed in defeat. "Well, she does live here and Culpeper isn't exactly a big metropolis. I guess we'd better get used to it." I shrugged, trying to be casual, like I didn't really mind. "Everyone I really care about has already given their opinion and by the time school starts everyone will be talking about you staying here anyway. You should know she isn't going to be the only one who thinks you'll change your mind about me."

He kissed the top of my head. "You don't know how surprised I've been summer after summer to know that some guy here hasn't already made a move on you. I was totally thinking I'd pushed my luck too far and by this year I'd be too late."

The waitress greeted us and pointed us to a booth, thankfully away from the Mantis family. I scooted in and he waited for my reply.

"Didn't you hear my dad today? We Cameron girls make up our minds early. I've been waiting on you to make up your mind since I was fourteen."

He grabbed a menu and handed it to me. "Well, I'm sorry I waited so long. Maybe I wasn't ready at fourteen, but I should've called you this past school year and told you what was going on in Alabama and that you were the only one I wanted to see. My mom didn't really want me talking to anybody here. She 'forgot' to pay the cell phone bill several times. I think she was scared I was going to call my dad to come get me. It doesn't matter. She made her choices and now I have to start making mine. This is where you are. It's where I've wanted to be for a long time now."

I was struggling with it the whole time he was reading the menu, looking for the right words to say so I could explain it. How could I tell him about Joy and the tunnel? And, worse yet—I'd kept it from him! Even before now we always shared secrets when we were home. I decided to enjoy dinner and show him my secret later. He'd have to see her and meet her to really understand—at least I know I would have.

Of course, he got something with steak in it and I got the vegetable plate and some rice. "This is so relaxing," he said, swallowing so as not to talk with his mouth full. "I hate going on dates where if there is even a moment of silence the girl feels like she has to chatter on and on. I can just be with you in silence, like today on the porch swing. I love that about you...about us." His beautiful eyes were luminous; the gold star dust around the stunning soft brown was shining against his reddish tan from being in the sun all day. His soft sandy curls were starting to grow back. I couldn't believe he really wanted to be with me. I had to say it. I had to get past it so I could really enjoy just being with him.

"Remember when you sneaked into the house and came to my room the other night?" His mouth was full this time, so he nodded. "Can you come back again tonight?"

He waited until he could talk again. "Aren't you too tired to go horseback riding?" I could tell he was.

"No, I don't want to go riding tonight. I need to show you something."

He raised his eyebrows with a look of mischievous shock on his face. "I thought I was supposed to be keeping my proper distance."

I rolled my eyes. "Not that, you'll be waiting 'til the day we say "I do" for anything in your head right now, but I do need to show you something. Please, will you come?"

He smiled before he answered me. My breath caught a little, I loved that smile. "I already knew that, besides I was going to make you wait regardless, my dad and Pastor Pearce taught me way better than that."

He looked at the spaghetti straps on my dress, for a second I saw him doubting his own resolve, but he regained it just as quickly. "Okay, but morals or not, I am still a guy and you are well...still...beautiful, you have to wear something big and baggy. I think this distance thing will be harder to do in your room if you have on that little red thing you had on the other night."

I blushed. He noticed immediately. He leaned over and said in a loud whisper, "Please don't be embarrassed. You definitely have nothing to be embarrassed about in that department."

"Thanks, I'll try to find the ugliest thing I own."

"Well, you don't have to go that far," he said. He happened to notice the waitress cleaning empty tables. Taking the hint it was closing time, he grabbed the check. I caught his hand before he got up to go pay.

"Around one, okay?"

He was curious why I was pleading for an answer, but knew me well enough to know not to ask here. He suddenly got serious, I suppose wanting to assure me he wouldn't let me down. He cupped my chin in his hand for a second. "Of course, sweet girl, I promise I'll be there."

I was too antsy to go home and go to bed. Even though I was tired, I didn't want to have to kill time alone pacing in my room 'til one. "Can we stop and see my mom for a minute?" When he looked at me to say "yes" I knew he was about to fall asleep, so I didn't let him answer. "You know what? Never mind, I'm beat too and we have a long day tomorrow."

He looked at his watch. "It's eleven already. If I'm meeting you in your room at one, I might as well stay up or I might not get back up. I'm fine, babe, really. Let's go."

"No, I don't want..." He cut me off. "You're not keeping me up. Besides, once we really get going on that roof, it might be a few days before we leave the farm again. Really, it's okay. We don't have to stay long."

"Thank you. I need to tell her something too." He keyed in on the word "too" and I could see the concern burning in his eyes. He'd figured out I had something really important to tell him back at the house, although he didn't ask. I thought he might now that we were alone. The look on my face must have mirrored my thoughts, begging him not to. I was starting to get very nervous about it. The last thing I wanted was for him to think I would keep anything this important from him. He knew me so well. He took my hand across the seat and let the questions drop.

I didn't mind going to see Mom at night. There were always so few people around it felt less hectic, less rushed. She was in her sleeping mode, eyes closed.

"Do you need something, Caimee?" It was Lisa.

"No, I just want to sit a minute and talk to her. What are you doing here at night?"

She looked tired and off schedule. "Oh, it's my day off, can't you tell?"

We really never got a chance to talk that often, but when I got to see her out of nurse mode for a second, she always made me laugh. I think she and Mom would have been friends. They're about the same age. She glanced around me to the chair where Ty was sitting. She cocked her head to the side just slightly, like she was either trying to remember his name or trying to figure out why he was here and not Dad.

"Visiting hours have been over for a while now, Hon, so sneak out quietly for me, okay?"

I nodded. She was cool. I knew she wouldn't make us leave. "I promise we won't stay long."

"Good to see you again, Ty." I could tell by the relieved look in her eye she had just figured out who he was. It was odd to me that he looked so different to everyone here. He looked like the sweet boy I'd always known—at least to me anyway. Maybe that's because no matter how much he changed physically, his good heart would always be the same. I didn't realize what seemed like a short time could make such a difference in him to the outside world, but it hit me here every time we came to this place that a few years could make all the difference as I thought of my mother, how many people who hadn't seen her in so long would recognize her now.

Lisa was about to leave when she caught my hand. She looked like she had something to say that would not have been easy in the daytime, surrounded by everyone. It was different on the quieter night shift. "She's lucky to have you, Caimee. As many years as we tried, I would have given anything to have a daughter like you."

She was too young to sound like she was giving up on the idea. "Maybe you still will," I said, trying to be encouraging. She nodded like she appreciated the sentiment, but there was no hope in her eyes.

"Don't forget...sneak out." I gave her a quick wave as she left and I went to see Mom. It kind of hit me all at once I was about to talk about personal stuff in front of Ty, I took note of what Lisa had just said. I never knew she wanted a child and I appreciated that she would reveal her vulnerability by telling me just to pay me a compliment. Her honesty gave me courage to say what I had to say. If she could, I could too. After all, Ty was not just an acquaintance, he was my life now. He should know everything.

Ty looked comfortable and so tired as he leaned on the arm of the big recliner style chair that Dad usually sat in. He was relaxed, but not sleeping. I hoped he was listening. It was easier to look at my mom and say what I was thinking and feeling than it was to focus on him and have to hide my face, blushing so deeply you could see it through my tan from across the room. I'm sure if he'd had a full view of me he would have noticed immediately. I wouldn't even have to glance sideways to make sure of that, I'd just keep looking straight ahead. I took a deep breath and started.

"Hey Mom! Ty's here. He came to see you again. I know you'd be glad to know that we're um...officially together. Now you don't have to listen to me go on and on any more about how much I miss him. He's staying at Cameron Manor this year instead of going back to Alabama. We're going be seniors together. I wish you could be a part of it all. I really can't wait for the Winter Ball and then Prom to get here. I get to dress up for both. I think this year is going to be very different now that he's back. Maybe I'll get to enjoy some 'real high school stuff.'" I looked over at him even though I promised myself I wouldn't and here came the blush. "That is, if he'll ask me to go." He smiled, so I knew he was listening. "I'm going to tell him about that other thing we talked about. I'm not sure how he'll take it, but it'll be nice for him to know."

He was rolling his head back and forth against the high back of the chair. "If you're going to tell me you really want to be a man or something, could you just rip that Band-Aid off right now and stop all this suspense?"

I ignored that. "See, Mom? He's really funny and sweet and guess what? I kissed him! It was *way* better than I thought it was going to be. He smiled again, this wasn't a conversation a boyfriend usually got to hear between a girl and her mom, but telling her meant telling him how I really feel. It was like he'd picked up the three-way line on our phone or actually like I'd handed it to him. I wanted to let him in, to make him a part of our private world. No more secrets. No more games. I figured I might as well really let him know what was in my heart. Why hold back now?

"Lindie was there. We rode her for a while. She misses you...I miss you. I've been telling you how much I love Ty for so long, but that was just a dream. Now that it's real, I love him so much more. He's really turned out to be everything I ever wanted." I sat in silence, just looking at her. Tears welled up in my eyes. I didn't even try to stop them before they started to flow. Some small part of me felt embarrassed, worried he might think this was weird, but I'd decided on the way over that he needed to know me, *really* know me—not as a child, but who I am now. I wanted him to know it all because I knew what it was like for the person you loved most not to share in any of it. I wanted to have all of that "knowing each other inside and out" in my life with her so bad. I wanted her to sit up and give Ty the "mother's lecture" the same way Dad had given him the one that fathers give. The silent tears turned to sobs. I'd been telling her about the things I wanted for so long, it was harder to miss out on telling her those dreams had come true. I wanted her to share in my real joy as well as my wishes. It had been a long time since I'd cried over our situation and our separation like that. It was hard to wrap my head around how she could be close enough to touch but might as well be miles away.

The next thing I knew Ty was behind me, rubbing my shoulders. "She hears you, baby. She knows in her heart. Don't worry, Mrs. Johnna, your Caimee will be the prettiest girl at that Winter Ball and the prom 'cause I'm going to take her. I promise I'll look after her because if I don't her dad and mine will let me know about it."

I wiped my eyes and looked up at him. He was sad too. He remembered her awake and laughing and riding and being my mom. "I know she'd be happy for us," he said, taking my hand and pulling me to my feet. "We should go, it's late," he whispered. I could hear his own sorrow in his voice. I knew it was because it hurt him to see me hurting. He'd listened to me cry over my mom many times, especially when we were little, but nothing like this. He'd never gotten to hear the secrets only she and I knew. I felt relieved now that he did.

I agreed we should go and followed him out to the truck. It was another time where silence was okay, peaceful. I was hoping he'd realize now that there's nothing I would ever keep from him. I was hoping my bare honesty would soften the blow when he found out about Joy. I was glad Lisa was there, working a shift that wasn't hers. Someday, I'd tell her that her openness gave me the courage I needed.

It was twelve-thirty when we pulled up to the house. He looked at me and laughed. "I'm going to go get in bed now, but just for my father's sake. I'll see you in thirty minutes. As long as you promise I'm not staying awake and walking all the way back up here just so you can tell me you're just being nice and trying not to hurt my feelings, but you don't want to see me anymore." He was only half teasing.

"Would I go so far as to tell my mom about you if that was the case?" I wasn't teasing at all. He'd always known that once I told my mom anything, it was not only important to me, it was the truth.

He seemed appeased by that. "Okay, I'll be back then."

I took his hand and squeezed it. "I'm afraid you might want to call it quits with me when you realize I've been hiding something big from you. Just promise me you won't freak out, 'cause it's pretty freaky, and remember that I didn't *not* tell you because I don't trust you and that I'm telling you now because we're finally together. I haven't said anything because I'm having trouble believing it myself."

He was totally curious now. "Caimee, just tell me already!"

"I can't. Your dad has to think you're home, so if you stay up here he may come and get you and he'll find out and I can't risk that. Please, just trust me, okay?"

"You know I do." He leaned over and kissed me. "I need one thing from you, though." I nodded and he knew my answer would be "anything." "Remember what I said about the pajamas you had on the other night. You're not to wear them." I nodded again. "Scratch that. Anything you have that looks like that and looks that good on you is okay with me...as long as I'm the only one who gets to see it, but don't worry, I won't let you take advantage of me." He laughed. I gave him a playful punch in the arm. "Seriously, I love you too much. We are waiting no matter what." I nodded in agreement, seeing a flicker of something in his eyes. I would have to ask him about it later; although maybe it was the one thing he wouldn't tell me.

Of course, I blushed, hoping he didn't see in the dim light of the truck's cab. "I have something else you might like. It'll give you a reason to get back here right at one, but keep your proper distance," I teased.

Ha! Ha! You're so funny! I got your proper distance right here." He leaned over, put his hand on the back of my head and kissed me again. He lingered there for a second as we shared the same breath. I almost couldn't let him go, but he promised to hurry back. He left quickly, saying if he didn't he wouldn't go at all.

I released his hand so he could jump out of the truck. I watched as he trotted off across the pasture to his house.

Joy was asleep, so I didn't wake her, but I had to sneak past her so I could at least brush my teeth and wash my face. I debated on which pair of pajamas to wear. He'd already seen the red ones, so I went with my just-above-knee baby doll nightgown with matching bloomer shorts. It was light cotton, peach-colored and off the shoulder with little pink flowers on it. Nothing like the spaghetti straps, but very cute in a girlie sort of way. I climbed into bed and didn't even realize I'd fallen asleep. He must have knocked, but I didn't hear him. He was standing next to my bed, stroking the side of my face and my hair. He didn't startle me, but I was surprised that I had drifted off given all I had to tell him.

"I almost decided not to wake you," he said, "but I don't think I can stand the anticipation for a whole 'nother day." He'd changed into green and white checkered sleeping pants and a white T-shirt. He noticed me appraising him in the dim light covered by the purple shade of my bedside table lamp. "Well, I couldn't very well 'pretend' to go to bed and not look the part and I didn't want to wake Dad up fumbling around getting dressed again. I do live right above him, you know."

I scooted over so he could sit down. He looked skeptical like "I don't want your dad or mine to kill me" kind of look. "Don't worry, I won't attack you, but I do think you look cute in your pj's.

"Well, the ladies do find me irresistible." He turned around, modeling them for me.

"Are you about done?" I asked, my tone was firm, but my grin gave me away.

He pretended to look dejected. "I guess if you're all out of dollar bills you want to throw at me."

I laughed so hard I had to cover my mouth. It took me a minute, but I finally got my composure. "Stop making me laugh, this is serious." I sat up. I could feel the weight of his stare on me.

"The only thing that's serious around here right now is how I feel about you."

My insides were shaking. For some reason, in this light, in this room, he made me nervous. Ty was sitting on the edge of my bed in my room at night about to kiss me and it felt like more of a dream than Joy sleeping in my closet.

"I love you, you know, and I'm glad you've been telling your mom everything you've been feeling."

I felt relieved. I was afraid he'd think me telling her in front of him was weird.

He grunted a short laugh. "I guess we're the worst secret keepers ever. We didn't even make it one week— not even hardly one day."

My laugh was more out of nerves than agreement. "Oh, I don't know about that. I have a pretty big one for you."

For the first time all night, he looked disinterested in whatever it was, he was preoccupied with some other thought. There was something deep in his eyes all the way to his soul, like disbelief or wonder, almost like a child realizing something new about life. "I can't believe I am sitting here with you, so many nights in Alabama I thought about you, I knew you would never give your body away, but I wasn't so sure about your heart. I thought over and over that I shouldn't even get my hopes up because I was too late...I had waited too long to tell you how I was really feeling..." He cast his eyes down like he was ashamed he had made me wait and doubt for so long, like his hesitation had hurt me. I couldn't let him feel that way.

He didn't have a chance to finish his thought because I leaned over and kissed him. I couldn't help but think what would happen if Mrs. Maggie walked in or Bo noticed him missing. I didn't care. I'd waited for him to tell me he loved me for so long. A thousand summer memories flowed through my mind of all the days and nights I'd sat out on the roof watching him work, watching him ride, and falling in love. I didn't even realize it was happening myself at first, but now I knew for sure. More than just a daydream of what I thought I wanted, I knew deep inside I wanted him forever. I hoped he felt the same—that this wasn't a passing crush. His loving me just for now would never be enough.

"Did you mean it?" I asked, trying to catch my breath, my voice was shaking, I was nervous. We had gone from sitting to reclining in one fluid motion. He was holding me tight, one hand behind my head, tangled in my hair as my head rested on his arm, the other moving slowly up and down my back. He wasn't forceful or pushing me too far, there was a certain gentleman's quality about him. I loved him even more for it. I had waited for him for so long, and I guess somewhere deep inside I still had a fear of losing him, there were a thousand ways it could happen, just like it happened to my dad with my mother's accident, or to Bo when Ty's mother just up and left. I didn't want this to be like a mirage, something I had been walking towards for so long but now that I was within sight...within reach it would disappear.

"Did I mean what?" he whispered gently into my hair above my ear. My heart was racing, pounding in my chest. I was glad the light was dim so he couldn't see the insecurity on my face. I didn't want him to get tired of me or annoyed because I needed his reassurance again.

"What you said to my dad about this being for keeps."

He pulled his face back so he could look into my eyes, no trace of impatience. "I've never lied to your dad, I will never lie to you, and this is for keeps. I promise." He kept his eyes on mine holding my gaze for the longest time, there was a pledge there, I had seen it before, but not quite this way, it was deeper, and more serious, it wasn't meant to convince our parents, this was a vow between us. He put his lips back to my ear kissing my cheek as he got closer, "I promise my sweet girl, with all my heart and soul I do."

I slid closer to him, keeping my head on his arm. I put my free arm around his waist. I had always wanted to touch his soft short curls, his lips, his face, and now I could any time I wanted. I was so engrossed in memorizing him, the feel of his skin, his face and my favorite pair of eyes in the world that I pushed the reason for his being here away. I wanted this part to last forever. I snuggled into his chest. He sighed a contented sound and held me tight. I was comfortable there next to him. I never wanted to move. He let me lie there a while. I'm sure he was fighting his curiosity about why I so desperately wanted him here. He stroked my hair. I took in a jagged breath and sighed. My mom used to do that to put me to sleep when I was little."

"I know," he said.

He paused, remembering something. The look on his face was like he was debating whether or not to tell me.

"Please, tell me what you're thinking." The pleading tone in my voice must have been enough to persuade him.

"Just a few days before the accident, I remember we were in the living room—me, you, and your mom. I was six, it was too cold to play outside so she told us to share our new Christmas toys, we were playing for a while she dozed on the couch. You started crying about something I'm sure I had done to you." He laughed at himself. "She opened her eyes and picked you up and left me sitting on the floor like I was in trouble or something. She laid your head on her lap and she put just her fingertips in your hair. I looked up during the next commercial and you were asleep, holding that pink rabbit you used to carry everywhere."

He kept stroking my hair and letting me remember. The next thing I knew he was rocking me a little to get his arm out from under my head. I opened my eyes to the sight of him memorizing my face. "I was tempted to watch you sleep all night," he said, "but I don't want to get caught up here because I do want to live long enough to marry you someday. Sorry, I was going to let you get in another hour or two, but my arm was asleep."

I would have enjoyed hearing the marriage part for the first time if I hadn't been so foggy, waiting for my body and my brain to meet somewhere in my sleepy "this has to be a dream" state. When my tangled thoughts came together, there was something else I wanted to ask before my eyes had finally closed. When we were sitting in the truck, I'd seen the flicker in his eyes when he talked about us waiting. It played again in my head. There was a story there and now was as good a time as any for me to see his soul the way he had mine at the hospital. I touched his face, running my fingers lightly over it. He needed a shave. I went from his rough skin to his soft lips and back again.

"Have you been here before?" He knew I didn't mean in my room in the early hours of the morning, he knew I meant in this situation.

He sighed. "I kind of figured you might want to know that. He took another deep breath, like he didn't want to tell me. I moved my hand up in his soft hair and waited. I'd already decided that no matter what his answer, I was going to stay composed. He was mine now and that was all that mattered.

"Once, with a girl named Candice." I looked down, my lashes covering the expression in my eyes. Maybe I didn't want to hear it after all. He lifted my chin with his fingertips, forcing me to look at him. "I was close to being in a situation neither of us was ready for and while I was kissing her, I um..." He turned away. "Oh no," I said, forcing him to continue. "Now you have to tell me."

"Okay, I um...I called her Caimee." It was at the end of our sophomore year. She got so mad, she hit me. But I'm glad it happened because it saved me from making the biggest mistake of my life and giving her something I've always wanted you to have—not exactly cool for a guy, huh?"

I couldn't believe it! Mr. Football, Mr. Popular waiting for me to catch up to him. I almost couldn't find the words to express what I was feeling. He waited, misinterpreting my silence. He looked like a little kid about to be in trouble.

I spoke quickly, wanting to let him off the hook. "Um...how do I say this? You waited for me, knowing I was younger, knowing I might say no, and knowing how our fathers might feel about it and taking a chance anyway. I would say that not only do I love you for it, I will always think you are the coolest guy ever. You just don't understand how much it means. What girl wouldn't want that from the guy she wants for keeps?"

He finally exhaled, relieved. "I'm glad you're happy about it. I took quite a bit of...let's say "teasing" from the guys on the team about it, but now that we're together, I really do want to wait. It may seem like a long time 'til we can be married." He saw the doubt in my eyes. "Yes, I really do want to marry you, but I just want it to be right...you know, so it really can be for keeps." I hugged him tight, pulling myself in close to him. I couldn't believe anybody had ever loved anybody as much as I loved him in this moment and then I thought of my dad and knew I had just caught a glimpse of what he lives with every day. My heart ached for him.

"Baby, you gotta tell me something now." His arms were wrapped around my neck. I heard him tap his watch. "Why am I here?"

I pulled my thoughts away from my parents before I started to cry over my mom again and focused back on the task at hand. I didn't answer, I had to show him. I sat up again, getting out of bed on the opposite side so he wouldn't have to move. "You promise not to freak out? You promise to keep an open mind and remember how you said you would never lie to me?" He nodded. "Well, I promise you the same. You know how much I love you and trust you, you saw it for yourself, how much more honest could I have been tonight, right?" He nodded again, acknowledging my candidness at the hospital. "This is real, even though it's a little hard to believe."

He walked over to me and put his hands on my shoulders, keeping us an arm's length apart so I could see the sincerity in his eyes. "I promise, baby. Nothing is so bad or so unbelievable we can't get through it. Okay now, what is it?"

I grabbed his hand and led him to the closet. "Please, whatever your reaction, you have to be quiet."

I opened the door slowly. Joy's face was covered by the blanket so he couldn't see who it was, but the stunned look on his face that I was hiding someone in my closet was unmistakable.

"Who? He started to ask, but I put my finger to my lips. "I don't want you to scare her." I leaned down and called her name. "Joy, it's me. I need you to wake up. I have someone here I want you to meet."

She opened her eyes sleepily. "What?" she asked, groggy and not fully awake.

"Sit up for me. I want to introduce you to Ty."

It took a minute. She was a heavy sleeper, but understanding crossed her face as she remembered our conversation earlier. She stood up, fixing her clothes, facing me in the back of the closet. I turned her around. "Ty, this is Joy. She's the girl from the painting."

He turned pale white, despite his tan, and stepped backwards until he bumped into the corner post of my bed.

"It's okay, Ty Look!" I walked over to him. He was gripping the footboard of my bed the way I'd dug my hands into the grass. He needed to touch something real, something concrete.

"Believe me, baby, I know what you're feeling right now. I was freaked out too when I saw her for the first time."

He wasn't looking at me, wasn't seeing the understanding of his confusion on my face. He couldn't take his eyes off her. It was like he was seeing a ghost.

"Joy, come here." I gestured with my right hand and wrist, instructing her to walk towards us while I kept one hand on Ty's chest. I could feel his heart beating, but it wasn't racing like he was afraid. I looked at his face more closely. It wasn't fear in his eyes either...more like curiosity or anticipation. The closer she came, the more he seemed to accept what his eyes were seeing. It must have been because we'd seen her all of our lives—either that or he was going into shock. She walked slowly, like she was in trouble. She was shy about meeting him.

"Where did she? I mean, when did she? He was struggling, trying to form a coherent thought.

"How long has she been here? Who is she?" He immediately assumed she was someone from our time. I know that picture has been up there for years. She should be much older. She can't be the same girl."

I was impressed that he'd kept his composure enough to keep his voice down. I slid my hand from his chest, down his arm, and took his hand. "Come on, let's talk."

I walked over to my bed, straightening my covers where he and I had gotten tangled in them. I patted the bed, so they'd come and sit down. They both picked a spot on opposite sides. We sat in a triangle—each of us in their own corner.

"Okay, talk," he said. I could easily hear the double meaning in his words—skepticism like "this better be good." He was going to need some convincing that this was actually the same girl, but he knew I wouldn't lie to him.

I started slowly, with the dogs barking that night and how the moon was so full it looked like I could touch it. Joy found her courage, even though her voice shook a little. She told him about the charcoal sketch she was doing of the house and how I'd scared her and she made as stray line. He nodded, quite familiar with the picture she was talking about. Typical Ty, he was calm. He didn't say a word until he had all the facts. The only time I saw him flinch was when I told him that I was afraid I might get stuck in her time. He looked at me and I knew without him saying a word that he was forbidding me to go back—not in a controlling way, but in an "I can't lose you" way. We told him the story, with all its unbelievable twists and turns, and by five o'clock he knew it all.

We really didn't have time to discuss it. He had to get back. He hugged me tight, but didn't kiss me goodbye in front of her before he darted out the door, not wanting to get caught. I knew that soon enough we'd be up on the barn roof alone. It was a relief, like a weight had been lifted, like the day Dad said we could stay. Joy was tired and went back to bed. The past few sleepless and late nights had begun to catch up with me. I set my alarm for seven and decided to get some more sleep. When I closed my eyes, I was expecting my brain to wander to what Ty would have to say to me later today, but instead it took me to places we'd been last night— my head resting on his arm, my arm around him, and endless honesty as we saw each other's hearts. I knew I needed the sleep, but two hours seemed too long. I wanted him to come back as soon as he was gone. I jumped up and ran to the window, hoping to catch a glimpse of him going back across the pasture, but it was too dark. I knew it was silly. He'd just left and I missed him already.

Chapter 23
"Close Call"

I stood there and watched anyway. I knew if I couldn't see him, I'd see his light. Bo had made the entire second story loft of his house a room for Ty when he was little so he'd have enough space to run around and play. So many nights when he was in Alabama I'd sit and wish I could see the light go on across the field, signaling he was there. I watched and waited to see that he'd made it back. He must have been running, trying to get inside, worried he'd wake Bo—or worse, run into him at the front door. It took about five minutes until I saw it—the glow of his bedroom light through the big window of his room facing the house. We used to flash our lights back and forth at each other when we were little. Now the sight of it brought me comfort, knowing he was here to stay, knowing he loved me and he knew the secret I'd been hiding.

At breakfast we were both so tired and preoccupied, Bo and Mrs. Maggie couldn't help but notice our silence.

"If you two are going to be out late, you need to call." Bo was trying to be a father to both of us in the absence of mine. Mrs. Maggie was in the middle of taking a sip of her coffee, but she nodded her head in agreement.

"I stayed to play the late game last night and you two were still out at eleven. I even checked Caimee's room to see if maybe you'd parked the truck down by your place and dropped her off here." I prayed she didn't see the "Oh my gosh, we almost got caught" look on our faces. I'm sure we were mirrors of one another. In that split second, I was trying to figure out what would have been worse—her finding Joy asleep on my closet floor if she'd decided to see if I was in the bathroom, or him in my room if she'd decided to come back later. I couldn't think about it. My face turning pale and then blushing red was about to give me away. I looked down at my plate and tried to think of something else. I was waiting for Bo to get started on his day and Mrs. Maggie to turn around and start the dishes so I could snag Joy some breakfast, but no luck.

I tried to hint without sounding too desperate or guilty. "Bo, don't you have to move the horses down to the lower pasture so we can get started?"

He didn't even look over to answer. "Already done." *Dang!* I couldn't catch a break here.

I cast my eyes down to my food and then quickly gave a meaningful look to Ty. He didn't get it at first. I mouthed the words, "Joy's hungry" while Bo and Mrs. Maggie were still engaged in conversation with each other, having given up on either one of us having anything meaningful to say. He nodded slightly, catching my drift. He was so sly I hardly noticed it myself. He took his napkin and put a crescent roll, some bacon, and some honeydew melon in it. He shrugged his shoulders. I knew exactly what he meant—not exactly a conventional breakfast, but it would have to do. He put it in an over-sized cargo pocket of his shorts. Now we had to think of an excuse to for him to go upstairs. Another quick lie. I could tell he had nothing. Neither of us were proficient liars. We weren't used to it, we'd been taught better, and we'd been caught enough so we gave up trying. This was going to be hard.

I put on my pathetic face. "Ty, I'm so tired, could you go upstairs and get my boots? I left them by the door in my room." He nodded and without a word, he stood up to go, not wanting to add to my fib and make it so big it was unbelievable. No need for him to even try. I didn't realize it, but I was about to get us caught all by myself.

Bo was instantly pulled from his conversation with Mrs. Maggie. "Pretty sure I tripped over them on my way in," he said, inclining his head towards the door. Mrs. Maggie was also suddenly interested. "You'd better hope he did and you didn't wear those filthy things in my house."

"It couldn't be my work boots. I wore them upstairs last night because I remembered as I was taking them off how mad you'd be if you saw the trail of dirt I accidentally left on the steps." At this point, all I could do was apologize because I didn't want her to go investigate. "Sorry Mrs. Maggie, I just wasn't thinking." I was trying to hurry because we were hungry and I forgot to take them off at the door." I doubted my own story. I was digging a hole here, I hoped I wasn't about to fall in it. Maybe I'd left them downstairs. I closed my eyes and took a deep breath. *Great. I'd just given her a reason to go up the stairs and into my room to clean the floor.*

Ty realized what I'd done, the second I did. He got up, walked around the table, and messed my hair, although I was so tired this morning I hadn't spent much time on it. He really didn't have that much work to do to make it look any worse. Mrs. Maggie was about to get on to me for causing her extra work, but he spoke first. "Don't you remember, babe, I stopped you at the door? I bet those were the ones you tripped over on the way in, Dad." He casually strolled out of the kitchen like he wasn't in a hurry, but I could just imagine him racing up the stairs two or three at a time to hand Joy the food he had hidden in his pocket, look for my boots, and then run back down. He was gone longer than I thought he would be, but not so long that anyone else noticed. Mrs. Maggie changed direction mid-thought before I could take whatever tongue lashing was due me. She was still pretty bent out of shape from the other day when she had to scrub the wood after I'd lied to her and said I had to go to the bathroom.

"Good thing he was watching out for you, young lady. That black stuff takes some elbow grease to get up off my floors and it doesn't just come off your shoes, it was on the banister and for some reason swiped up against my kitchen counter.

"I was thirsty and got some tea on my way up," I said, lying again, remembering that I'd also snagged a sandwich off the bar. I closed my eyes for the second time and leaned back against my chair. They must have thought I was tired when really I was trying to cover the lie I felt blazing in them. Mrs. Maggie would have been the first to notice if she'd been paying attention. I didn't realize I'd left a trail of black shingle dust that almost led her right to Joy.

Ty passed the wide square opening to the kitchen, holding my boots. Bo and Mrs. Maggie didn't notice him. They were talking horse DNA and the stock we had in the barn, and when Thor would be ready to start his racing career. "I'm finished," I said, hoping it was quietly enough to keep their attention on each other.

Neither of them seemed to care as I slipped out.

"They were in my room, weren't they? Sorry, I'm so tired I just got confused when your dad said he'd seen them. He must have tripped over my Chuck Taylors. They're high-top and if he didn't look he would've just assumed they were my boots." He was sitting on the top step, re-lacing his own dirty Timberlands.

"Yeah, don't worry though, I covered—and Joy got breakfast."

"How did you get your shoes off so fast to run and get mine *and* give her breakfast?"

"Let's just say I hope she doesn't mind fast food and faster conversation." I'd really needed his help this morning. Seems like I'd almost kept my secret a little too long."

"I hope Mrs. Maggie doesn't see the dirt trail up the steps and go find her. That was a stupid, rookie mistake, man, I just forgot." He held up one of my soft, what used to be yellow, hand towels. It was covered in black smudges. "Sorry, it was the first thing I could find."

Yeah, well, so was this with my eyes half open this morning." I gestured to my outfit. It was okay for work on top of the barn, but nothing close to what I wanted him to look at me in all day. Lime green running shorts and a light orange T-shirt.

"I did notice you look a little like one of those multi-colored popsicles today."

"This isn't much better," I said, pulling the hot pink hair tie out of my pocket. I had my hair pulled up into a ponytail—only pulling the last bit halfway through leaving it shorter and off my neck. "I was just going for something that wasn't black."

He patted me on the leg when he was finished with his boots. "Come on, let's get rid of this before she asks why I ruined it."

He ran over to the pile of shingles on the ground around the big dumpster, put the towel in the middle of the debris, and threw it over the side with the rest of the trash with a wide shovel. Anyone watching would have thought he was just cleaning up. The yellow towel was so black and dirty it would never be noticed. Even Mrs. Maggie wouldn't be looking in there.

It didn't take long for Ty to get us all harnessed up and tied to the top of the roof. We were shoveling again in no time. "I want to go with you when you take her back under the house. I really want to see the tunnel for myself." I nodded. "If I hadn't seen it, I still wouldn't believe it. You should have seen her when we first met. She was so trusting, even though it had closed until midnight that day, she believed every word I said when I told her how I had fallen through. I can't believe she went back night after night trying to come here."

He gave me a "tough break" look. "Sounds like you have a friend." He made it sound like I'd found a stray puppy that followed me home. I gave him a look that said I knew it.

"She's nice and yes it's nice to have her here. She's a good friend, but I'll be so glad when all this sneaking around is over, I mean let's face it we stink at all this truth stretching. I still have to show her the painting and I'm not sure how I am going to do that, but I think I'd better try while Dad is gone—at least we're the only ones that will be upstairs."

"Oh no, you don't get to do that without me. I gotta see her face when she sees it. No offense taken. Being told you're a terrible liar is kind of a compliment." He smiled at me like he was proud of himself. I just shook my head and laughed, he was right. We kept shoveling. I knew if we stopped to discuss it Mrs. Maggie and or Bo would look out the window and ask us at lunch what was so interesting we had to stop moving to waste time and chit chat about it.

"Besides, I did the math. Your dad is still going to be gone for quite a few days right? She'll be leaving about the same time he gets home, that gives us some time. I don't know about you, but these past few late nights are starting to get to me, I gotta get some sleep tonight. Can't it wait 'til tomorrow? It's Sunday and at least we won't have to work all day." I agreed.

"On one condition, we finish early and go get you a phone. It would be nice not to have to string cans between our houses to have to talk to you. He didn't miss the "throwing your phone in the pond was stupid" so I didn't need to say it. "And I don't think Bo would appreciate me calling at midnight or one in the morning to tell you to come over. If you didn't want to talk to your mom, you could have just blocked her number."

This time he stopped working. "I didn't want to just not talk to her, I didn't want to have anything from her that she was paying for. She uses that to try and control me and make me feel guilty because she gave it to me and paid the bill. I don't think you're quite getting how miserable she's made my life this past year. It was like having an electronic leash. When I first got here I thought Rainsville and Alabama were the problem, but the truth is, I did have a life there. The real and only problem was her. She ruined everything." He shoveled harder, thinking of her during his rant. Bo was right in the beginning he did want to blame the whole town, at least this was progress, Rainsville wasn't the enemy anymore, he was at least focusing on the truth with his feelings more focused on what was really bothering him.

He was irritated with the whole turn the conversation had taken. I didn't answer. Talking about it seemed to aggravate him more. My normally calm Ty can handle anything, but this rattled him a little. It didn't do any good to rehash it, his mind was made up. I felt guilty, he felt judged.

"I'm sorry, I shouldn't have said anything. You're right. It was your decision to make. You know her a lot better than I do." I glanced at him, not wanting to see if he was really mad at me. In that second I realized I couldn't take it. This wasn't childish bickering, this was a serious issue that might be construed as a fight and I didn't want our relationship to be like that. He knew I was really sorry. Even I could hear the remorse in my voice, its taste on my tongue. "I would never want you to think I was judging you for anything."

He stopped and motioned for me to come closer to him. "I'm sorry too. I know I take my frustration with her out on other people. Dad said I've been doing it to him since I got here. It's not you, babe, it's her." He leaned down and kissed me. "I want you to be able to tell me anything, no matter what, even if we don't agree, okay?" He saw the skeptical look in my eyes. "Promise me, no holding back ever. It only leads to resentment. Trust me, I know." I promised and we started shoveling again. There was peace in the working silence.

We worked until it didn't matter what color my clothes were. They were all black from the dirt and dust and sticky from the glue where we had to put down the felt. I made another bathroom excuse at lunch to take Joy some food while Ty occupied Bo and Mrs. Maggie. We had scraped off and put felt on one whole side of the roof and had started on the other half when we noticed it was too dark to work anymore, that two weeks Ty thought it would take us was almost right, but we were a few days ahead of schedule. He stopped and assessed the moon. It was still a little less than half full. He looked at his watch. "I think we missed it."

I stopped and gazed up at the sky. My heart nearly leaped out of my chest thinking he meant we'd missed Joy's opportunity to get back home. Just thinking about that made it feel like my insides twisted into a knot. As much as I was glad she'd come, I knew how much she needed and wanted to go home.

"She says it has to be either at its fullest or completely dark for the tunnel to open. It's not even close."

He took a swallow of water, hung his water bottle back on his belt, and shook his head no. "I mean I think we missed the phone place. I believe it closes at six, but even if it's open later, I'm too tired to go."

"It's okay, we can wait another day or so." He agreed. We had bridged our first gap. It was a little thing, but we came out fine on the other side. I lifted my bottle to take a drink not realizing it was empty, he saw me just clip it back onto my harness resigning myself to the thirst and handed me his last swallow.

He nodded back up to the moon. "That reminds me of something I've been meaning to tell you. I think you can't let her find out too much about her future it could scare her to death, the Civil War and all. It could change things here. She has to be exactly who she would have been if she'd never come here."

He stopped short when we heard a noise behind us. Neither of us had noticed Bo come through the open hatch door. "Hey Ty, can we go get the phone tomorrow? I'm beat and Maggie has supper waiting."

"I know," he agreed. We had the same thought." *Had he heard our discussion about the moon?* I held my breath, waiting for him to ask. "We can go tomorrow after church. It's cheaper for me to put you on my plan. For some reason, they give you a discount if you have more than one line." We were safe, he didn't ask. I slowly let the air out of my lungs.

Ty started to protest. Bo saw it coming before he could get a word out. He held up his hand to stop him. "I know you want to pay your own way, just let me help you get started, okay? I'll take the monthly charges out of your pay for working around here, but in the long run it's a better deal for both of us."

Ty saw his logic and conceded, but then thought better of just giving in. "As long as our sharing a bill doesn't mean you're going to make me give her the number, I know I told her I would text it to her, but that was kind of just to get her off my case."

Bo sighed in defeat. He knew Ty wasn't going to talk to his mom again unless it was on his own terms and no amount of grunt work could make him. "It's your business, son. You handle it the way you see fit. Just remember, you should never cut her out of your life." He glanced at me as if to remind him anything can happen and it might be too late to apologize. Ty nodded, but didn't comment. "Now you all come on down. Maggie says your food is getting cold on the porch."

Ty walked over and took my shovel. "Can you take these while I untie us and get Caimee down?"

Bo took the shovels without another word. That was the end of Bo pushing him to talk to his mom.

Chapter 24
"The Painting"

"I guess your sentence is over," I said, watching him hang my harness back on the wall. I was more than a little put out. I figured after this job I'd hold the title of "Ms. Free Labor" 'til the end of the summer, only now I'd be working alone. Even if Ty wanted to be with me, Bo would be giving him something else to do. I wasn't looking at him so I didn't see him run over and nearly tackle me until I was already in his arms. He swung me around the barn by the waist 'til I was dizzy, just like he'd done in the yard the day April came over. It worked. I laughed.

"I told you babe, we finish together." He must have seen the "Yeah, but what about the next crummy job?" question in my eyes. "I'm saying we finish *all* of it together. Okay, Dad may give me some stuff to do at night, but I'll be with you during the day." I could tell he didn't want to say it out loud, but emphasis on the word *all* meant getting Joy home too. We never said it, but we'd both learned a lesson about talking freely about her, the moon, or the tunnel. We had nearly gotten caught. That was twice in one day, counting the whole breakfast lie I nearly got busted telling.

He took my hand. "Come on, let's go see what we get to eat outside like we're hounds too."

I laughed again. "I love you so much." He didn't have to answer—the "me too" was deep in his eyes and all over his face.

Our plates were empty lying on the porch beneath the swing that was becoming our favorite place. Hillbilly and Bumpkin were lounging each on their own step; their low snoring made the mood all the more peaceful. I laid sideways with my head on Ty's lap, staring out into the yard between the porch rails, while he kept us gently swaying back and forth. I was watching the lightning bugs light up around the bushes while he almost slept. I allowed myself to daydream about watching our kids run around the yard with mason jars trying to catch them like we used to when we were little. I noticed Bo look at his watch out of the corner of my eye and it brought me back to reality. I immediately started thinking about how I was going to get some food for Joy, which was getting harder to do by the day.

"You two just gonna leave my good dishes out here all night to get eaten on by bugs or stepped on in the morning by your boots or those lazy hounds?" Mrs. Maggie glowered at us when she came out to collect our plates.

Ty had an answer ready. "We didn't want to step on your clean floor. We both held up a dirty shoe for her inspection. "I wouldn't want anyone to think we don't live in a museum. Can you just imagine the scandal? What if someone came over and saw a stray shoe print in your kitchen or on your steps." He was so tired he'd turned his filter off. It was rare he was sarcastic with Mrs. Maggie.

Bo was sitting on the top step and turned around to answer him on Mrs. Maggie's behalf. For a second I thought he was going to be mad. He didn't put up with disrespect from Ty where she, or any woman, was concerned. "Hey, you watch your tongue, boy! How do you think the townsfolk would react if word got out we couldn't eat off Maggie's floors? Just imagine, what if there was a cleanest floors in Culpeper contest and she lost because one of the two of you was careless?" The tree of us laughed at her expense.

In silent indignation, she gathered up our dishes and took Bo's plate away, even though he was holding his fork, about to take another bite of the piece of chocolate cake still on it. She let the screen door slam behind her, but then she came right back. None of us moved. We stayed in our spots, knowing she wouldn't let it go.

"If even one of you is late for church in the morning, not only will I leave without you, you'll all be scrubbing my floors on your day off, dirty or clean."

We answered in unison with a tired unenthusiastic, "Yes ma'am."

She wasn't mad. There was no bite to the threat. Bo must have been just as exhausted as we were. His filter was off too. It was show season and he was going nonstop from sun up to sun set, not only was he the trainer he was the vet, working with the jockeys and keeping the horses in top condition was more than a full time job.

"That woman will shine the gold on the streets of Heaven if there's a mop lying around."

Our laughter was silenced when we heard her good-natured, "I heard that." More proof we needed to talk about Joy in secret. She could hear one of the lightning bugs I'd been watching land on a bluebell if she was listening hard enough.

Bo and Ty headed across the pasture around nine-thirty. Ty helped him get the horses back into the barn.

I dusted myself off as best I could, took off my shoes and went into the house to figure out how to sneak something up to Joy. Mrs. Maggie was in her room watching TV, but her door was open and she could see right into the kitchen. As soon as I opened the refrigerator, she was standing in her doorway. "You can't be hungry."

I turned to face her so she'd see I was carrying my dirty boots and trying not to touch anything.

"Just thirsty." This lying thing was getting harder and easier the more I did it—easier to hide my dishonest expression, harder to keep coming up with something new and harder to feel good about myself for doing it. She seemed satisfied with that and went back into her room. Now all I had to do was get whatever food I could find up the stairs without her noticing I was carrying it. I knew she'd be able to see me from her bed when I rounded the bar to leave. I was going to have to get a bottle of water. It was the only thing I could carry and not spill while trying to balance the Tupperware container of leftovers from lunch. The containers were a road cone orange color so I wasn't sure what I had until I got upstairs, nor was I sure she wouldn't see the color in my hand as I flashed by her door. I didn't have time to look, all I could do was hope it was something that wouldn't be too gross cold. I found out later that I'd lucked out—tuna salad and fruit cocktail. Using the microwave definitely would have been too noisy. As it was, I had to slide the silverware drawer open as quietly as possible. It was a miracle she didn't hear that. Fortunately for me, her television was up loud. She was watching a quiz show, trying to beat the contestants with her answers.

"I'm sorry I'm so late," I said to Joy. She laid her book aside. She looked sad, almost pained, the hurt in her eyes ran deep into her soul. She was shaking down to her bones. I was filthy and wanted a shower more than anything, but couldn't leave her with that look on her face. She hadn't eaten in eight hours or more, but she ignored the food, so I knew it must be bad.

"There's a war coming." I didn't understand until I followed her gaze to the book she had been reading— my eighth grade American history book. Another mistake. How could I have left that one out? I should have thought, I should have known. I couldn't sugar coat it now. She had read all about the Civil War.

"Yes, Joy, but your family...our family survives; otherwise, how would we be here now? The Camerons made it through and so did this house."

She nodded with tears in her eyes. "Yes, but all those other people, so many deaths, starvation, homelessness. It looks awful."

Again, more truth. "Yes, it was awful, but..." I didn't know what else to say. I couldn't finish my own sentence. I mean, I have no idea how any American would have responded if we had been given a history book that told us about September 11, 2001 years before it happened, with no way to prevent it. I didn't have any words. I took her hand. "I'm sorry, I didn't mean for you to find out too much about your future while you were here. I was hoping to show you around my time without telling you about your pressing tomorrows. I handed her the container of food again. "Please try to eat something. It isn't anything you need to worry about right now. It's still years away for you. I guess the one good thing about you knowing is you can prepare yourself and your family. It will be hard because you won't be able to explain to them how you know, but it still gives you an advantage."

She nodded. There was nothing left to say, no way to make her feel at ease. War was coming and there was no way to relieve her fear.

I fell into bed after my shower. I didn't even bother to dry my hair, even though I hated going to bed with it wet. It made my pillowcases damp in the morning. Joy fell asleep while I was in the shower. Streaks of tears were clearly visible on her face, the food barely touched. She must have been really tired to want to sleep with all that new knowledge and pictures floating around in her head. I figured she'd been sitting there reading and studying all day. I picked up the book and hid it in the drawer of my bedside table before I got under my covers. No special pajamas tonight—plain white cotton tank top and teal boy shorts. I knew Ty wasn't coming. We'd already decided to take her to see the painting on Sunday. No need to stress over going to bed a little more casual and more comfortable than fancy. We hadn't had time to really talk about anything except getting some sleep tonight. My last conscious thoughts were more guilt over not showing Joy the portrait today. I had been putting her off because I was so busy, tired, and focused on myself. The remorse for spending so little time with her nagged at me. Taking her up to the Rapunzel room sooner rather than later like I'd promised might have at least put her mind on something else. She didn't say it because of her little history lesson tonight, but I knew she missed her mother terribly, even more so than before, likely worrying one or more of her family would not survive the coming conflict.

I must have been dead to the world for a long time when I felt it. I was so tired I hadn't been dreaming, not even of Ty—at least not until this second. I was still in the same position I was in when I collapsed onto my soft bed. I had to have been sleeping deeply because my body picked up on the sensation, but my brain chose to ignore it for what seemed like a long time, pushing it away. When it finally registered somewhere in my subconscious, it scared me half to death, but as with any nightmare, I couldn't wake up. The part of my brain that would have been motivated to move me was still sound asleep and in my dreams it was a spider, then a cockroach, then some type of reptile, all of which I was afraid of. Somewhere on the edge of the dream, in some small part of my conscious mind it dawned on me that I needed to get away fast. I sat up and flew to the other side of the bed. In my stupor, I knew I had to put as much distance between myself and whatever vile creature it was that was touching me. I shook out my hair, not sure what might be about to fall on the covers, but I couldn't feel it anymore. I was breathing heavy, like I'd been running. It had been in my bangs and on my face. The longer I couldn't find it the more frightened I became that it was still on me, touching me, but I couldn't fully wake up.

Something wasn't right. Suddenly I couldn't move my hands either. They were bound around my wrists with some type of tight restraint. I struggled to see in the dim moonlight, continuing to shake my head. I didn't realize it at the time, but I was also kicking my feet. My blankets were on the floor.

"Babe, wake up! It's me, Ty." My heart was racing and I was gasping for air. I couldn't make it make sense.

He held my wrists firmly so I'd stop flailing. I couldn't let go of the feeling that something was crawling in my hair. I was trembling, on the verge of a scream.

"Caimee, look at me! It's me, Ty." He let go of my hands and took hold of my face, forcing me to look up through the tangled mess of my damp hair. I focused on his face, but still couldn't quite get my heart or my breathing under control. "Shhhh, baby, you're making enough noise to get Mrs. Maggie up here. It's just me." He started clearing my hair away from my face and leaned away, unpinning my legs.

"I'm so sorry, baby. I didn't mean to scare you." He was talking fast, trying to explain himself.

"I was feeling so guilty. The only thing she wants is to see the painting and we've been putting it off. I couldn't sleep. I kept thinking about it. I thought we could take Joy to see the picture tonight. She asked me again this morning when I brought her breakfast. I forgot to tell you, but it kept coming back to me every time I closed my eyes." I practically threw the food at her and left. Our being tired just felt like a lame excuse, it has got to get old fast sitting in that closet all day."

I was almost fully awake now and I realized how stupid I must have looked fighting him and trying to get away. I could see between the light and shadow coming in through my plantation shutters that his face was really red on one side. I was horrified. "Did I hit you? I am so sorry, sosorry." I reached up to caress the spot where I'd hit him. I knew then it must be true it was the same size as my palm, I felt terrible.

He laughed. "Yeah, well at least we know you can defend yourself. It's okay, sweetie, it doesn't hurt." He stopped and thought about it for a second. "On the other hand, maybe you can't." He found that amusing, I didn't think it was funny at all. He was right, he'd subdued me in seconds. I said it before I could stop myself. "I thought there was a bug or something. It felt like a nightmare." It came out a little whiney and pathetic, which didn't help anything.

I didn't get the sympathy or the hug I was hoping for. He rolled over onto the side of the bed I'd been sleeping on and covered his face with my damp pillow. The bed was shaking he was laughing so hard. I slapped his rock hard abs with my hand and all I did was hurt my own wrist. That made him laugh harder.

"You about done with all that?" I asked, annoyed that he could hardly catch his breath. He removed the pillow and when he saw my face, he was singing a different tune.

"Come here, baby. I'm really sorry. I promise I'm all done laughing." He moved to hug me, but I turned away. It was a game now. He had to be really sorry and mean it. He got up on his knees and crawled around me so he could see my face.

"Babe, I promise I am sorry I scared you. I was moving your hair out of your face because you looked uncomfortable."

I let him put his arms around me an unspoken acceptance of his apology. He moved my hair and started kissing my neck and shoulder. "I promise I will never, ever pretend to be a bug again." He started laughing quietly this time and I playfully tried to get away, but no chance. He wasn't letting go.

Suddenly, he stopped kissing me. For a minute, he was frozen and his breath on me made me quiver. I was disappointed that he was finished until I realized what was happening. We only had seconds to move. He heard it before I did. Slow, quiet creaking up the stairs. Mrs. Maggie. He pulled back from me without a sound. I pointed towards the closet.

"Get rid of her," he whispered before he silently moved into where Joy was asleep. I was praying he didn't startle her. Most certainly she would have made noise.

My door knob turned and the door opened slowly about half way. When she saw me sitting up in the middle of my disheveled bed, she pushed it the rest of the way open without the same finesse. "Sounds like you're wrestling a grizzly up here. What are you doing awake at this hour?"

I tried to sound like my nightmare was still fresh. "Sorry, I had a bad dream. I dreamed I was falling off the barn roof. I woke up sitting over here. I was trying to get my bearings when you came in."

Fortunately, the light was still off and the only illumination was dim, coming from the window behind me. If she'd seen my face and how flushed I was from across the room, no doubt she'd have called me on it.

"Well, you're okay. Can I get you some warm milk or something?"

Great, now I was feeling totally guilty. I lie to her and she offers me warm milk. "No, thanks. I'm really tired. I'm going to try to go back to sleep."

She stood there looking at me for a second. I could see her much more clearly than she could see me with the bright hall light surrounding her. She seemed doubtful, not that she distrusted me, but more like she was truly worried about my getting back to sleep.

"Really, I'm fine. I think I've been working too hard

lately. I'm glad I have tomorrow off."

She seemed to accept that. "If you're sure you're okay," she said, taking a step as if she was about to leave.

"I'm fine," I repeated, trying to get her to go. I stretched forward off the high bed to reached down and pick my blankets up off the floor and straighten them so she would have no doubt I was going back to sleep.

"Night then," she said, closing the door softly and heading back down the stairs.

I waited a few minutes before I went to the closet. I wanted to give her plenty of time to get back down to her own bed.

Ty was sitting across from Joy. "This girl can sleep through anything," he said, noting she hadn't even so much as flinched.

"Do you think we should wake her? I've been promising to let her see the painting for days now. I hated to let her down again. You must have read my mind from your bed, I was feeling bad about it too, but Mrs. Maggie's awake now."

He stood up and walked me backwards to my bed with his arms wrapped around me. "Let's give her about half an hour and then we'll go up." He nodded towards the Rapunzel room.

I was skeptical. "Are you sure? What if she wakes up again?"

"I think we'll be fine, as long as we don't wrestle anymore grizzlies up here."

He helped me put my covers back into place. We laid on top of the quilt, me on my stomach and him on his back. I sat up and moved closer to put my head on his chest. His T-shirt was soft and smelled like fabric softener and cologne. That's when he noticed it. He could see about a quarter of an inch of the end tab below my shorts.

"Babe, are you still wearing a Band-Aid on that scrape? You should let it get some air or it's never going to heal."

"I was just trying to keep it clean." I raised my head and strained to see it.

"Keep it clean on the roof and leave it open to the air when you can. Trust me, I've had enough road rash type injuries from football to know." Before I could stop him, he reached down, pulled up the bottom of my shorts, and ripped it off. I covered my mouth. "Sorry, sorry, I know that hurts, but the last thing you need in a weird spot like that is an infection. You would have to get Mrs. Maggie to put ointment on it and I know you don't want to have to explain who cleaned it and took care of it in the first place. He looked down at the precarious location suggestively, just below my panty line, just above the top of my leg. We both knew Mrs. Maggie would not consider him touching me anywhere near there to be "keeping a proper distance."

He sneaked down the stairs in his pajamas, his thick socks cushioning his steps against the wood. I didn't hear him the way I had Mrs. Maggie when she came up. I waited quietly by my door. I was nervous he'd get caught. I shuddered at the thought. What could he have said to get out of that situation? 'Sorry, I was sleepwalking?' Yeah right, no problem getting Bo and Mrs. Maggie to buy that one. It was only a few minutes before I saw the door handle turn. I stepped back, afraid it wasn't going to be him, realizing that was silly. If he'd been caught I would've heard it from up here. I'm sure with the raised voices his presence here would have caused, it would have been loud and clear.

"I could hear her snoring through her bedroom door," he said. "She's really going to town down there. Sounds like a battalion of lumberjacks working in the forest."

I scoffed in the back of my throat. I'd had this conversation with her a few times when I encountered her taking what she called "a short break" in the middle of the day. "Well, don't ever call her on it. She denies being a snorer. You wait here. I'll go get Joy." I left him standing in the threshold of my doorway still looking out.

Once I woke her and told her where we were going, she was so excited I had to remind her to keep quiet. The three of us sneaked around the square, following the banister around past my dad's bedroom door. *Good thing he isn't home.* I thought unlike Mrs. Maggie and Joy, any noise wakes him right up.

We stopped at the narrow door that led to the round staircase and up to the Rapunzel room. Joy recognized the route and could have led the way. "It's all the same shape and everything," she whispered. It's strange how different and how much the same this house can look."

Ty opened the tall skinny door slowly. Luckily, Bo uses it so much that the hinges opened silently. The stairs to the round room were another matter, narrow and creaking with every move we made. There wasn't even room to try and balance on one side or the other because the space was so tight. Every inch of the wood whined with age. It had been overlooked in the renovation. Leading the way with the same tiny flashlight he'd used the first night he came here, Ty started skipping them, taking three at a time. He turned and silently instructed us to do the same. Easier said than done, given our height difference. We stretched our much shorter legs to keep up. Thankfully there were not nearly as many stairs as there were to get from the bottom floor to my room. He opened the next door at the top of the staircase. It had dead bolt on the handle, but Bo always kept it unlocked.

Once we were inside, Ty closed the door so we could talk a little more freely. The room was set off the back of the house and not directly over any others. My mother used to say it was the best place for us to play and make noise because they couldn't really hear us downstairs. Now wasn't the time to test that theory. Joy and I stood motionless in the dark, leaning against the door, waiting for Ty to turn on the lights. He pointed the tiny shaft of light down at the floor, careful not to make even the slightest noise while he followed it to the opposite side of the room. I don't know how he could see anything. The tiny beam could not have been illuminating a circle larger than a quarter in front of him. Silently, he lowered the custom built rounded shade that covered the one window. I couldn't see my hand in front of my face once he walked away with the only source of light. Luckily, he'd been in this room so many times he had it memorized.

"Hang on, I'm almost there," he whispered in a way that made me feel safe, like the confidence in his low pitch when I almost fell off the ladder in the barn. I could tell by his voice he was getting closer to us and the light switch, wherever it was. I'd been feeling the part of the wall I could reach, trying to light his way back. No luck I couldn't find it, with good reason I realized later, it was on Joy's side of the door, I felt her lean into me when he stood just inches away from her to flip it on. She either didn't want to be in his way, or his sudden close proximity in the darkness had scared her. We all squinted into the sudden brightness that filled the room when he hit the switch, our eyes adjusting from the pitch black.

"It's over here," I whispered a little too loudly in my excitement as soon as I could see.

There was no mistaking Joy's excitement. Her blue eyes were wide and shining with anticipation. The picture was partially covered with a tarp. I moved the covering aside. She stood in front of it, mesmerized, and then moved to a sitting position without ever taking her eyes off her mother.

"It looks just like her," she said, reaching out but not quite touching the painting. She looked afraid, as if she might damage it. "It looks so old now. The painter showed us the frame before he actually put the picture in it. It was much shinier and sturdy looking."

Ty and I sat beside her, looking at her family. "We've been making fun of Caimee for years. The older she got, the more you two looked alike," Ty said, kidding us both. "We all thought it was creepy and strange, but I think this is even more strange—the three of us sitting here, looking at it *together*." Joy and I looked at each other taking in again just how identical we were and both nodded in agreement.

"I can see now how you knew me that day. It must have been strange for you to see my face and not know anything about me." I got up and dusted off my shorts, remembering my scrape was exposed and this was the only floor Mrs. Maggie didn't insist on keeping spotless as it was Bo's domain.

"Look at this," I said, reaching behind the big painting and pulling out her smaller charcoal drawing. "See the stray line? Now we understand it."

She was shocked. She'd never seen it finished. "I guess I finished...or will finish it when I get home."

The weird reality of her own words hit her and twisted her expression into one of disbelief.

"It's so odd. That's my ma's china cabinet and that blue blanket folded on the shelf belongs..." She shook her head, knowing that wasn't right. "I mean *belonged* to my brother, Nicholas."

Hearing the past tense from her own lips, in her own voice with regard to her brother brought sudden tears to her eyes. "I wonder if he will make it—you know, through the war." Her eyes shifted from her family's belongings to both of our faces.

Guiltily, I looked down at the floor, not wanting to meet Ty's scrutinizing gaze.

"What war? What makes you think there's a war?" I could feel his eyes on me, waiting for an explanation. He was asking her the question, but looking at me. He didn't really want an answer from her.

"I'm sorry. She read my eighth grade history book today. I forgot. I didn't mean for her to find it."

Ty stood up, serious now. "Babe, we agreed, the less she knows about the future the better. We're trying not to change things too much here. Who knows what it could affect in our time? Maybe we won't have this place. Maybe we could screw things up so bad we never meet. I can't live with that."

He was more frustrated than angry with me. His saying that we could make it so we never meet made me shudder. He realized that just the thought of it scared me and he was instantly sorry he'd even thought it, much less said it out loud and worried me. It was too much for either of us to think about losing each other just when we realized we had a future together. He stood up and walked over behind me, putting his arms around my shoulders and resting his chin on my head.

"I know, Ty. I really didn't mean for it to happen. I wanted to tell you earlier, but I got to thinking about what might happen. What if she goes back and everything changes here the second she goes through that wall? I started shaking again and he held me closer, pulling me into his chest, Joy didn't seem to notice. She was far away in the painting again, thinking about war.

When my momentary rush of panic passed, he let me go and went to sit in front of her, his eyes boring into hers. He was deadly serious, but kept his voice even and low, trying not to scare her. "Joy, you have to go back and act as if none of this ever happened. You have to go back and live your life exactly as you would have if you had never met us, or come here, or found out anything. If you don't, it could change all our lives forever."

She nodded with grave understanding. "I know and I will. Caimee told me Sheriff Garrick's log said I made it home, no mention of where I had been, so maybe nobody will even ask me."

Ty shook his head. "No, even if the Sheriff or people you know don't ask I'm sure your mother will, we have to come up with something other than the truth. They can't know. First of all, they won't believe you unless you show them and we can't have more people from your time coming here. That would really mess things up. We have to come up with a story they will trust."

The three of us looked back and forth at each other. No ideas, no good lie came to any of us. The silence put a look of dread in Joy's eyes. She was the one who was going to have to tell the story. She was the one who was going to have to pull this off and pretend to "unknow" what she had learned and we were absolutely no help. I squatted down beside her, not wanting to get any dirtier. "Don't worry, we'll think of something."

I looked at Ty. He caught my drift and my expression of "help me here, please." He reached across our little huddled circle and took her hand in comfort. For a split second I was jealous. I knew it was ridiculous, but she looked just like me, an easy replacement. "She's right, Joy. We'll have a plan before you go."

I don't know if it was his being older, or male, or the fact that the sheriff's log already gave us a clue as to how things would go, but Ty exuded confidence in his promise and it appeared to reassure her. She seemed satisfied that everything was going to be alright, but uneasy with him touching her. We both noticed how she managed to slip her hand away and fold her fingers together as if to protect the other hand. I moved my face away and mouthed the word "shy" to Ty. He nodded so slightly that only I would have noticed it. Neither of us said anything about it because it would have embarrassed her even more.

The last thing I wanted to show her was something Mrs. Maggie and I had debated about many times.

"Who made this?" I held up the unique artwork. It was four sticks put through each side of a tightly stretched piece of fabric that had the words "THE LORD IS MY SHEPHERD" on it. She walked over and took it from my hands. "I always said that the lady in the picture—your ma—made it, but Mrs. Maggie thinks it's older than that. She had it appraised. The guy at the auction said it was at least 200 years old."

She stopped tracing the raised words and looked at me, almost alarmed. "Auction?" She was upset and hurt thinking we had considered allowing it to go outside of the family.

"No! No! We never intended to sell it, just to see how old it was." Relief crossed her face and settled into her eyes. "Please keep these things. They belonged to Ma. She was fond of all of them. She made this when she was expecting Nicholas. The doctor said she had to rest and she did it to occupy herself while she was in bed. The fabric was old. It came from a quilt Ma had as a child. It was just a corner scrap that was accidentally ripped. Ma repaired the quilt and made this out of the piece she had to cut away. That might account for some confusion about its age. The thread was newer."

The memory seemed to disturb her in some way. It seemed a benign enough statement that shouldn't or wouldn't normally cause the look of pain on her face – or was it resentment? Ty noticed it too. She saw our questioning look.

"Pa didn't let her rest as long as she needed. Nicholas came early because she was working too hard. We're lucky to have him." She turned and looked at the canvas, the smiling little boy in her mother's arms.

I changed the subject. "I knew I was right. I knew your mom made it. It just seemed to belong with the rest of this stuff. Do me one favor when you get back, have her put the date on the back of one of these pieces of wood. Mrs. Maggie put so much stock in her friend's opinion, it will be great to finally prove her wrong."

Even Ty, who was so opposed to changing anything, agreed. "Joy, you have no idea how long Caimee and I have waited to prove her wrong about anything. She's always right, putting a date on it would be great. Besides, that shouldn't change anything too much here, except for once Mrs. Maggie will have to eat a little crow."

Joy looked at him confused, like why we would want her to eat a crow. We got it at the same time. "It's just a saying, it doesn't really mean anything," he said, taking the stitched picture from my hand and examining it himself. "What are their names?" he asked, nodding towards her parents in the painting. That would help too, if Caimee is going to put together a history of this place."

Joy walked over and pointed. "That's my Pa. His name is Brodie. His family is Scottish. She was catching Ty up on the information she'd already given me. "He looks so different in the painting than when I was growing up. Just before he went to Virginia—you know, when he got the house, he shaved his heavy beard and mustache. That's Ma. She's Italian. Her name is Norina. That's how Nicholas got his name. She wanted him to have her initials since Pa always made a big deal about his son carrying on the Cameron name. She wanted him to have some part of her name too. Pa was upset because she'd already named him, but when Nicholas came early, Pa wasn't home. Ma said he was working, but that was before he got his job with the railroad, so I'm not sure where he was. We still lived in Georgia at

317

the time. Ma never said what his job was."

Ty and I looked at each other. She didn't notice the knowing look on both of our faces because she was concentrating on the likeness of her mother. She'd been staring at her over and over from the moment we entered the room. I figured they were more than close, they were best friends. Ty wouldn't understand because I hadn't told him about that part of my relationship with my mother yet, but I knew Joy's pain. How many times had I talked to the picture of my mom, wishing for an answer. At least Joy got to go back to her mother, but I still felt sorry for both of them. From the sound of it, Brodie was doing everything but "working."

Given the poker game story, Ty and I were silently betting he was a chronic gambler—or worse, had a mistress somewhere. Joy's time had kept her so innocent and naïve, we were easily cynical and suspicious and I was willing to bet we were also right.

We uncovered the rest of the things we had under the tarp. Joy identified Nicholas's cradle, her mother's bible, her father's pocket watch, and the peach dress I'd seen her wearing the day we met. It was tattered and worn, not well-preserved at all until Mrs. Maggie had it vacuum-packed in a special plastic bag. It had stopped the decay enough for it to still be in one piece.

"How strange that anyone would want this," she said, holding it up and appraising its condition. "It's just an old dress."

"Joy, I promise that Ty and I will make sure we keep all or your...I mean *our* family's history, even the things that seem..." I looked at the dress again, searching for the right word. "Tattered."

She walked over and gently ran her hands along the top of Bo's desk. "This belonged to my Italian grandfather."

She turned and addressed Ty. She must have been getting more comfortable around him. "Your pa did such a great job making it new again. It would make Ma very happy to know someone still uses it."

"Caimee and I were four and five years old when he did that. I remember I wanted to help him finish it, but he said it was too old and importan. He let me watch, but not touch. He refinished each piece and put stronger nails in it to hold it together exactly like it was." She turned her attention back to the desk, thinking of something she didn't share, I assumed about her grandfather.

Ty looked at his watch. "Lucky it's Sunday and they're sleeping in. It's almost six. I have to go." With the shade drawn, we hadn't noticed the early morning rays of the sun. He quickly kissed me goodbye, almost forgetting Joy was in the room. It was a kiss on the cheek, but somehow still seemed like too much in front of her. He'd been so careful last time to give me a hug. He didn't look her in the face when he said, "I'll see you both later."

I was guessing he didn't want to scare her if we hadn't already. I mean, if holding her hand was too much, then him kissing me must have been way out of her comfort zone.

"You should get back down to your room before Mrs. Maggie comes up to make sure you're awake," he said and then slipped out. I didn't even hear him go down the stairs.

We sneaked out a few minutes after. Across the pasture, we saw that the light in his room was on. He hadn't been caught, but I wondered if we weren't pushing our luck. I was afraid that sooner or later Bo was going to hear him sneaking in and it was putting us all in danger to have Joy and me walking around side by side in front of the window. I closed the plantation shutters and got back into bed, all the while thinking of ways we could see each other without taking unnecessary risks.

"You're lucky to have such a nice boy," Joy said before she closed the closet door to get a few more hours of sleep herself. It was hard for her to say it. The compliment came out almost a whisper. No wonder she felt like she wasn't getting anywhere with the guy she liked, she could barely be around one that was just a friend. I felt sorry for her wishing I could help, but I had no real idea how to do that.

"I know," I answered her as humbly as possible, realizing how right she was, remembering the days I thought Ty would never be mine. I nestled down into my covers. I could still smell his cologne on my pillowcase. I closed my eyes, knowing the scent would make for excellent dreams.

Chapter 25
"The Plan"

Mrs. Maggie was sitting on the bench behind us and had to hit us both for slumping down and leaning our heads back like we were getting comfortable enough to go to sleep.

"I'm gonna have to find a different church if the two of you don't stop leaning all over each other and nodding off," she said on the drive home. "I suppose the girls will ask about it at lunch today."

Ty and I were sitting in the back seat in nearly the same position as we'd been in church—my head on his shoulder, both of our heads leaning back against the rounded headrest. Ty scoffed a bit before he answered.

"Tell them the baby kept us up all night." We both laughed, knowing how unrealistic that was after all the warnings we'd gotten, and the promise we had made to honor our upbringing and each other.

Bo gave him a disapproving look in the rearview mirror. "That's not even a little bit funny." Mrs. Maggie turned around and gave him a scathing glare. "You're worse than your father or Caleb ever was."

She looked over at Bo. "When you're done working him to death, save me a little of his strength 'cause I've got a few things I can think of that need doin' too."

We both sighed. "Great, more slave labor," he said, smiling at me, not quite picking his head up off his makeshift pillow. I knew what he meant—more time together. He picked up my hand and interlaced his fingers with mine. All the while, Bo kept a close eye on us. He shook his head like he was worried, but the little smile on his face said different...we had all heard the same sermon today and deep down he knew Ty got it, not just today but all the times he had talked to him outside of church. I was right about what I told Ty that first night, Bo knew he had raised a good man, despite the sarcasm.

~~~

I couldn't believe it. We were alone and were finally going to have a chance to do something I was hoping we'd have time for while Joy was here. Since I had seen the duck pond in her time, I wanted her to see it in mine. I wanted her to see what had been done with her favorite tree. Mrs. Maggie was having her usual Sunday lunch with her bingo buddies. Bo and Ty had gone to get Ty's phone.

"We have to hurry," I said, digging through my bathroom, looking for my big blue beach towel with a picture of a huge yellow sun smiling and wearing sunglasses in the middle of it. I couldn't get her into anything less than jeans and a T-shirt.

"I can't believe you're going out like that." She was looking at the same bikini I'd worn to teach her how to shave her legs. I checked in the mirror to make sure the bows of the ties around my hips were even. I rolled my eyes at her, reminding her she had to lighten up. "It's not like we're going to the mall or a water park, we're going to be out by the pond alone. I need to work on my tan. My arms have gotten so much sun while I've been up on the roof working on the barn that I'm starting to look like a real farmer."

She started to ask, but then thought better of it. I wasn't sure which part she wanted me to explain first—the concept of a mall, a farmer's tan, or a water park. I didn't have time to put any of the concepts into plain words.

"Here it is," I said, grabbing my towel from the cabinet under the sink. "Let's go."

We ran down the stairs but I paused in the front doorway and looked around before we took off across the yard and the pasture, just to make sure nobody was around. The coast was clear.

"Go quick," I said, almost pushing her outside onto the porch. She had carved out her own path to the pond in her time and I had no idea where she was going. This time she was the one who was lost. She went left up toward the iron gate and I went right toward the pasture. We were a good fifty paces apart before I noticed she wasn't following me. "This way," I said, trying to whisper, but it came out loud. I felt kind of stupid for trying to be quiet. Nobody else was here. She stopped and looked a little scared at the distance between us, like she could get lost and never find her way back. Things here must have looked as foreign to her as they had to me when I was surrounded by apple trees.

It didn't take us long to run together once we were going in the same direction. She spun around like I had seen "Alice in Wonderland" do in a cartoon once. "Wow! It looks like another place entirely." I didn't say anything right away. She seemed overwhelmed and I wanted her to take it all in. She stopped spinning and focused on the gazebo. "I told you, remember? It's your favorite old cottonwood. Grandpa Nathan had the wood treated so it wouldn't age anymore and then he put this here instead. He loved it too and wanted to remember. The dock is the same, except Bo and Ty built it out of the scraps left over from the gazebo."

"It's beautiful," she said, walking up into it and looking around. I am so glad it is still here even if it is different now, there was something special about that tree."

I walked over and up the two steps into the gazebo and stood next to her. "I have a feeling it's going to look brand new again soon. I think re-staining it is on Mrs. Maggie's list. I'm sure Ty and I will get around to it in the fall, the way things are going." She could tell I was getting a little sour on the whole "work Caimee to death" thing. She started to comment but instinctively knew there was nothing she could say that would make me feel any better.

"Come on, we have to hide you before we get caught, being out in the open like this makes me nervous, I hate to take a chance after we have gotten away with it for so long." I sat her under the weeping willow my dad had planted years ago. It was so big now its summer branches were thick and reached to the ground. She was all but invisible. I found a sunny spot just outside of its shade, kicked off my flip flops and spread my towel out. She gasped when I turned onto my stomach, reached back, and untied my bikini strap.

"Nobody's around for miles. I don't want a tan line." I turned my head sideways so I could look at her and we could talk. She was shaking her head. "It's just so different here some things are so nice and others seem so odd. I miss home so much. I imagine everyday what my mother must be going through."

I thought for a second how great it would be if Joy's mom, Norina, could have just a little bit of what my mom has right now, not forever like mine, but just for a little while—long enough for us to get Joy home...no ability to remember. If she could just sleep through the worry and fear, she must be feeling the way my mom does. I thought about the blank stare on Mom's face. It is a blessing that she has no idea what she's missing out on in life. If she knew how I'd grown and changed, how we'd all changed over the years, I know it would make her sad. That's when it hit me. I started to sit up, but remembered in the nick of time my suit was untied. That would have really freaked her out.

"I've got it. I know what we can do when you get home. It will be noon when you come up, so you have to stay hidden until dark."

She instantly objected. "Why? That leaves Ma wondering for another whole day."

My plan was forming more clearly now. Ty would be so proud. "Just a few hours until the sun goes down. You'll come staggering out of the woods. Wait! Are there woods close to the house, I didn't notice."

She nodded. "Yes, behind the house is mostly woods. You didn't see that part."

I was getting excited now that I had it all worked out. "We'll rip your dress a little and get it really dirty." She looked very upset at the idea of that and started to protest.

"Just wait," I said, holding up my finger, trying not to expose myself. "This will work. Sometime after dark, you sneak around to the back of the house and come out of the woods. You tell them that you got lost and you remember falling and hitting your head on a rock."

The similarities to my mom's accident turned my stomach. I had to swallow back the hurt before I could go on, but it worked. Nobody expected Mom to wake up and remember anything...ever. Joy could use the same excuse.

"Then you say that you can't remember anything after that. Tell them you're not even sure how you found your way home. Keep it simple like what your mom tells the people in town about how your Pa got the house. As long as you tell the same story over and over, after a while people will stop asking." She lit up when I compared her lie to her mother's; after all, she'd seen that theory work.

"I can do that, I really can. I think that might work." Relief flooded her face. She leaned down, mimicking my position and rolled on her stomach under the shade of the tree. She let out a deep sigh as if a weight had been lifted. She thought about it for a few minutes in silence "I think it's a great idea. I know it will work. If I say I can't remember, how can they keep asking me where I was?"

We were both silent now, lost in thought, picturing how things would go in her time, the day she just stumbled out of the woods. Before I knew it, we were both asleep.

Chapter 26
"Bribes"

It was glorious. My mind fluctuated somewhere between the first night Ty came to my room and the summer breeze blowing across my back and weaving itself through my hair. The sun wasn't too hot, appearing and disappearing behind small clouds that provided intermittent relief from its warm rays and the air was cool enough to let me lie there wandering in and out of my fantasy world. It was pure peace and relaxation, somewhere between deep sleep and sweet dreams. Joy seemed to be in the same state, only deeper. On the edge of my thoughts I could hear her deep, even breathing. In my subconscious I was hoping she was somewhere peaceful with her mother.

I'm not sure how long I'd been lying there. I didn't even hear his footsteps.

"Don't worry, I'm not a bug, or a lizard, or a frog," he said, chuckling low and whispering into my ear. When I opened my eyes, I realized he was doing it so as not to wake Joy. Forgetting that my bikini top was untied, I almost sat up. I was excited to tell him about the plan I had devised to help Joy when she got home. He saw me bend my arms to push up and face him, but he gently put his hand in the middle of my bare back and stopped me. He kissed my back up and down my spine and then moved my hair and started on the back of my neck, making me shiver despite the heat.

"I think you want me to do this before you do that," he said, picking up the ties to my top and tying them in a bow. I blushed deep scarlet. He laughed in a low voice. "Like I said, sweet girl, you've got nothing to be embarrassed about in this department. He waved his hand over the entire length of my body referring to my shape.

When he was done, I rolled over and propped myself up on my elbows. I wasn't expecting him to take my picture with his new phone. He had a Styrofoam box in the other hand. I brought lunch." He nodded towards Joy. "I thought she'd be upstairs, so I made an excuse to bring it up and give it to you. This was my next guess. I had to order something without meat so dad wouldn't ask. I hope she doesn't mind. Mrs. Maggie is home too. She seems a little put out. She didn't say, but I'm guessing the whole church and probably the whole bingo league knows we're dating now. I'm also guessing her Mississippi mud pie was not the talk of the luncheon" I reached up so he could help me stand up.

"She'll get over it. Her desserts have been the star of the show long enough."

I looked over at Joy. "I hate to wake her, but she's going to have to stay out here 'til we can sneak her in after dark, since everybody is home. Any ideas if she doesn't feel comfortable with that?" He shrugged, sweeping a few stray strands of my hair away from my face that were blowing in the light breeze. "I guess we could come up with something, but I think she will be fine here."

"I'll bring her with me when I come up tonight." He looked self-conscious, like presuming we had a two a.m. date every night might not be okay with me.

I held his beautiful face in my hands. "I can't wait," I said. My words wiped that uncertain look off his face. Things kept going slowly from there...we were walking on the edge of a very dangerous cliff.

We didn't realize Joy was watching. He started kissing me and everywhere his hands touched was skin—a new sensation for both of us because I was usually wearing pajamas or my regular clothes. Without any conscious decision to do so, we sat down facing one another on my towel. The box of food was quickly forgotten.

He hugged me tight to him, my hands in his hair, his hands touching my face, my back, my legs, but he wasn't being harsh or groping me, he was soft and kind, which made it harder for me to let go. It was more my fault than his. I leaned closer into him, only this time there was no saddle between us and I was able to slide myself against him so he could put his arms around me.

"I missed you," he said, laughing at himself. "I know it's only been a few hours, but I did."

"I missed you too." I took his hands locked around my mid-section and interlaced my fingers with his. This was so different than any experience we'd had before and as soon as his hands were in mine, I kissed him again.

I'm not sure how long she'd been standing there. Ty noticed her first.

"Hey Joy." His voice had an "oh no" tone.

She was standing behind me. I was so mortified that I turned my face and buried it in his chest, hiding my blushing in his shirt.

He wasn't fazed or ashamed—or maybe he was covering it better than I was. I knew him too well to know he wouldn't be a caught off guard. I could tell by the way his demeanor changed instantly. It wasn't like we were out there making babies, cuddling on a towel, but in this outfit I knew I was on the verge of going past my own limits, so I was definitely way...way past hers. My skin still tingled from his touch. He kept his voice even and refocused her attention. I think he had to because her obvious discomfort was making him self-conscious too. I was sure there were a million questions in her eyes, but he simply didn't address it—like it was nobody's business but ours.

"I brought you some food, Joy. Everyone is home, so you'll have to stay hidden out here for a while if that's alright with you."

She was either too shocked or intimidated to say anything. I gathered my courage and finally met her stare. Ty hadn't let go, so I was still in his arms. I was grateful, I needed the support. I could tell immediately that she had retreated into her shell—shy Joy was clearly back.

I also saw something new. It was on her face, in her eyes and the way she stood and inched away from us—as much as she wanted to be with this Kade guy, men scared her; not just because she was shy like I thought, but there was something deeper. It was like puzzle pieces fitting into place in her expression, deep in her eyes. There was something else there—a story she hadn't told me yet. I knew it had to be her father; a fear that affected her so profoundly had to come from somewhere close. What I knew about her relationship with him was just the tip of the iceberg so to speak...that had to be it, but I hoped I was wrong.

Ty reached behind himself and grabbed the box. It's bread and pasta with Alfredo sauce."

Great, something else she didn't understand. "Like noodles." I explained, but she still didn't seem to get that clarification either. I took the box from his hand. She was suddenly looking at Ty like a man and that intimidated her. She didn't reach for the food until I took it, scooted over to the far end of the big towel away from Ty and handed it to her myself. He looked at me confused, unsure why she looked frightened and perplexed, the last thing he would want is for her to be frightened of him. I gave him a look and shook my head a little, like 'Don't ask, I'll break it down for you later.' As it turned out, I didn't have to—he was already trying to put it together. It was dawning on him slowly. I could see the wheels turning in his head.

We stood up together and I picked up the beach towel. "Ty will come and get you after the sun goes down." Before we realized that she'd have to stay out here 'til dark, I had intended to wrap myself in my towel for the walk home, but I felt bad leaving her here with nothing to sit on. I moved the towel to the shade and cover of the tree. She was absent-mindedly moving like a wooden doll, but nodded in agreement. I was surprised when she spoke. It looked like it took all her courage to say anything at all.

"It's alright with me. I want to stay out here. It reminds me so much of my time and I'd rather stay awhile in the fresh air and sunshine, even sleep under the stars than spend time in that little room today. It gets stuffy in there and it's so nice today."

I instantly felt guilty. I know. I'm sorry. I'm glad this place is special to you and you're used to spending time here. The only other thought I had was to put you in Ty's room, it would be easier to sneak you in there since Bo is usually at the main house." She immediately turned red and shook her head no, I knew it was pushing her boundaries way past the limits to even suggest she be in a boy's room, especially after what she'd just seen. "I'm fine here, really. I love this pond and I don't mind staying. I didn't argue even thought I knew she would be here a while.

"I think you'll like this. It's one of my favorite things to eat. It's Italian food." I opened the box to make sure there was a fork in it. She seemed okay with it after I said it was Italian, maybe she imagined it was something her mother would eat. Ty stood back, finally sensing that he more than...we...had scared her. She'd likely never seen anything like it—no TV, no movies, and I'm sure no live making out show amongst the 1840 kids in Culpeper. We hadn't done anything obscene or wrong according to our time, but clearly we'd crossed some lines in hers and if I was being honest, in ours too. I was ashamed. I knew better. Ty took my hand to help balance me as I put my flip-flops back on and we started to go.

"Oh wait! I almost forgot." He pulled a bottle of water out of his over-sized cargo pocket. "I snagged this from the kitchen when I didn't find y'all upstairs."

Once again I had to take the bottle and walk it over to her. I sat on the other end of the towel trying to assess how much damage we had done and how she saw me now. I felt like I'd gone from being the big sister that was to be admired to someone she was seeing very differently. I tried to cover, even though I didn't really believe it, so the effort was half-hearted. "It's okay, Joy.

We can talk about it later. It's normal for our time, I promise." Okay, maybe not "normal" for Ty to be caught making out with me while I was wearing a bikini. If it had been Mrs. Maggie who had walked up or perish the thought—one of our fathers, Ty would be in a bad way right now and I'd be locked up somewhere wondering where Dad was going to hide his body, but I couldn't exactly tell her that, so I just went with "it's normal." That word seemed to comfort her the most.

She nodded again, keeping her silence. I wasn't sure if it was because she was offended or simply without words. She took the water, opened the box, and started to eat. I took the bottle of water back, opened the top, and showed her how to use it, realizing she might sit here and go thirsty looking at it, not being able to figure out how to actually drink it. I was over-compensating, of course. She would know how to drink it because we'd already been over it. I was lingering, hoping she would look at me and smile. For the first time since she arrived, our roles were reversed. I wanted her approval and acceptance—or maybe it was forgiveness I was looking for. Either way I hoped the whole thing would just blow over, but right now no amount of making light of it was working. I decided I best take Ty and give her some space and alone time.

"Stay here. Promise."

"Promise." That's all I could get her to say before we left.

We held hands all the way back, discussing how guilty we felt.

"I think she has some deep-seated fear of men, although there's one boy back in her time—Kade. She seems to like him a lot, but I don't think she's done anything about it yet. He's the sheriff's son."

Ty thought for a minute, finally realizing what I'd seen by the willow tree. "Well, just think about it, look at Brodie. He doesn't seem to be a real stand-up guy where her mom is concerned. Maybe she's afraid of ending up like Norina, married to a gambler and if you ask me, a real good candidate to be a cheater as much as he was gone while they were expecting her brother."

I stopped walking and pulled on his hand 'til he made the two steps back to where I was standing. "Did I tell you today, how lucky I am?" I really meant it. There was no part of a man like Brodie Cameron, in Ty.

"You have no idea how many times I thought that about you the night we went riding on Lindie." I caught his drift, no part of a woman like his mom in me. He was pulling me forward. "Come on, we gotta get back. With you dressed like that, Mrs. Maggie will be backtracking the minutes I've been gone."

"Yeah, speaking of which you can't keep that picture on your phone. What if your dad sees it—or worse, some guy at school takes it out of your football locker while you're at practice?"

He smiled at my assumption. "How did you know I was going out for the team?"

Because I know you...and you know I'll be in the front row for every game."

"Well, then you should also know me well enough to know I have already put a password on this phone. No worries, sweetie. It's just for me and I promise it's just of your face. I'll show you later, but right now we have to hurry. But I do need to say that I am sorry while we are still alone. I was way out of line back there and you don't even have to tell me it was awkward for you to face

Joy. I could see it all over your face and you're blushing. I tried to play it off to make you feel better, but I love you too much...." He looked down and shifted his weight, folding his arms across his chest. "I respect you too much to put you in any light where anyone would question your character and I'm sorry. It won't happen again." I started to protest and take the blame, but he stopped me. "I know what you're thinking and don't even say it, okay? It was my fault, so just let me take the responsibility on this one. I know what my father and yours expect of me." He got quiet, like the next part was harder to say. "I know what God expects of me and I'm going to live up to that, I promise." I knew that look. No matter what I said, it wouldn't change his mind so I just took his hand and headed home.

Normally I would have trotted up the porch steps and changed clothes immediately, but I couldn't get to them given the unexpected crowd gathered in front of the house. Dad never said anything about me walking around in my bathing suit as long as it was just family there and Ty was usually working in the barn, so it just never came up; but these people were not family or friends. I didn't recognize either vehicle.

Mrs. Maggie was standing next to Bo. They looked as confused as Ty and I did as we approached. There were two pickup trucks parked one behind the other, blocking the entrance to the house. One was a new, shiny, charcoal black, double-cab Chevy. The other was dull green, a much older model. They'd just driven up because the dust hadn't settled. Bo didn't say anything but patiently waited for them to state their business prepared to shake their hands in welcome. I stayed a foot behind Ty wanting to disappear. I couldn't go around as they had literally made a parking lot in front of the porch steps and the trucks were too close together for me to walk between them. Mrs. Maggie was looking at how close they had parked and was not happy about her bushes being crushed. It was almost intentionally rude and obtrusive. There was plenty of room in the driveway for them to have moved over at least ten feet.

By the time the second man was just turning off his engine, the one driving the black truck had already gotten out and closed the driver's door behind himself and been standing there for a few seconds, I was betting it was in the first one he had noticed me. He was short, but muscular, with a thick build, greasy-looking blond hair and blue eyes that didn't stop roaming over my body for even one moment. In his lustful preoccupation with me, he'd missed Bo's extended hand. The second man trotted up fast so as to not be as uncouth as his friend and accepted Bo's gentlemanly greeting. Noticing the first man's expression, Ty shifted slightly to his right, an unsuccessful attempt to hide me. His smile made me feel like I was being molested. I noticed Ty's jaw flex and he crossed his arms in front of himself another attempt to block the looks. The second man was more discreet, but followed his friend's gaze. He was cleaner, clean-shaven, also blond, but taller and lean. He immediately started spitting tobacco into the center of the tight circle. Mrs. Maggie gave him a dirty look and stepped back. Neither man took their eyes off me when the second man started to explain why they were here. Mrs. Maggie looked mad. Bo was being careful not to show any emotion, but I knew him well enough to know whatever Ty was about to say in my defense, he would back him up. Their leering was just plain gross.

The tall one only looked away from what I hoped was my face to spit again and take a small step toward Bo, but he didn't even attempt to hide that he wasn't done looking at me yet. He leaned to the side to look around Ty as he took a folded piece of paper out of his top pocket. "Lookin' for Titus Christopher Bohannon," he said. He was clearly in charge. The other one didn't move, just stood there with a smirk on his face. He ever-so-slightly made a kissing gesture at me, pursing his lips and then licking them. Mrs. Maggie shoved her hands deep in her apron pockets, I'm sure to keep from smacking him. Bo moved in closer to Ty, putting his shoulder in front of him, in part to help block their view and in part a silent warning to keep Ty from doing anything. It was an "I will handle this" gesture. I thought I saw Ty nod slightly.

It all happened in seconds, before Ty could identify himself, but before he did so he took off his T-shirt. Never taking his eyes off the men, he flexed his arm back and handed his shirt to me. Gratefully, I put it on. It came almost to my knees. Mrs. Maggie smiled. I knew she was thinking we'd just avoided a brawl right here in the yard. Together or not, Ty respected me and wouldn't allow the behavior of either of these men to continue, no matter how he had to stop it. Thankfully, all he needed to do this time was give up his shirt.

Bo looked prouder than a peacock. Ty hadn't needed him to step in and stop another fight. He just took care of it as any Southern gentleman would have— with dignity. Bo stepped aside, giving Ty the unspoken go ahead to handle it, but he never left his side. "That's me," Ty said, stepping forward now that I was covered, which didn't seem to deter the short one whose intense glare wouldn't let me look away until Ty stepped closer.

"Got a delivery for you here," he said. He started focusing on his reason for interrupting our Sunday. He handed Ty a large envelope with the word "TITLE" written on it in black, now that they were almost side by side I could see even the tall one was smaller than Ty. "Sorry, it has some miles on it, but the woman who purchased it insisted that it be delivered as soon as possible, so we had to bring it here all the way from Alabama; otherwise, it's showroom new. We tried to get here yesterday, but hit some bad weather. No hail or anything. The paint doesn't even have a scratch. She'd have bought one from a local dealer instead of having this one driven all the way here, but this color with the dark interior was custom built and they didn't have one readily available at your local Chevy dealer."

Ty opened the envelope and read its contents. I caught a glimpse of the handwritten note inside. All I could read was "Love, Mom" at the bottom, written in big sweeping letters—the same handwriting I had seen in our mailbox a hundred times on envelopes addressed to Bo with Ty's report cards inside them. Ty put the note in his other hand and inspected the other paper. It had some kind of seal on it and boxes with typed information in each one. He scoffed and handed all of it to Bo.

"Take it back," he said to the tall one. "Tell her I refused delivery."

The short one finally had a reason to engage in the conversation and stop trying to see through the T-shirt Ty had given me. "Can't take it back, boy. Truck's bought and paid for—already paid cash up front for delivery too." Mrs. Maggie put together what was going on before Bo handed her the papers.

"He said he doesn't want it." She was stern and serious, and a bit incredulous. Being a mother herself, she could not believe Ty's mother would stoop so low as to try and bribe him with a new truck into coming back to Alabama. The tall one agreed with his buddy. "It's all registered in your name. Title is even signed over to you. Woman who bought it doesn't own it, it's yours. I can't take a truck that belongs to you and just give it to someone else now can I? 'Specially after she paid my boss at the dealership extra for us to drive it down here."

The short one tossed Ty the keys. "Looks like you got yourself a truck, kid."

Ty caught them. "I'm not a kid and I don't want the truck." Given what he looked like without a shirt on with his height, broad shoulders, clearly defined abs and angled waist, nobody there was about to disagree.

"Nothing I can do about it. Come on, Kyle, let's go." He walked back to the truck he had driven up, but Kyle, the short one, was not quite ready to leave. He stopped to light a cigarette before he followed. He tilted his head back and blew the rancid-smelling smoke in the air, taking one last opportunity to look at me like I was a juicy burger or something. "Nice to meet you...I mean all of you," he said, finally turning to follow his partner. I knew that was only for my benefit and that was when Bo grabbed Ty's forearm. Even though he made no move toward either one of the strangers, he knew I wouldn't have wanted him to. Ty yanked his arm away from Bo as soon as the two men were out of sight. I now saw what he meant about taking his frustrations with his mom out on Bo.

Ty was angry. "So now she thinks she can buy me?" He took his mother's note from Bo. His tone was full of disdain, saturated with anger. "Here you go, honey. This is so you can come back home. Hope to see you soon, LOVE, MOM." He took the envelope and the keys and pushed it into his father's chest. "Mary Ellen Davis is a lot of things, but a mom isn't one of them," he said. Ty's mother was using her maiden name, now that she and Bo were divorced. I hadn't realized that. It just never came up and until this summer he really didn't say too much about her while he was here.

Now that the space had been cleared in front of the house, Ty went inside. I started to follow him, but looked at Bo first in case he wanted to talk to Ty before I did. "Go on," he said. "I'll put this thing somewhere else for now. Mrs. Maggie just stood there with a disgusted look on her face. I'm sure whatever she said to Bo was not flattering to Mary Ellen at all.

I was expecting to find Ty in the kitchen, so I walked right past him. He was sitting in the small living room just to the right of the foyer. He didn't say anything when I went by. When I couldn't find him, I turned around and went back to the front. He looked like he needed a minute to himself, so I turn to go and let him be.

"Brewster's?" he said. He forced a smile for me.

I took off his T-shirt and threw it at him. "Gimme five," I said, "I need to change."

I tried to hurry before Mrs. Maggie could come in. I knew she'd mean well, but she'd also try to give him some teacherly/motherly advice to try and make him feel better. I grabbed my old faded blue jeans with the holes in the knees, put my flip flops back on, and pulled on a powder blue sweater that Grammie had crocheted for me. It was like hers with quarter-sized holes between each knot, so I left my bikini top on underneath, not wanting to waste time finding the right-color tank top. I took a few minutes to fix my hair and put on some make up. I was breathless from running down the stairs.

"Sorry that took so long."

He adjusted the cap on his head, stood up, and walked towards me. "As always, totally worth the wait." He kissed the top of my head and lingered there, I put my fingers through his belt loops. "I love you so much." He nodded moved to my face and kissed my forehead. "I know." he said, I love you too, always have, always will, please tell me you already knew that no matter what I am not leaving you, it doesn't matter what she, or anybody else, including another girl does to try and get me to, you are my family, the only one I ever want." I just looked up at him and nodded. "I know I need reassurance sometimes, but that is just because I have seen how loving someone can turn into tragedy, I guess I need to hear promises of forever because somewhere deep inside I am afraid it will be cut short, not because I doubt your feelings for me." The look on his face said he finally understood. "So it isn't because I waited too long." I kissed him again, "With you there was never a time that was "too long" I would have waited forever." He hugged me close one hand around my waist the other turning my head sideways against his chest, his fingers in my hair and stroking my face, I could hear his low steady heartbeat. "Just promise me something okay? When we have a daughter, you won't even bring up naming her after my mother." There was a little bit of sarcasm and a whole lot of serious behind his words. "No way," I promised. When he turned away from me to walk out the door I was smiling, blushing and about to burst inside. I had imagined our children a million times, thought of their names and even wondered how many we would have.....maybe he hadn't done all that, but he *had* thought about it.

Bo and Mrs. Maggie stopped talking as soon as we walked out onto the porch—no doubt a conversation they thought we wouldn't pick up on. We both knew they were talking about Mary Ellen's bribe. Bo had moved it, but I didn't take the time to look and see where.

"Can I have the keys to the truck?" He wasn't angry anymore, just like always we had leaned on each other this time it was my turn to comfort him, like he had done for me a thousand times. It felt good to know that I could be his rock too, all he wanted....needed was me in his arms for the storm to pass, my strong steady Ty could get through anything without me but today I knew, he didn't want to, he wanted me.

Bo didn't even bother to ask which truck. He tossed him the ones I'd seen a thousand times, still on a key chain with a small plastic horse on it that my mother found years ago.

"We're going to Brewster's."

I waited for Mrs. Maggie to tell us not to eat too much and spoil our dinner, but she didn't say a word.

~~~

We pulled into the overcrowded parking lot. It looked like the high school lot. I recognized almost every car, of course. It was a hot day in July. I should have known every kid in town with a way to get here would be here, I was just hoping maybe we would catch a break since it was between lunch and dinner. It was even more populated than the last time we'd come. We had one of our "comfortable silence" car rides over. No need to rehash the obvious. I knew how he was feeling, he knew I loved him and would be here to listen anytime he was ready to talk about it some more, or would be okay with it if we just let it drop. I slid over in the seat and rode pressed close to him. Except when he had to shift gears, his arm was around me.

"You wanna go somewhere else?" he asked on his second pass around looking for a place to park. "Whatever you want, I don't care, but I know you want a hotdog."

He smiled a genuine smile that lit up his eyes. "You know me too well, sweet girl." Just then, he found an empty space. When we got inside I noticed it wasn't just any group of kids from school that was here it was pretty much all of the football team, if I hadn't known better I would have thought we were in the locker room after a game.

Oddly enough, the only table open was the one that seated two, where we'd sat the last time. The waitresses were running around so we settled in and expected to wait a few minutes.

"I do have some good news for you," I said, putting my hand on the top of his menu and lowering it so I could see his face. "I figured out a story for Joy for when she gets back."

I quickly explained the whole head injury amnesia plan to him quietly, in case anyone was eavesdropping.

"Not bad, baby, not bad at all. We just have to ruin her clothes so people will believe she's actually been living outdoors, wandering around.

"I know she really didn't like that part, but what are you gonna do, it has to be that way."

He nodded in agreement. "I'm sure we can trash it up just enough to be believable."

I could see the wheels turning in his head. I knew he'd come up with something.

We were almost home free. We had our food and drinks when in walked April, Jenna, Ericka, and a guy I hadn't seen all summer—Steven Goodwin. Ty had his back to the door so I saw them first. When I sighed, he turned to see what had put such an expression of dismay on my face.

"Great. Eat faster."

"I don't think it will help," I said just as Steven scraped a chair across the floor, flipped it around backwards and straddled it at our much-too-small-for-three table.

No greeting, no hey, glad to see you, he just launched right into whatever stupid thing he was going to say. April was standing behind him while the twins had gone to order.

"You know what the great thing about summer school is, Ty?" he asked, not waiting for a response. We both looked at him, anticipating whatever bomb it was he was about to drop, given the conceited look on his face. He wasn't bad looking, but he was no Ty. I guess April had decided to opt for second place, but factor in his personality and it was more like tenth. He was tall, but a few inches shorter than Ty, not nearly as well built, hazel eyes and a cute face when he didn't have the mean expression he was wearing now. We sat in silence and let him continue as neither one of us cared to respond.

"Well, I figured you might not know so I'm going to let you in on a little secret. See, when your mom works at the school..." He tilted his head back towards April, "...and she's not in her office all day because she's subbing to teach the morons who failed math, her computer is left unattended. I'll bet you didn't know that all kinds of things get emailed to her about...oh say, new transfers—you know, kids coming here from other schools?"

We'd figured out exactly where this was going, but not quite how far he was going to run with it. I saw Ty's knuckles whiten as he gripped the edges of the table. Steven didn't turn. Keeping his eyes on us, he reached over his shoulder and April handed him a small stack of stapled papers. He cleared his throat and started to read like we were in a formal court hearing or something. "Titus Christopher Bohannon." That was the second time I'd heard his full name today. "Grade point average, three point four...not bad!" The comment was so artificial and condescending I almost hit him myself to save Ty the trouble. "Excellent student to have in class, participates well, natural leader." Your teachers really did like you there—except one. This is the part that gets really interesting," he said, flipping to the back page. "Titus will be transferring out at the request of another student's parents for fighting. His family situation in regards to his mother having an inappropriate and open relationship with a married faculty member, in addition to his aggressive behavior, has become a distraction. Although he has played varsity football in the position of quarterback since he was a freshman and has led his team to the state championship two years running, at this time our coach and staff feel it is in the best interests of all parties that he be removed from the team to reduce the disturbance that both his and his mother's actions have caused amongst the players, as many of them have taken sides in this issue, some of them opposing the coach's decision to have him removed."

Steven folded all the papers back together and scraped them under Ty's chin. "It looks like you've been a bad boy, not to mention your mom. So, let me fill you in on how this is going to go. Our first string quarterback finally graduated last year and I've been up for that slot since I was a sophomore. You ain't taking my spot, got it? You even so much as show up for tryouts or come near *my* field, there won't be enough of you left to play a game of touch with your family in the backyard, much less a real game with a real team. This is my senior year too and I don't have any problem putting you in the hospital to keep you off my team. I haven't waited this long to be starting quarterback, been on this team for three years to have some outsider come and think he's going to take what is mine. You show up at tryouts and this goes public."

April stood behind him with a self-satisfied grin on her face. This wasn't about Ty for her, it was about getting back at me.

Ty unlocked his grip on the table and I held my breath. *Please don't hit him! Please don't hit him!* I said to myself over and over, but Ty was calm, which shouldn't have surprised me. He'd never been a fighter until that one time.

"You can print a thousand copies of that and hand it out to every kid who walks through the doors on the first day of school. Pass it out to the teachers and tack it up on every telephone pole in town if you want to. Publish it in the paper if you feel the need, but save your energy, because when you're done with all that, you're gonna need your strength to bring me water while I'm out playing and you're warming the bench."

Steven didn't say a word. The look on his face was plenty—somewhere between murderous hate and disbelief. April gave me a similar look. She took the papers back from Steven and stepped out of the way when she saw Ty get up. She was expecting—no, she was *anticipating* a fight. They'd planned for it. No wonder the rest of the team was here. They knew Steven had some gossip he wanted to share, no doubt to get them all on his side to keep Ty off the team. He'd spread the word about everybody meeting at Brewster's. Our showing up was just a lucky coincidence for them. I was hoping after they saw what a jerk Steven was that at least some of them wouldn't want to be involved.

Ty gathered our trash on his tray and walked over to the trash can and threw it away. Steven pushed him as soon as his back was turned. *What a coward.* He didn't see the two cops on break having dinner in the corner. They both stood at the same time, catching his eye. He put his hands up, signaling it was over and walked out, pushing the swinging door with unnecessary force. The cops looked at Ty as if to ask if he wanted to press charges. Ty waved, shook his head "no" and kept walking before there was more trouble. The cops sat back down, but watched us walk out, making sure there wasn't going to be a fight in the parking lot.

April had managed to slip out of the way, but that

didn't stop her from noticing the tie of my bathing suit top out from beneath the wide scoop neck of my shirt. If I hadn't put my hair up to eat my messy cheese fries, she never would have seen it. I was following Ty, trying to be discreet, but no such luck. She pulled the string and untied it. I felt my bathing suit falling underneath the wide weave of my sweater. Laughter erupted from all the guys around me, a couple of them clapped and a few more whistled. It didn't matter that I'd caught my strings before anything showed; it was the gesture that made her friends think she was that much cooler and that much more a force to be reckoned with. I grabbed the neck of my shirt from the outside holding the strings up though the thin yarn.

I was holding the strings together behind my neck with my other hand, unable to tie them because my hair was tangled and in the way. I pushed the door open with my hip, glad that Ty hadn't seen the final insult because there would have been a fight if he had. He saw me coming when he turned to make sure I was behind him, I was holding myself together and understanding crossed his face. He was angry. The two cops were still eating. Ty shot them a look through the big window and held his hands out, palms up, like "don't you see this?" He hadn't wanted their help for himself, but when it came to me, he felt very differently. He walked around, opened my door, and helped me in. Since I was using both of my hands to hold my clothes together, I had to scoot in sideways on my hip. The motion tugged at the scrape on my backside and I grimaced, feeling the newly healed flesh pull open again against the denim of my jeans. I turned my back to him once we were both inside the truck. I kept hold of the bikini top strings with my left hand, scared to move my right from my collar as the top had slid down another couple of inches in the front as a result of my efforts to get into the truck. Ty moved my hair out of the way, took the strings from my shaking fingers, and tied them himself. "I am sorry sweetie, I should have let you go in front of me, I would have stopped it, I should have seen it coming" "It wasn't your fault, and if you had stopped it Steven would have won, no way would they let you tryout if you had gotten into it with all those players in there." "I don't care about that. You don't need to be in the middle of this, I need to handle it." I turned when he finished tying the strings. "You did handle it babe, you let that idiot walk out of there in one piece which is more than I would have done if I was you."

"Two bribes in one day and both stamped with my stupid mom's name all over them."

"I can't wait to see you pummel that idiot on the field." The thought of it brought a smile to his face.

"I might even "accidentally" overthrow and hit Blondie in the back of the head while she's standing on the cheer line." The thought of that made me smile even bigger.

"Do you really think you can beat him and take over the quarterback spot?"

He looked at me almost in disbelief that I would even have to ask. "Babe, please." Heavy sarcasm. "No doubt. You don't get the spot I had as a freshman if you stink, don't you remember dad had me out there on peewee teams when I was four."

My thoughts turned to the rumors that were clearly going to be flying. "I'm sure by the time this gets around I will have left Brewster's naked with everything showing. I couldn't help but feel as dirty as I had while being gawked at by those two men today. There was no mistaking the shame on my face.

"You know, most of the kids are content to just let me be, not my best friends, but certainly not the jerks April and her crowd are, the sympathy on the pretty red headed girls face sitting alone in the corner didn't escape my attention on my way out the door, she knew all too well what I was feeling, for a second we were kindred spirits. I don't get it. Why does she hate me so much? Isn't she in the least bit worried that her mom could get into trouble because she stole private records from the school?" It was more a statement of indignation than a question. I wasn't waiting for him to answer, but he did anyway.

"She hates you because you're everything she's not, which makes her hate herself. And. if she doesn't care about herself, what makes you think she'd care about her mother's reputation at the school?"

I shrugged, realizing he was right. "How do you know so much about it?" I asked, wondering about his insight into girls. "Because my mom is just like her— hates herself enough to be selfish and makes everybody else around her miserable."

That was enough said. I slid over and pushed myself as close to him as I could. He leaned over and kissed the top of my head.

"I was wondering what that smell was," he said, absent-mindedly breaking into my thoughts about Joy's time growing short as we rounded the last curve before Cameron Manor Road. We left the incident at Brewster's behind and were content to just be with each other.

"What smell?" I said, not having noticed anything. I

kept smelling it while I was in the living room, waiting for you to come downstairs. It's you—the smell of your hair on my shirt. I think maybe I might not wash this one for a while. I looked up and smiled at him. He could see my cheeks turning pink.

"What? Babe, you smell good."

"It's not that," I said, realizing we were in front of the house now. "I have a pillowcase I'm keeping for the same reason—only it's your cologne and you. It smells like you."

He kissed me before he cut the engine. "I'll get Joy something from my house and bring her up when everyone is asleep. You look tired. Why don't you go to bed early? We have another long week starting tomorrow."

I sighed and nodded. "Yeah, I know." I looked at my nails, all broken and chipped. "This is going to be a long few weeks of summer we have left." I started to get out, but I couldn't leave without saying it. "Thank you."

He looked confused. "For what, babe?"

"For not fighting with Steven. I don't want them to think that's how you are."

"Caimee, I didn't start the other fight—in Alabama. I got in trouble because I finished it. You know that's not my style to jump up and beat some idiot down."

"I know, but now so do they and maybe they'll stop trying to provoke you."

The look on his face said he doubted it, but he tried to be hopeful for my sake. "Maybe, now go take a hot shower, relax, and get to bed early, okay?"

I kissed him again and went inside.

Chapter 27
"The Accident"

When I woke up the next morning I was confused and alarmed. Joy. I ran to the closet. She was asleep in her usual spot. I had no memory of her coming in last night. I must have looked really drained after our week of sleepless nights and the incident at Brewster's, so Ty didn't wake me. I shut the closet door and tiptoed back over to my bed. Half way there I saw there was a note on the pillow on the side I didn't use.

"I had a talk with Joy when I walked her over. I sort of smoothed things over so she wouldn't be freaked out by me anymore—at least I think I did. It wasn't easy. You were right. She was pretty shaken up, but I just told her how much I love you and I didn't mean to embarrass either of you by showing it too much, I kept it simple. You looked too beautiful to wake up, but I have a new picture of you on my phone now. See you at breakfast. Love, Ty."

I picked up the picture of my mom on my nightstand and told her all about it.

~~~

I was right—the next week dragged on and on. We finished scraping off all the shingles and laying the sticky felt on top of the bare wood. Now we had to start covering it with row after row of the new shingles. The July sun beat down on us during the day and every evening we noticed the moon getting fuller and fuller.

Joy woke on the morning of her last day, excited to be going home, sad to be leaving. "Can I take an extra-long shower today? I want to shave my legs extra good." It was funny how she'd picked up my habits and lingo in such a short time.

"I'm really going to miss you, you know—and of course you can. Take all the time you want." We talked about our plan for her to stumble out of the woods and fake amnesia and also about how she was going to start flirting with Kade.

"I'm going to make him notice me as more than the girl on his way to school," she said. "I've learned so much from watching you and Ty together. Ty is such a nice boy. I think I've found one too." Whatever he had said to her on their walk back from the pond that night worked, but I think it was the apology that really helped her get over her fear. I reckoned "I'm sorry" wasn't something she had ever heard out of her father's mouth.

She stuck her head out of the shower curtain, her hair dripping on the floor to hear what I'd have to say. I cringed, remembering what she'd seen under the weeping willow tree. Even I knew that had almost gone way too far.

"Well, just remember, it's a different time and situation on your side so just be careful. Be yourself. He can't help but fall in love with you if you act like yourself." I felt like her mother for a second, but going down the mental list I had tabulated of all the great things about her I wasn't wrong, she was pretty amazing and this Kade guy would be lucky to have her. She nodded like she understood, but anybody could have seen the mischief in her eyes. What I really wanted to say was, 'Hey, don't put on a bikini and start kissing the guy in the middle of nowhere and not expect things to get a little out of hand. Lucky for me, Ty has some self-control. I couldn't help but wonder what would happen if Kade didn't? I didn't really know how to tell her not to do what I had done. She'd been watching Ty and me fall in love and I couldn't find the words to tell her not to do the same without sounding like a hypocrite.

"Just promise me you won't do anything that belongs in my time and not in yours," I said as she shut off the water. I handed her a towel.

She blushed. "Of course not, Ma wouldn't like it." I was relieved she'd gotten my point. "To be honest Joy, neither would mine."

~~~

Bo looked like the cat that had swallowed the canary at breakfast. Mrs. Maggie was putting her pecan waffles on the table, looking at him like he was crazy. Ty and I weren't far off her expression.

"Um...what's up, Dad? You look a little too happy for this early in the morning."

Before he could answer, we heard the front door open and footsteps in the hall. We all stopped to look up. Mrs. Maggie was the only one in the know...of course. "I didn't tell them you called and said you were coming back early." He gave her a quick smile and nod appreciating that she let it be a surprise.

"Dad!" I said, jumping up and running over to him. I was a little too old, but he picked me up like I was a little kid. He did that sometimes after an extended trip. I squeezed him tight.

"You're a few days later than you said you'd be, I was getting a little worried," said Maggie.

"Storms in Paris had everybody delayed," he said,

looking over my shoulder to see what she had on the table. 'I'm starving!"

I grabbed his hand and towed him to his chair. Mrs. Maggie smiled. There wouldn't be any leftovers today. Ty and I exchanged worried looks that was going to be bad news for us...well, Joy anyway. I was glad it was almost over, no way could I lie to my dad and now there was another person to hide her from, it made me nervous. It was going to be harder to sneak her out to get home with him upstairs and it was getting tiresome trying to come up with new reasons to get up and sneak some food into Ty's pockets. I did what I was best at and pushed it away for now. Mrs. Maggie set out orange juice and Dad said grace.

"I want tea today," I said, jumping up and going to the 'frig to get it before Mrs. Maggie could complain about how we need to appreciate what she'd set on the table instead of getting something else, she shot me a disapproving look, but that was the end of my scolding today, dad was home and there was too much to catch up on. I grabbed the pitcher which was heavy and full. Everyone was ignoring me except Ty. He knew exactly what I was doing. By now, we almost had it down to a science. Bo and Mrs. Maggie were too involved in asking Dad about his trip, and catching him up on show season to notice. Ty slipped out of his chair, came over and took the tea from my hands while I stuffed a banana and a blueberry muffin into his cargo pockets. Those shorts were becoming more and more handy. Two days ago Bo had commented how he was wearing them out because he washed and re-wore them every day. We had discovered over the past week they were excellent for getting meals to Joy. Ty gave some lame excuse about not wanting to ruin everything he owned working on the barn and just kept wearing them. Bo didn't comment again he just shook it off Ty's pants were the least of his worries with his busy schedule, there was always something to do with the horses.

Ty sat back down and when they finished talking I noticed Bo still had that goofy grin on his face.

"So Bo, you were just about to tell us why you're so happy this early." I just *had* to ask. He leaned back in his chair the way he always does when he thinks whatever he's about to say is going to be good.

"Well, I went to the sun up sale at Clarke's Hardware store this morning. Some of the fellas in there were talkin' about a friendly wager going around town. Seems there was some hubbub down at Brewster's the other day that got it all started. Ty and I just looked sideways at each other, not turning our heads, suddenly concentrating a little too hard on our waffles. Neither of our fathers was fooled. Dad played right into Bo's story. "Really? What kind of hubbub where the kids hang out would possibly lead to a wager among grown men?" He genuinely wanted to know, but his tone said he knew this had either Ty's name or mine written all over it. High school football and the south, another bad combo that would be drawing attention to us, it was all people talked about when the season started, whether they had a kid in school or not.

"It seems that someone is going to try and take Steven Goodwin's place as quarterback on the football team this coming year. Steven's dad has been going all over town talking to pretty much everybody who'll listen, saying that just ain't gonna happen. He says his boy's been at this school longer and it isn't right for the coach to even consider it. I guess the coach got wind of it, looked up Ty's stats from his old school, and says he's gonna give the job to the best man. Mr. Goodwin says that's just a rumor. Nobody's really sure if the coach will let Ty even try out. No surprise the kids have gotten involved and pretty much everybody has picked a side, at least most of the other players have, but not all of them. When Mr. Goodwin left, the other guys in the store kept talking and apparently quite a few of them have sons that play and would love to see Steven bumped to second string. He's a bully and that comes first-hand from their kids. You care to confirm or deny any of that, son?"

We all looked at Ty, waiting. "Since I've been prisoner here, tied to a roof every day, what makes you think I'd know anything about it? The guy was a jerk to me and his stupid girlfriend was really mean to Caimee. I just told him I was gonna to try out after he told me I couldn't. He got all mad, tried to start a fight, and we walked out."

I knew Dad would put it together. Why did he have to be so intuitive when I needed him to be silent, eating, and glad to be home? "Okay, then how does everybody know what school you came from and all about your football career there? As far as I know, nobody even knew what town you lived in—at least nobody ever asked me. Did you mention it, Bo?" Bo chewed and thought for a second. "Not that I recall, I just said you were in Alabama on the rare occasion anybody ever asked."

I knew Ty didn't want to talk about it. He got up and scraped his plate and set it in the sink.

"Caimee, can I use your sunscreen? My face is a

little sore from all the sun yesterday." Obviously it was a lie, but they let it go as they were focused more on his avoiding the subject at hand than him going up into my room.

"Sure! It's in my bathroom on the shelf where I keep my makeup and stuff."

"Thanks," he said and he was gone.

I tried to refocus my attention on my food, but it was impossible with three pairs of eyes on me. Now that Ty was gone, I was kind of taking the heat. I knew if I didn't tell them Mrs. Maggie would hear about it sooner or later. I mean, if the men at the Clarke Hardware were talking, it was a miracle her bingo BFFs hadn't already heard the whole story. With their eyes boring holes into the top of my head I finally had to look up at the three curious faces, none of whom were going to take no for an answer.

"April Mantis used her mom's computer access at the school and stole his transcripts and other files from his old school—all his grades, stats from football, the reason he was kicked off the team, and a narrative about his mom were on it. I'm sure all the kids know by now. Steven came into Brewster's with the stolen transcripts and read them to Ty. He told Ty he'd better not even show his face at tryouts, or he would make everything public."

Bo was instantly angry and so was my dad. I held up my hand, trying to think of something to smooth things over on the fly—not my best skill. "Okay, okay, just wait before you two form a posse and go kill somebody. Ty handled it. He's going to tryouts anyway to just see if the coach will allow him to play. Hey, maybe this is a good thing. April and her zombie followers have been making people's lives miserable for too long at that school. If the meek, sheep-like masses are taking sides, maybe this means we're all done taking her ruling our school like 'Iron Fist Barbie.'" I was proud of that one. It made me smile to think of them hanging next to each other in a toy store. "On sale now, last chance before they go out of style—Iron Fist and Broke Nose Barbies, both of them a perfect likeness of April."

Bo was still angry. I hadn't appeased him at all. "Well, he'll get the chance to try out. I don't care what Steven Goodwin's father thinks. If they didn't know he could beat him they wouldn't say anything about it at all."

Dad slapped him on the back. "He'll get his chance, even if we have to go down there and raise the roof off the place."

I rolled my eyes. "Nothing like sports to get grown men acting like little boys," I mumbled under my breath. They were so busy coming up with a "plan" that neither dad paid me any attention, but Mrs. Maggie nodded her head in silent agreement. She must have seen the sarcasm all over my face. I tried again to bring them to reality. 'I wouldn't worry too much about it. The coach has to let him try out—his grades are good and he's eligible." Then I put my foot in my mouth and made things worse. "Unless they try to say he can't play here because he was kicked off the other team, which I wouldn't put past Steven or his dad to try and pull." *Dang! Why did I say that?* I thought wishing I could suck the words back into my mouth. Too late! I'd set things in motion now.

Bo stood up. "Caleb, I got some errands to run, wanna come? The horses are already down in the lower pasture." He looked at me letting me know that in no way should their plans keep us from working. I nodded keeping my mouth shut, I had done enough damage.

Suddenly Dad had all kinds of energy. "Give me a minute to change," he said, handing Mrs. Maggie his empty plate. Ty came back just in time to see his father looking like he was on a mission.

"I'll be in the truck, Caleb."

"Five minutes!" Dad answered, calling back down the stairs. He must have run in his excitement to help Bo with his undertaking. He was only gone a few seconds before I heard his door close. Ty had only been gone a few minutes, but everyone had already finished eating. Bo was walking toward the door. "Don't worry, son, I got this one," he said before Ty could protest. It was obvious they were going to see the coach, no matter how far they had to go to track him down.

"I'm sorry, babe, they forced it out of me," I said as he buckled my harness into place and helped me into my knee pads.

"It's okay, sweetie. I was just hoping to handle this on my own. I don't want the guys on the team thinking 'Daddy' handles my problems."

All I could think of was 'Okay, I need a guy thing here to make him feel better." "Don't worry, baby, you can do your talking on the field."

He winked at me and we went up the ladder to get started. First time I'd ever gotten lucky with my thoughts on the fly like that.

~~~

It was around eight when Ty and I took turns pounding in the last nail. It had taken nearly two weeks, but we'd done it.

"I hate to admit this, but it is much prettier than the old one," I said, taking in the sight of the sea of shiny black we had place over the entire barn.

"I don't know about prettier, but it's going to keep the horses dry and I'm proud of you." He put his arm around me. You hung in there and really helped."

I sat down carefully so as not to cut myself again. We were on top of the rounded peak looking up at the moon. It was so full from up here it looked like it was about to fall out of the sky right on top of us. It was the same as it had been the night I'd plunged through the wall—low, bright white, and ready to lead Joy home.

Our dads were sitting on the top porch step admiring our work when we finally had all the tools away. As was our custom, we sat on the porch swing and waited for Mrs. Maggie to bring us our dinner. The new "No filth at the table" rule was hard and fast now. She'd had to clean up our mess too many times.

"I'm proud of you kids," Dad said as he saw us coming up the dirt path to the house.

"It really does look great," Bo added.

We were both waiting for an explanation of what they'd done today. We hadn't seen either of them since breakfast. It came while we were eating. Mrs. Maggie sat in the rocker on the other side, lingering and waiting to hear.

"I had a talk with the coach today," Bo said, turning to lean on the stone pillar so he could see Ty's face.

"Yeah, he was really a nice guy," Dad added. Not having a son and never having a reason, he had never really spoken to him other than for a few seconds here and there at parent-teacher night.

Bo continued. "We sat in his office while he called

your old coach, who vouched for your character and said the only reason you were asked to leave is because the other parents insisted. Once he had the full story and Caleb here told him what a great kid you were, he was convinced. I'm glad he went. They figured as your father I'd be biased. He was my impartial third party." He reached over and slapped my dad's shoulder. That had to be a joke. No way was my dad impartial when it came to Ty.

"Coach said he'd always intended to give you a chance, given your record, but now he can defend his decision to the school board and the Goodwin's. Your old coach is going to send a letter clarifying the situation. No real way to keep your mom out of it, though. Seems like everybody knows all about it anyway, so between her actions and the fight, people were thinking you'd turned into some kind of thug or something."

"Great," said Ty. There was a hard edge to it. He wasn't too thrilled about his story spreading all over town, but there was nothing we could do to put out the fire now. It was started and blazing hot.

Stupid April! I wondered how they avoided getting her mom in trouble today. They wouldn't have wanted to do that, but I thought it was better not to ask given the look on Ty's face. It was better to just let it drop.

With Bo getting up at the crack of dawn for the sale and Dad not having had any sleep, everyone decided to turn in early. The house was quiet and dark by ten—except for Joy and me.

"Please promise you'll come and see me soon," she said, "even if it's just to say hello through the wall. I'll wait for you next time the moon is dark, okay?"

She was sitting there in her dress like she was about to go on a big trip or something—all smooth and wrinkle free, hair combed and tied neatly in her ribbon styled appropriately for her time. It dawned on me that there was something really wrong with this picture when Ty knocked and came in.

"Man, my dad is snoring up a storm over there. I could have marched out with a band."

"Look at her," I said, hoping he'd catch on to the obvious. He shrugged, "Yeah, so? She looks um..." He took in the sight of her odd clothes, then said "...nice."

"We have to rough her look up a little bit, remember? She can't stumble out of the woods all clean and smelling good like that."

He nodded, "Yeah, I did forget that with everything else going on today. You're right, let's take her down to the barn, plenty of dirt down there and she definitely won't smell good."

"But I don't want to be dirty. I just took another shower and put on lotion," she said, showing us her clean, smooth legs. Obviously, we both had rubbed off on her more than a little bit. Two weeks ago she would have been mortified for Ty to even see her ankles.

"Joy, you can't go like that, nobody will believe you," I said, taking her hand and leading her out of the closet. "We have to go to the barn and get you dirty. You have to look like you've been living in the woods and you can't remember anything. That's the only way this will work. Ty was already looking out my door, making sure the coast was clear. "And remember, tell them you hit your head the first day. That will explain why you don't have any bruises and why you can't remember any of the other days you were gone."

It was nerve-wracking sneaking her out of the house. It was the first time we risked being seen together with the family home, but we really had no choice. Ty went out onto the porch first to have a look around. He made it to the edge of the steps before he waved us forward and the three of us sneaked outside and ran for the cover of the barn.

"Okay, don't get mad," Ty said. "This isn't meant to be mean." He was much more careful with his actions around her since he'd scared her that day at the pond. Even though she seemed to have gotten over it, we were always mindful never to cross those lines again. He grabbed the sleeve of her dress and gave it a hard pull. It ripped right on the puffy part. Of course, she teared up. "Ma made this dress."

I smeared some wet dirt on her shoes and onto the hem of the white dress she had on underneath her cotton dress. It looked like a nightgown an old lady would wear. I stained it with dirt and mud until it looked like she'd been walking in it. Next, I took her hair down and wiped as much of the mud as I could off my hands. Making sure my fingers were still dusty, I combed them through until she looked like she hadn't had a bath in a quite a while. Ty put some streaks of dirt on her face. By the time we were done, she looked positively homeless. He looked at his watch, an hour to go," he said. "Maybe we should go under the house and wait, just to make sure we don't miss it." I could tell he was excited. He hadn't seen the wall shimmer or felt the room spin like we had.

Thor was getting agitated having a stranger in there. He'd been bucking a bit and kicking the gate. I could tell Joy was afraid of him. So was I, but I didn't want Ty to see it. It didn't matter, he could tell by the way we both jumped at the sound of the wooden gate rattling under the strain of Thor's powerful foreleg thrust. We were both a little shaken.

As soon as we turned to go, one of the harnesses fell off its peg. The metal clanking sound of the buckles hitting the ground got our attention. Ty turned and towed me with him to go back and hang it up. The sound set Thor off. He kicked again, even harder than before. It shook the wooden rail holding the gate closed out of place and he bolted out of the stall. I didn't see it clearly, but I heard her scream. Thor had trampled Joy.

We only had a few minutes before her screaming would wake everyone. Her right ankle was obviously broken. It was twisted and deformed. I could see over the top of her shoe that it was already starting to swell. I knew it had to hurt, but I also knew we had to keep her quiet. If Dad or Bo had come in here and seen her next to me in those clothes it would have been all over. We would have changed our time and hers.

I held her head up, trying to comfort her. "Listen, Joy, you have to stop screaming. Please listen." I put my hand over her mouth. She sobbed, helplessly reaching for her lower leg, but unable to move. I looked at Ty, waiting for him to say something. Any plan would do at this point—any plan that kept our secret. He looked at me as serious as I'd ever seen him and said something that made absolutely no sense to me.

"Quick, take off your clothes. We can't worry about the tunnel now, we have to get her some help. We'll figure that part out later."

I sat there, trying to quiet Joy and looking at him like he'd lost his mind. "Do it now!" he said, running back to the wall and grabbing a rope to go get Thor before anyone heard him running around the ring. I didn't get it, but I obeyed.

"Okay Joy, I have to move my hand. Please trust me and don't scream. We're going to help you." I had no idea why I was asking her to trust me, I had no idea what we were about to do, but I trusted Ty. I stripped down to my underwear in seconds, just as he came running back in with Thor. He put him away and shut his gate securely. "We have to change her clothes." I nodded, only half catching on.

Joy was in so much pain she would have let us strip her naked and wouldn't have even noticed. Her crying was quieter now, but her breathing was rapid and shallow with the agony. Her ankle was turning black and blue. Her foot was flopped over in an unnatural position. It turned my stomach to look at it. "Don't move her," he said, his frenzy slipping through his command as he took off running to get a small pair of pruning shears from the tools hanging on the wall. They were a little bit of overkill for the job we needed to do, but Ty was careful and they were all we had. We were working as fast as we could. He cut her dress off and then looked at me.

"I need *everything* you have on," he said, knowing I'd be mortified. I took what was left of Joy's dress and covered myself as I handed him my under clothes. I didn't notice it before because I was so self-absorbed, but she had stopped moaning and crying altogether. I looked at Ty, terrified that she was dead, he read my thoughts. "She passed out," he said. "I need your help to get this stuff on her." He was holding up my clothes. Once again he gave me his shirt. I hesitated to take

Joy's dress away from in front of me to take it, but I knew I couldn't really maneuver around her to dress her and hold her dress in front of me unless I had both hands free. His shirt was the only solution. He read the panic on my face. He turned his head and closed his eyes while I put on his clothes. Next we worked together and put everything I'd been wearing on her. I was happy I'd had on shorts. No way would we have gotten jeans on over that break. We slid them up carefully and managed to get them buttoned without moving her too much.

Once she was dressed, we had a minute to think. "Go get my dad and please don't tell him it was Thor. He'll shoot him for sure and you too for bringing me in here." He nodded, I'll think of something," he said, "but I need my shirt back, I can't go get them like this."

I knew he was right. I put the scraps of Joy's dress around me under his shirt and then maneuvering out of it handed it back to him. That gave me a second to think. "I've got it. Tell them you were coming out here, getting to know Thor, and didn't know I went back up on the roof to get my watch. I took off the watch the little fairy in the middle pointing to the time slipping away and the pink band clearly visible against the hay and dirt. It killed me to leave it there, but I laid it next to her. They know I'd never lose it up there. It means too much to me. "I wear it every day. They'll believe I'd go back up alone to get it. Tell them I fell off the ladder and made it this far and told you everything before I passed out."

Ty nodded and made some drag marks in the dirt so it looked like I'd walked dragging my broken, twisted foot to the spot where Joy was laying on the ground.

"Hide in Lindie's stall. When you hear us drive off to the hospital, go to my room and wait for me."

I promised and he took off running towards the house. I knew at the speed he was going I only had a few seconds to get hidden and settle Lindie down enough so she wouldn't draw attention to me.

Chapter 28
"The Storm"

I could hear the commotion from the shadows in the corner of Lindie's stall. I'd picked up every stray scrap of Joy's clothes and had her shoes in my hand, holding them against me while trying to hold her dress in place. Ty played his part perfectly. Dad was yelling, "What was she doing out here?" He was hollering, but not at Ty. He was frantic.

"Quick, go get your dad. We need to carry her to the car. Joy had started to come back around. I was hoping she wouldn't say anything coherent, like ask for me or something that would ruin everything. All I could hear was her crying, "Help, it hurts! My leg!" She was screaming. Each word got louder and louder as she started to come to. It physically ached in my stomach and my chest to hear it. Ty was back in minutes with Bo, sticking to the story. I wasn't sure if he was panicked sounding because Joy's screams were starting to get to him too or because he was still acting out our plan. It wasn't like him to lose his cool like that. Bo must have been horrified at the sight of "me" lying there broken and screaming.

"What was she doing in here?" he asked, repeating my dad's question, only he was yelling at Ty, demanding an explanation.

"I don't know! She said something about getting a watch and that she fell off the ladder." I saw Bo's boots go by the slats in Lindie's gate. I held my breath, terrified I would be discovered—naked, wrapped in the shards of a dress from 1840, while my twin lay in agony a few feet away.

"She must have dragged herself this far," he said, noting Ty's well-placed marks in the dirt. The next scream I heard was Mrs. Maggie's. "I'll get the car," she said, not even bothering to ask what had happened. The four of them picked her up and laid her in the back seat, all the while she was screaming shrill, piercing sounds. I didn't even realize I was crying until I heard them leave.

I waited about five minutes to make sure they were gone. I patted Lindie out of the way, opened and securely closed her gate, and then took off across the pasture. I held my rags in place as best I could, not stopping to breathe until I got to Ty's room. I dug through his dresser and found a pair of sweat pants with a draw string and a T-shirt. As soon as I pulled the shirt over my head, I noticed the clock on his bedside table. Five minutes past twelve. We had missed our window. We only had one more chance to get her home, but how would she explain the cast? My mind was spinning, racing, grasping at any straw that might be a good plan—a believable lie to get us out of this mess. I couldn't come up with anything. I couldn't believe we were able to pull off what we did, given the stress we were under. Ty was everything I ever thought he'd be in crisis. He had really saved all three of us.

It was four in the morning when Ty came in—at least I hoped it was him. I wasn't asleep. I was sitting there in the middle of his bed, in the dark, afraid to turn on a light or his TV. I had no idea when I heard the door open if he was alone. Then it occurred to me it might be

Bo, so I ran as quietly as I could, climbed into his bathtub and pulled the curtain. I heard the sound of boots hitting the hardwood floor, the creak of the closet opening and next came the whooshing of the curtain being pulled back.

"It's me," he said, slumping down on the edge of the tub. "It's bad. She had to have surgery. They had to realign the bones in her lower leg and put in some type of rods to hold them straight. The doctor said she'll be in bed for months. I jumped up from the tub and dropped in front of the toilet. Ty held my hair while I threw up. I was shaking so badly, I couldn't control it.

"What are we going to do?" My teeth were chattering from the panic. "She said if her mother couldn't live in this house with her children, she wouldn't stay here without them, they are her life, I mean look at what kind of husband she has. I don't think she has a motive to stay if Joy is gone. What if this changes everything? What if the sheriff's log is wrong, what if her coming here already changed things? We never accounted for any reason she wouldn't go back. I can't lose this place. Ty, I can't lose you."

He got down on the floor with me. "I know, babe. Don't worry, we'll think of something. I'm supposed to go pick up Grammie. She was too upset to drive and I have to get back to the hospital. I have to be there so she doesn't say anything when she wakes up, but I had to see you first." I nodded, hating to see him go, but knowing he had to leave.

I huddled down in his blankets and tried to sleep. The smell of him and being in his room was comforting. I felt like it took forever, but eventually I drifted off. The next thing I knew it was four in the afternoon—twelve hours later. I couldn't believe I'd slept that long. Ty was lying next to me with his arms around me. He must have been up all night. Even asleep, he looked tired. I slipped out of bed, trying not to wake him. I was starving, but unsure if I was alone. I looked over at him again he looked so peaceful and perfect, my heart melted when I noticed my watch on his nightstand, in the middle of everything he must have picked it up and saved it for me, I walked over and kissed him lightly, but he didn't even flinch. I stayed clear of his huge window and made my way back to his bathroom. I used his toothbrush and quietly took a bath.

The hours passed slowly, but Ty slept on. I watched the moon rise and the hours ticked by as our last opportunity to get Joy home slipped away. Ty finally moved around one in the morning. He held back the covers and invited me to come lay next to him.

"Sorry, they gave me a sleeping pill at the hospital and told me to take it when I got home. Dad insisted. He said I looked too upset and that I needed some rest. Dr. Little came by, so he called the 24-hour pharmacy and told them what to give me. I drove through to pick it up on my way back. I must have played my distraught boyfriend roll well. Normally Dad would never agree to me taking a medicine like that. I did have a few minutes alone with Joy. She's pretending to be you. Luckily you all seemed to have swapped enough information about your lives that she's pulling it off. I told her the story we came up with about her falling, but I didn't get to talk to her alone very long. Grammie is so upset she barely leaves the room. Last thing I heard her say is how this place took her daughter and she wouldn't stand idly by while it took you too. She's going to be a problem."

I didn't speak. I wasn't sure if I could get the words out. Somewhere in my dreams, in my much needed sleep, the answer had come. I started to accept it while sitting in the warm bath water. I thought I was going to throw up again. I knew what we had to do. It was the only thing that made sense—the only thing we could do. It was just a blurry outline of a plan that became clear after the tunnel closed. I rolled over and put my face against Ty's chest. My tears wet his shirt. "I know how to fix it. I know how to keep things from changing."

He sighed. "Me too. I just don't know if I can get through that."

"I'm scared." My voice shook as I said the words admitting it made it so much more real. He responded by stroking my hair and holding me close. "I know baby, I know, you're okay, just be here with me right now."

~~~

The storm I feared was coming when dad wanted to leave was circling around me now. I could smell the rain and hear the thunder the same way I felt the lifeblood of this place coursing through my veins weeks ago. The fear was almost unmanageable, but I had two weeks to get myself together, to hide here with Ty, waiting until the dark of the moon when I could go back in her place. Dad hadn't pulled me away, but even still I was leaving. The Manor was pushing me back, forcing me to turn back time so we could stay here forever. I shivered and Ty kissed my face, my lips, my hair, any part of me he could reach. There was no room between us, but I managed to get closer. "Tighter," I whispered and I felt his arms tense. I was the only one who could do it. Nobody else could make it right. It was the same fear I'd had before only stronger because leaving was no longer just a possibility as it had been when dad wanted to go, it was certain, if I couldn't do this now. Losing this place... not being here meant losing all of my memories, all of my dreams. There was no way to save them except to go back for her.

"I love you," he said.

"I love you too," I whispered in the dark.

His love, our lives here together, something else I had to leave to save. I realized I could live without any of the rest, but I couldn't lose him. Cameron Manor was the canvas we were painted on. We had to have it. Fear turned to determination, I would find a way. All I could do now was hope and pray.

ABOUT THE AUTHOR
(in her own words)

I was born in Japan, the child of military parents. We moved to Georgia where I spent my early years. We traveled the world until I was eleven, and then returned to Georgia, the first place I lived in America. There we "put down roots" and I received my education. I started writing at age twelve. I love the South and its rich history. Although my life's career was not spent as a writer, over the years I discovered that the art of storytelling—the weaving together of history and fiction—is part of the southern culture that was engrained in me from childhood. Although I now have my own military family—my husband and children, the South and its people still provide the inspiration for my stories. Every storyteller leaves a bit of themselves in their stories, whether written or told aloud and handed down through successive generations. I hope you find a bit of yourself in mine.

OTHER BOOKS BY THIS AUTHOR

The Crickets Dance

A passionate story about loyalty, friendship, cruelty,
tolerance, forgiveness, and love.

* * *

CAMERON MANOR
The Hope and the Harvest

The Cameron Saga
Book 2

Coming soon to Amazon.com

Made in the USA
Coppell, TX
24 February 2022

74028684R00225